"WHAT MAKES YOU THINK I AM YOUR MAN?"

Sabrina glanced up at him in surprise. "Why, given your outrageous reputation, you are exactly the sort of man I require."

Hunter inclined his raven head. "I am flattered."

"Think nothing of it. Any man who could . . . could . . ." Her voice trailed off. Two blotches of red stained her cheeks.

One dark brow drifted upward. "Could . . . ?" he prompted.

Her pert little nose wrinkled, and she leaned forward to whisper, "Well . . . you know."

He shook his head. "No, I don't." He folded his arms over his broad chest and gazed down at her. "I hate to disillusion you, but I make it a rule never to prey on young innocents."

Her eyes went wide. "Never?"

"Never."

"I see." Forlorn, she bit her lip and pondered her situation. "What if . . . I were willing to pay you?"

To his credit, he did not laugh. "You're that desperate, eh?"

She pulled a miserable frown. "I'm afraid so. I simply must destroy my reputation."

BOOK YOUR PLACE ON OUR WEBSITE AND MAKE THE READING CONNECTION!

We've created a customized website just for our very special readers, where you can get the inside scoop on everything that's going on with Zebra, Pinnacle and Kensington books.

When you come online, you'll have the exciting opportunity to:

- View covers of upcoming books

- Read sample chapters

- Learn about our future publishing schedule (listed by publication month *and author*)

- Find out when your favorite authors will be visiting a city near you

- Search for and order backlist books from our online catalog

- Check out author bios and background information

- Send e-mail to your favorite authors

- Meet the Kensington staff online

- Join us in weekly chats with authors, readers and other guests

- Get writing guidelines

- AND MUCH MORE!

**Visit our website at
http://www.zebrabooks.com**

RACING TO RUIN

Stacy Brown

ZEBRA BOOKS

KENSINGTON PUBLISHING CORP.

http://www.zebrabooks.com

ZEBRA BOOKS are published by

Kensington Publishing Corp.
850 Third Avenue
New York, NY 10022

All Kensington Titles, Imprints, and Distributed Lines are available at special quantity discounts for bulk purchases for sales
promotions, premiums, fund raising, educational, or institu-
tional use.

Special book excerpts or customized printings can also be created to fit specific needs. For details, write or phone the office
of the Kensington special sales manager: Kensington Publishing
Corp., 850 Third Avenue, New York, NY 10022, attn: Special
Sales Department, Phone: 1-800-221-2647

Zebra and the Z logo Reg. U.S. Pat. & TM Off.

First Printing: April, 2001
10 9 8 7 6 5 4 3 2 1

Printed in the United States of America

Chapter 1

England, 1820

"Are you quite sure you truly wish to do this?" Lady Amanda Somers whispered fiercely in her younger sister's ear. She darted a nervous glance over her shoulder at the nearby group of babbling debutantes to make certain they were not eavesdropping. Gathered by the rhododendron bushes bursting with pink blossoms, the giggling group was engaged in an avid search for potential husbands and took no notice of anything out of the ordinary. Each of them had attended this weekend party in the hope of attracting the interest of an eligible male.

"Of course I'm sure I want to go through with it," Sabrina snapped, letting her gaze survey the myriad guests milling about Lord Holmes's perfectly manicured gardens.

Very shortly now, the enormous ballroom would bubble over with enthusiastic guests who, doubtless, would later enjoy a hearty meal in Holmes's lavish dining room. Sabrina wondered how many of the two hundred guests were planning to spend the weekend. Having heard rumors of the wicked liaisons that often took place on such occasions, she wondered with titillation if she might be privy to anything as exciting.

As she watched the liveried servants carry torches to illuminate the balcony and gardens, she realized with a surge of triumph that the defining moment of her life had finally arrived. In a few hours, her grandfather would be thoroughly disgusted with her. He might banish her to the country. A smile played around the edges of her mouth. Oh, yes. The far-reaching ramifications of tonight's actions were simply too wonderful to contemplate.

"I fear it's too risky," Amanda complained tersely under her breath, "even for you. Heaven knows, you dare more than the law allows."

"Nonsense." Sabrina's voice rang with impatience. But she managed to essay a bright smile in acknowledgment of Lord Whitehead's impertinent perusal. Inclining her riotous red curly head, she made a mental note of his attention. He might come in handy if the Earl of Greystone failed to perform. "You only say that because it has never been done before," Sabrina told her nerve-wracked sister quite calmly.

"Oh, it's been done," Amanda muttered and caught sight of Whitehead's searing gaze. Fixing the audacious rake with a stern frown, she grabbed Sabrina by the arm and propelled her down the balcony steps. She traversed the sprawling gardens—disgruntled sister in tow—in search of a secluded spot. A white stone bench flanked by two towering hedges came into view. She steered her foolhardy sister, none too gently, in that direction.

Amanda sank down on the stone bench and drew her sister near. "Really, Sabrina, I must protest. Your intended course is entirely deplorable," she insisted in the harshest elder sister voice she could muster. "You must stop this folly. Immediately."

Sabrina rolled her eyes heavenward. "You are wasting your breath," she replied with bold impudence. "I have no intentions of changing my mind."

Amanda clutched her recalcitrant sister's arm. "I implore you, do not allow your emotions to rule your head. I beg of you, consider your future, dearest."

"I am thinking of my future," Sabrina fired back and wriggled her arm free. "I know exactly what I am doing."

"I can well imagine what Grandfather is going to say." Amanda moaned and clutched her forehead. "He'll blame me. I just know it."

"Nonsense, he knows you have no control over me."

Sabrina's lips twisted. For that matter, neither did her grandfather, regardless of the power his controlling nature wielded most of the time. Tonight, she planned to prove to that narrowminded, domineering old goat that she was her own woman. She would make him regret his implacable overbearingness.

"He can be very persuasive, you know," Amanda cautioned with trepidation. "Have you thought of what this evening might mean? The recompense you will face?"

Sabrina turned on her sister. "How can you ask me that?" she cried, her clear blue eyes clouding with emotion. "You know *exactly* why I am doing this. If I don't take action now," she declared, her voice wavering, "I shall go mad. I just know it."

Amanda was instantly contrite. "Of course, dearest," she said, patting her sister's arm with care. "I know. But surely there is another way to achieve your objective?"

It was Sabrina's turn to sigh. "I don't see how. I must go through with this. Nothing you say or do will stop me."

Amanda clasped her sister's hand tightly. "Sabrina, for once in your life, pray think before you act," she implored.

Sabrina snatched her hand away. "We have gone over this a thousand times. It is the only course of action that will achieve my end. If you cannot bear to watch," she announced, getting to her feet, "then I suggest you don't." Without allowing her poor, bedraggled sister the benefit of a reply, she turned on her heel and trudged down the expansive lawn in search of the notorious Hunter. She hoped he, at least, would not disappoint.

Hunter Lancaster, Earl of Greystone, retrieved Lady Declaire's slender arms from around his neck. Pulling the crisp, white linen handkerchief from his breast pocket, he wiped it across his mouth, removing the wet evidence of her clinging, aggressive kisses. It was little surprise Lord Declaire had died last year of a stroke, Hunter thought with a rueful smirk. The old man clearly lacked the stamina to satisfy his wife.

The object of his thoughts giggled and twined her arms around his neck. "I simply cannot wait," she breathed, grinding her hips against his suggestively, "to lie beneath you."

Hunter grimaced and pushed her gently away. She had seemed eminently more kissable and, for that matter, beddable a fortnight ago when he had initially expressed interest in her. Looking at her bony, narrow face now, he wondered if he ought not give up drinking brandy, for under its influence his judgment was woefully inadequate. "Let's not rush our fences. It's early yet."

She pulled a bratty frown. "You certainly do not live up to your reputation, my lord. I expected, from all accounts, to be exhausted by morning." She ran her eager palms over his chest. "You've barely touched me, and it's nearly dark." She glanced over her shoulder at the shadowed shrubbery maze. "You could take me right here and now," she suggested, breathless with lust.

He frowned. Subtle, she was not. Where was her sense of

decorum? Everyone knew the proper way of approaching a midnight tryst. One did not blurt out their expectations in graphic detail. Nor did they reference past illicit liaisons as a sort of sexual endorsement. And the lady in question never made overt sexual demands, not unless she was already in bed.

"You know, my dear," he drawled with dry mockery, "there is a great deal to be said for subtlety. Or at least, the vague appearance of it. Have you never considered the coy approach?"

She shrugged and flashed a provocative smile. "Who has time to wait? I see something I want—I go after it," she assured him, letting her hands slide lower. "And I want you."

Suddenly, revolted by the woman before him and the entire sordid event, he snatched her hands from his waistband and held them firmly against her chest. He wasn't sure what disgusted him more, her or the fact that he had played this part before.

It was always meaningless.

Always empty.

And utterly boring.

Was this all there was to life? he wondered with irritation. Just a series of shallow exchanges between two uncaring people? At the ripe old age of two and thirty, he found he no longer had the stomach for it.

"No," he said sharply, furious with himself as much as with her. "You've overplayed your hand, my lady."

Evidently, rejection was something new to Lady Declaire, for she stared at him, her vulgar mouth gaping wide. "You bastard!" she spat at him. "How dare you spurn me?"

He inclined his dark head in mock contrition. "My apologies, madam, consider it a postponement if you like. We can enjoy a passionate rendezvous somewhere more private, at a more convenient time."

"When?" she asked, running her tongue over her lips with lascivious anticipation.

"How does the twelfth of never sound?"

Her face fell. "Why, you," she snarled and raised her hand to slap his face.

But he caught her hand before it flew to his cheek. "Uh, uh," he muttered and squeezed her bony wrist between his thumb and forefinger. "No, my dear. That pleasure is reserved for a lady whose honor has been insulted." He let out a derisive chuckle. "You and I both know you have none. Now," he said in no uncertain terms as he released her gruffly, "be a good girl and go away. Or I'll have our esteemed host throw you out."

"You haven't heard the last of Harriet Declaire," she said through her teeth before she disappeared in a huff of garish gold silk.

He shook his head. "I sincerely hope I have," he muttered to himself and raked his hand through his thick raven hair.

Distant laughter, echoing against the backdrop of the orchestra playing a Mozart concerto, beckoned his weary bones. It was high time he joined the party. This evening had the earmarks of a total disaster, and it hadn't even begun yet.

Sabrina was mentally preparing her witty introduction when she caught sight of the notorious Hunter emerging from the dimly lit shrubbery maze. A current of excitement ran through her. Excellent! He was alone. A tiny smile ruffled her mouth. If Greystone was everything she had heard, her troubles would soon be over.

She tugged as hard as she could at the modest lace neckline of her pink muslin gown, in an effort to bare a small amount of what she hoped would be enticing cleavage. Picking up her hem, she hurried along the outside hedgerow in search of a good spot to intercept her prey. She ducked through the break in the hedge and plunked down on a small, round bronze bench that vaguely resembled a mushroom top.

She drew a deep breath and waited. The tiny white pebbles crunched beneath his immaculate, shiny black Hessian boots. Any minute now, they would meet. She could barely suppress her smile or contain the exhilaration that coursed through her veins. This was easier than she imagined. Her plan was working splendidly. Had she really worried it would be a challenge to garner an introduction? Silly girl.

As he drew near, she glanced up at him from beneath what she believed were coquettish lashes. Her eager gaze slid over the length of him. Her pulse quickened. My, he certainly did not disappoint. He was taller and *much* bigger than she imagined. And startlingly ... older, more sophisticated than any imagining could have been. And she had devoted a considerable amount of time envisioning this particular rogue.

Why, he looked at least thirty. The perfect age for her purposes. She needed an experienced, mature man who knew how to get the job done. He was dressed impeccably, as she knew he would be. His valet must be as patient as the devil, for the neat, intricate folds and tucks in his cravat were awe inspiring. Not to mention the delicate, flawless fabric of his cambric shirt and enviable wrist frills. She estimated he had paid a fortune for that soft, blue-velvet cutaway with claw-hammer tails and satin, embroidered waistcoat that fit his formidable chest like a second skin. A wave of dizzy excitement overtook her.

In that instant, she knew exactly why he had earned the reputation of notorious rakehell. He was beautiful. A Greek Adonis to be sure, she allowed, as her hungry gaze devoured all six feet something of him. Could those buff-colored buckskin breeches fit his muscular thighs any better? she wondered with a surge of warmth. Were there ever such well made shoulders? Or finely chiseled features?

A slight smile touched his lips, softening the normally forbidding lines around his mouth. He inclined his raven head in her direction.

Now, here was a man who had sampled all the world had to offer and found it mildly boring. His carriage, his countenance, everything about the man fairly oozed arrogance and self-assurance. To her surprise, she found that extremely—unbelievably—alluring.

She donned her sweetest smile, lowered her lashes demurely and waited for him to fall at her feet.

And waited.

And waited.

Her head snapped up. She found herself staring helplessly at his broad-shouldered back. She blinked. He hadn't stopped. He had walked right past her. Her mouth fell open. He wasn't even tempted. Remotely. She bit her lip in frustration. So much for her well-laid plans. What on earth was she going to do now?

Self-recriminations were a waste of time, for if her eyes did not deceive her, the notorious Hunter was getting away. And she was no closer to achieving her goal. She hopped to her feet. Hauling her elegant dress above her knees, she ran after him, looking very much like the hoyden her grandfather accused her of being.

"M-my lord," she cried. "Wait!"

At the sound of her voice, he stopped and swiveled around to face her. Even in the purplish twilight glow she could see— no, actually *feel*—his gaze on her. His blatant perusal lingered for a moment on her bared legs, savoring her shapely calves before ebony brows hiked up in silent query.

Color flooded her cheeks. So, that was what a pair of bedroom eyes looked like. She dropped her skirt. No wonder the man was considered England's premiere rake. She felt an unfamiliar rush of heat overtake her, and all he had done was look at her.

"May I be of some assistance?" His deep, silky voice swirled around her in seductive inquiry.

It was a wonderful voice. Deep and rich and sensual.

"Oh . . . yes," she managed on a sigh. What was the matter with her? She could barely catch her breath. She hadn't run that far or that fast. "You certainly may," she told him, breathless with excitement. "I'd like you to ruin me, if you please."

He must have stared at her for a full minute before the impact of what she had just said sank in. Piercing gray eyes narrowed into silver slits. "I beg your pardon. *What* did you say?"

"You know, ruin me. Make me ineligible for balls, marriage, or for that matter, any decent society at all." She smiled up at him brightly. "I should very much like to be firmly installed on the shelf. And I think you are just the man to do it."

"I know what it means," he almost snapped at her. "What evades me at the moment is why?" he asked, his tone decidedly cool.

Her back stiffened. What ailed the man? He was supposed to suggest a more secluded spot, not question her motives. "I have my reasons," she imparted with stiff civility. "Would you like to ruin me or not?"

He looked at her askance. This was by far the most bizarre exchange in recent memory. And he had had quite a few. Amused, and more than a little baffled by the fetching sight before him, he decided to play along. "With such a generous offer," he drawled softly, "how could any man refuse?"

She breathed a sigh of relief. "I was hoping you'd feel that way," she replied, grinning from ear to ear.

"I am afraid you have the advantage of me. I don't believe I have had the pleasure of making your acquaintance. And you seem to know me rather well." He looked down at her with an indulgent lilt of his lips. "That doesn't seem quite fair, now, does it?"

She hesitated for a moment before she stuck her hand out. "My name is . . . Juliet."

The warmth of his large hand enveloped her much smaller one. He raised an ebony brow. "Juliet? As in *Romeo and Juliet?*" he clarified, his tone faintly mocking. He knew she was lying, of course. But why? She was either an incurable romantic or a naive twit. To his surprise, he discovered he had a marked preference for the former.

She donned a puckish grin. "Naturally."

Glancing down, he realized he was still clasping her hand and promptly released it. "I think," he said with a hint of derision, "as you've approached me with your *very* tempting offer, you should explain why you wish to throw away what I presume is, at present, a perfectly good reputation."

She squared her shoulders. "I have no need of a pristine reputation," she told him in curt tones, her chin arched in defiance.

"Indeed." He crossed his arms over his chest and appraised her with keen interest. "You must be the first and only member of your gender to feel that way."

She snickered at that remark. "What good has it ever gotten any woman? Save for landing her in the dreaded marriage mart," she muttered with obvious disgust for that unfortunate state. "Besides, I have asked you to ruin me, my lord. Not court me. The less we know about each other, the better."

He bit back a smile. Her guileless nature was utterly charming. That she was a refreshing change from the Lady Declaires of his acquaintance there could be no doubt. Besides, it did his jaded heart good to find innocence was alive and well and talking to him.

"I see your point," he murmured thoughtfully. "And I appreciate the difference," he added with a sardonic grin. "Still, I am curious. If I am to be the man to do the deed, I must know why a charming young girl such as yourself would deliberately seek to ruin herself?''

She expelled an irritated sigh. ''I cannot see what difference my reasons could possibly make to you,'' she snapped, her impatience mounting. ''You are either willing, or you are not.''

He studied her for a long moment, his hooded, languid gaze roaming over her. She looked all of about twelve years old. Bold as brass, she practically demanded he tarnish her fine reputation on the spot. ''You understand, of course, the gravity of what you ask?''

''Oh, yes,'' she replied, clearly enamored of a state considered by most members of her sex as tragic. ''It is my understanding that there are three traditional ways to achieve total ruin,'' she added in a flourish of barely contained excitement.

''I can think of several,'' he muttered with sarcasm.

''Oh, good,'' she said, a gleam of anticipation in her eye. ''I felt certain you would know the most efficient way. I want to be totally ruined, mind you.''

''Irrevocably?'' he queried with amused tolerance.

She nodded her curly head. ''Completely. Let there be not a shred of decency left to my name.''

His forehead crinkled in speculation. ''What makes you think I am your man?''

She glanced up at him in surprise. ''Why, given your outrageous reputation, you are exactly the sort of man I require.''

He inclined his raven head. ''I am flattered.''

''Think nothing of it. Any man who could . . . could . . .'' Her voice trailed off. Two blotches of bright red stained her cheeks.

One dark brow drifted upward. ''Could?'' he prompted.

Her pert little nose wrinkled, and she leaned forward to whisper, ''Well . . . you know.''

He shook his head. ''No. I don't.'' He folded his arms over

his broad chest and gazed down at her. "Why don't you tell me?"

She swallowed audibly. "Suffice to say," she replied, clearing her throat to conceal her awkwardness. "I shall not be the first debutante to fall from grace."

"Nor the last," he snorted with derision. This charade had gone on long enough. It was time to set the impetuous little miss straight. "I hate to disillusion you, but I make it a rule never to prey on young innocents."

Her eyes went wide. "Never?" she asked, crestfallen.

"Never."

"I see." Forlorn, she bit her lip and pondered her situation. "What if . . . I were willing to pay you?" she asked, glancing up at him from beneath speculative lashes.

To his credit he did not laugh. "You're that desperate, eh?"

She pulled a miserable frown. "I am afraid so," she muttered on a restless sigh. "I simply must destroy my reputation."

"Mmm," he murmured indulgently, "that is quite a vexing problem. But I sincerely doubt you could afford me," he drawled with barely cloaked sarcasm. "And in any event, I couldn't possibly accept your money. Just for future reference," he advised in a sage whisper, "it is usually the other way around."

"Oh." She sounded utterly dejected. Her forehead creased in thought. "I was given to understand it worked both ways."

He shook his head to the contrary. "Afraid not."

"Oh, very well." She shrugged off her misunderstanding. "Still, I do wish you'd reconsider, my lord. Could you not make an exception in my case? Just this once?" she practically begged him.

She was unlike any woman of his acquaintance—in, or out, of the bedroom. Nothing short of temporary insanity, however, could induce him to shatter her chaste existence. No matter how tempting a morsel she was.

"No," he said at length, "I do not think I will."

"Why ever not? Surely," she sputtered, her tone harsh with frustration, "I am eminently worthy of ruin."

He inclined his dark head in agreement. "Eminently."

Her eyes narrowed on his faintly amused face. "See here, you *are* Lord Lancaster," she asked, rancor sharpening her tone, "known over half of London as the notorious Hunter, are you not?"

His lips curled slightly. "I have heard that unfortunate euphemism used to describe me, yes."

She slapped her hands on her narrow hips. "Then, it is true that you've charmed more women than you can count out of their virtue and husbands cleave to their wives the moment you enter a room?" she demanded hotly.

He winced. By Jove, was his reputation as bad as that? "Do they?" he asked on a bored sigh.

Exasperated and clearly at the end of her tether, she burst out, "I cannot credit how a man capable of unholy wickedness with his own stepsister will not grant me one insignificant favor."

His jaw turned to granite. So, the vile gossip mongers were still whispering about poor, sweet Julia. No one dared suggest the child was his—publicly. They did not have the mettle to meet him on the field at dawn. But they would damn well hypothesize in private. It sickened him to hear of it.

"That episode," he ground out, "of which you so cavalierly speak, is not founded in a shred of truth."

Two delicately arched brows shot upward. "Not a smidgeon?" she asked, clearly amazed by the discovery.

Devil take it! The little chit actually sounded disappointed. "Not a one," he told her, his voice like ice. "It is, however, a painful subject for me and my family as a whole. Something I do not wish to discuss."

By God, if he could lay his hands on the blackguard responsible for his stepsister's decline, he would make him pay. He had scoured Julia's possessions for some evidence as to the bastard's name, but he found nothing more than a love letter and an insignia ring. Not much to go on. But he was determined to seek retribution. If it took him years, he would make the blackguard pay for destroying his beautiful stepsister.

"I . . . apologize," she managed to get out. "But I can hardly be responsible for tales of your disreputable past, however exaggerated. Believe me," she griped, crossing her arms over her chest, "it comes as no small disappointment to me. Am I to assume that episode in the Thames last month is also pure fiction?"

His lips twitched ever so slightly. "No. But the lady in question was fully clothed at the time."

She arched an inquisitive brow.

"Her aquatic abilities were woefully lacking," he went on to explain. "I had no choice but to jump in after her."

"I see." Deep worry lines marred her otherwise perfect forehead. "In that case, my lord, I simply cannot understand why you have refused my offer. What's wrong with me?" she asked, gazing up at him with guileless blue eyes.

His slow gaze slid over her, lazily assessing the creamy expanse of her neck, her nicely rounded shoulders, her soft, supple breasts. His hooded stare lingered on the neckline of her simple garb. "Nothing that the next few years won't remedy," he drawled out.

She gawked at him. "Are you suggesting," she asked, bristling from the top of her curly head to the tips of her tiny toes, "I am too young?"

"Precisely." He took her by the shoulders, turned her around and patted her on the backside. "Now, why don't you go back to the nursery where you belong, before you get yourself into some real trouble?"

"Go back to the nursery!" She spun around to face him,

hands balled into fists. "I'll have you know," she averred, nearly bursting with indignation, "I've acquired a wealth of experience well beyond my eighteen years."

"I've no doubt you have," he imparted with dry sarcasm. "Being ruined by me, however," he told her with a note of warning in his voice, "shall not be one of them."

"I must say," she sputtered angrily, "you certainly do not live up to your reputation. You, sir, are clearly not the notorious scoundrel I hoped. In fact," she added with bristling contempt, "you are not a whit like the man of whom I heard so much."

He shook his head. That made twice. He really needed to do something about his reputation. Whatever happened to a man sowing his oats? And the sanctity of the boudoir? Perhaps his father was right. If Hunter continued on his current course, no reputable family would admit him. Either he decided to live up to his wickedness or marry before it was too late to acquire a bride worth having.

"Sorry to disappoint you," he uttered with a cool smile, "but my answer is final."

Her spine straightened. "Obviously," she said with as much dignity as she could summon under the mortifying circumstances, "I misjudged you."

"Obviously," he concurred with a nod of his perfectly groomed head.

Dozens of unruly, fiery red ringlets bounced every which way as she haughtily tossed her head back and said with an imperious air, "I see no reason to continue our brief acquaintance."

"Nor do I." He etched a mocked bow. "Good evening, Juliet."

"Good-bye, Lord Rakehell," she barked and hurried past the uncooperative rogue.

Her legs could not carry her down the narrow garden path fast enough. She had never been more insulted in her life! Back to the nursery, indeed. She would like to send him back to school to learn some manners.

Humiliation mingled with outrage. Her cheeks burned. How dare he spank her as though she were a child? She pressed her cool palms against her hot cheeks. What utter embarrassment!

Tonight was becoming a perfectly ghastly affair. Nothing was working out as she planned. She hadn't considered he might be selective. A rake was a rake. Any woman would do. Wouldn't she?

Her mouth twisted. Apparently not. He may cut the most impressive figure of man she had ever encountered, but that did not give him license to be rude. The man was beyond contempt.

"Oh, bother!" She snatched a blossom from the nearby peony bush and tugged at the soft white petals. She had to come up with a replacement for that offensive boar. Fast. At this rate, she would never get ruined.

Chapter 2

Hunter managed to slip into the crowded ballroom without encountering any more female interlopers. Gad! What a strange evening this had turned out to be, he thought, channeling his way through the swarm of popinjay suitors and frivolous females. Up until an hour ago, he would have wagered he had heard it all. Precious little could shock him. The outrageous baggage in the juvenile pink gown, however, was something he had never before encountered.

He shook his head and smiled to himself. She was quite an adorable little thing. At least, what he could make of her in the dim light. Nice legs too. Pity, he wasn't sufficiently ignoble to accept her offer. Just the same, he couldn't help wondering who she was.

He was about to see how much money he could lose in a friendly game of commerce when yet another woman intercepted him. This one was tall, blond and slim. And she looked extremely distraught.

Devil take it, was he to be accosted by distressed females all night long? He glanced longingly at the mahogany tables, the deck of gleaming crisp cards, and the poker chips that beckoned. He drew a weary sigh and looked away. Forcing a polite smile to his lips, he asked the beautiful blonde in his path, "Madam, are you unwell?"

"Indeed I am, my lord." She wet her lips nervously. "We are not formally acquainted. But I wonder if I might not impose on your good nature to assist me?" she asked in a soft under-tone.

He frowned with displeasure. Damn and blast. Not again. "Of course," he managed with a stiff civility. "What is it that troubles you?"

"You are," she whispered, "I believe, familiar with my husband, Ian Somers?"

"Ian?" He breathed a sigh of relief. Lady Somers would scarcely be interested in a romp in the bushes. Or total ruin. "Of course. We fought on the Peninsula together. I'm afraid I haven't seen him in ages." Hunter glanced around the densely populated ballroom. "Is he in attendance this evening?"

"Unfortunately, no. His father is ill. He could not come away just now. I am here with my younger sister."

"I see. I hope you and your sister are enjoying yourselves?"

"Tolerably well." She hesitated for a moment before she asked, "Might I impose on your friendship and take you into my confidence on a rather grievous family matter?"

Ian had saved his neck more times than he could recall. No matter how much he wanted to lose himself in a bottle of brandy and a good card game, Hunter could hardly abandon Lady Somers in her hour of need.

"If there is anything I can do to alleviate your discomfort, I will gladly do it," he assured her.

She cleared her throat. "The matter which weighs so heavily on my mind concerns my sister. Have you perhaps made her acquaintance?'' She looked positively ill as she explained, ''I fear she would not be easy to forget. She has . . . a rather singular request.''

His lips twitched. *That* was an understatement. So, the little scamp had an older and, he hoped, wiser sister. ''I believe I have had that pleasure.''

She gulped. ''You did not comply with her—''

His eyebrow lifted. ''Request?'' He shook his head. ''I should sooner rob the cradle, madam.''

She released the breath she had been holding and splayed her hand over her chest. ''Thank heaven.''

His lips curled ever so slightly. ''I take it her name is not Juliet?''

Lady Somers's forehead creased. ''No. It's Sabrina.'' She shot him a queer look. ''Why did you believe her name to be Juliet?''

He chuckled softly. ''For the simple reason that I was cast in the role of Romeo.''

Her face turned a whiter shade of pale. ''Oh, dear. How embarrassing for you. I must apologize for my sister; she is younger than her years. Due perhaps to the fact that she has led a completely sheltered life and has an unfortunate headstrong streak.''

''Think nothing of it,'' he replied with an amicable smile.

She looked visibly assuaged and managed a smile for the first time. ''I felt sure you were a man of honor. That is why I suggested she approach you.''

A deep crevice marred his forehead. ''*You* suggested?'' Was the entire family eccentric?

Her smile blossomed. ''As you must have noticed, my sister is bound and determined to destroy herself. I could think of nothing else save offering a man whom I believed would not—''

''Accept her offer?'' he interjected archly.

"Exactly." She glanced at him tentatively. "You are not . . . angry, I hope?"

Was he angry? Diverted was a better word. His brief encounter with the little baggage was sure to be one of this evening's highlights.

"Not in the least. Although," he muttered dryly, "I cannot say the same for your sister."

"That's what worries me." She caught her lower lip between her teeth. "I feel certain she will approach someone less honorable. I cannot very well continually intercept her invitations and beg abstention, my lord."

"Quite," he murmured pensively. "I see your dilemma."

"What am I to do?" She gazed up at him with enormous, miserable doe eyes. He knew he could not refuse her aid.

"Allow me to assist you, Lady Somers. Rest assured, your sister shall come to no ill this evening."

Relief flooded her features. "I felt certain you would do us good," she said, clutching his hand. "I cannot thank you enough for your kindness. I know Ian will be eternally grateful when he hears of your kind intercession."

"Think nothing of it." He bowed politely over her hand. "It will be my very great pleasure to assist you in any way that I can."

He told himself it was because he owed an old friend a favor. And that he was helping a beautiful damsel in distress. He even thought of poor, dear Julia so brutally wronged. He dared imagine himself as a savior, halting a foolish innocent's leap into utter misery.

Whatever the reason, he found himself in search of the damned chit with an aim to protect her. The notorious Hunter, who had graced more matronly thresholds than he cared to remember, was off to save an innocent from ruin. If it wasn't so damned ironic, it would be hilarious.

* * *

It did not take long to find her. She was in a secluded alcove, batting her eyelashes at Lord Whitehead, whose wolfish tendencies were legendary. An irritated frown touched Hunter's lips. What on earth women saw in the man, he could not fathom. He was blond, pale, taller than a bean pole, and twice as spindly. He found himself wondering if the wimpy Whitehead had accepted the little chit's outlandish offer. A black scowl crossed his face. His gait quickened.

"Ah, there you are," a deep voice uttered softly against her ear.

Sabrina looked up. Her gaze collided with the sultriest pair of roguish eyes she had ever seen. Her breath caught in her throat.

"Hunter!"

Her eyes widened owlishly at his lazy, sensual smile. It was far too warm. The way he was looking at her reminded her of Grandfather's hunters licking their chops before a good meal.

He etched a mocked bow. "None other. I wondered where you'd gotten to."

"You did?" she gulped.

"I've been looking for you everywhere," he murmured and pressed a kiss to her hand.

Her mouth dropped open. "You have?"

He inclined his head imperceptibly in Whitehead's direction. "Forgive me," he drawled, an icy edge to his voice, "but the lady promised this dance to me."

Whitehead arched a dubious brow. "Did she, indeed?"

A dangerous glint shone in Hunter's eye. "Are you perchance suggesting I have mistaken the matter?"

Whitehead looked taken aback. "O-of course not."

Hunter bared his teeth in a predatorial smile. "Good. I

shouldn't like to have to call you out. It is so damp and chilly at dawn.''

Whitehead's scrawny Adam's apple bobbed up and down. He bowed his head in a curt farewell. Obviously, Sabrina was not worth fighting over. She could do no more than stand helplessly by while Whitehead mumbled something about it being a pleasure to meet her and disappeared with his tail between his legs.

Her furious blue gaze collided with Hunter's indolent silver orbs. ''I never promised you anything,'' she hissed under her breath, ''least of all the next dance.''

He ignored her censure, clasped her by the hand and dragged her toward the dance floor.

''See here,'' she cried, struggling to keep pace with his long strides, ''who do you think you are, barging in where you are not wanted?''

''Think of me''—he pulled her into his arms and gathered her close—''as Romeo.''

She scowled up at him. ''Very amusing, my lord. Kindly leave me. I have no intentions of dancing.''

''That's too bad,'' he countered with icy determination, ''because you are going to dance, with me, right now.''

Thoroughly annoyed with the meddling man, she glared up at him and dug her heels mulishly into the floor. ''No,'' she countered firmly through clenched teeth, ''I am not.''

Heedless of her objections, he placed one large, masterful hand on her waist and drew her flush against him. Before she could utter an objection, he had whisked her small frame onto the dance floor. As the music sent the couples twirling around the enormous ballroom, she felt her feet leave the floor. Her lips thinned with displeasure. Another domineering beast, he and Grandfather would get on famously.

His strong, masculine grip grated on her. She detested the

hot flourish of pleasure that threatened to consume her. It was entirely due to the uncooperative rogue's proximity.

"Has anyone ever told you," she whispered in a fierce under breath, "you are a brute?"

"You're the first." He whirled her around as if she weighed less than a feather.

The unnerving warmth of his hand seeped through her thin dress, searing her flesh. Her discomfort increased tenfold. "Doubtless," she grumbled with irritation, "I shall not be the last."

"I cannot tell you how heavily that weighs on my mind," he drawled, his voice laced with mockery.

She glanced up at him from beneath beetled brows. "You are a vexing man. I was doing rather well before you interrupted."

"Mmm. I noticed." He glanced down at her upturned, petulant face. "Just what the devil did you think you were doing back there?" he asked roughly.

"Throwing myself at Whitehead. What did it look like?" she muttered testily.

His jaw clenched. "That's what I was afraid of."

"You can hardly blame me, my lord," she said, an irritated edge to her voice. "What choice did I have? Besides being the only other rake I could find on such short notice, he was available. And interested."

"I wager he was," he snorted with derision.

She gave him a mulish look. "This is all your fault, I hope you realize. If you hadn't been so stingy with your favors, I'd be well on my way to achieving my goal."

"My fault?" he repeated, agog at her temerity. "In case you have misunderstood," he growled against her ear, "I just rescued you from the lion's den."

"Oh, pish posh!"

Pish posh? What the devil did pish posh mean?

"You must see in what impossible position your lack of cooperation places me."

"I am afraid to ask what position that might be?"

She expelled a deep sigh. "Now I shall have to move down the list. Approach someone new. Make another introduction. And I sincerely hope *he* will be a rake worthy of his reputation."

"The list?" he echoed incredulously. "You have a list?" His face darkened. "What blasted list?"

"Naturally, I have a list," she snapped. "What do you take me for? I'll have you know, I've researched the subject thoroughly. You were my first choice, of course. But as you are unwilling to oblige and you've seen fit to interfere where you do not belong," she reminded him tersely, "I have no other option but to pursue Lord Carew."

Momentarily stupefied, he gazed down at her. "By God," he breathed, "you are a most singular girl."

"Thank you," she replied primly. "But I think you miss the enormity of my current predicament. I've lost valuable time. Worse yet," she said, exasperated, "I do not know what Carew looks like."

His arms tightened around her, crushing her delicate frame against his hard, lean body. "Listen to me," he growled, fully intending to pound some sense into her addled brain. "You little fool! This is not a game. Do you have any idea what could happen to you if you offer yourself to every stranger you meet?"

His breath was warm against her temple. A tingle of excitement ran down her spine. "I was not offering myself, as you put it," she muttered, wriggling to no avail against his hard, muscular chest. It was most disconcerting to be pressed against a warm wall of manly flesh. "I merely want to be ruined."

He snickered, tightening his grip on her small waist. "It amounts to the same thing to a man like Carew."

An unbidden current of pleasure swept over her, causing her

mind to draw a momentary blank. "Yes . . . well . . . as you are not going to be involved," she replied, clearing her throat, "kindly unhand me and let me go about my business."

"No."

She quit struggling and looked up at him. "No?" Her eyes searched his handsome face for some clue to his intentions. "What do you mean, no?" She eyed him with suspicion. "What are you about, my lord? Have you perchance . . . reconsidered?" she asked, breathless with longing.

He cast a dark look in her direction. Devil take it! No, he had not reconsidered. What kind of imp ran around offering herself to men without the slightest idea what her offer actually entailed?

He ought to leave the little chit right where she stood. Let her learn her lesson the hard way. What was she to him? Nothing. Just another foolish henwit. London was full of them this time of year.

His mouth thinned with anger. Hell. How had he gotten dragged into this ridiculous situation in the first place? It was rather like asking the wolf to mind the sheep. He smirked and glanced down at the rambunctious bundle in his arms: an innocent, wayward little lamb, more like. Painful memories of his stepsister's folly tugged at his heart, softening him. Julia had been roughly the same age when she made her grand faux pas. If only she had had a dark angel to guide her.

His critical gaze swept over Sabrina's face. It struck him suddenly that she was quite a beauty. Not in the traditional sense, of course. Most would not appreciate her untamed red hair, which curled about her face in reckless disarray, or the sprinkle of freckles across her nose, which should have been doused with lemon juice. But she had a wild, unvarnished innocence that was strangely engaging. Those enormous blue eyes fairly sparkled every time she smiled at him, as she was doing right now. And she had dimples. The cutest pair of dimples he had seen in a long, long time. Oh, yes, she was very appealing.

"I might be persuaded," he told her softly. His gaze slid over her flushed face and settled on her soft, supple lips. Another man might be tempted to taste that sassy little mouth. *Only a dishonorable bastard,* came a harsh mental reminder. He tore his gaze from her soft parted lips. They were far too inviting. What the deuce was wrong with him? She was a mere child, completely naive to the ways of the world.

"Might you be?" she asked, all eagerness and excitement.

"Naturally, I will require full participation on your part," he told her in a low, husky voice. "That is absolutely necessary to achieve total ruin."

"I assumed as much." She craned her neck back to look him squarely in the eye. "You do understand, of course, time is critical?"

"Trust me," his silky voice held a sardonic note. "What I have in mind won't take long."

"Oh, good," she said, bubbling over with enthusiasm, "I must say, I am pleased that you are the one to do the deed."

He fixed her with a curious gaze. "Why?"

"If you're going to be ruined, my lord, who better to do it than a man who is the envy of every woman in town? You are considered by far the most handsome rake of the season," she told him in a blunt manner of which he was growing fond.

He stared down at the adorable scamp and managed to utter a dry, "Thank you."

"Don't mention it."

He shot her a rueful look. "I hope you won't be disappointed when you find out what I've planned for you."

"Oh," she replied in heartfelt earnest, "I feel certain I shall not be."

Those huge, artless eyes of hers tugged at his conscience. What the devil was the matter with him? He wasn't actually lamenting his decision, was he? Devil take it, no. But he didn't have the heart to disappoint her either. She looked so deuced eager, standing there like a willing victim in his arms. Devilishly tempting, too. The least he could do was give her something to remember and giggle about with the rest of the debutantes of her acquaintance. Taking her petite gloved hand in his, he weaved through the scads of guests and led her from the dance floor across the marbled foyer.

"Where are you taking me?" she asked, barely able to contain herself as she trotted along behind him down the long hallway.

"In here," he told her and opened the door to what appeared to be Lord Holmes's library, for the walls were covered with countless volumes of leather-bound books.

Closing the door, he swung her around and pulled her into his arms. Gasping in surprise, her eyes flew wide. He bent his head to press a kiss to her lips. His mouth was a mere hairsbreadth from her own. He did something he never had occasion to do—he hesitated—and found himself gazing into the most gorgeous pair of blue eyes he had ever beheld. Two innocent, startling blue eyes searched his. It was more than the striking color, he realized. It was the expression. He knew exactly what she was thinking. Or very nearly. She was undeniably startled and a little apprehensive. But what struck him most was the trust shining up at him. A frown crossed his face. It made him feel like a real cad. No woman had ever looked at him that way. He reckoned he did not deserve to be trusted.

Her softly parted lips were a stronger temptation than he would have liked.

"What are you doing?" she whispered.

His hands slid up her arms, drawing her closer against him. "I am going to kiss you."

She wrinkled her brow. "Why should you want to do that? And in the library of all places?"

He stared down at her for a moment. He had never met a woman who talked so much. "I prefer to sample the merchandise before buying, so to speak," he imparted dryly.

Her mouth formed the word, "Oh."

She did not appear the least bit excited by the prospect.

He arched one dark brow. "I presume you have no objections?"

"No. None at all," she replied. "You may kiss me if you like."

An easy grin played around his lips. "I am so glad you approve."

Closing her eyes, she lifted her dainty little chin and offered her closed mouth to receive his kiss. He wondered if he were not a debauched cad, for this was the most endearing sight he had ever witnessed. Slowly, he covered her enticing mouth in a tender kiss, pressing his lips gently against hers. He lifted his head and waited for her to swoon.

She did not swoon.

She frowned.

"Is something amiss?" he asked, his ego slightly deflated.

"Oh, no," she replied politely, but her expression was all disappointment.

"Apparently, my expertise is lacking," he averred with a sardonic smirk.

"Well, it was not what I was given to understand it would be," she allowed.

Mildly insulted, his lips twisted with displeasure. "Am I to assume your first kiss was not everything you hoped?"

"No." She told him frankly. "But it was not my first kiss."

He blinked in astonishment. Devil take it. His jaw clenched. What the hell did she mean, not her first kiss? She was a child barely out of the schoolroom. His gaze darkened. "Who's kissed you?" he demanded, his tone brusque.

"I was kissed by Jeremy, our stable boy, two years ago. I

must confess," she went on to say, "he put a bit more effort into it than you, my lord. It was rather wet and sloppy, but infinitely more exciting than what just passed between us."

Impertinent chit! Infinitely more exciting. The hell it was. Since when did stable boys go around kissing ladies of the manor? He had never been so piqued in all his days. The little baggage thought he fell short of the local help. "I am sorry to hear it," he muttered in a churlish tone.

"I don't mean to complain," she rushed out, "and I am more grateful than I can say for your cooperation. But—"

"But what?" Irritation made his voice grate.

"Well," she said, wetting her lips in an enticing manner, "it strikes me that you chose a rather inopportune moment."

She never ceased to amaze him. First, she critiqued his technique. Then she argued over his timing. Something could be said for jaded women. Ironically, they were much easier to please. His temper flared. "How's that?" he asked her roughly.

"If you were planning to kiss me, might it not have been better to do it earlier, for the benefit of the other guests?"

He gave her a speculative glance. "Possibly. But I have something else in mind for you. Provided, of course, you still want to be completely ruined."

"I do hope it is more exciting than kissing," she remarked with a disappointed pout.

He smirked at that remark. "I'll try not to disappoint you." Smarting from the little imp's setdown, he suggested amicably, "Perhaps, if you gave me another chance, I might garner higher praise than a common stable boy?"

She shrugged one slender shoulder. "If you like. But quite honestly," she imparted on a bored sigh, "I cannot understand what all the fuss is about."

"You will," he vowed in a low growl and slid his arms around her small waist, pressing her close enough to feel the pounding of her heart. "I promise," he whispered against her mouth.

Her soft curves molded to the masculine contours of his muscular body. He felt her tremble. A smile of male satisfaction spread over his lips. She was not wholly unaffected. As his mouth lowered to devour her sweet, supple lips, he realized with a jolt that he was far from immune.

The moment his lips brushed against hers—caressing, melding her lips beneath his—he knew his mistake. She gave herself up to the kiss, opening like a budding flower. Soft, sweet and eager. She was like a perfect rose, delicate and full of exquisite promise. As his mouth, warm and wet, opened to taste her fully, his arms, strong and sure, tightened around her. One hand slid down her back and settled in the soft indent. His palm splayed against the small of her back, pressing her closer.

Her ardent response surprised him. And his first taste of her left him wanting more. Much more. The kiss turned fervent, hungry. His mouth twisted and turned over hers, devouring her as if he had been starving for years.

Sabrina had never experienced anything quite like Hunter's kiss. The touch of his lips seemed to set her aflame. Every inch of her body awakened to his caress. A warm wave of pleasure engulfed her, rendering her incapable of rational thought. Floating adrift a sensual, soft cloud, her arms crept around his neck. The feel of his soft, persuasive mouth—hot, wet, and overwhelmingly sweet—made her quiver. She leaned into him, desperate for more of this delicious ambrosia. Currents of desire rippled through her. Clutching at his hard, muscular arms for support, she met his fervor, welcoming her foray into the sensual world.

His hands moved in a slow caress over her enticing body, caressing her firm, round breasts, small waist and narrow hips with a precision that elicited a soft moan of pleasure. She twined her fingers through his ebony hair and met the deep, erotic thrusts of his tongue with equal pleasure.

She was an apt pupil. And that pleased him more than he cared to admit. She followed his passionate lead with remarkable finesse, savoring every sweet, tantalizing, provocative movement which served to heighten his pleasure. In fact, in no time at all, she had turned his seductive skill on him! Her tongue was doing the most unbelievable things to him. Those sexy little half sighs, half moans of pleasure threatened to stretch the boundary of self-restraint. And the way her fingertips caressed his ear and his nape was driving him mad. Her instinctive, uninhibited response was nearly his undoing.

To his stunned disbelief, he acknowledged he was losing control. If he did not end the kiss, he would end up obliging the little chit. She would be irrevocably ruined on Holmes's library floor.

When at last he tore his mouth from hers and came up for air, she expelled a deep, dreamy sigh and, to his surprise, nestled against him as if she never wanted to leave the succor of his embrace.

"That was very pleasant indeed, my lord," she whispered, in awe of what had just transpired, and rubbed her cheek against his broad chest. "I never knew kissing could be quite so . . . wonderful," she said on a breathless sigh.

It sure as hell was! What the devil had just happened, anyway? he wondered with a frown. How could this little slip of a girl affect him so? It was damned disturbing. He was old enough to be her father. Well, not quite. An elder brother, at the worst.

She buried her face in his neck. "I feel so strange," she murmured in a soft, warm breath against his throat.

Devil take it, so did he. His arms closed around her. He rested his cheek against her vibrant red tresses and drew a deep breath. She smelled wonderful, like a fresh summer's day. And the way she fit in his arms, nothing had felt this right in a long, long time.

He shuddered at the direction to which his thoughts had turned. He was depraved. He had to be. She was fourteen years his junior, a mere girl . . . a girl with a woman's body. And a deeply passionate nature. If he did not release her luscious little body right this minute, he would be tempted to drink more deeply from that sweet fountain of tempestuous youth.

"Meet me outside the front entrance in fifteen minutes," he murmured in a warm breath against her mouth and abruptly set her away from the serenity of his embrace.

She opened her mouth to object, but before she could utter a single word, he quit the library. Heavens, she thought on a wistful sigh, she dearly hoped his plan involved more demonstrations of his rakish expertise. She would be severely disappointed if it did not.

Sabrina could barely contain her excitement as she bounced down the stone horseshoe steps and waited for the instrument of her ruin to appear. The notorious Hunter would see to it that not a shred of decency was attached to her name. She had no idea in what way he hoped to achieve his ends, but she found herself extremely curious to experience whatever it was he had in mind. If it was anything like the way he had just kissed her, she was bound to reel. One thing was for certain, she thought, rocking on her heels with delight, Grandfather would be livid.

A sleek black carriage rounded the drive and came to a halt where she stood. She smiled to herself. How clever he was! By tomorrow morning, she would be well and duly ruined. And what fun she would have tonight. A tingle of excitement rushed over her. This was more fortuitous than she ever dreamed.

She would have to come up with a way to show her gratitude

for all he had done for her. Or was about to do, as the case might be. To think, earlier this evening she had imagined he was the most vile sort of person. And now, here he was, gallantly coming to her aid. And kissing her. Soundly. Passionately. Deliciously. She drew a dreamy sigh. Life certainly had odd twists of fate. And she was never as glad of anything in all her born days.

The object of her admiration jumped down from the carriage. She smiled up at him with warmth. "My lord, I cannot thank you enough for what you are about to do," she gushed.

His lips twitched. "You may not always think so highly of me."

She clutched his arm. "Oh, but you are wrong." She gazed up at him with artless eyes. "I could never form a dim view of your character. Not now."

He frowned slightly. It was about time she learned a rogue's kiss meant nothing. He just did not like being the cad to teach her that bitter lesson. Regardless of how pleasurable he found the dalliance, after tonight, he would never see this adorable little hellion again. He had discovered intoxicating innocence was a bit too tempting, even for a seasoned rake like him to resist entirely. He removed her hand from his velvet sleeve.

"I shall bear that in mind."

"Where are you taking me?" she asked, jubilant with anticipation.

"Home," came his curt retort. He tugged open the black lacquered door and motioned for her to climb in.

A gurgle of laughter escaped her throat. "I hope you don't plan to abduct me and demand ransom," she teased lightly. "I doubt Grandfather would pay a farthing for me."

His eyes turned a dark slate gray. "Don't underestimate yourself," he snapped at her.

She smiled a little ruefully. "I'm not. I know exactly what I am worth in his eyes. Still," she said, her smile turning impish, "it might be fun to be kidnaped. Is that what you are planning?"

He shook his head at her. "Nothing nearly as exciting. Now, get in."

She hiked up her hem, baring two lovely ankles, and climbed into the carriage. Two things struck her almost immediately. First, his carriage was quite elegant, with purple satin walls and velvet squabs. Second, her sister Amanda was sitting smack dab in the middle of those comfy seats!

Her brows knitted in confusion. "Amanda? What on earth—"

"It's for your good, dearest," Amanda insisted, reaching over to give her hand a sisterly pat.

Sabrina pieced the scenario together with lightning speed. The notorious Hunter had never intended to ruin her. Amanda, her so-called loyal, devoted sister, had conspired with the black-guard from the start. No wonder she had plied Sabrina with wicked stories prior to their arrival this evening. Her despicable scheme was now patently clear. It was insulting. It was hurtful. It was mortifying.

Fixing her sister with a wrathful look, Sabrina burst out, "How could you?"

Amanda smiled at her sister's wounded expression. "Some day, you'll thank me and this kind gentleman, too, for saving you."

"Saving me?" Sabrina gawked at her sister. "Gentleman?" Vile rogue more like.

He had tricked her.

And he had used her.

She should never have trusted him. And she definitely shouldn't have kissed him. It rankled her most to know Amanda had enlisted *his* help. Her own sister! These days a girl could not trust her own flesh and blood. It was deplorable.

She opened her mouth to issue a rounding set down, but was deprived of that pleasure by the wretched rogue.

He slammed the carriage door shut. Without so much as a sideways glance in her direction, he instructed Amanda in a curt tone, "See she gets home safely. Next time, she might not be so fortunate."

His hateful voice rang with condescension in Sabrina's ears. One burning desire consumed her. She wanted to murder her sister. Slowly.

"I cannot thank you enough, my lord," Amanda's insipid voice grated against Sabrina's nerves.

"I am only to happy to be of service, Lady Somers," came his disgustingly polite rejoinder.

How could she have clung to him like that without at least some guarantee of ruin? Heat crept into Sabrina's cheeks as she recalled their torrid kiss. Amid her self-recriminations, a thought occurred to her. She could still achieve ruin. All was not lost. A slow, devious smile crept across her lips. She would give this arrogant interloper the resounding set down he so dearly deserved.

A gleam of mischief lit her eyes as she remarked with brazen cheek, "I am sure my dear sister would love to hear all about what just transpired in the library, my lord."

Piercing gray eyes glinted dangerously into amused blue. The air fairly crackled with tension. Her mouth broadened into a triumphant smirk. She had cornered him rather nicely.

Amanda glanced from one to the other. "In the library?" she queried in dismay.

"Pray, do tell, my lord. I, for one," Sabrina chimed in, verbally tweaking his arrogant nose, "am dying to hear your explanation."

Amanda turned the full force of her questioning gaze toward his lordship. "My lord?"

His furious gaze locked with Sabrina's. "A momentary

diversion," he imparted on a bored sigh. "Nothing more. Your sister is young and has a flair for the dramatic. I fear her imagination is overactive. Where she cannot find scandal," he added with a nonchalant shrug, "she invents it. A foolish and childish game," he intoned with a meaningful glint in his eye.

Sabrina glowered at him, outrage lurking in her furious gaze. He crossed his arms over his chest and leaned one shoulder against the carriage door. He had the audacity to smile.

"As you must know," he told her sister with maddening composure, "such a circumstance leads to embarrassment for the lady's family and little more than an imposition for the gentleman."

"I am relieved beyond measure to hear that was all there was to it," Amanda replied with a sigh.

Sabrina gave her sister a dubious look. How she could swallow that rogue's Banbury tale, like an empty-headed twit, was beyond her. The man was as slippery as a snake, and twice as dangerous. No wonder he was notorious. He avoided culpability with amazing deftness.

Ignoring the repellent bounder, she gave her sister a forsaken look. "I thought S. K. Hughes was as important to you as he is to me," she blurted out, hurt written all over her face.

"Oh, he is," Amanda insisted with what struck Sabrina as poorly feigned earnest. "Truly."

"You know how important this is to me. How could you?"

"Please, Sabrina," Amanda urged with a furtive glance at his lordship, "don't fly up in the boughs."

"I shall never forgive you," Sabrina replied with strong conviction.

She felt the notorious Hunter's gaze flick over her. "Oh, I think you'll recover sooner than you think. Good night, fair Juliet," his deep, masculine voice was heavy with hateful mockery. "It's been an education."

Sabrina's head snapped up. Blue shards of ice impaled him. "Rot in hell, Romeo," she imparted with a frigid smile.

Amanda drew in a shocked breath. *"Sabrina."*

His smile broadened into a roguish grin. "Possibly. Just make sure I don't meet you there, my impetuous little one."

He hit the roof of the conveyance with his palm. "Drive on," he commanded and stepped back.

Hunter watched the carriage creak along the gravel drive until the dark of night eclipsed its shadowy form, then shook his head and started up the steps. A smile tugged at the corner of his lips. He could not credit the way that outrageous hoyden had just tried to entrap him. She was more resourceful than he had given her credit for.

An unfamiliar twinge of regret gnawed at him. What fun it would have been to soil that precocious imp's reputation. Who the devil was S. K. Hughes? And why did that blasted name seem oddly familiar?

Chapter 3

A fortnight later, Hunter drew his pensive gaze from the prowling caged animal in the menagerie at the Tower of London. With a critical eye, he examined the woebegone-looking Bow Street Runner he had hired. He had been eager to take his leave of the country and return to London in the hopes that Mr. Crawford would have good news. But what the Runner had to report was worse than Hunter had imagined.

"What you are saying," Hunter said in a lethal tone, "is that you've taken my money and provided none of the information I sought."

Crawford raised his hands in self-defense. "Now, 'old on a minute. I done like y'asks. 'Tain't me fault naught came of it, now is it, milord?"

Hunter sneered at the scruffy-looking man. "No, it isn't. The fact remains, however, I am no closer to learning the identity of the blackguard who led Julia to her ruin. You have your fee, regardless."

The Runner cleared his throat. "That ain't strictly true, milord. I done some pokin' 'bout." He dug into his pocket and retrieved a tattered hankie. Carefully, he unfolded the material to reveal a gold signet ring. "Dunno know what the insignia means yet. But I do know 'twas crafted at a shop on Bond Street. The craftsman remembered casting several rings. His last customer was a fellow by the name o' Paine. Canno' say I remember anyone o' that name among your stepsister's acquaintances, though."

"Several rings, you say?" Hunter remarked, examining the ring thoughtfully. It was an ugly piece. The significance of a snake wrapped around a naked maiden evaded him. Why would anyone sport such a hideous piece on his finger?

"Find this man Paine," he said with harsh impatience and flung the ring into Crawford's grimy paw. "He may know the names of the other owners. I don't care what methods you employ. I want the man responsible for Julia's downfall. Do I make myself clear?"

"Aye, milord, that you do," he said, nodding confidently, and slipped the ring back into his frayed pant pocket. He lifted his shoulders in a defeated shrug. "Don't mind tellin' ye," he muttered, scratching his balding head, " 'tis a strange case this one. I've look into all her dalliances—"

"My stepsister did not have dalliances," Hunter corrected bitingly. He refused to accept that notion. Whoever had destroyed his stepsister led her astray, of that he was certain. Julia's character was above reproach. Her one flaw was that she trusted too easily. And, for that trait, she had paid dearly.

The Runner dragged his red, bulbous nose along his sleeve. "Beggin' yer pardon, milord," he said with a gruff snort. "I meant no offense. Simple fact is, I canno' find nothin' out o' the ordinary."

"Mmm," Hunter intoned. He hadn't been able to unearth any incriminating details of Julia's life either. A somber expression overtook him. "I suppose a signet ring and a love letter are not much to go on." He heaved a sigh. "Keep at it. Let me know as soon as you come up with something."

Mr. Crawford donned his shabby cap. "Right you are, milord," he replied, and tipped his brim in farewell.

As he departed the Tower of London, Hunter's mood was understandably foul. He was not a bit closer to solving the mystery of his stepsister's ruin. He had searched for six long months. Half a blasted year. Tirelessly, he had probed for some clue, some inkling of the scoundrel who had taken her under his spell.

His mouth curled downward. Obviously, he wasn't looking in the right places. For the first time since little Annabelle's birth, he wondered if he would ever discover the identity of her father.

His mouth twisted with contempt. What sort of man would leave a woman to fend for herself and her child without any means of support? Even the most nefarious rakes of his acquaintance paid for their byblows. He winced at the thought of dear Julia involved in such a circumstance. How could the sweet, innocent girl he knew and loved more dearly than anyone in the world have gotten involved with that ilk of person?

Guilt consumed him. Perhaps his father was right. Bad blood did run in the family. It was little wonder Hunter's unheralded return from Italy after nine months with a newborn baby girl in his arms was steeped in controversy. It was difficult to find anyone among the *tonnish* elite who did not believe him capable of such corruption. The fact that Julia had married an obscure Italian count, and her daughter was a countessa, assuaged the vicious rumors not at all.

Hunter's fingers tightened around his walking stick. In retrospect, he wished he had squelched his fierce temper rather than endlessly berating poor Julia for the blackguard's name. Clearly, she had been afraid of Hunter's punitive reaction;

frightened that he, like their father, would judge her actions. No wonder she had refused to offer any explanation for her condition, let alone name the miscreant responsible. Hunter's constant badgering for details during her confinement must have confirmed her worst fears.

Hunter drew a heartfelt sigh. How she must have longed for a confidant, but found an interrogator. It was a wonder she had not grown to despise him over those long, difficult months. No matter how well intentioned, he knew he had behaved badly. It haunted him.

He stabbed in frustration at the cobblestones with his walking stick and swore under his breath. He despised feeling powerless. One thing he would make damn sure of: Annabelle would never know she had been born on the wrong side of the blanket. He would kill the first person who suggested it.

"I think it only fair to tell you," Amanda Somers informed her sister when the two were alone in the rose salon at Morely House on Berkeley Square, "I have written to the Earl of Greystone and thanked him for his intercession."

Sabrina sprang to her feet. "You did *what?*"

Amanda gave her sister a stern look. "I thought someone should."

Sabrina expelled a miserable sigh and plopped back down in the chair beside her sister's escritoire. She knew her sister's note would be a source of amusement for the cad. Thank him! Thus far, the wretch had kissed her, in a most unseemingly— albeit wickedly exciting—fashion and tricked her in a most dishonorable manner. The scoundrel was hardly worthy of gratitude.

"You know Lancaster has caused me no end of misery," she muttered, and hooked her leg over the arm of the chair in a most unladylike manner. "It is extremely disloyal of you to be kind to the vile man."

"It is *Lord* Lancaster. And he is not a vile man," Amanda replied, preoccupied with the arduous task of penning responses to dozens of social invitations. "Ian is very fond of him. I told him how obliging Lord Lancaster was in helping us to avoid total social disaster. He was ever so grateful. As we all should be," she averred with a reproachful look in her impertinent sibling's direction.

Sabrina was not green enough to miss the pointed reminder. Ian had been livid when he learned of Sabrina's quest for total ruin. She received the customary lecture on her wild, compulsive nature. Worse yet, he vowed to put an end to her association with S. K. Hughes should she ever try anything foolish again.

"Lord Lancaster has promised to be as silent as the grave. We owe him a debt of sincere gratitude. If you are embarrassed by the unfortunate incident, you have no one to blame save yourself," Amanda remarked, unmoved by her sister's plight.

Sabrina pouted. "I am not embarrassed in the slightest," she remarked, and raised her chin a notch. "Why should I be?"

Amanda laughed softly. "I can think of several reasons."

Sabrina's lips thinned. While her conduct verged on unconventional, it could hardly compare to the shocking liberty that rogue had taken. She chose to overlook the salient fact that she had enjoyed his kiss thoroughly.

"I am amazed he has the nerve to speak to Ian after the way he comported himself," she intoned with a scowl. "His manners are not at all agreeable, to my way of thinking."

"As I collect," Amanda remarked with poorly disguised mirth, "it was *you* who approached *him*. He can have no reason to be ashamed. If memory serves, he refused you outright."

Sabrina blanched at the reminder. "You were instrumental in his decision to be sure," she said bitterly. "I seriously question the wisdom of speaking to you again after your horrid betrayal.''

Amanda flashed an indulgent smile and pushed back her chair. ''Yes, dearest,'' she murmured as her slippered feet padded across the deep rose-colored Aubusson rug. ''And I was ever so pleased you changed your mind.'' She tugged the tapestry bellpull beside the fireplace.

''You are supposed to support me, and all you ever do is criticize my judgment,'' Sabrina grumbled.

''When you demonstrate to me you have a level head on your shoulders, I should be very happy to pay you the compliment of trusting your judgment.''

Frowning, Amanda lifted her sister's leg off the arm of the Queen Anne chair. ''At some point, dearest, I should very much like to see you comport yourself like a lady for more than one hour at a time.'' She took in her sister's disheveled appearance and sighed unhappily at the sight. ''You are scarcely the epitome of manners, I daresay. You are always the last down to dinner. And you are lucky if your dress is ironed and buttoned,'' she lamented with dry humor.

Nettled by the reprove, Sabrina tossed an irritated glare in her sister's direction. It was, of course, true. Garbed in a pleated, brown silk gown with mameluke sleeves and triple shoulder ruffles, Amanda was the epitome of fashion. How she could be remotely comfortable exercised the mind. Sabrina's wrinkled, light blue muslin gown, however, paled in comparison. No hope for it. Sabrina simply was not a proper lady. Nor did she have any wish to be.

Loosely translated, feminine demeanor equated silent complacency. But that would never do. With so many different thoughts and feelings inside her, threatening at any moment to burst forth, how could she ever hope to squelch them all?

She could not.

Still, she thought on a sigh, it was vexing to live among

people who required total submission of her spirit. How could she ever hope to attain the proper female state? It was useless to try. Her mind was simply too occupied with intellectual quests to trifle with inconsequential details like whether or not her dress was ironed.

"Is it my fault I was born with a natural inclination toward intellectual pursuits?" Sabrina asked her sister.

"No. It is not your fault. But you don't have to slouch in your chair, use outrageous slang and act like a man, when you clearly are not."

A knock sounded at the door, cutting Amanda's lecture mercifully short. "Ah, Alfred," she said, handing the pristine pile of ivory parchment missives to the butler, "see these are delivered."

"His lordship's afternoon paper has arrived, my lady. Shall I leave it with you?"

She smiled and accepted the freshly ironed newspaper from the silver tray. "How well you know my sister's habits, Alfred."

He inclined his salt-and-pepper head in tacit agreement. "Will that be all, my lady?"

"Yes. Thank you."

Etching a dutiful bow, he closed the door, leaving the two sisters alone once more.

"Your paper." Amanda tossed the coveted item on the table beside the porcelain tea set and tempting cakes.

Sabrina's mood brightened. "Thank heavens." She rushed over to peruse the latest edition. "Something interesting to occupy my time, instead of fancy work. It is beyond my comprehension," she remarked, and unfolded the newspaper to pore over the articles, "how you manage to produce scads of those wretched things when all I ever end up with is lumps and knots."

Amanda gave her sister a dubious look. "It's an acquired

art," she remarked dryly. A mischievous glint came into her eye. She sank down on the rose velvet settee beside her sister. "Sabrina, I can scarcely believe you hold no affection whatsoever for our magnanimous earl. I think you are withholding something."

"He is not *our* earl, Amanda," came Sabrina's curt rejoinder from behind a wall of newspaper print. "I don't suppose such a man could ever really belong to anyone."

"Oh, I don't know," Amanda sighed dreamily. "I must confess, I rather thought Lord Lancaster cut a fine figure of a man." She poured a liberal portion of piping hot tea into two porcelain cups etched with tiny pink roses. "That he is uniformly charming, intelligent and exceedingly well heeled, there can be no doubt." She placed a slice of cake on a plate. "Kindly remove your nose from the paper and drink your tea," she said in an irritated tone as she handed her petulant sibling a cup of tea and cake. "What more could a lady ask of a gentleman?" she asked, savoring a bite of the buttery treat. "I, for one, find him exceedingly agreeable, good-looking and a gentleman. How you cannot agree is a mystery to me."

Sabrina placed her cup on the table with a loud clatter. "It just so happens," she imparted hotly, "that hateful rogue, whom you seem to regard as an honorable gentleman, kissed me in the most improper fashion in the library."

Amanda arched a golden brow. "Did he, indeed? I suspected as much," she murmured with a conspiratorial smile. "Was it wonderful?" she asked, her eyes dancing with devilment.

Sabrina gazed at her sister in blank surprise. "Are you not shocked? I think you should be shocked," she said, nonplussed. "Or at the very least, outraged."

Amanda paid no heed to her sister's dismay. "I've heard tell," she said, a wicked gleam in her eye, "Lord Lancaster has been known to leave women swooning."

"I did not swoon," Sabrina countered sharply, and snapped

open the newspaper to conceal the color that had crept into her cheeks, for she very nearly had! "Really, Amanda, your curiosity is most unbecoming. You are a married woman, after all. Remember yourself."

"I am not dead, dearest," Amanda retorted in a dry tone.

"I don't see why you are interested in Lancaster's overtures," Sabrina barked, growing impatient with her sister's preoccupation. She found the topic unnerving. She did not like to dwell on the vexing Hunter. It was an impossible circumstance. She turned the page and perused an advertisement for leather vamp boots. "I assure you," she averred, giving what she hoped sounded like a banal sigh as she placed her feet on the table top, "he bored me to tears. I doubt if the man is serious half the time."

Amanda swept Sabrina's feet off the table. "Come now," she remarked over the rim of her cup. "Even a bluestocking like you cannot be wholly unaffected by a man like him. Confess to me, you harbor feelings for him," she coaxed with a sly grin.

"He is an amusing diversion, nothing more," Sabrina mumbled in a failed attempt to appear preoccupied with the paper.

"Are you possibly in love, do you think?"

Sabrina refused to dignify that question with a reply. She shot her sister a quelling glance over the corner of the newspaper and was rewarded with an amused chuckle. Her mouth turned downward. Was there no way to deter her meddling sister? She never noticed before what a stubborn, determined nature Amanda possessed.

Reaching over, Amanda turned down the edge of the newspaper. "Are you listening to a word I am saying? I asked you if you thought you were in love. And you offered no reply. That simply cannot be normal," she muttered with a frown.

Sabrina glared at her and resumed her feigned reading.

"Why can you not be more docile and malleable like the

other debutantes your age?'' Amanda asked with a miserable sigh.

''Because, they are insipid and annoyingly dimwitted,'' came Sabrina's nonchalant rejoinder from behind the crisp newspaper. ''A dreadful combination guaranteed to produce a perennial headache, Ian always says.''

''Yes, but could you not try for a modicum of normalcy? Most would be thrilled by the mere thought of a man like Lancaster expressing interest.''

Her sister's suggestion gave Sabrina pause. Expressed interest? She caught her lower lip between her teeth. Had he expressed interest?

It was preposterous. Certainly, he was not interested in her. Her forehead creased.

Or . . . was he?

A man like that simply did not have the inclination to marry. She frowned slightly.

Or . . . did he?

Her breath caught in her throat. Could it be?

No. She shook her head. It was unconscionable. He simply was not the marrying sort. Of course, being his mistress was no dull prospect either.

A warm flush swept over her. How would it feel to be courted by the notorious Hunter? The idea was undeniably exhilarating. He could provide an extensive sensual education, bar none. That was definitely an alluring quality in any man. Particularly if one had to suffer marriage.

She knew he would never understand her attachment to S. K. Hughes, and that greatly diminished his appeal in her eyes. Doubtless he would force her to give up her intellectual pursuits. She could never do that. A rueful smile ruffled her lips. Well, it was a nice reverie while it lasted.

Shaking off her fanciful thoughts as empty-headed, romantic

notions, she mentally chastised herself for being as foolish as her fanciful sister.

"Must we discuss this?" she demanded with barely cloaked hostility.

"Dearest, you act as though you never hope to fall in love." Amanda's voice was nearly shrill with frustration.

Rolling her eyes heavenward, Sabrina lowered the paper to her lap. She opened her mouth to verbally lambast her meddling sister when a tap sounded at the door. Alfred appeared.

"I beg your pardon, my lady, but Lady Merryweather is waiting to see you."

Amanda and Sabrina exchanged a look of blank surprise.

Constance Merryweather was a middle-aged woman who had a well-earned reputation for knowing, or instigating, the most scandalous pieces of gossip in all London. Other people's lives were the bane of her existence.

"What can Lady Merryweather want with us?" Amanda asked her sister.

Sabrina shrugged her shoulders and tossed the newspaper aside.

"Show Lady Merryweather in, Alfred," Amanda instructed.

A second later, the plump, gray-haired woman floated into the sitting room on a sea of voluminous lavender silk.

"Oh, my dears," she exclaimed, breathless with excitement. "I simply had to come. I must tell you. You will never believe it when you hear."

Amanda glanced at her sister and frowned slightly. "Pray, be seated, Lady Merryweather. You look overset."

Lady Merryweather collapsed on the rose velvet settee in an exhausted lump. "I am all out. It has been such a morning." She waved her pudgy hands in the air.

Amanda's forehead creased with worry. "What is it that has made you ill?"

Lady Merryweather mopped her brow with her white lace

handkerchief. Her eyes fluttered shut. "There's been a terrible . . . murder," she said with a shudder.

Amanda looked stunned.

Sabrina was stupefied. In general, people of her acquaintance were not murdered.

"A murder?" the two sisters echoed in unison.

"It was grizzly," Lady Merryweather said with a sob of horror.

A shiver ran over Sabrina as the elderly woman recited the hideous details.

"The victim, you will never believe it, my dears," she said, her eyes wide with fascination, "she was a young woman of some means. They found her body early this morning, in Cheapside. She had been strangled. Her body tossed in the river," she exclaimed, throwing her beefy arms in the air.

Amanda drew in her breath in shock. "Who would have done such a thing?" she asked, abhorred by the violent crime.

Before Lady Merryweather could impart further details, Sabrina spoke up. "Don't keep us in suspense. Who was she?" she demanded with a mixture of excitement and morbid curiosity.

Amanda shook her head at her sister.

But Lady Merryweather was just as eager to impart the gruesome details as Sabrina was to hear them.

"Lady Jane Greenly, a debutante like yourself. You might even be acquainted with her family. Her father is the Earl of Bellingham," she cackled. "A highly respected family to be sure. She'd come up for the Season from Essex. We all had great hopes for her to make a suitable match." She clutched at her breast. "When I reflect that she was at Almack's just last Wednesday. Lady Jersey greeted her in person. Imagine how bright her future would have been. And now . . . this!" Her eyelashes fluttered shut. "It is unfathomable."

"I should say so," Amanda mumbled, dazed by the news.

"I know Jane," Sabrina remarked with a pensive air. "Or knew her. She was a quiet, shy girl. Certainly not the sort you'd expect to end up—"

"You are correct, Lady Merryweather," Amanda interjected, giving her sister a forbidding look, "when you suggest we are acquainted with the poor, unfortunate girl. She and my sister came out together. They were presented at court on the same day, I do believe."

"Yes, we were. What I want to know is, what is being done?" Sabrina asked pointedly, eliciting a look of censure from her sister.

Lady Merryweather shrugged her portly shoulders. "What is to be done? The poor gel is dead. The family is beside themselves with grief, that I can tell you." She wagged her sausagelike finger for emphasis.

"It is little wonder," Sabrina remarked.

"Who could have done such a heinous deed?" Amanda asked, hugging her arms around her midriff.

"Who, indeed?" Lady Merryweather commiserated. She clutched her hankie to her mouth in abject distress. "It is unthinkable."

"Certainly inquiries will be made to discover who perpetrated such a vile crime," Sabrina conjectured.

Lady Merryweather blinked at Sabrina over the top of her frilly handkerchief. "I've not the slightest notion. Such matters are best left to men, my dear," she said with a dismissing wave of her corpulent hand.

"That is the wisest course, naturally," Amanda chimed in, fixing her wayward sibling with a quelling glance.

Sabrina scowled, but fell silent.

"You are quite unwell, Lady Merryweather, as we all are upon hearing such news. Is there something we might offer you to bring you some relief? Tea, perhaps?" Amanda inquired politely.

"Gracious no," the rotund matron said, and struggled to heave her great bulk from the narrow settee. "I must be off, my dears. I must extend my sympathies to Lady Jane's father this very day."

Amanda showed their guest to the door.

As soon as Sabrina was alone, she snatched up the paper. Her eyes could not move fast enough over the black print.

"Whatever are you doing?" Amanda asked upon her return.

"Reading about the murder," Sabrina replied, her hungry gaze devouring the contents of the article.

"Your avid curiosity is abominable. Really," Amanda scoffed, "I think it shows the poorest taste."

Sabrina shot her a withering glance. "Oh, stop being such a ninnyhammer. Come and have a look at what it says."

"Very well, if you insist." Amanda scurried across the room and snuggled on the settee beside her sister. "What does it say?"

Sabrina bit her lower lip. "Not much more than Lady Merryweather explained. But I am sure they know more than they are printing. They must. I could find out more . . . if S. K. Hughes were to write to Mr. Hammersmith at *The Chronicle*. He might be able to make some inquiries."

"Are you mad?" Amanda burst out. "Ian would be shocked to know we read the story, let alone intend to snoop about for gruesome details."

"*We* won't," Sabrina replied calmly. She folded the irrevocably wrinkled newspaper and placed it on the table. "S. K. Hughes will." Her lips ruffled with sly machination. "Ian cannot possibly have any objections."

"Oh, no." Amanda shook her head in grave disapproval. "It is out of the question. You know as well as I that he would never approve."

Sabrina looked peevish. "You are just as curious as I am to hear more about it. You know you are. It is merely your strict sense of propriety that prevents you from admitting it. Someone murdered Jane Greenly, a woman with whom we were both acquainted. I happened to like her quite well. We cannot just sit back like docile idiots and pretend it hasn't happened. Besides, as young women living in this city, we should know. If only for our own protection.''

"If you would cease to cavort about without a proper escort, you would need not fear for your safety,'' Amanda snapped crossly.

"If there is a madman roaming the streets,'' Sabrina tossed back tartly, "I, for one, would very much like to know about it. If only to allow for caution on my part. Someone has to find out who killed poor Jane. If it were me, I would want you to care enough to discover the perpetrator, at the very least, enlist the help of someone who could.''

Amanda heaved a weary sigh. "Why do I feel myself being drawn into another one of your outrageous schemes?'' she groaned, rubbing her temples.

A slow smile of satisfaction crept across Sabrina's face. She knew her sister was weakening.

"I am not asking you to lie,'' Sabrina cajoled, "just . . . omit the more incriminating portions.''

"Oh, very well,'' Amanda said in a harassed voice. "But, this time, if you get yourself into a spot of trouble, I won't come to your rescue,'' she imparted strictly.

Sabrina shrieked with delight and threw her arms around her sister.

"Do be careful,'' Amanda whispered, hugging Sabrina tightly. "This entire episode has chilled my blood.''

"I confess, it has me unnerved as well. But you mustn't worry. I am always the epitome of caution.''

Except where the notorious Hunter is concerned, an irritating voice whispered in her head. She chose to ignore that voice. At the moment, Hunter was the very least of her concerns. She could ill afford to waste precious time and energy on him. Regardless of how incredibly attractive he was, she had far more important things to contemplate. How on earth she planned to investigate that ghoulish murder was a far more formidable challenge. It promised to be quite a feat, even for her.

Chapter 4

As the clock in the hallway of Hunter's elegant Upper Brook Street town house struck midnight, the master of the house settled comfortably before the fireplace in a large winged-back chair. Tugging at his cravat until the knot gave way, he placed his black, mirror-polished Hessians on the ottoman. Taking a sip of the pleasantly warm amber liquid from the crystal balloon glass cradled in his palm, he laid back his head and expelled a tired sigh.

His frustration was boundless. This evening's meeting with Mr. Crawford had not yielded any news. Lord Paine had proved a trifle uncooperative. After a week of surveillance, all Hunter knew about the illusive man was that he had a marked preference for base and corrupt pastimes, which would land him very shortly in debtor's prison.

Hunter yanked his cravat from around his neck and tossed it over the arm of the chair. Irritated fingers fumbled with the buttons at the neck of his linen shirt. He couldn't dwell on the paucity of information. Not tonight. He needed to find some measure of relaxation or he would go mad.

He was about to delve into Walter Scott's latest adventure novel, *Ivanhoe,* when he heard commotion in the front hallway beyond the dark mahogany library door. As the argument grew louder, he scowled and threw the book down on the ottoman.

Was he never to have a moment's peace? He was seriously considering spending a month in the country despite the appalling society. A little fox hunting could be just the thing he needed to rejuvenate his blood. At least in Derbyshire he held some hope to find something vaguely resembling tranquility.

Crossing the darkened library in three angry strides, he yanked open the door and demanded of his elderly butler in a disgruntled growl, "What the deuce is going on out here, Evans?"

The butler straightened his crisp white collar and cleared his throat. "My lord, this . . . *woman,*" he muttered, looking down his gargantuan nose at the petite female shrouded by a black hooded redingote, "is demanding to speak to you. She *claims* it is urgent."

The intruder, who was standing in the middle of the dimly lit foyer, removed the hood from her head to reveal a mass of golden tresses.

Hunter stared at the woman in mute confusion. His piercing grey eyes narrowed on her face. "Lady Somers?" he asked, stupefied.

A smile softened the worried look on her face. "My lord, I was hoping you would agree to see me." She rushed forward to clasp his hands in greeting. "I would not have come were I not in desperate need of your help."

Her hands were like ice, he noticed with a pensive frown. "What on earth possessed you to venture out on such a night? And at this ungodly hour?"

She glanced furtively over her shoulder at the butler, who

was firmly entrenched by the door, a look of contempt on his forbidding face.

"That will be all, Evans." Hunter's voice held a note of curt dismissal.

The butler cast a disapproving glance in Lady Somers's direction. "Very good, my lord." He turned on his heel and disappeared down the dark hall.

Lady Somers heaved a sigh of relief. "Oh, my lord," she whispered, and closed her eyes, "you are good to be sure."

His lips twisted. Good was not a word that leapt to most people's minds where he was concerned.

"How this must look," she muttered with a miserable groan. "What you must think of me."

His concerned gaze drifted over Lady Somers's drawn countenance. She looked ill, indeed. He could scarcely turn her out.

"Come, warm yourself by the fire," he commanded, dismissing her trepidation. He led her into the library. When she was sitting comfortably before the warmth of the firelight's glow, he said, "Tell me what has brought you here?"

She was wringing her hands. "I did not know to whom I should turn." Her voice was agitated.

"Could your husband not be of some help?" he prompted, wondering where the devil Ian was whenever his wife needed him.

She shook her head. "I left him asleep in his bed."

Hunter felt a twinge from the hairs on the back of his neck. He dearly hoped Ian was not a jealous husband, for his skill with a dueling pistol was formidable. Hunter would hate to wound his friend over a silly misunderstanding.

Mystified by a seemingly happily married woman throwing herself at his mercy in the middle of the night, he asked bluntly, "Why should you want to do that?"

"I had no choice. You see"—she looked away—"something . . . untoward has occurred." Her voice climbed an octave as she explained, "I am at my wit's end. I have not the slightest idea what to do. Given the current predicament, I had nowhere else to go. I regret imposing on your kind nature—"

"Calm yourself," he interjected with some force, "and tell me what has happened."

Trepidation ruffled her brow. "It's . . . Sabrina. I couldn't go to Ian," she rushed out. "After that debacle at Lord Holmes's party, he vowed to punish her most grievously and tell Grandfather if she ever did anything stupidly foolish again which . . . I am very much afraid she has."

He expelled an irritated breath. Somehow he had known the impertinent little baggage was behind her sister's distress.

Getting to his feet, he demanded in a voice that rang with curt impatience, "What has she done now?"

Her gaze fell to her lap. "She has attended Lord Hobson's weekend party under false pretenses," she said, her voice horribly small. "Her conduct verges on infamous most of the time. I am persuaded, tonight, her behavior is beyond the pale. I am grieved, indeed, to impart such shocking news. You see, she has not been invited."

Hunter's jaw clenched. "I see."

Apparently, near ruin was not sufficient excitement for the little hellion. She had moved on to more intriguing surroundings. So much for heeding his sage advice. Damned chit was bound and determined to get herself in trouble.

He glanced at Lady Somers's blond head hung in shame. He had been down this road once before and had no intentions of bailing the headstrong hoyden out of another mishap.

"Why come to me?" he queried with his back to her while he filled his glass with brandy.

"You must realize, under the circumstances, you are the only person to whom I can turn."

Uttering a scornful chuckle, he tossed the brandy down his throat. "Happily, I haven't seen your sister since she demanded

I ruin her reputation. Allow me to assure you," he imparted with heavy sarcasm, "I am not eager for another encounter."

Lady Somers's eyes widened in dismay. "Y-you must see the indecency of her behavior."

He nodded sagely. "Indeed. But what has it to do with me?" he asked, and dropped into the chair opposite the fire.

She cast him a look of reproach. "I cannot believe you truly intend to stand by and allow my sister to fling herself into another scandal, my lord. Not after the way you interceded so gallantly at Holmes's weekend party. You will never convince me of the contrary."

His mouth set in annoyance. The woman had a knack for employing compliments to her advantage. No amount of flattery would induce him to rescue that ungrateful little wench. Not this time.

"She is by nature headstrong and rash. I fear she may be in grave peril. Please, my lord, I beg of you, will you not help?" she beseeched him.

He looked away and gazed pensively at the fire. His lips thinned. The devil only knew the trouble that silly chit could get herself into with her reckless antics. He still hadn't fully recovered from her outrageous request that he ruin her on the garden path.

He scowled at the flickering flames. Confound it. He would do it. Against his better judgment, he would save her. One last time. But he would not touch her. No matter what the inducement.

"What *exactly* do you think she is planning to do?" he asked with ill-concealed rancor.

"I believe she has gone to do some investigating regarding that ghastly murder."

"Murder?" He almost fell off his chair. A mantle of furious color spread over his taut features. "What murder?" he bit out.

"That poor unfortunate who was thrown in the Thames."

"Good Lord." He vaulted to his feet and paced the room. "That was in Cheapside, was it not?" His ebony brows slanted in a frown. "What the devil does she hope to find sneaking about in Hobson's home?"

Lady Somers heaved a woeful sigh. "One can only imagine. I am afraid my sister is endowed with a rather singular character. Anything is possible."

"Madam, you have a gift for understatement," he uttered coolly.

"What are we to do?" she asked, her voice anxious.

"You," he intoned meaningfully, "will do nothing."

Relief flooded her features. "Oh, my lord." She clasped her hands together. "You are a saint. I knew you would not disappoint."

He gave her a dubious look. "I sincerely doubt that I am a saint, madam. But I will help you find your recalcitrant sister."

"How do you intend to fetch her without creating further scandal?" she asked with concern. "Have you, perchance, an invitation?"

He gave her a sideways glance that told her he did not. "I will manage. Somehow. Are you capable of returning safely home on your own?" he asked as he escorted her to the dark green marbled foyer.

A smile graced her tired countenance. "Perfectly. Given the delicacy of the situation, my lord, I believe it would be better if I showed myself out. My carriage is waiting near the corner." She raised her black hood, concealing her identity once more.

"Excellent. Never fear. I'll return your sister safe and sound by morning light."

He opened the front door and met a gust of cold night air that sobered him like no douse of cold water could. His lips curled ruefully. Once again, he found himself racing after the wild harridan in the middle of the night.

He couldn't quite believe it himself. On this occasion, he couldn't use the excuse that he owed Ian a debt of gratitude. In fact, he couldn't produce any rational reason for his actions at all. Lady Somers squeezed his hand. "We are forever in your debt, my lord." She wet her lips nervously and cast him a furtive glance. "There is just one more matter that bears mentioning. Although, I hesitate to mention it. . . ."

The chilly night air swirled around him and stung his cheeks with icy mockery. He wondered what had possessed him to agree to this ridiculous adventure. He longed to be nestled comfortably in his library. Damn and blast! When he found the headstrong little urchin, he fully intended to give her a paddling on the backside.

"Yes?" he prompted, his irritation waxing by the minute.

"This unfortunate incident must remain between ourselves. It would not do for Grandfather to catch wind of her escapades. He is not the understanding sort. Heaven knows what would happen should your involvement come to light. He would undoubtedly take a dim view." She glanced up at him from beneath sly lashes. "He might even call you out—or at the very least disown her—were he to catch wind of her antics."

Staring at the woman before him, Hunter tried to fathom what she could mean by such an odd comment.

"Indubitably," he murmured with a nod of his head. "Never fear, madam. You may rely on me to be the soul of discretion."

"Thank you, my lord."

Ian would have to be told at some point. Hunter did not feel right keeping a midnight visit with his friend's wife a secret. But he needed to find the scandalous little hoyden first. He was itching to pound some sense into her addled brain.

He waited in the bone-chilling dead of night until he was certain Lady Somers was safely deposited in her carriage. As he closed the door, he shook his head. His mouth curved into an unconscious smile. Women as a rule did not trust him. And with good reason. It was pleasant to encounter one who thought him worthy of esteem.

Forty-five minutes later, a tired and thoroughly vexed Hunter debarked from his carriage behind Hobson's garden wall.

"Wait here," he told his beleaguered driver.

"Right you are, milord," the driver replied, and hugged his collar around his neck to ward off the night's chill.

As Hunter tramped across the shadowy thicket toward the estate, he shook his head. "I am definitely getting too old for this," he growled under his breath. Never before had he attempted to slip into a ballroom uninvited. In fact, to his knowledge, it simply was not done. At least, not until this evening.

As he hoisted himself over the marble balustrade and landed with a hard thud on Hobson's deserted balcony, he told himself there was a first time for everything.

Fortunately, the scores of guests were so engaged in idle gossip and romantic conspiracies that they took no notice of him as he strode from the dimly lit balcony and mingled with the swarming crowd. He managed, to his great relief, to traverse the mobbed dance floor without being accosted by droves of giggling women looking for their next dance card entry.

It shouldn't prove terribly difficult to locate the headstrong chit, given that she was the only woman of his acquaintance with vibrant red hair. With any luck, he would whisk her from the premises before she caused any more trouble. Of course, the fact that the room was packed did little to aid his search.

Sabrina adjusted her pearl choker for the tenth time and tugged her white gloves over her elbow. She glanced down at her pale green silk dress and worried that it was too simple compared with the gowns of the other members of the *ton* present this evening. She did not wish to look out of place for fear of calling attention to her presence. Drawing a deep, calming breath, she wondered why her nerves were overset.

Her pulse was throbbing like a wild thing for the simple reason that in very short order, she was going to slink from the throng, creep upstairs and search her host's bedchamber for damning evidence. She was not at all certain she was prepared for what she might find.

Ghoulish details of poor Jane being strangled flooded her mind. She took another sip of watery lemonade and wondered if the stress of the evening was too much for her. If her eyes did not deceive her, the notorious, undeniably gorgeous Hunter was standing not ten feet from her.

Her breath caught in her throat. Gracious heavens. This was no illusion. He was real. He looked more beautiful than a man should. He was wonderfully tall, dark and handsomely forbidding, she thought with appreciation. His well-defined muscles, accentuated by his snug, black velvet cutaway, had her mewing with admiration.

She bit her lip and sighed, remembering exactly how it felt to run her hands over his rock-hard chest and strong, virile arms. It was pure nirvana.

It was then that he saw her. His gray tempestuous gaze drifted over every inch of her with excruciating thoroughness. Her pulse soared.

A thrill of excitement rippled through her as she watched him saunter purposefully toward her. Why, the man behaved as if *he* were the lord of the manor. But that was what made him so alluring, she acknowledged with a surge of warmth. He was always in command of any situation. A quality she found utterly irresistible.

He inclined his dark head in tactic greeting. "The honorable Miss Bennett, I do believe," he said, his tone sharp.

A rush of pleasure washed over her. Not in the least put off by his brusque manner, she quickly forgot about her nefarious mission and dropped into a polite curtsey that would have made even her stodgy grandfather proud. "My lord."

Silver eyes gazed deeply into blue. He clasped her slender hand in his and pressed his lips to her skin. Tingling currents of raw attraction ran up her arm.

"It is a delightful surprise to see you again," he said in a voice smoother than velvet. "Our last encounter was quite . . . unique. I wonder what you have planned to charm me senseless this evening?"

Good gracious. The sensual promise his hooded gray eyes conveyed made her knees turn weak. Her heart slammed against her ribs. "You are too kind, my lord," she demurred.

"Indeed, I am. I have been scouring the ballroom for you for the last half hour," he said in a curt undertone that belied his anger.

She pulled a frown. So much for another romantic interlude. She should have realized he gazed at every woman with equal hunger. "What on earth brings *you* here of all places?" she asked in a terse under breath.

"I'm saving your foolish neck," he fired back. "You ought to know it is considered outrageously bad conduct to go where you are not invited."

She glared at him. "You are being absurd, my lord. No one knows I wasn't invited."

"Keep your voice down," he hissed, "or everyone will know we're *both* here uninvited." His breath was warm against her ear. She hated herself for quivering.

"If you'll be so kind as to go away," she whispered crossly, "no one need know."

"As much as I'd cared to," he told her sarcastically, "I am afraid I am not at liberty to oblige you."

Her mouth pinched. "Why is it, my lord, that I continually

encounter your unwanted presence at the worst possible moments? Have you nothing better to do than poke your nose into other people's private affairs?''

"As it happens," he drawled with chilling curtness. "I would be enjoying all the comforts of home were it not for the ramshackle existence *you* lead."

She gave him a petulant glare. "My life is not in the least ramshackle," she flung at him. "I do not desire your intervention and would do quite nicely without it."

"It grieves me to hear it," he muttered dryly. "At the moment, however, we need to connive a way out of here. I am persuaded your poor sister must be fretting excessively by now. If I do not get you home before the dawn, there will be the devil to pay."

"I might have known Amanda was behind your sudden appearance," she fumed angrily. "We used to be utterly devoted to one another. Marriage has done dreadful things to her. She's lost all sense of loyalty."

A sardonic smirk touched his lips. "I do believe it has an ill effect on most people. Now, why don't you and I slip away before we are noticed, shall we? And forget this unfortunate experience like a bad dream?"

"You are all kindness, my lord," she imparted with biting sarcasm. "But I have no intention of leaving here without getting what I came for."

His eyes turned a dark slate gray. "You," he said through his teeth, "are a naive, dangerous child with a penchant for getting yourself into trouble." He raked his hand through his hair and expelled an irritated sigh. "I'm the damned fool who constantly seems to get you out of it."

"I never asked for your help," she barked back, oddly hurt by his disgust of her.

He regarded her as a childish nuisance. Nothing more. She regarded him as . . . as what?

She wasn't sure of anything at the moment, except for the currents of excitement that raced through her whenever he was near. She couldn't think why. Now, however, was not the time to delve into her feelings. Hunter was a formidable opponent. She needed all her wits about her.

"No," he replied coldly, "you haven't the sense. Thank goodness your sister has a level head on her shoulders."

Sabrina could well imagine the impression Amanda had given his lordship. Headstrong. Impetuous. Foolish.

"Come, my little hoyden," his voice rang with maddening command, "you are going home to bed where you belong."

Shooing him away with her hands, she told him, "Just . . . take yourself off."

"Not a chance," came his acrid retort.

She stamped her slippered foot in frustration. "You are spoiling everything."

His eyes narrowed on her petulant, upturned face. "Exactly *what* am I spoiling?"

"My investigation, if you must know." Her tone was decidedly peevish.

Hunter drew an irritated breath and prayed for patience. And self-control. He needed self-control. Desperately. The desire to take the damned gel over his knee and paddle her senseless very nearly overpowered him. Even more disturbing was the group of disapproving onlookers interested in the heated discourse.

A disgruntled frown touched his lips. "Are you in the habit of creating scenes everywhere you go?" he growled against her ear. "You look overly warm," he averred with admirable civility, and extended his arm in polite invitation, "allow me to escort you onto the balcony."

She glared down at his arm with disdain. Short of causing a scene, however, she could do nothing else but accept him. The wretch was relying on it.

"Oh, bother," she grumbled. "Must you make every circumstance work to your advantage," she gritted under her breath as he led her toward the double doors that opened onto the secluded balcony and private gardens.

Oh, bother? He bit back a smile. She sounded older than his childhood nanny.

"Do I manage all that well?" he murmured. The warmth of his breath against her ear made her shiver with unwanted pleasure. "I was under the impression that was your penchant, dear heart."

"Fustian," she snapped, and stepped back from his overwhelming presence. "I am no slowtop. I know what you are about, why you connived your way onto the balcony."

His lips quirked. "Do you?"

She looked up at him, her gaze soft and languid. "You are planning to kiss me again, are you not?" she breathed with ill-concealed anticipation.

He cocked a dubious brow. "In full view of Hobson's guests? No." He shook his head decisively. "I am not."

Embarrassed heat flooded her cheeks. She averted her gaze in an effort to hide her disappointment.

"Oh," she said in a small voice. "I cannot tell you what a relief it is to know your intentions are, at last, honorable," she added with brusque sarcasm.

He smiled down at her with an indulgence she detested. "As I told you once before, I am not in the habit of ravishing young innocents."

That was a lie. He would like nothing more than to offer her a stylish town house, expensive wardrobe, lavish jewels, and his protection in exchange for just one night of passionate lovemaking. What he wouldn't give to hear her call out his name on a breathless moan of pleasure.

A fierce frown marred his face. What the deuce ailed him of late? He was definitely not the sort to lose his head over a woman. Especially not one with a mind of a child and a preponderance for scandal.

His burning gaze drifted over the fetching creature at his side with lazy precision. She was a delight. She was a hellion. Quite the most unusual person he had ever met.

"Do not be disagreeable, Sabrina," he coaxed gently. "You know as well as I you'd best slip away before our esteemed host finds out about your peculiar lack of protocol and you get yourself into real trouble." He inclined his raven head toward the ballroom. "I daresay dear old Hobson would take a dim view of our being here without the benefit of an invitation."

She crossed her arms under her bosom. "If you wish to leave, you may. I am staying."

He vacillated between the urge to throttle the little baggage and to kiss her soundly. "The devil you are!"

"The devil I am," she tossed right back at him. To her chagrin, she had to step back from his hard, tense maleness. "Stop . . . interfering in my private affairs. You've no right." Acutely aware of his overwhelming masculinity, she swallowed and willed her stomach to cease its somersaults.

His searing gaze raked over her. "By God," he breathed, "you are an outrageous hellion."

Her frosty glare drifted over him. "I cannot credit your concern for my well-being. As I collect, my lord, you forfeited the opportunity to assist me in my moment of need."

A sardonic smirk touched his lips. "Disappointed, were you?"

She wet her lips. Oh, dear, his hard, lean body was intimidating beyond belief. Craven coward that she was, she had to quell the urge to scurry back inside. "Verily, my lord," her voice quivered horribly, "it seems rakes are not to be trusted. In, or out, of the library."

He smiled at that. "Ah, yes," he said in soft, dulcet tones that had her tingling right down to her toes, "the library." His hand reached out and caressed a smooth tendril of coppery red hair that had fallen haphazardly down her ivory neck. "How could I forget?"

One look in those sultry gray eyes and she knew he had not forgotten. Not one single, solitary moment. Neither had she. Heaven help her. He was remembering their all-too-fleeting moment of wild, abandoned passion with obvious relish. Good gracious. She was, too.

Wetting her suddenly parched lips, she forced her gaze lower. That was a mistake. She found herself staring at his sensual, full mouth. She knew she was in serious peril of being kissed.

He reached out, drawing her against his dangerous heat. Bending his head, he pressed his soft, parted lips against hers and kissed her fully on her quivering mouth. Liking the riotous sensations pulsating through her, she grew bold and touched her tongue to his. A muffled sound escaped his throat. His arms tightened around her. He pulled her against him, devouring her lips with savage hunger.

His mouth trailed hot, wet kisses down her neck. Tilting her head, she basked in the delicious sensations his searing touch evoked. A tiny sigh of exquisite pleasure escaped her throat. Her fingers tightened around his shoulders, clutching to him for support, for her legs felt suddenly too weak to hold her.

He captured her mouth, smothering her moist lips in a slow, drugging kiss. His hand slid up her waist and covered her full, impudent breast. Cupping the round, soft mound, he teased her sensitive nipple with the pad of his thumb. Pleased by her beautiful, uninhibited response, he smiled with satisfaction as her breast peaked beneath his touch.

"*My lord,*" she gasped.

He chuckled at her use of formality in the very informal circumstances. He felt rather like a lord of the manor seducing an innocent governess. But he wouldn't think about that just now.

It might be madness, but it was also the sweetest pleasure he had found in ages. His open mouth captured hers, moving with startling ardor over her pliant, sweet lips.

She returned his kiss with equal longing. Her lips intoxicated his senses. Her incredibly soft, supple body was more than any hot-blooded man could resist. With a concerted effort he managed to tear his mouth away from the enticing feast.

He had thought the first time he had kissed her was an aberration. Now he knew it was not. They were beautifully matched. Their compatibility was undeniable.

Sexually.

In all other ways, the impetuous little miss drove him closer to committing murder than anyone he had ever met.

Breathless and weak, she pressed her cheek against his chest and clung to him. She felt his lips brush her hair and smiled to herself. The pounding of his heart beneath her ear pleased her. It spoke of his passion for her. Her hand slid over his chest, and she pressed her palm against his thundering heart.

He lifted her chin to stare down at her. His gaze swept over her passion-flushed face. His chiseled features darkened into an angry scowl. "Stop looking at me like that," he snapped at her.

"Like what?" she asked, gazing up at him with a dreamy smile on her soft ruby lips moist from his torrid kisses.

His frown turned sardonic. "Like I'm your dream lover and you're madly in love with me," he said cruelly.

She stepped out of the warmth of his embrace. "I was not aware that I was looking at you in any particular fashion. And I am most certainly not madly in love with you."

He snickered at that remark. "I'd hate to see how you kiss a man when your feelings are involved," he drawled as he ran his knuckles over her flushed cheek. "I doubt he'd survive."

Jerking her face away, she arched her chin defiantly. "I've not the slightest notion what you are talking about," she told him curtly. "You provide little more than a passing amusement for me, my lord. As an avid student of life, I regard our encounters as merely experiential. Every woman should be kissed by a rake at least once in her life. But you may believe me when I say my feelings could never be invested where you are concerned."

"Good." The encroaching sounds of couples conversing wafted through the night air. He dropped his hand to his side and quickly stepped a respectable distance away from her. "Let's keep it that way, shall we?"

She blinked at him, all innocence and confusion. "I cannot imagine how else it could be."

"I sure as hell can," he growled.

Her ingenuous gaze searched his face. "Whatever do you mean?" she asked him, wide-eyed.

He shook his head at her. "Never mind. I'll save that lesson for another time."

Her expression soured. "My lord," she imparted in a crisp tone, "you appear to be under a grave misapprehension. Allow me to make my feelings patently clear. I desire nothing from you, much less, as you put it, another lesson."

"I sincerely doubt that," he snorted with a sardonic edge. "At present, you may satisfy me with an explanation. What the devil do you think you are doing slipping into Hobson's ballroom in the middle of the night?"

Chapter 5

His imperious tone rankled Sabrina to the core. She turned away from him and leaned against the stone balustrade to gaze up at the diamond-scattered night sky. "Surely," she said, resentment making her tone bitter, "my distraught sister wasted no time in relating the circumstances which precipitated my appearance here tonight."

His hand slipped around her upper arm. The warmth of his touch singed her bare skin. He turned her to face him. "I should very much like to hear your explanation." His gaze flickered over her hectic face. One end of his mouth curved slightly. "I am persuaded it will be quite colorful."

She drew a deep, impatient breath. "Very well, my lord. As you appear to be bent on ruining everything, except for me a second time, you leave me no choice. I must take you into my confidence. I am a journalist."

His dark brows snapped together. "A journalist?" he repeated, dumbfounded. "The devil you say! I don't believe it. You're having me on."

"It is all perfectly true," she replied coolly.

He gave her a dubious glance. "What Banbury tale is this?"

"It is no Banbury tale," she countered firmly.

He scoffed at her. "No reputable newspaper would employ a woman."

"I never laid claim to being employed by a newspaper. You merely assumed it."

He gave her a disparaging look. "Then, pray," he asked pointedly, "how do you write articles?"

"Ian visits the office on my behalf."

He looked startled. "Ian?" he echoed in amazement.

"Most of the time. If he is too busy, he gives my articles to his secretary, Mr. Bridges, who delivers them to *The Chronicle* newspaper office on Fleet Street."

Hunter went dead still. "Not the *London Chronicle?*" he asked, shock mingling with incredulity.

"Yes. Are you familiar with it?" she asked brightly.

"Vaguely," he muttered pensively. Why was he shocked? Nothing about this wayward changeling should surprise him. This, however, he had not expected.

"Perhaps you have read some of my articles on fossils and nature?" she asked, eager for his opinion.

"What?" he mumbled, his thoughts preoccupied.

"Have you read them? My articles, I mean."

"Er, no"—he shook his head—"I haven't."

"Oh," she said, dejected. "Well, they are quite good. Some of them."

"I'll bear that in mind," he retorted, an acerbic edge to his voice.

"I am particularly proud of the account of my visit to the Royal Stables," she was saying.

He pulled a frown. "Royal Stables? I was given to understand women wrote about fashions from France or, at the very worst, the latest *on-dits?*''

She gave him a crushing look. ''As far as I am concerned, horseflesh is far superior to fashions, my lord.''

He raised his eyebrows. ''Ah, I see. How the devil did you manage to get yourself hired?''

She shrugged. ''It wasn't terribly difficult. Ian was immensely helpful in securing the position.''

Hunter rubbed his chin thoughtfully. ''He must have been very persuasive to convince the proprietor.''

''I don't think I could have done it without his kind intervention. Not that I lack talent,'' she hastened to add, ''but it is a very competitive field. As you know, women are barred from anything interesting altogether.''

''Somehow,'' he replied with dry indulgence, ''I am not the least surprised you feel that way. Tell me, what does your precious S. K. Hughes think about this unconventional pastime of yours?'' he asked, his silver gaze gently mocking her.

She laughed out loud. ''He is quite devoted to it.''

Hunter's jaw tightened. Her devotion to that miscreant infuriated him. Devil take it! He wasn't jealous, was he? Over a girl who had a positive knack for getting herself into compromising situations? Hardly. ''Is that so? How convenient,'' he muttered.

''Yes, it is, rather.''

''You are saving yourself for him, I take it?'' he asked, observing her with a keen gaze.

She hesitated for a moment. Her lips curled slyly. ''In a manner of speaking,'' she allowed, ''I suppose I am.''

One brow arched in mild inquiry. ''Marriage, I assume, is out of the question?''

She wrinkled up her nose. ''Suffice to say, it is not welcomed.''

His lips thinned. Obviously, the blackguard was a married man who preyed on naive innocents. ''He sounds like a charming fellow," he averred with scorn. "Your future husband may not take kindly to your avid preoccupation, what then?"

Her eyes widened to the size of china saucers. *"Future husband?"* she sputtered, and burst into gales of laughter. "Oh, my lord," she managed to say, her shoulders shaking with mirth. "You are under a grave misapprehension."

"What, may I ask, is so diverting?" His voice held a distinct chill.

"I fear you have misunderstood the circumstance entirely," she told him, struggling to maintain a straight face.

His eyes narrowed on her bemused countenance. "And what circumstance might that be?" He liked being at a disadvantage about as much as he enjoyed being the object of laughter.

"It is quite simple. There is no such person."

His intent gaze searched her face. "What do you mean, no such person?" he barked. "I was given to understand that you were in love with the cad."

A gurgle of incorrigible laughter escaped her throat. "In love? I don't see how that is possible."

Unamused, he asked roughly, "And why not?"

"S. K. Hughes does not exist. Well," she amended, serious at last, "not in the flesh."

The fact that the little chit had misled him—deliberately— and he had fallen for it irked him no small degree.

"What the devil do you mean?" he snapped, angry with himself for believing her wild, amorous tale in the first place, "he does not exist?"

"I created S. K. Hughes as a pen name."

"You what?" he practically roared at her.

"I made him up," she said with pride. "He enables me to write my articles. Very helpful fellow, don't you think?"

"Mmm," he muttered, "quite." No wonder the blasted name Hughes had been oddly familiar to him. He had probably seen it countless times and never made the connection.

"As you so aptly pointed out, I couldn't very well use my real name."

"No. You couldn't." He flashed an approving smile. She was more clever than he had imagined. Resourceful, too. In spite of his firm conviction that she was a headstrong fool, he could not help but admire her tenacity. He was right about her. She was an original.

"Dashed clever of you. I don't suppose the newspaper proprietor has any inkling?" he asked archly.

She gave him a forbidding look. "Heavens no. It would not do for him to learn of it. I hope I may rely on you to remain silent?"

"I think I can manage that," he said, his tone exceedingly dry.

"Thank you, my lord," she said with an obvious rush of relief. "I am enormously gratified that you understand what it would mean to me to have the opportunity to prove myself both as a woman and a journalist," she said, youthful exuberance etched on her face.

He eyed her skeptically. "It means that much to you, does it? You actually fancy yourself a serious journalist?"

"My work is the most significant part of my life," she told him solemnly. "Why else do you think I approached you and asked that you be the instrument of my ruin?"

"As I recall, you hedged a bit on that minor point," he uttered dryly.

She blinked at him. "I should think it would be obvious. I will do anything to be free, to be able to pursue my intellectual interests. Quite simply, my lord, I wish to live a contented life quietly in the country, permanently installed on the shelf. I wish to write serious stories. Something more interesting than the Rosetta Stone and Lord Elgin's Grecian marble statues at the British Museum."

"I see," Hunter remarked, stroking his chin in thought.

"Well, in that case, perhaps you ought to pursue a really intriguing story for the paper. It might not be as outlandish as murder, but it would garner the respect you seek. Say, something on Thomas Brown. He is giving a lecture this week on his "Philosophy of the Human Mind." You might attend and summarize his discussion for the paper."

She gazed up at him, her clear blue eyes brimming with admiration. "Do you honestly believe such an article would secure me a foothold among serious journalists?"

He flashed a complaisant smile. "It is a start. And certainly well worth a try. He is well respected among his peers. I think you'll find his theories rather interesting. Such an article will go a long way toward proving you a capable writer."

"I do hope so, my lord," her soft, breathless voice rang with longing.

His gaze drifted over her sparkling eyes and rosy cheeks, then captured her languid blue depths. Of its own volition, his hand reached out and caressed her cheek. The pad of his thumb traced her cheekbone. Her full, moist lips, parted in warm invitation, were too strong a temptation. Dragging air into his lungs, he summoned his self-control and dropped his hand to his side.

He cleared his throat. "What lurid information are you in hot pursuit of at the moment?"

"It just so happens," she explained, warming to her subject, "I knew that poor, unfortunate girl who was murdered. Her name was Lady Jane Greenly. She was the debutante daughter of the Earl of Bellingham, who has suffered a serious attack upon hearing the grievous news. No one seems to be doing anything to catch the killer. So," she said on a shrug, "I decided to take action."

He cocked an intrigued brow. "Oh, you did, did you?" Shaking his head at her, he crossed his arms over his chest and leaned back against the balustrade. "I expect I should have my head examined. For the moment, you have my attention. Proceed.''

"Whose company do you suppose she was keeping most recently?" she asked with titillating suspense.

"Hobson's."

"You are quite adept at this, my lord," she mocked lightly. "Jane was last seen alive at a party given by Hobson himself."

He gave her a quelling look. "I presume you've come to the ludicrous conclusion based on their brief association that Hobson killed her?"

She shrugged. "I haven't the foggiest idea. Three other men have danced attendance at her side over the last few months as well. Notably, Lord Everly, Lord Grimes and Viscount Lindsey. All three were present the night she disappeared. I think each warrants further scrutiny, do you not agree?"

Hunter shook his head. What the devil had come over him of late? Was he actually giving credence to this preposterous theory?

"No. I do not. Just because a gentleman dances the cotillion with a lady does not necessarily mean he's strangled her."

She stiffened at his harsh rebuke. "I did not say it did," she replied, her tone crisp, "I merely suggested it was worthy of further inspection."

"For an intelligent woman," he snorted derisively, "you are remarkably naive."

"Why do you say that?" she asked peevishly.

"For the simple reason, dear heart," his voice was laced with acrimony, "no one cares about that poor, unfortunate girl. Members of the *ton* do not care to read about murder and mayhem." He paused to snicker. "In fact, they rather prefer to ignore it altogether."

Greatly distressed by his cavalier attitude, she imparted crossly, "I don't know how you can be so callous. Do you not care a whit about poor Jane?"

He dragged his hand through his hair. "With your penchant for brotherly love," he remarked dryly, "why didn't you join a religious order?"

She looked slightly taken aback. "I scarcely think I am a proper candidate for a religious order, my lord."

"I collect you are right," he drawled with heavy sarcasm. "You lack the self-discipline."

She chafed at his condescending tone. "You really are a heartless brute," she snipped.

He flashed a rakish grin. "Quite right, my dear. A rogue and a cur." He etched a mocked bow. "I plead guilty to both counts. At the moment, however, I think it imperative that I get you home before you get yourself into a quandary beyond your capabilities."

She blinked at him in astonishment. "I've yet to undertake my inquiries," she sputtered in dismay.

His voice brooked no disagreement as he told her, "You won't, either. Let me assure you, my dear girl, this story of yours will never grace the pages of any newspaper. Ever."

Squaring her shoulders, she tossed back tartly, "Anything is possible."

"Verily," he growled, "it might snow in summer. But that doesn't mean you'll ever get to write that blasted story."

Her chin lifted a notch. "Murder should be a matter for public concern. Whoever committed this heinous crime is obviously a desperate, undesirable sort who attacked a helpless, young woman. He might strike again."

"Rubbish," Hunter barked. "It was an isolated event. A simple case of a poor, unfortunate girl being in the wrong place at the wrong time. Where do you come up with these ill-conceived notions of yours?"

Her fiery blue eyes sparkled with temper. "They are not ridiculous. My theory is every bit as plausible as your explanation."

"Perhaps you should confine your pursuits to more feminine issues," he imparted with an infuriating air of superiority. "I do believe it is best to stick to what one knows."

Slapping her hands on her hips, she flung at him, "Next, I suppose you'll be claiming that my constitution is too delicate to delve into such things."

"As a matter of fact—"

"Poppycock!" she blustered angrily.

Hunter seriously questioned the wisdom of conversing with someone who used the expression *poppycock*.

"If I had been tossed into the river, I'd want someone to care enough to find out who'd done it," she cried with energy.

He heaved a weary sigh. Wasn't that precisely his rationale for pursuing Julia's malefactor? His lips thinned. Dash it all. She had him on that point.

"What the devil do you hope to find poking about Hobson's estate?" he demanded roughly.

She gave him a petulant glare. "Clues, naturally," she muttered dryly.

He shook his head at her. "Forget it. You, my headstrong little hoyden, will gather nothing. Least of all clues. Henceforth, you will confine your powers of investigation to the mundane. I, for one, would sleep a lot better. It is high time we were on our way. I've had enough of your foolishness."

She heaved a frustrated sigh. "Have you not heard a word I've said? I cannot leave now. I may be close to uncovering some very important information."

"I don't give a damn," he muttered in a low, terse tone. He reached out and took her roughly by the arm.

She dug in her heels. "If you think to drag me from the premises," she intoned sharply, "I warn you, you will regret it. I will scream. Loudly. And, I will cause the most outrageous scene you have ever witnessed. Do you fancy a scandal, my lord?" she taunted.

His dark, angry gaze threatened to impale her. "You little . . . witch," he breathed.

She flashed a puckish grin. "I thought you'd see things my way," she said, retrieving her arm from his clutches. "Now that you have arrived," she remarked, adjusting her long, white gloves, "you might prove useful. I do believe you are the perfect choice to aid in my investigation."

The muscle leapt in his cheek. "Why is that?" he bit out.

She cocked a brow. "Who better to connive his way to the upstairs bedchamber than a notorious rake?" she tossed back saucily.

He gave her a hard, menacing look.

A few minutes later, the pair slipped from the packed ballroom into the front hall, which was blessedly empty, save for two footmen who flanked the front door. It was with relative ease that the two sleuths managed to pad unobtrusively up the winding staircase.

A quick visual inspection down the long hallway confirmed Hunter's worst fears. Damned place was probably lousy with inner and outer corridors, not to mention adjoining rooms, he thought, uttering a string of oaths that would have put a sailor to the blush.

"My lord," Sabrina gasped in dismay, "I am shocked at you." Her brow knitted slightly. "And not at all certain I know what you mean by those words, precisely."

He dismissed her shock with an icy glare. "Has it occurred to you," he asked through gritted teeth, "that we may well have to search all of the bedrooms? It could take half the night to locate Hobson's room."

Gazing about her, she chewed pensively on her lower lip. "Mmm, quite."

But she was not daunted by the prospect. Oh, no. Wild horses would not keep her from her moral quest.

"We'd best get started. You take the left side and I'll take the right."

Grunting his assent, Hunter trudged down the hall to make a cursory inspection of the first room, which he dearly hoped was vacant. Twenty minutes later, a frown of consternation touched his lips. He had searched three different bedrooms with no success. Sooner or later, he was bound to stumble upon an occupied room. What then?

Devil take it! Creeping around Hobson's home in the middle of the night was utterly insupportable. How the deuce had he gotten into this outrageous situation? He did not relish the notion of being caught. He raked his hand through his hair. This had gone far enough. He would find the damned wench and toss her over his shoulder if need be. But they were leaving.

He opened the door to the next bedroom and froze. Someone was inside. Lord, he hoped it was not some unsuspecting guest preparing for bed. He strained to get a good look at the occupant's face through the crack in the doorway. His view was partially obstructed by the back of the door. It was definitely a woman. As she got down on her haunches to rifle through some papers, his gaze ran over the narrow waist and nicely rounded bottom.

Tilting her head to one side, her profile came into his view. A slow smile spread across his face. Only one person of his acquaintance had an adorable upturned nose and blazing red hair. Unless he was greatly mistaken, the silly chit had actually stumbled upon Hobson's bedchamber.

Hunter slipped inside the room and quietly eased the door shut. Creeping on tiptoes, his arm snaked out and snatched her against him. She let out a shriek and fought her would-be assailant, kicking and squirming toward freedom. Her heel connected painfully with his shin bone. He let out a strangled groan and clamped his hand over her mouth.

"Hush," he snarled angrily against her ear. "It's me, you little fool."

She stopped squirming.

"May I assume you found Hobson's bedchamber?" he whispered softly against her cheek.

She quickly stepped away from his treacherous warmth. "Indeed, I have," she said, clearing her throat. "Look what I have discovered," she exclaimed with pride, holding up a gold signet ring with a snake coiled around a naked maiden.

Hunter's dark brows snapped together. "Where did you get that?" he demanded, snatching the object from her fingers.

"It obviously belongs to Hobson. Does it appear familiar to you, my lord?" she asked, studying Hunter's pensive frown.

He glanced at her. "Why do you ask?" he queried with trepidation.

She shrugged. "Unless I am greatly mistaken, I thought I saw the light of recognition in your eyes."

"Did you?" he asked nonchalantly, and handed the ornate gold piece back to her.

She examined the ring with curiosity. "It is a perfectly hideous piece, I must say," she murmured rhetorically. "Is it of significance, do you suppose?"

He shook his head. "I doubt it."

An impish smile tugged at her lips. "Well, you'd be mistaken. What would you say, my lord, if I told you that a gold medallion with the same insignia was found clutched in Jane Greenly's hand?"

Momentarily stunned, Hunter quickly recovered himself. "I'd say you have an overactive imagination."

Reluctantly, Hunter admitted tonight was not a complete loss after all. He had stumbled onto a very important element in his quest for Julia's malefactor—or rather his wild, impetuous hoyden had. His initial assumption that the ring was an important link was entirely correct. Apparently, signet rings like the one in his possession were not as rare as he had once believed. The snake and the maiden were obviously a symbol. But of what?

One woman was dead, and another disgraced and abandoned. The ring must signify something untoward.

Quite an interesting development in the case, one about which Mr. Crawford would shortly hear. Of course, Hunter had no intention of telling the wayward chit the truth. The last thing the little hellion needed was encouragement.

"Well," she said on a sigh, "I doubt it was Hobson who killed poor Jane. He'd scarcely have a ring and a medallion with the same hideous insignia. What *do* you think the snake coiled around the maiden is meant to signify?" she asked, examining the disgusting piece with a critical eye. "Why would two separate men wear the same emblem? It is no coincidence. The symbol is some sort of link between the two. It must be."

"I have no idea. Put the ring back. Let's get out of here before someone takes exception to this lamentable interest of yours."

She looked at him as if he had suddenly sprouted six heads. "We cannot leave now, just when we've stumbled onto something valuable. Hobson may not have killed Jane. But you can be certain he knows who did. For all we know, other rings or medallions like this one exist."

Hunter was impressed. She was clever and resourceful and playing with fire. "Possibly," he imparted, his tone curt, "but I, for one, I've no wish to be waylaid by one of the guests and forced to issue what promises to be an exceedingly embarrassing explanation for our presence."

"We've got to find the owner of the medallion," Sabrina affirmed, her voice determined. "Who do you suppose it is?" she asked, almost to herself. "Everly, Lindsey or Grimes?"

"At the moment," Hunter grumbled irritably, "I don't suppose anything save for the fact that we are treading on perilous

territory. We are in grave danger of scandal." Grabbing her
by the hand, he threaded his fingers through hers and dragged
her toward the door. "With any luck, we can slip out down
the back stairs, and no one will be the wiser." He opened the
door a crack and peered out into the hallway.

Their hasty departure was interrupted by the untimely arrival
of a lively group of lords and ladies meandering up the stairs
to seek their beds.

"Damnation!" he spat under his breath. Ducking out into
the hall, they sneaked into what Hunter prayed was a deserted
bedchamber and closed the door.

He crossed the darkened room to inspect the way down
through the window. It was far too high to jump without breaking a leg.

"Thanks to your damned foolishness," he tossed over his
shoulder, "we're stuck here for the moment, if not the night."

At seeing his dark, angry scowl, Sabrina blanched. "There
must be some way out," she offered in a panicked voice, the
enormity of their predicament sinking in at last.

He eyed her coolly. "Nothing leaps to mind. What do you
suggest?"

"I—"

"Hush," he snapped, silencing her effectively. "Someone
is coming."

Muffled sounds of conversation drew closer. Footsteps shuf-
fled along the carpet beyond the door and came to a standstill.
He could hear feminine laughter and the hushed murmurings
of voices.

Darting a glance around the room in search of somewhere
to hide, his gaze came to rest on the mahogany armoire. He
shook his head. "First place they'd think to look."

She gave him a startled look. Planting her hands on her
slender hips, she asked, "Precisely, how many times have you
been faced with this particular dilemma, my lord?"

He slanted her a dark frown. "Get under the bed."

"Under the bed!" She recoiled in disgust at the mere idea. "It is dark and dusty under there. I-I'll get filthy. And I'd ruin my best gown."

He emitted a furious growl. They were about to be discovered alone in a bedchamber, and she was worried about soiling her damned dress!

"Over here." His fingers bit into her wrist as he dragged her across the room toward the enormous trunk against the far wall.

"What on earth are you doing?" she whispered fiercely.

He threw open the top. "Saving your honor and what is left of my reputation," he replied, and shoved her none too gently into a sea of silk and satin dresses.

Her face was mushed into a billowing satin gown that threatened to suffocate her. Gracious, she thought, struggling to disengage a whalebone stay from her rib cage, this investigative work was decidedly unglamourous.

"Squeeze in," he hissed, and pushed her farther into the satin abyss.

"I cannot breathe!" she squealed.

He slammed the lid shut behind her, but it would not close.

"Damnation," he growled, and yanked her out of the encroaching fabrics that threatened to suffocate her.

"Where should we try next?" she asked, sputtering feathers that seemed to have invaded her mouth.

His glance shot quickly around the dimly lit room. "The drapes," he said, propelling her toward the large casement windows.

"What about you?" she cried, casting a nervous glance over her shoulder at the door that was about to spring open.

"Don't fret," he said, and shoved her behind the green velvet drapes. "I'll think of something."

She opened her mouth to protest, but he silenced her and snapped the drapes shut.

The click of the bedroom door latch found Hunter without a place to hide. Casually, he leaned his palm against the window ledge and essayed an indolent pose.

"Hunter Lancaster?" A shrill, horribly coarse, vaguely familiar female voice pealed through the dimly lit room.

He shut his eyes for a moment, hoping the obscene creature was an aberration. She was not. He swore under his breath and cursed his bad luck.

Of all the bedchambers to get caught in, why did it have to be Harriet Declaire's? Never before had he lamented the small, intimate social circle to which he belonged.

She flashed a wicked smile. "I don't believe it." A derisive chuckle rent the air. "I thought I saw your head duck into my bedchamber. But I wasn't sure."

Curiosity got the better of Sabrina. She edged the velvet drapes apart and peered around Hunter's shoulder. Gracious heavens! Bedecked in the most ostentatious purple and pink silk gown, the woman fairly wounded the eye.

"Who is *that?*" Sabrina whispered, appalled by the obstreperous creature cannoning toward them.

"That," he bit out under his breath as he snapped the drape shut, "is Harriet Declaire."

"Of course it is, darling," the object of his disgust remarked. She drifted across the shadowy room to where he stood guard before the bulging drape.

"Who were you expecting?" Lady Declaire asked with a leer as she ran the tip of her ivory fan over his muscular, broad shoulder. "How clever of you to slip inside when no one was looking. I had no idea you were here tonight," she mused, her hungry gaze sliding over him with licentious delight.

The muscle in his jaw clenched. "Nor I you," he retorted with a tight smile. He couldn't quite fathom his ill fate. The last place he wanted to get cornered was in Harriet Declaire's bedroom. How the devil was he going to emerge unscathed from this debacle?

She pouted playfully. "You will tease me, you wretched man. But I don't mind. I do like surprises. We both know why you sneaked up here. Let's not pretend."

"I hoped you'd understand," he murmured noncommittally as he wracked his brain for an escape route.

Her lips curled provocatively. "I knew you could never resist a night in my arms. You won't regret it, I promise you," she crooned, running her palms over his chest.

Hunter's face set in stone. He might have known the crass woman would jump at the chance to vindicate the dent in her otherwise colossal ego. How the devil was he going to escape without obliging her ferocious appetite?

"Be rough with me, Hunter. I like it hard and fast," she moaned, and pressed a kiss to his mouth.

A squeal of shock emanated from behind the drapes.

Lady Declaire reeled back. "What was that?" she asked, a suspicious gleam in her eye.

Hunter crossed his arms over his chest. "What was what?" he returned blandly.

"I heard a noise. It was coming from behind the drapes."

"Oh, that. It was nothing." He prevaricated badly. "Probably just a field mouse."

She fixed him with a dubious look. "Mice? This close to London?"

He shrugged. "A rat perhaps?" he offered lamely.

"In Hobson's guest chamber?" She shook her head. "I think not. You're hiding a woman behind there."

"Don't be ridiculous," Hunter scoffed at her. "You said it yourself: I snuck up here to be with you."

Her eyes narrowed contemptuously on his guileless facade.

"I think you slipped in here looking for a bed and I surprised you. Don't look so innocent; it's been done before."

"Has it?" he asked in poorly feigned ignorance.

"Move out of my way," she snarled.

"Now, Harriet, calm yourself. I am sure we can—"

"I'll raise the house," she vowed acidly. "We wouldn't want that, now, would we?"

Hunter expelled a defeated sigh and stepped aside. Lady Declaire tore back the drapes. Sabrina etched an embarrassed half smile.

"I knew it!" Lady Declaire shrieked. "You vile bastard!" She turned on Hunter, fists clenched. "How dare you use my room to bed a cheap tart."

Sabrina blinked at the vulgar woman in shock. She turned her stunned gaze toward Hunter. "Is she suggesting—"

"Yes," came his curt reply, "she is."

"That is the most insulting thing I've ever heard," Sabrina declared, the picture of righteous indignation. "For your information," she imparted in a huff, "we are not on intimate terms. Well," she amended, "at least, not in the manner *you* suggest."

Hunter's eyes drifted shut. He stroked the bridge of his nose with his thumb and forefinger. He dearly wished she would quit while she was ahead. Flattered as he was by her attempt to save him from total disgrace, the situation was rapidly deteriorating into total mayhem. A timely exit was imperative.

Lady Declaire eyed the impertinent chit with keen interest. "I know you," she snarled, her eyes pinched with loathing. "You're the strumpet he was with at Holmes's garden party when he might have had me."

Hunter emitted a miserable groan and rolled his eyes heavenward. At this rate, he would be lucky if Lady Declaire did not rouse the house with her shrewish ranting. News of his sneaking into Hobson's ballroom and cavorting with Sabrina Bennett in an upstairs bedchamber would be just the sort of thing to put his reputation over the edge.

And Harriet Declaire was just the sort of woman who would do it. If this evening's scandal ever reached his father's ears, Hunter would be banished from the single familial event he was welcome to attend—Christmas dinner.

Hunter's arm slid around Sabrina's waist. "Time to leave."

But she did not look inclined to heed him. Her statuelike stance could best be described as horrified. Apparently, scenes like this were something of a novelty for girls who lead sheltered lives. Hell! It was not exactly a normal occurrence for him either.

"*She* called *me* a strumpet!" she sputtered in shocked dismay.

"I know. I heard," came his clipped reply.

Before Sabrina knew what he was about, his arm slipped under her knees, and he swept her off the ground. As if she weighed little more than a feather, he cradled her against his chest.

Flabbergasted, she cried, "My lord, put me down right this instant."

Seething, Lady Declaire watched as the object of her fantasies whisked the infantile tart off her feet.

Ignoring the squirming bundle in his arms, Hunter addressed the irate Lady Declaire in a remarkably calm voice given the outrageous circumstance. "Good evening, madam, I apologize for the misunderstanding." With that he marched from the room, Sabrina securely nestled in his arms.

"This is the second time you've refused me, Hunter Lancaster," Lady Declaire screeched, and threw a pillow at the door through which he had escaped her clutches.

Her fisted hands flexed with rage at her sides. It was too much to be born. She would make him pay.

Her fingers drilled against her upper arm. As she paced the

room in a furious prowl, a scheme took root in her mind. She knew exactly how to fix that rogue. A wicked smile spread across her feline face. He would be sorry he ever insulted Harriet Declaire.

Chapter 6

Sabrina objected strenuously to his hands intimately clamped over her rib cage and thighs. It was most disconcerting to be pressed against a brick wall of pure masculinity. He smelled wonderfully male—like soap and a hint of lemon, she noticed with a rush of warmth. Disconcerted by how much she enjoyed her current position, she wiggled with energy to be set free.

But it was of little consequence, for his iron fingers dug into her flesh with renewed energy.

"I suggest you act the part of the damsel in distress if you wish to avoid a confrontation with our undoubtedly dismayed host," came Hunter's lethal warning against her ear.

His breath was warm and soft along her neck. She gulped. "Oh, dear." Her eyes grew round. "I see your point."

"I thought you might," he murmured, his tone dry.

Her arm swooped through the air in a wide half circle. She clutched her forehead in a melodramatic fashion and uttered a painful moan.

"*Ooh,* I am in agony, my lord," she groaned, and winced as though in pain. "I shan't be able to manage on my own. How kind you are to lend me aid."

"Much better," he said, his voice husky and low. She found herself enjoying the moment far more than was proper under the mortifying circumstances.

Hunter hurried down the hallway past the crowd of astonished guests toward what he hoped were the back stairs. He emerged inside the bustling kitchen. The servants all stopped what they were doing and stared at the finely clad gentleman hoisting a lady in his arms.

"Sprained ankle," he explained as he headed for the servants' entrance.

"Ooh!" Sabrina moaned, and let her eyes drift shut in agony. "I shall never walk again."

As soon as they reached the garden entrance, her performance drew to a close.

"You may now release me, my lord," she instructed in a prim voice. She was far more affected by his proximity than she showed. It was unseemly to be held by a man who was not a lady's brother or, the very least, her husband. It was also wildly exciting. The last time she had felt so deliciously wicked was, not surprisingly, in Lord Holmes's library.

Hunter's carriage was waiting in the dark, sheltered foliage of Hobson's trees. Yanking open the door, he plunked the rambunctious bundle down on the black leather seat. Before she had the chance to reprimand him for his outrageous conduct, he disappeared. Her mouth snapped shut.

Scrambling to set herself to rights, she heard his voice firing unintelligible orders at his driver.

Mortification consumed her. Gracious, had he actually swept her off her feet and tramped through the house with her like a sack of potatoes? He had. She bit her lower lip. My, it was quite a disturbing feeling to be manhandled.

"Just what gives you the right," she blazed when he appeared at last, "to parade through Hobson's home treating me like a wrapped parcel from Bond Street?"

Seated opposite her, he crossed his arms over his massive chest and regarded her with a cynical smirk. "Age, wisdom, experience and the undying conviction that a scandal must be avoided at all costs despite the fact that a wealthy, spoiled brat like you is out for a perverse, cheap adventure," came his scathing retort.

His caustic remark wounded her to the core. She was glad the carriage was dark, for it concealed her red, hot cheeks. Had the excitement of the challenge overtaken her senses completely? No. Certainly not. How like him to overlook the salient facts. She had made a great discovery this evening. Hobson was somehow involved with the villain responsible for poor Jane's death.

She turned away from his haughty countenance. "I scarcely know what to say in the face of such utter humiliation."

"Now, that is an occasion, to be sure," he drawled out.

"Was it strictly necessary for you to carry me from the house?"

His eyes glinted dangerously. "How else would you suggest I extricate the two of us from the disastrous circumstance?" he gritted.

Before she could utter a response, the conveyance hit a deep rut in the road. Her shoulders slammed against the black leather squabs. She heard him chuckle at her efforts to stay upright. His lordship, she noted with irritation, had scarcely moved a smidgen. She glared at him.

"No gentleman would have dared."

He turned the full force of his piercing gray gaze on her. "I've told you before," he said, his tone ominous, "I am not a gentleman."

She was too annoyed to heed the subtle warning he had

issued. "So I've noticed," she flung at him. "I've never been so mortified in all my life!"

Unruffled, he muttered in an exceedingly dry tone, "I find that very hard to believe," and settled back comfortably on the seat across from her.

She crossed her arms over her chest and fixed him with a mute look of burning contempt.

"Is this all the thanks I get for saving your scrawny neck?" he queried with mild sarcasm. "You really are going to have to do something about your manners. They are deplorable."

"I do not know how you have the nerve to speak to me of manners when you keep such lovely company yourself, my lord," she commented on a derisive snicker. "Who was that horrid creature?"

He shrugged his broad shoulders slightly. "No one of consequence. At least," he murmured with a pensive air, "not before tonight."

She blinked at him. What did he mean by that cryptic remark? "I am all astonishment, my lord. That *woman*," she averred with disdain, "insulted your honor and thoroughly offended my sense of decency. If she were a man, you'd have called her out, would you not?"

He flashed a sardonic smirk that conveyed his opinion. "No. I would not. In any event, she is not a man. In fact, she is not even a lady. Let's just forget the entire sordid event, shall we?"

"Very well, my lord, if that is the way you feel about it. But I must say, I am surprised you are not more enraged."

"May I remind you"—his voice held a barbed note—"if you hadn't been argumentative, that charming scenario could have been avoided entirely."

"I am not argumentative," she tossed back tartly. "Your arrival caused that unholy scene."

"I beg to differ," he countered coolly.

It was dreadfully late. She was exhausted and lacked the

energy to launch into recriminations. She peered out the window at the dark, misty, abandoned city street.

"Where are you taking me?" she asked with a sleepy yawn.

"Home," he told her, his tone like ice.

Closing her tired eyes, she laid her head back to rest. "Good," she said crisply, "I should like to be dropped off around the back near the gardens, I've left a window open in the servants' quarters. My maid, Fanny, will be waiting for me—"

"Your sister's home," he interjected curtly.

"Oh."

Then it struck her. *Her sister's home!* She sat bolt upright. She could never explain her disappearance in the middle of the night when she was supposedly tucked in her bed at Grosvenor Square.

"Stop this carriage immediately. I have no intentions of going to Morely House. Fanny will be worried sick. To say nothing of what Grandfather will say."

Hunter's soft, derisive chuckle cut through the darkness. "That is your quagmire. Perhaps in the future you will consider your actions before behaving so rashly."

"I am not going—" she began in a fury, but he leaned forward and pinned her against the seat. Sandwiched between the leather squabs and a wall of pure male muscle, her heart flopped around in her chest.

"I—" Her startled blue gaze collided with the virile, strikingly handsome man looming over her. Her voice died in her throat.

"I will brook no argument from you, little one. I cannot risk being seen with you in the dead of night." He flashed a crooked smile. "Seeing you to the garden entrance, servants' quarters or the front door is definitely not an option. I promised your sister I'd return you safe and sound. And I intend to do just that. It's quite a nice ride back to town," he said in a voice like steel cloaked with black velvet. "We will have plenty of time to have a nice, cozy little chat, you and I. I am eager for you to satisfy my curiosity."

Her temper ignited. How dare he order her about like a child? Who gave him the right to whisk her off in the middle of the night without so much as a by your leave?

"Well, then, by all means," she said, her voice dripping with sarcasm. "Ask your fill. Obviously, I am completely at your disposal."

He snickered at that remark. "So you are." His dark, hooded gaze slid over her with seductive slowness. Her pulse soared. "Why did you lead me to believe you were Hughes's lover?" he asked, his voice low and husky.

Her eyes widened slightly. *Hughes's lover!* Heavens, he was direct. And improper. Most improper. But that did not deter the tingle of excitement in the pit of her stomach.

"I did nothing of the sort," she fired back.

"Oh, yes you did." His soft, seductive tone swirled about her wickedly like a satin caress. Her heart lurched madly. She pressed back against the seat.

"You led me on," he murmured huskily, his penetrating gaze holding her captive. "Why?"

The smoldering flame lurking in his silvery depths made her heart jolt. "I—I did no such thing. I am scarcely responsible for what erroneous conclusions you draw about my character," she said with a hard swallow, and eased, to no avail, away from the encroaching figure of overpowering, raw sensuality.

"You went out of your way to put me off, didn't you?" he asked, leaning closer.

Heavens. She could feel the warmth of his breath tickle her cheek. "I—I did nothing of the sort," she stammered, her senses careening.

He planted his palms on either side of her thighs, trapping her between his arms. "Was it because you were afraid I might decide I rather enjoyed our previous assignation and pursue you?'' he asked, a seductive glint in his eye.

Telltale color crept into her cheeks. "No, I never—"

"Never what?" he asked, his sinfully provocative gaze flickering over her flushed face as he leaned over her. "Imagined I'd want a girl like you?"

She wet her lips. "Why would you?" she asked on a soft sigh of anticipation.

He smiled and dipped his raven head. "My wicked, perverse nature, I guess," he murmured before he covered her mouth with his.

The hardness of his lips, strong and sure, made her quiver. With a soft groan of surrender, she gave herself freely to his savage kiss. Mindless of everything but the feel of his mouth slanting over hers, she wiggled closer to his hard, rippled chest and kissed him back.

His hands stroked her hips and thighs and slipped beneath her hem to caress her stockinged legs. Easing her hem over her knees, his palms slid over her hips, caressing her thighs and in between. She trembled. His lips pressed against hers, hard and searching and deeply passionate, while his roving hand stroked her inner thighs and grazed over her soft, feminine core. Tilting her hips, eager for his roving caress, she met the sensual invasion of his tongue with her own, twisting, stroking, loving. His hands tightened on her thighs, and he dragged her across the seat, pinning her against him. She gasped at the feel of his hard arousal.

His mouth grazed her earlobe. "See what you do to me?" he whispered thickly.

An involuntary tremor of desire washed over her. Arching her neck back, her eyes fluttered shut. She sighed. She could not understand what was happening to her, but she never wanted this moment of exquisite pleasure to end. He pressed her down on the seat and bent his head to kiss the hollow of her neck.

She angled her neck, welcoming his hot, wet mouth against her burning skin.

"I want to touch you," he whispered hoarsely on a deep sigh of requited passion. She expelled a breathless half moan, half sigh and arched against him. His fingers fumbled with the buttons on the back of her gown. Yanking her bodice loose, he tore through to the thin barrier that concealed her soft ivory globes.

His tortuous palm caressed her breast, now barely concealed by the filmy cotton of her chemise. Gently, he kneaded her soft mound until she nearly ached from the sensation. She felt herself peak beneath his roving hands.

Completely taken under his sensual spell, she could do no more than stare at him, longing mirrored in her torpid blue eyes.

"Kiss me," he whispered, his voice rough with emotion. "Kiss me," he urged thickly, his mouth hovering above hers.

Her arms wound around his neck. She lifted her face to his. As if they had a mind of their own, her softly parted, moist lips pressed against his. Groaning, he crushed her to him, devouring the sweetness she offered. A muffled sound escaped his throat. He deepened the kiss.

As his open mouth trailed hot, wet kisses down her neck, she clutched at his shoulders, desperate for more. Tilting her head, she basked in the delicious sensations his searing touch evoked. His hand moved down the length of her back, pressing her against his warm, pulsing body.

"Hunter . . . Hunter," she whispered on a breathless sigh of pleasure, and covered his mouth with her own. Her soft, supple lips parted to receive his kiss. He covered her burning lips with his, devouring her mouth with bruising hunger. She met the strokes of his tongue, welcomed the sensual invasion and thrust deep into the sweet recesses of his mouth.

The soft fabric of her chemise gave way as the warmth of

his mouth covered her soft, creamy orbs. His tongue teased and laved the rosy, taut marble. Her fingers dug into his hair. She arched against him, convinced she would go mad from pleasure. When his mouth closed and sucked hard, desire overrode all reason.

She was on fire. Waves of ecstasy throbbed through her, radiating from his persistent mouth suckling at her breast, culminating in a dull ache in her soft, feminine core where the hard evidence of his burning desire pulsed against her.

She moved against his tormenting thrusts with some primal need she could not identify or understand. She thought she would die if he ever stopped touching her. His hand tugged at the thin cotton barrier until the material gave way. He found her honeyed warmth with his probing fingers.

"Hunter," she breathed against his mouth. As her body responded to his tormenting strokes, she let out a cry of ecstasy and was carried away by the waves of pure rapture his touch created deep inside her.

His mouth found hers once more for a savage kiss. He parted her legs with his hard, muscular thigh. Her eyelashes fluttered open. She gazed up at his passion-flushed face looming above her.

Their eyes met. Time stood still. She could hear their ragged, uneven breathing. Dark, penetrating shards of silver stared down at her searching her soul. Then he pulled back, leaving her suddenly devoid of his warmth. He raked his hand through his hair. Taking a deep breath, he closed his eyes and shuddered.

"Get up," he said, his tone cold and strangely taut with anger.

Staring at him in stunned disbelief, hurt written all over her face, she pushed herself up on the seat. "W-what's the matter?" she stammered in a mere whisper. "What have I done?"

He turned on her, baring his teeth in a furious snarl. "Cover yourself."

"But I—"

"Cover yourself," he gritted, and drove his hands through his tussled black hair.

Numbly, she sat all the way up and tugged at the hem of her dress, dragging it over her legs. Clumsy fingers fumbled with her chemise. She felt as if she had ten thumbs.

The carriage was silent, save for the uneven creaking of the wheels against the furrowed road. She did not dare so much as glance in his direction. Oh, God. Lord God. She wanted to die, to crawl out of the carriage and die. Simply die. Hurriedly, she straightened her bodice.

It was horrible. Every fiber in her body screamed out for his touch. Her breasts hurt. Her normally soft cotton chemise stung against her hard, achy nipples still moist from his hot, searing mouth. The dull, throbbing ache between her legs had not subsided. And she had the most mortifying urge to burst into tears.

The carriage mercifully ground to a halt. Without a word, he reached out and thrust the carriage door open. He looked at her as if he hated her. "Get out."

She managed to jump down from the carriage. How, she wasn't quite sure, for her legs felt like lemon pudding. She heard the door close with a resounding click behind her. The carriage wheels creaked forward. The sound of the driver cracking his whip penetrated her addled brain like a hard slap of reality.

Her breathing settled down to a more even beat. Slowly, her mind returned to some semblance of sanity. He had warned her that he was no gentleman. Tonight he had proven it. Tears of shame rolled down her cheeks. She couldn't blame him entirely. She was shocked and humiliated by her body's eager response to his scandalous touch. She should be thankful he had put an end to it when he did, for she had passed the ability to think clearly long ago. She had slipped into that beautiful, sensual haze where all that mattered was lover touching lover. Of course, it wasn't beautiful. And they weren't lovers. They were virtually strangers.

She sobbed even harder. Had she actually lain back in his carriage and let him do those things to her? Let him touch her intimately? Kiss her passionately? She had. The memory burned indelibly in her mind. What was more, she had reveled in every moment of it.

What hurt most was his absolute disgust of her. The look of contempt on his face made her heart ache. She drew a ragged sigh and sniffled. On the other hand, she realized, wiping her nose on her dress sleeve, she despised him. At least, she told herself she had every reason to.

She took a deep, steadying breath. Scrubbing away the tears that stained her cheeks with her palms, she swallowed the painful lump in her throat. Slowly, she pushed open the wrought-iron gate and crossed the darkened courtyard that led to the sleepy Morely House.

Hunter expelled a furious growl and smashed his fist against the carriage wall. Damn her! How could he have lost all control over an innocent young chit? Resting his elbows on his knees, he dug both hands into his hair and squeezed his skull between his palms. What the hell was wrong with him? Had he really come that close to having his way with her on the seat of his carriage? What the devil had possessed him to act so rashly? He, who had brought his mistresses to the peak of excitement without ever losing control, had been consumed with mindless lust. Never in his entire life had he been so carried away by the woman in his arms that he had lost his ability to reason.

He had never experienced such overwhelming passion, such all-consuming desire.

Thank God he had come to his senses.

Furious with himself, he pounded the leather seat with his fists. Squeezing his eyes shut, he swore under his breath. How could he have been so damned stupid? He never made mistakes. Not ever. At least, not where women were concerned.

Except for tonight. Another moment, and he would have made the biggest mistake of his life. He would have plunged inside her soft, wet, tight welcoming sheath and lost himself completely. Hell, the mere thought had him aroused. Her navy blue eyes brimming with unbridled passion, her soft, wet lips eagerly parting to receive his kiss, and her luxurious, fiery red hair spread across the dark carriage seat all beckoned him into the sensual fray. And he had gone. Eagerly. Unable to resist tasting her, touching her, the burning need to possess her had nearly overwhelmed him. In his haste, he had forgotten her age and inexperience.

The only thing that kept him from making violent love to the little baggage was the thought of dear Julia seduced and abandoned. He would not wish such an ill fate on Sabrina. He chafed at the memory of looking down into those deep blue, artless eyes, slumberous with desire, in awe of what were undoubtedly new sensations. Suddenly, he saw the willing, eager woman he had held in his arms as the beautiful, trusting, young innocent she was. And it stopped him. Cold.

He massaged his forehead. Sabrina. She could teach *him* a few things about seduction.

It was hard for him to believe that the woman who had burned with desire at his caress was a complete novice. As a rule, he had never paid any attention to virtuous women. He sure as hell never came close to deflowering a virgin. Now he knew why.

A firm conviction took hold in his mind. He must never see Sabrina Bennett again. He must never be alone with her. He could not trust himself. He snickered at his admission. A fair slip of a girl, a complete innocent, tempted him like no other woman he had ever known.

Chapter 7

It lacked a few minutes before the hour of ten o'clock the following morning when Hunter received his unexpected caller. Prying his eyes open, he instructed Evans to send Mr. Crawford into the dining room. Clad in his navy brocade dressing robe, Hunter sat sipping a cup of strong, black coffee and tried, with little success, to wake up.

By the time he had finally got that damned silly chit out of his system and found sanctuary in sleep, it was nearly five. He had fallen into bed and would probably still be there if not for Mr. Crawford's arrival. The blasted man had better have a good reason for hauling Hunter out of the depths of much needed slumber.

"Mr. Crawford, my lord," Evans announced with stiff displeasure.

"Ah, Crawford," Hunter said, and motioned to the chair to his right. "Sit."

Evans's eyes threatened to pop out of his head. He cleared his throat and extended his hand for the offensive man's tattered cap. The nervous Mr. Crawford chose to clutch the mangy object between his fingers instead. A look of barely concealed awe crossed his face as he looked around the elegant room. Evans dropped his hand and cast a disdainful glance at the man who was ogling with envy the gold candelabras perched on either end of the walnut sideboard.

"Tell me, what has brought you here at this ungodly hour," Hunter asked, rubbing the sleep from his tired eyes.

The Runner dragged his gaze from the plush surroundings and frowned a bit. "It's near' eleven, milord," he mumbled, shifting from foot to foot. "I thought you'd be up by now."

Hunter yawned hugely. "I do hope your powers of observation are better than your judgment. Take a seat and tell me what you've come to say. Your visit is not inauspicious, as I, myself, have some developments in the case to relate."

Clearing his throat, Mr. Crawford bumbled his way into the expansive dining room and pulled back the richly carved walnut chair. Evans watched in horror as the short, stocky visitor slid—grimy, torn pants and all—onto the gold velvet seat.

Hunter shook his head at his outraged butler. "That will be all, Evans. I doubt Mr. Crawford intends to abscond with the Lancaster silver. It would scarcely be a sound endorsement for future clients," he drawled.

Evans cleared his throat and etched a stiff, dutiful bow. "As you wish, my lord."

"It's right nice of you to offer me a cup o' coffee, milord," the Runner said when they were alone.

After imbibing a large gulp of hot coffee, Hunter muttered over the rim of his fine white porcelain cup, "Get to the point."

"Lady Jane Greenly were that girl we found floatin' in th' Thames not too long ago."

Sabrina would be pleased, Hunter thought with a slight smirk. At least Bow Street was interested in her dear departed friend. ''Go on.''

''Guess what's so special 'bout 'er case.''

Hunter rested his elbows on the table, slowly sipping his coffee. ''I am not certain, but I've a feeling you are about to tell me she was murdered by a man who is fond of wearing a certain gold symbol of a naked maiden and a snake.''

Scratching his balding head, Crawford sat back and stared blankly at his employer. ''How'd y'know that?'' he asked, astounded.

''For the simple reason she was found clutching a gold medallion with that disgusting insignia. I do hope you have something relevant to relate,'' Hunter muttered testily.

''As a matter o' fact, I 'ave,'' Mr. Crawford said, slurping his coffee. Doused with four lumps of sugar and an ample slopping of heavy cream, the concoction looked revolting.

''Night afore last, our man Paine went to some meetin' at a fancy-lookin' place owned by a certain Lord Everly.''

Frowning pensively, Hunter traced the edge of his coffee cup with his forefinger. Everly was one of the names on Sabrina's list. How very interesting. ''And?''

''There were five other men who'd gone, too. I could see from the street they was havin' a terrible row 'bout somethin'. Paine was none too popular with the likes of 'em. I can tell you.''

Hunter's brow drifted upward in surprise. ''Five men you say? Were you able to ascertain their identities?''

''Just Paine and Everly. I'm still working on the rest.''

''Everly warrants further scrutiny, I should think. He may well have done away with the Greenly girl.''

''What makes y' say that, milord?''

Hunter shrugged his shoulder. "Consider it a hunch. Am I correct in assuming a stout, gray-haired gentleman was among the group of men you saw?"

The Runner look astonished. "Right you are, milord. He was sittin' back watchin' the proceedin's."

"Mmm. That would be Hobson."

Mr. Crawford blinked at Hunter. "Now, how y' know that, milord?"

A slight smile tugged at the corner of his mouth. "I paid an unexpected visit to his home last evening. He was in possession of a certain ring that I have seen once before."

"So," the Runner murmured thoughtfully, "he's in on it, too. That was right smart o' you, milord."

Hunter uttered a dry, "Thank you." Truth be told, he could not actually take credit for the discovery. His feisty little accomplice was definitely onto something. Of course, it was far too dangerous for her to pursue. Still, he could not help but admire her intellect. She was a most unusual sort of girl.

"Milord?" Mr. Crawford asked his wistful employer. "Shall I tell you what 'appened next?"

Hunter dragged his thoughts back to the present. "By all means. Proceed." He frowned slightly and took another gulp of coffee. The deuced gel occupied too much of his thoughts.

"Paine was right angry, he was. He tore something off his finger, threw it down on the table and stormed from the place."

"The signet ring," Hunter supplied.

"Aye, milord," the Runner remarked, helping himself to another cup of coffee, heaps of sugar and a generous portion of cream. "I waited and crept in after they'd left to do some pokin' about." He shivered. "Somewhat evil is goin' on up there, milord, that I can tell you."

Hunter's brow furrowed. "Evil? What do you mean, evil?"

"I went into the room and couldna believe me eyes. The whole place was covered in shrouds of black and deep purple."

Hunter nearly choked on his coffee. "The devil you say?"

The Runner nodded. " 'Twas downright eerie, that I can tell you. But I kept on lookin'," he boasted with a proud posture, "coz I always do me job no matter what the perils."

Hunter nodded. "So you do. I am sure there will be a bonus in it for the risk you took."

"Thank ye, milord." Mr. Crawford's gratified grin was followed by another loud gulp of the sickly sweet, creamy contents in his cup. "What I found next sent a shiver down me spine, let me tell you. Manacles, chains, whips and several large ropes lying about."

"Sounds delightful," Hunter drawled in disgust. "What else did you find in this dark, forbidding room?"

"Ain't that enough?" Mr. Crawford exclaimed, incredulous.

Hunter sat back and contemplated what he had just heard. "It is not much more than a bizarre occurrence. What does it actually tell us?"

"There's a group o' men who wear them there rings, that's what."

Hunter refilled his cup with much needed coffee. "I've already deduced that. It is hardly significant," he said with a dismissive wave of his hand. "We still do not know which one was involved with Julia."

"I'm workin' on it, milord."

"Not fast enough," Hunter snapped, his patience wearing thin.

"What about that there book?" the Runner queried with pride in his discovery. "That's worth me fee, surely."

Hunter's eyes narrowed on the man's weathered face. "What book?"

"Almost like a Bible, it was lyin' open on a pulpit, draped in purple satin, like a shrine o' sorts. Someone 'ad been makin' an entry just afore I come."

Hunter frowned pensively. "What was in this nasty little book?"

"Names, like the bettin' book you might find at Whites."

"Yes, well, I doubt the members of that particular club are in peril of parting with their much coveted honor."

"You ain't heard the worst of it. Your stepsister's name was in it. And quite a hefty bet was placed on her, I don't mind tellin' you. O' course, I dunno who did the deed, just how much blunt he got for it."

Hunter's face contorted with rage. "*Julia's* name?" he exploded, and slammed his cup down hard enough to smash its saucer. "Who the devil would put my stepsister's name in such a vulgar book?"

" 'Aven't got the foggiest." The man shrugged and filled his cup for a third time, repeating the nauseating cream and sugar ritual. "But I've a feeling I know why."

"Unfortunately," Hunter gritted, his brow darkening, "so have I." What the devil had his sweet Julia gotten herself into?

"I shudder to think what goes on in such a vile sort of place."

"Mmm," Hunter sighed, drumming his fingers on the table. "Torture, I should think. Or perhaps something even worse." He slapped his napkin on the table and got to his feet. "I want to know which one of these men put Julia's name in that damned book."

The Runner was quick to slurp down the remainder of his coffee and hastily get to his feet. Hunter glanced at the now empty sugar bowl and creamer. It was little wonder the man lacked a full set of teeth.

"Find out all you can about this nefarious group of men, especially the last two," Hunter ordered sharply. "I should very much like to make their acquaintance." *And plant my fist in the blackguard's face who dared enter Julia's name into such a disgusting sort of book,* he added silently.

* * *

A knock sounded at the door. Inside the ornate dressing room, which boasted four cheval mirrors and a plush red velvet settee, the tall, blond man standing before a mahogany highboy called out, "Come."

His dark brown eyes caught sight of Lord St. John Everly in the mirror. He frowned slightly and dismissed his valet with an impatient wave of his hand. Gazing in the mirror, he adjusted his neck cloth to perfection, heedless of his friend's obvious agitation.

"How can you be so calm?" Everly demanded in a fierce under breath as he approached the spot where the man stood fussing over his neck cloth.

The blond man shrugged his shoulder. "I see no reason to panic."

"You know, of course, *he* was at Hobson's last night? Just barged right in without an invitation," Everly blustered, waving his pudgy arms in the air. "The nerve of the man. It simply isn't done. But he did it."

"Who?" the man asked, gazing into the mirror as he smoothed his blond hair with his palms.

"Lancaster, of course," Everly snapped.

He turned to face the room. "Tut, tut, St. John. You promised not to mention that name to me," the man replied, his voice deceivingly calm.

"What do you think he was doing there?" Everly asked, ringing his sweat-soaked palms. "He doesn't even know Hobson socially. You realize, he could cause a lot of trouble for us," he bemoaned, pacing to and fro like a frightened hound.

The blond man shrugged his olive green superfine coat over his shoulders and tugged the ruffled cambric shirtsleeves over his wrists. "What trouble can he cause?"

"You know as well as I do what kind of trouble he can cause," Everly snarled, fisted hands at his side. "Don't forget, you're responsible for Lancaster's sister's death. If you hadn't gotten her with child, none of this would be—"

Before Everly could finish his sentence, the tall man's hand snaked out and tightened around his throat. "I told you," he hissed through his teeth, "never mention that name to me again." He tightened the flesh-and-bone noose around Everly's neck. "I won't be shouted at by the likes of you. You're not fit to wipe my boots," he added with a vicious sneer. "I've twenty-six maidens to my name. How many have you?"

Everly's beefy fingers clawed at the iron clamp around his throat that threatened to crush his windpipe. He issued a pathetic plea for his life. Sniggering with disgust, the man released him. Everly collapsed on the settee in a lump. Gasping for air, he rubbed his sore neck and tried to catch his breath.

The man adjusted his ruffled sleeves. "Women find me irresistible. There isn't a woman born I cannot seduce." A smile graced his flawlessly handsome face. "Where is the sport in that, I ask you? The majority of the men in our circle frequent brothels, don't you know? Who wants to plow a well-worn path, I ask you? I must confess," he said, splaying his hand across his chest, "Julia was different from the rest of my conquests. I allowed myself to indulge in a momentary diversion with her. I must be even more potent than I realized." A proud smile touched his lips. "She was breeding after a mere few weeks in my bed. Of course, then she was useless to me." He waved his hand in the air in a dismissive fashion. "I had to rid myself of the clinging chit. Such a nuisance. All that muttering about love. Of course, I never imagined the damned chit would die birthing the babe. That was another thing entirely."

"What are you going to do about that deuced Runner?" Everly asked at last, still gulping for air. "Paine insists he's after you."

He tucked his gold watch and chain into his pink-and-green brocade waistcoat. "Does he? How very flattering. I cannot imagine why. You killed the girl."

The color drained from Everly's paunchy face. "You—you promised not to say anything about that!"

The man flashed a cool smile in the face of his friend's hysteria. "So I did. I cannot think why I should. Unless, of course," he said with a dark, menacing glare, "you continue to annoy me. As to the other, all our clandestine meetings are held in that disgusting room of yours."

"You founded the damned society."

"Mmm," he replied, and leaned closer to the mirror to scrub a spot on his pearly white teeth with this thumbnail. "And you took to the notion quite well as I recall. I must say, you surprised me with your sordid perversions. You'll soon have all the members using manacles." He glanced at Everly skeptically. "I do wonder I ever let you in. Deflowering virgins takes skill, St. John. I have my doubts about you. Still," he said on a bored sigh, "you are good for your losses and pay promptly on all my completions." He slipped the gold insignia ring on his third finger. "But you worry overmuch. Why should anyone assume I am guilty of anything?" he asked, glancing with admiration at his reflection in the mirror. "No law against seduction. And it is so much more amusing to have a club where one can discuss and benefit so fittingly from one's conquests. If a stupid gel gets herself ruined, that's her problem, now, isn't it?" he asked, meeting his ignoble associate's stricken expression in the mirror.

"There is one person who may not feel that way," Everly pointed out, his voice wavering with trepidation.

The other man *tsk, tsk*ed. "Leave Lancaster to me."

Everly gulped audibly. "Do you think it was wise to excommunicate Paine?" he asked, nervously chewing on his fingernails. "He's been one of us since the beginning. It doesn't seem quite fair."

The lean, masculine figure plucked at an imaginary piece of lint on his sleeve. "Of course we should have done. He's been a problem from the first. Far too flamboyant for my taste. I don't like indiscriminating Corinthians belonging to the club. He attracts too much attention. He is the source of all your anxiety, I daresay. What with that inquisitive Runner on his tail. He's a liability none of us can afford, least of all you," he remarked pointedly in the face of his friend's distress.

"I don't know why you say that to me. I am not the only one guilty of wrongdoing."

The blond man uttered a satirical laugh. "You are the only one fretting, old boy."

"I—I think we should all stick together," Everly whined, running his pudgy fingers through his thinning hair. "We should operate like other societies do. As a-a brotherhood."

One sardonic brow elevated slightly. "Brotherhood? Come, come now, St. John, you are scarcely *my* brother. Ours is a secret organization. Not exactly like a missionary society."

"That may be, but we've got to be careful, protect each other's identity. Paine might talk. He's in a bad way."

One blond brow cocked. "And say what? That you killed a girl and tossed her naked body into the Thames?"

Everly's normally fish-belly face turned a whiter shade of pale. "It was an accident. I didn't expect her to fight me."

The man shrugged and admired his profile in the cheval mirror. He smiled at Everly's tortured reflection. "Stop fretting. I know what I am about," he remarked, the picture of calm placidity.

*   *   *

The black carriage with the gold-and-red Somers crest gleaming on the door practically flew through the streets of London. Inside, Ian Somers contemplated murder. He still couldn't believe what he had heard an hour ago when he had stood in the house his wife had once made her home and listened to her grandfather's tirade.

As the carriage ground to a halt outside the stylish brick town house on Upper Brook Street, Ian did not wait for the footman. He threw himself down from the carriage and marched up the stone steps. Angry fists pounded against the door, dispensing with the customary bronze lion's-head knocker.

The door swung open. "Where is his lordship?" Ian demanded to know.

Evans looked slightly taken aback. "His lordship is bathing and does not wish to be disturbed," Evans replied, easing the door shut.

Ian would have none of it. He wedged his booted foot between the door and the casement. "That is indeed unfortunate," he said through his teeth, "because I intend to disturb his lordship presently."

Evans cleared his throat. Seeing no other avenue, he opened the door to the large, encroaching figure. "Who shall I say is calling?" he asked with stiff civility.

Ian shoved the door wide and stormed into the foyer. He strode past the stunned butler and started up the front stairs.

"B-but, my lord, you must be announced!" the outraged Evans cried, and scurried after the intruder.

Ian glanced down the hallway. Hearing the muffled sound of male voices to his right, he trudged down the hall. Not bothering to be admitted, he threw the door to Hunter Lancaster's private sanctuary open.

Reclining in a large copper tub, the master of the house was relaxing in a hot, steamy bath. His valet danced attendance at his side. As the door swung open, Hunter looked up in surprise.

"Ian? What the devil are you doing here?" he asked, and motioned for his valet to get his robe.

Getting out of the tub, he wrapped the full-length robe around his naked, glistening body and caught sight of his friend's dark scowl. "Is something amiss?" he asked, and dismissed his astonished valet, who happily took his leave.

Wordlessly, Ian marched up to the man he once considered a friend and planted his fist in his jaw. Taken completely unawares, Hunter fell backward and landed in the middle of the floor. He blinked up at the ferocious man looming over him.

"You bloody bastard," Ian hissed, his fists balled in anger. "Get to your feet."

"I would be happy to do so if I knew why the devil you just tried to break my jaw," Hunter countered coolly as he took himself off the floor, his pride damaged no small degree.

"As if you don't know," Ian scoffed. "You just couldn't keep your hands off her, could you?"

"Who?" Hunter asked, dreading the answer he knew was to come. His preoccupation with the fiery redheaded trouble-maker had mercifully been eclipsed by Mr. Crawford's disturbing report earlier this morning. Naturally, he had presumed he could rely on her to remain silent. He had been mistaken.

He had misjudged the damned chit. Her quest for ruin was at last realized. He might have known she would divulge his foolhardy indiscretion. Unless he missed his guess, she had chosen to omit her willing response. Not that it signified. In such matters, the man was ultimately responsible and, therefore, culpable.

Talons of dread clutched at his heart. Precisely what portion of their torrid encounter had she related? Not . . . all of it? Hell, he hoped not. This could prove to be a scandal he would not easily weather.

"Sabrina. Damn you! My sister-in-law. The complete innocent you ravaged last night."

Hunter's jaw clenched. "I did not ravage her," he bit out.

"Are you going to deny you were caught with my sister-in-law in one of Hobson's guest bedchambers last night?" Ian thundered. "To add insult to injury, you saw her home in your private carriage? Alone?"

"No," Hunter snapped, his tone low and controlled. "I do not deny that I rescued her, in the nick of time I might add, from another one of her hapless plots. My propitious intervention was at your wife's bidding."

"I am aware of my wife's foolish entreaty. I apologize for it," Ian retorted with curt civility. "It was not Amanda, however, who beseeched you to seduce her sister in the middle of the night!"

Hunter winced. Even to his prejudicial ears, he had comported himself like a dishonorable cad. Taking a deep breath, he tried to retrieve his character from the brink of moral disaster. "Upon my honor, the last thing I wanted was another encounter with that headstrong little minx."

"Do not dare mention honor to me," Ian replied with venom.

"If you must know," Hunter said, testing the damage done to his jaw, "I vowed never to see her again. She is far more trouble than she is worth."

Not in the least persuaded, Ian crossed his arms over his chest and regarded Hunter with a cynical smirk. "But you just couldn't resist taking full advantage of the fact that she is a total innocent who is infatuated with you, could you?"

Hunter snickered harshly. "Infatuated? I sincerely doubt it. Your outrageous sister-in-law is an avid student of life, don't you know?'' he averred sarcastically. ''Such persons do not suffer from infatuations.''

''You are not in a position to mock me, Lancaster,'' Ian gritted, hands fisted at his sides. ''I am closer than I ever thought I would be to calling you out. I've heard the ugly rumors circulating around your name. But I refused to believe them. I judged you an honorable, decent man incapable of siring a child on his own stepsister. Evidently, I was mistaken. It was a grave error, for it has brought disaster upon those I love most. The gossips have etched an accurate portrait of your character. It would seem you enjoy preying on young innocents.''

''You were not mistaken to bestow your good opinion upon me,'' Hunter replied, his tone as cold as a winter's morning. ''I do not prey on virtuous women. In general,'' he muttered with contempt, ''I avoid them like the plague.'' That was the truth. He dearly wished he had clung more firmly to his habits of old.

Of course, he had never met a wild, bewitching creature like Sabrina. Most virtuous women of his acquaintance were plain, shy creatures. Hardly the sort to make him burn. But she had. With a vengeance.

''I await your assurances that this was all a terrible misunderstanding and you will make immediate retribution.''

Hunter opened his mouth to refute the accusations and frowned slightly. What the devil could he say? He hadn't laid a hand on her? When his hands and mouth had been all over her? He plowed his hand through his midnight hair. Hell. He had better make a clean breast of it.

One objective burned clearly in his mind: he was going to enjoy beating the little baggage senseless for the trouble she had caused him. If she had not displayed such pathetic lack of judgment in going to Hobson's in the first place, he would not be facing the dreaded parson's trap. The fact that he was equally to blame, he dismissed as irrelevant. He was never particularly rational when he was angry. Right now, he was livid.

He cleared his throat and stood tall in the face of utter ignominy. "I can only say that while her virtue is intact, her honor, I fear, has been badly tarnished."

Ian slanted him a scornful glare. "That is putting it mildly."

Undaunted, Hunter continued, "You, of course, are free to name your seconds. But pray, allow me to assure you that I intend to offer for her. Posthaste. I shall procure a special license and meet with her guardian this very day. Will that satisfy you?"

"It will," Ian replied with a stiff nod.

"Good." Hunter's entire body seemed to relax. He bared his teeth in a smile. "I should hate to have to put a bullet through your chest."

Ian was not amused. "For God's sake, man, why did you wait for me to force your hand? Where is your sense of honor? It was your duty to make amends. You should have offered for her the minute you'd disgraced her."

Hunter stiffened at the rebuke. "I suppose," he said, clasping his hands behind his back, "it was momentarily diminished by my hatred of the matrimonial state."

Ian shook his head at him. "Gad, you really are a rogue. Cheer up," he remarked, and slapped Hunter on the back none too gently. "There's still an outside chance she'll refuse you. All your worries may well be over."

Hope dawned. Hunter hadn't considered an avenue of escape from this unholy mess. But of course, she could refuse him. She was free to do so. She would be saving them both from a fate guaranteed to be worse than death. After all, it was total ruin she sought, not marriage.

* * *

Half an hour later, Hunter's valet returned. Despite his master's foul mood, he saw to his lordship's ministrations with admirable skill. Donning a pale blue silk waistcoat and soft, gray velvet cutaway, Hunter hoped he looked sufficiently contrite, although contrition was an emotion altogether alien to him.

He heaved an impatient sigh and tore the neck cloth lose. "No. Not this one," he muttered, and tossed it on the floor. His valet stood patiently by while Hunter fought with his third uncooperative silk neck cloth.

Hunter was dreading this afternoon's interview. The discomfort irritated him. Of course, the fact that he had slept badly was not helping matters. He was not by nature an insomniac. Images of a fiery redhead lying beneath him, her blue eyes languid with passion and her wild, erotic hair scattered over the pillows, had haunted his sleep.

What the devil would the chit say when he proposed? Would she dare refuse him? Lord, he hoped so. Even if she did not refuse him outright, she might cry off after a short betrothal, claiming he was too disgusting to be borne and beg to be released from her promise. He would happily comply.

God knew he would make the world's worst husband. What did he know about marriage? Not a damned thing. Save for the impressions he had received during his early boyhood. Vicious fights behind closed doors. Ugly words expressed at dinner. His mother, dear sweet mother, blatantly cavorting with countless men in front of his father until he could not abide the sight of her any longer. His father was glad when she took up with a Frenchman and left for the Continent, never to be seen or heard from again. It was rumored she died shortly thereafter from the pox.

Not that his father's second marriage had fared much better. His wife's inability to bear his children came as a bitter disappointment, one he made no effort to hide.

No, Hunter thought with firm conviction, he would not inflict such a state on his worst enemy. It was with a heavy heart that he realized he had no choice but to issue a marriage proposal, this very day, to the most unconventional woman of his acquaintance. It would be farcical were it not so damned infuriating.

Chapter 8

Hunter waited, in what he presumed, from the pale yellow upholstered couch, matching chairs and shards of warm golden sunlight streaming in through the large casement windows, to be the morning room. The illustrious Grandfather Bennett was scheduled to appear at any moment.

Hunter couldn't help but wonder what tactic the old fossil planned to take. Without a doubt, affiancing his wayward grand-daughter to the Earl of Lancaster was the best outcome for which the old curmudgeon could hope. Given that Hunter was honor bound to offer for the little hellion, everything should work very nicely, provided she showed the good sense to refuse him. Yes, everything should work out splendidly. She would have achieved her coveted state of ruin, and he would have done the noble thing.

His fingers clawed at his neck cloth. It seemed to be restricting his breathing. His forehead creased in a deep frown. Dash it all, he sincerely hoped the virago had the good sense

to refuse him. It could prove a trifle disastrous for the both of
them if she actually decided to go through with it. He rubbed
his chin and contemplated the workings of Sabrina's mercurial
mind. No woman in her right mind would ever agree to wed
a notorious rake like him. Besides, she had expressed an aversion to marriage, had she not? He was certain she had.

He breathed a little easier. His bachelor way of life would
remain entirely intact. He admonished himself for the sense of
dread that had threatened to upset his normal calm.

He lifted one leg across his knee and drummed his fingers
on his immaculate black Hessians. By nature, he was anything
but a patient man. This deliberate attempt to make him stew
in his immoral juices grated on his nerves excessively. He got
to his feet and prowled the room. Stopping to take note of the
time on his gold pocket watch, his jaw clenched.

Twenty minutes. He had been waiting for a full twenty minutes. His lips thinned. Another five, and the damned chit could
suffer scandal before he would offer for her. He replaced his
watch in his waistcoat pocket and continued his restless pacing.

At the sound of the doorknob turning, Hunter swung around,
expecting to encounter the irate Viscount Bennett. To his surprise, the butler stood in the doorway. "Lord Bennett will see
you now. In the library, if you please."

Hunter's features turned to granite. It took all his self-control
not to turn on his heel and storm from the house. Self-control . . .
and the unhappy truth that he was responsible for the current
debacle. Stiff-backed, he strode from the room. He followed
the butler across the carpeted hallway into the white-walled
library.

The door shut behind him. He stood, feet slightly apart, and
braced himself for the tirade he felt sure would ensue.

Old was not the word to describe the tall, willowy gentleman
who occupied the seat behind the enormous walnut desk. It
struck Hunter that dear old Grandpapa looked to be in mourning,

garbed as he was in black from head to toe. He wondered with a rueful smirk if the forbidding man dressed in the macabre color routinely, or if the demise of Sabrina's honor was the reason.

"So, you have come," the brittle old man said at last. He allowed his disapproving gaze to sweep over the Earl of Lancaster. "I must admit, I am surprised," he remarked with obvious disdain and retrieved a small snuff box from his pocket. "I did not believe wastrels capable of restitution." He pinched a bit of snuff and half shoved, half snorted it up his nose.

Hunter's silver gaze narrowed on the shriveled old man. Wastrel? The war waging between the desire to rein in his temper and the need to issue a rounding set down was very nearly lost. Then Hunter reminded himself that he had come here to do his duty. Given half the chance, he fully intended to issue an offer.

"You see, my dear," the old man remarked with a chilling smile to someone seated in the corner of the room, "you were wrong; he has come."

Hunter's head whipped around. A scant distance away sat a young woman who he knew must be Sabrina. Her identity, however, was scarcely ascertainable from her disconsolate countenance. Her normally straight, delicate shoulders were slumped. Her unruly curls adorned a head that was grievously bowed in submission. She did not resemble, in the vaguest manner, the feisty harridan he had come to know. She looked pale and drawn as if she had aged ten years overnight.

The situation was, indeed, dire, for what else could eclipse her eternal flame of tempestuous energy? Hunter had no idea she would be present for this humiliating interview. It was a cruel exercise that increased his dislike for the old man tenfold.

"Ian must have been more persuasive than I gave him credit for," her grandfather averred, rudely disregarding Hunter's presence. "I assume that is why he has made an appearance. He certainly felt no compunction to do so before."

Before? What the devil did he mean by that? The idea of this disagreeable man being privy to his private indiscretions made Hunter decidedly uncomfortable. He did not take kindly to being referred to as the disparaged "he." His desire to get this blasted interview over flared anew. Clearing his throat, he clasped his clenched fists behind his back and launched into his well-rehearsed speech.

"I have come to ask for your granddaughter's hand in marriage. I fear, inadvertently, her honor has been—"

"Destroyed. Yes, I know."

Hunter winced inwardly and cast a furtive glance in Sabrina's direction. She looked positively ill. Her fingers clutched at her knees hard enough to turn the knuckles white.

"But I highly doubt it was inadvertently done," the viscount added with a derisive grunt. "It is impossible for me to assume otherwise. We must all lament your wickedness. Hopes of a decent match for my granddaughter are irrevocably dashed."

Hunter's spine straightened. Decent match? For a viscount's wayward granddaughter, she was doing quite well by Hunter's estimation.

"An alliance between my granddaughter and a rogue like yourself would heretofore have been insupportable. But now, what can I hope for?"

"Grandfather, *please*," Sabrina beseeched in a tiny, miserable voice. "Do not do this, I beg of you."

"Be silent!" he exploded, slamming his fist down on the desk.

Recoiling from his fury, she lowered her gaze to the floor.

"Now, young man," he muttered, addressing Hunter once more, "you will explain yourself."

Young man! No one dared call Hunter young man. Even if Bennett was older than Methuselah, he was still a blasted viscount. Hunter was the Earl of Greystone for God's sake. He deserved a measure of respect.

"Constrained as you obviously are to offer for my grand-daughter, you should feel compelled to be honest." His disparaging gaze swept over Hunter. "If nothing else, it will be a novel experience for a scoundrel like you."

Scoundrel! Hunter clenched his jaw hard enough to crush his teeth. He had heard more than enough. Were it not for the promise he had made Ian, Hunter would have issued the verbal laceration the old man richly deserved.

"If I were the scoundrel you suggest," Hunter gritted, "I would scarcely offer your granddaughter the protection of my name."

The viscount waved his blue-veined hand in the air. "Your name," he scoffed. "What consolation is that? You, sirrah, are a renowned rake."

Every inch of Hunter's body went rigid with anger. It took supreme self-discipline to squelch the powerful urge to throttle the disagreeable man.

"Given your granddaughter's outrageous conduct," he said with icy precision, "you would be fortunate to receive a single offer."

Out of the corner of his eye, he saw Sabrina's sharp intake of breath.

"As to the rest," he continued in a voice that held a distinct edge, "my family, to the best of my knowledge, is completely above reproach."

"It is bandied about all over town that you fathered your own sister's child."

"She was my stepsister," Hunter corrected through his teeth, "and I am not the child's father. But we digress," he imparted sharply. "I have the means, and the desire, to care for your granddaughter in a fashion, I daresay," he remarked, casting his disdainful gaze around the modest room, "that far exceeds the manner in which she was raised. That should satisfy you."

The old man vaulted to his feet, shoving the leather chair against the wall with a loud thud. "She was raised with the finest influences!" he exploded in a white-hot fury.

"Indeed?" Hunter queried with a dubious brow. "Then what, pray, was she doing in the middle of the night with a man who was not her husband?"

A cry of abject misery tore from Sabrina's throat.

"Enough! I have heard more than enough," she interjected with surprising energy.

Both men stopped to stare at the petite woman who had spoken with such force. Drawing a deep breath as if the words were difficult to express, she addressed Hunter, "I thank you for coming, my lord," she said quietly, "but it was not necessary. I shall be quite content to retire to the country. You've no need to worry that I shall capitalize on scandal."

"Do you see what a headstrong, disobedient hoyden she is?" the old man blustered angrily. "I am not a bit surprised she's disgraced the family."

A look of pain crossed Sabrina's face. "Grandfather, *please.*"

Her plea went unanswered. He merely regarded her with a look of disgust. "She is a severe disappointment to me. She takes after her father. *He* was a commoner." His voice rang with abhorrence. "It does not do for the classes to mix. *That,*" he muttered savagely, motioning toward his granddaughter, "is the vulgar, earthy result of such a union."

Sabrina sank into the chair in a crumpled mass of hurt humiliation.

Hunter did not miss the grimace of pain that contorted her face. He was filled with compassion for the spirited young thing. How difficult it must have been for her to be raised by a brutal man who made no secret of the fact that he harbored nothing but contempt for his own flesh and blood. Hunter well knew the humiliation of being the brunt of disdain. His need to rescue her from a life of utter misery mounted with a vengeance.

"Amanda takes after her mother," the disgruntled viscount went on to say with pride. "She is everything a woman should be: gentle, obedient and graceful. And beautiful. Not like *her*." He eyed the girl, who now wept softly in the corner, with cold dislike. "That hair," he bristled in revulsion, "it is shocking. So wild and unruly. A perfectly hideous color."

"It is very beautiful," Hunter heard someone say softly in a voice that sounded remarkably like his own.

Sabrina's head lifted. Astonished, she blinked at him through glistening tears.

"It is vulgar in the extreme," Bennett countered firmly. "Jezebel offspring," he hissed under his breath. "It comes as little surprise to me that she destroyed her reputation. Given her character, it was merely a matter of time. But to what extent has she been compromised? Have you taken her virtue as well as her honor?"

Hunter's nostrils flared. "I've already offered the protection of my name." His voice was taut with anger. "All that is left is for *Sabrina*," he intoned with meaning, "to decide if she will accept me as her husband."

"Her wishes do not enter into it. She will do as she is told. Or be brought to heel. I am her guardian. *You* will deal with *me*," Bennett bellowed vehemently.

Hunter's eyes glinted with blistering contempt. "I have no intentions of gratifying your voyeuristic tendencies with graphic details," came his acrimonious reply.

Accustomed to getting his own way, the domineering man thundered, "You have brought ruin upon this house." He pounded his fist on the desk. "I demand a full explanation. By God, I shall have one!"

"I have no explanation," Hunter replied, cool and remote in the face of pure rage. "I freely admit I behaved abominably.

I have indicated that I am prepared to make restitution. More than that, I will *refuse* to do.''

"This is an outrage!" The aged viscount raised his fist in the air. "I have the right to know."

"I am persuaded your granddaughter has already told you all you need know. Her confession is, after all, why I am here. Surely," Hunter imparted with a decided chill, "it was sufficiently sensational to satisfy you."

Casting a speculative glance at Sabrina, Hunter noted she had dried her eyes and was beaming from ear to ear. Evidently, she was thoroughly enjoying the rounding set down he had just issued. It struck him as odd that her grandfather did not know already what had transpired. He frowned slightly. What had she told the churlish old goat?

"If by that you mean she behaved like a common trollop," her grandfather's voice was bitter with loathing, "then I quite agree with you."

Hunter's features hardened into a glowering mask of rage. "You have said more than enough," he snapped in a lethal tone. "I warn you, have a care. You are speaking of the woman soon to be my wife."

"You think *her* worthy of your esteem?" Bennett asked with heavy mockery.

Hunter gave him a hostile glare. "Eminently," he imparted with conviction.

The old man sniggered viciously. "Mark my words, she will wreak havoc on your ordinary existence and drive you to distraction."

"She will no longer be your concern," Hunter bit out, his tone like ice.

His rejoinder took the wind out of Bennett's sails. He sank into his chair. "You are steeped in scandal. It is a wonder you dare show your face in polite society," he muttered.

"Nonetheless, your granddaughter will shortly be wed. A

scandal will have been averted. And you may hold your head up once more in polite society."

The old man's thin lips pursed. "Very well, I give her to you with my compliments. In my view," he sneered, "you deserve each other."

Hunter's jaw might have been hewn of iron. But he managed to control his temper. "It is my wish to speak to my betrothed. Alone. Surely," he said, baring his teeth in a frigid smile, "you can have no objections to such a minor request?"

"She is yours. Do with her as you please." Leaning heavily on his black cane, he managed to get to his feet and walk across the room. Opening the library door, he cast one final glare of censure at his mischievous granddaughter and quit the room.

Sabrina released a weary breath and lowered her gaze to the floor. She was certain today ranked as the worst day of her short life, for it very nearly felt like the end of her life—life as she had known it. She felt as if she were in a dream state, the part when one realized the disturbing direction their dream was taking and wanted to wake, but couldn't break free from the gripping nightmare.

When Grandfather had summoned her to the library earlier this morning, she never imagined she would encounter the last person on earth she wanted to see. Lancaster's presence astounded her. And his impassioned declaration for her hand dumbfounded her. Despite the fact that she was certain his proposal was born from a strict sense of honor rather than genuine affection, she reveled in that fleeting moment of triumph. The notorious Hunter had actually come, defended her honor, and gallantly offered for her hand in marriage. She truly had not believed he would come. Why would he? After all, a girl like her was scarcely worth any man's trouble, particularly not one as beautiful as Hunter. He could have any woman his heart desired. Why *had* he offered for her? Rakes never suffered from moral dilemmas. He could not truly wish to wed her. He was merely being kind, or perhaps, at the very most, dutiful. She would refuse him, of course, and thereby save herself from the embarrassing truth. He did not really want her.

She could feel the instrument of her once coveted ruin staring at her. His dark gaze weighed heavily upon her bent head. Glancing up, she meet his eyes. Color flooded her cheeks. She quickly looked away.

Clearing her throat, she managed to say shyly, "You should not have come, my lord. I did not expect it."

He reached out his hands to her. Of their own volition, her palms slipped into his. Dark gray eyes gazed down at her. Unnerved by their intensity, her own gaze skidded away.

"I had to come," he said, giving her hands a squeeze.

Of what? Affection? Encouragement? She wasn't quite sure. But she was pleased by the gesture. It made her feel safe. She frowned at her strange train of thought. Safe with the notorious Hunter? How utterly bizarre.

She shook her head. "No. You did not. I am as much to blame as you. If I—"

He pressed his finger to her lips. "It is all arranged," he told her, his voice full of tenderness. "I have purchased a special license. We will be married this coming Saturday."

She looked blank with surprise. Was he in earnest? No. He could not be. Besides, even if he were, she would never make the Earl of Lancaster a proper wife.

"Married," she repeated softly, "this Saturday. But . . . that is the day after tomorrow!"

He smiled down at her staggered expression and affectionately tucked a stray curl behind her ear. "There are some advantages to being the Earl of Lancaster," he remarked dryly.

Retrieving her ice-cold hands from the warmth of his grasp, she wandered over to the window. He wasn't making this any easier. No girl in her right mind would refuse a man of his wealth and stature—except Sabrina. "My lord, you are kindness itself,'' she managed with a hard swallow. "I thank you for your offer. I know it was graciously meant. But there is no reason for us to wed.''

In three purposeful strides, he crossed the room to where she stood. She was acutely aware of him, a blatantly masculine presence at her side. She tried to step away, but he would have none of it. Grasping her by her shoulders, he turned her to face him. "On the contrary, there is every reason,'' he countered with a measure of force. "You were alone with me, in the middle of the night. I took shocking liberties. Touched you, intimately. As only a husband has the right.''

Embarrassed color suffused her cheeks. She lowered her lashes.

"I have no choice but to offer you the protection of my name.'' His fingers curled under her chin and tilted her face upward. His compelling silver gaze beseeched her. "You must accept me as your husband.''

"Very well done, my lord''—she tried to smile and failed— "but completely unnecessary. I assure you, I have no intentions of accepting you.'' She sighed woefully. "I am entirely to blame. If I had not insisted on unearthing details about that recent murder, neither of us would be facing this pathetic state of affairs.''

Pathetic state of affairs? His jaw tightened. "Your honor has been compromised,'' he said stiffly. "The blame lies with me. You are innocent. I took full advantage of the situation. The fault lies entirely at my feet. I am willing to make amends. I *insist* on making amends,'' he added, his voice firm in its finality.

"To save me from ruin?'' she asked, fighting the absurd need to laugh.

"Yes. Preposterous, is it not? But that is the situation in which we find ourselves.''

"But it need not be," she insisted in earnest appeal. "You have done the noble thing. I have refused you. You are free."

Hunter scowled at his own conduct. What the devil was the matter with him? She had given him his freedom precisely as he had hoped. But he knew he would not—could not—accept it. He would marry her. If only to deprive that walking fossil the pleasure of gloating. After meeting the hateful man, Hunter understood immediately Sabrina's aversion to him. He was narrow-minded, judgmental and domineering to the point of suffocation. Hunter felt an irrational need to rescue the fragile bird from the claws of a vicious cat.

He framed her face with his hands. "Do you think I could walk out that door and never look back?" His eyes, tender and compassionate, searched hers. "I am wholly responsible for your plight. Marry me," he urged softly.

She shook her head and pulled away from him. "I cannot accept you. It is out of the question."

His features hardened. "The devil it is!" he exploded hotly. "I don't intend to give that curmudgeon the satisfaction of knowing you refused my offer."

Pride! His damnable pride would be the death of him. He was galloping toward utter disaster without a thought to anything but his unswerving desire to shove his nuptials down the brittle old man's throat. That, and the notion of saving the pale, unhappy woman he had grown decidedly fond of from the depths of utter misery.

"It comes down to this," he imparted roughly. "Marry me, or face a life of drudgery with that domineering old goat."

Sabrina gulped, clearly revolted by that horrid prospect.

"Imagine your life, your miserable future, enduring endless days and nights of solitude with your grandfather. He will be the ever-present vicious reminder of your grand faux pas."

She looked simultaneously frightened and repulsed by the prospect. "You make your point all too clearly, my lord."

"Then, accept me as your husband," he urged thickly, "and all will be well."

She gave him a whimsical smile. "How confident you are. You make it sound facile with your charming proposal and romantic words. But I know very well that I'll never be a proper wife to you." She rested her head in her hands. "I'd go mad living in the country, breeding endlessly. I want more out of life than that. Perhaps I don't deserve it, but I want excitement, intrigue, challenge. You can offer me none of those things." She drew a deep sigh. "Even if I were foolish enough to marry a notorious rake—which I am not—I would scarcely choose you."

His hands fell to his sides. "Obviously," he uttered coolly, "your aversion to me was not strong enough to ensure secrecy. Let's not forget," he averred bitingly, "it was your unconventional behavior that brought this on both our heads."

She turned increasingly pale. "You are entirely correct. I am truly sorry. I never thought it would come to this." She looked utterly depressed. "I must confess, total ruin is far worse than any imagining could have been. It is not at all what I had hoped."

His lips twisted with rancor. "Marriage to me is a fate worse than death, is that it?" he asked her bitterly.

"You cannot possibly want this," she cried, willing her voice to remain steady.

"What I want is irrelevant," he snapped, his tone curt. "It is what I must do. The honorable thing must and will be done."

A look of disbelief crossed her face. "You're a rake of dubious repute," she sputtered in frustration. "You are not supposed to be honorable."

His mouth curved into a cold smile. "Sorry to disappoint you."

She shot him a rueful look. "I would be a fool to trade one

domineering master for another.'' *Especially one who does not love me,* she added silently.

His sharp, gray gaze bore into her. ''You mistake me,'' he told her, his voice like steel cloaked with velvet. ''I offer you no choice. Saturday, St. George's Church, you will become my wife.''

She gaped at the dark, forbidding stranger before her. ''Are you saying you love me?'' she asked softly.

''Of course not,'' he snapped impatiently. ''How could I?''

How, indeed? she thought with a pang of sadness. A man like him would never love a woman like her. Why was she forlorn? It was not as though she ever expected to find love. She wasn't a romantic fool like Amanda. Why, then, was she being oversensitive? He had merely stated the unvarnished truth. He did not love her now, nor would he ever.

That was all right. She was no frivolous female. It was just that she could not help remembering how wonderful it felt to hear his fervent expressing of his intentions. To learn he was not sincere was a slight disappointment. But she would survive. Hadn't she always?

''Accept me now, and be done with it,'' he urged her, his breath warm against her temple. ''Believe me when I say, I have earned my reputation. Once decided, my mind is set. I will make you my wife.''

Her shoulders slumped. She expelled a deep sigh of resignation. Marriage did have one saving grace. Freedom. If she could wangle it. ''Very well, my lord, you seem bound and determined to wreak havoc in both our lives. I will marry you . . . on one condition.''

His steely gray eyes threatened to impale her. ''Condition?'' His brows snapped together. ''What damned condition?'' he growled at her.

She clasped her hands together demurely at her waist. ''It is quite simple. You have no real desire to gain a leg shackle.

I have even less desire to be dominated. We will agree to allow each other to continue as before.''

His piercing gaze narrowed on her pale face. "What precisely do you mean by that?'' he ground out.

Her tongue darted between her dry lips. "I mean,'' she said with a swallow, "you may continue to-to . . .'' Her cheeks turned a lovely shade of pink, and her voice trailed off.

He cocked a brow. "To?''

Her gaze skidded away. "Well, do whatever it is you do with, um, your mistresses or whomever. I shall be permitted to pursue my work. Uninterrupted.'' She stole a glance at his forbidding expression. "Agreed?''

He crossed his arms over his chest and regarded her in taciturn silence. "Allow me to paraphrase. You are giving me leave to bed countless other women, to enjoy my rakehell existence to the fullest, heedless of the fact that henceforth I shall be a married man, is that it?''

Her cheeks brightened. "Yes.''

"All this you will graciously allow, provided, of course, that I overlook your bluestocking tendencies and do not interfere with your work. Is that the bargain you wish to strike?''

"Yes. I believe you have the gist of it, my lord,'' she murmured, not meeting his eye.

"I suppose I should consider myself fortunate,'' he said on a derisive chuckle. "I imagined I would gain a soul mate, a confidante, a wife and a lover. A kind, caring mother for my children. In actuality, however, I am merely going through the motions of matrimony so that we may both continue to live as before.''

She bristled at his tone. "I think it is a very sound solution to our problem. Besides, it is hardly the thing to be in each other's pockets, now, is it?''

"Heaven forbid,'' he mocked. "But what of the Lancaster

heir?'' he asked, arching one ebony brow in query. ''I will at some point have to fulfill my obligation to the title.''

She squirmed with discomfort. ''Yes . . . well. We will have to . . . to—''

''Renegotiate terms?'' he supplied.

''I should imagine so, yes.''

''Ah. How clever you are.''

Her eyes sparkled blue fire. ''I think it a sound solution to both our problems,'' she declared defensively.

His slow, seductive gaze slid over her with shocking thoroughness. ''You think that your cozy little arrangement would be mutually satisfactory, do you?'' he murmured huskily.

Gulping, she stammered, ''I—I don't see why not.''

His lips curled into a wicked smile as his finger caressed her cheek. ''You don't think you'd mind my pleasuring other women while you devoted all your energies to intellectual pursuits?'' he asked, his voice like a satin caress.

''Why should I?'' she croaked, and hastily cleared her throat. ''It goes without saying that you will be discreet,'' she said, brushing past him, eager to escape his dangerous heat. ''No one need know about our private affairs.''

''Oh, yes, you are quite right on that point. Discretion is the better part of valor. Don't I know it,'' he drawled out amusedly. ''Very well, my dear, I accept your conditions. With one addendum.''

She whirled about to face him. ''What might that be?''

His lips twitched. ''That I may be free to make alterations to our agreement should I see fit.''

She gave him a startled look. ''Why should you wish to do that?''

One end of his mouth lifted slightly. ''I have my reasons. What say you?''

Frowning, she glanced at him dubiously. ''I cannot think why you should wish for such an arrangement.'' She cocked her curly head to one side. "I must say, my lord," she remarked, studying his handsome countenance, "I can never tell if you are serious or not."

"I assure you," he intoned gravely, "I have never been more serious in my life."

She sighed and shrugged her shoulders. "Oh, well, I suppose, in time, we shall get to know each other's idiosyncrasies." She stuck her hand out to seal their bargain. "I will wed you, my lord. As you wish, Saturday at St. George's Church."

He squashed the urge to smile. His large, masculine hand closed around her small, delicate one.

"Don't be late," he said, gazing deeply into her clear blue eyes. "I don't like to be kept waiting."

"I make it a habit always to be punctual, my lord," she said softly.

"Capital notion," he murmured, smiling down at her. "You see we are off to an excellent start. We shall leave for the country directly," he assured her, his gaze tender and serene. "You will like Lindhurst, my dear. Very much." He caressed her pale cheek with the back of his hand. "The color shall return to your cheeks and the sparkle in your eyes. I will see to it that you are happy."

She returned his smile. In that moment, she felt that all would be well between them despite their differences and the manner in which they had been thrown together. At least, she would be free of her grandfather's cruel yoke. How much worse could it be to marry a man who harbored no affection for her whatsoever?

Chapter 9

As it turned out, St. George's was not available for Saturday. In fact, that fashionable site where most *tonnish* marriages were celebrated was not available for several months. Hunter assured himself as he stood at the altar in the comparatively small Grosvenor Chapel that it was not an inauspicious beginning to their nuptials.

What was undeniably peculiar was the paucity of guests. Neither his father nor Sabrina's grandfather was in attendance. Hunter had not seriously expected his father would make an appearance. In a way, he was glad he had been spared the usual disparaging looks and derisive remarks. A mere handful of men and women occupied the first two rows. Even at that, the small, pitch-pine pews looked stark and empty.

He forced his gaze from the meager surroundings and turned to face the altar. His forefinger slipped between the crisp silk cloth and his moist neck and tugged. In a matter of minutes, he would emerge from the dimly lit brick edifice a married man. A condition that would undoubtedly feel . . . odd. A frown touched his lips. More than odd. Terrifying. Bizarre. Damned unnatural.

What the deuce was he going to do with a wife? What grated most was that he had brought this calamity on himself. His bride-to-be had been understanding itself. Why in heaven's name had he not bowed out gracefully when she had given him the chance?

After meeting her oppressive, despicable grandfather, he knew why. Somewhere in the recesses of his cold heart, he felt responsible for her. No matter how much she might deserve to suffer the ramifications of her foolish quest for ruin, Hunter couldn't very well abandon her to wallow in abject despair. Not when he could save her with a measly—easier said than done—proposal. It was not as though he was sacrificing himself. He needed to marry at some point; it was expected. His obligations to the title had to be considered. He just had not envisioned the matrimonial noose tightening quite this soon around his neck. Particularly not to a headstrong, unpredictable girl of eighteen.

He blew the air out of his cheeks. Where the blazes was she? Everything seemed to be moving far too slow this morning. He wanted to get the ceremony thing over with. He longed to retire to the country for a few weeks. He clasped his hands behind his back and gazed aimlessly at the reredos and traceried windows looming above him. He hated to be made to wait. Hadn't he told her as much?

His lips thinned. Their marriage was definitely off to a bad start. Marriage, to his mind, offered paltry benefits. One thing was for certain; he intended to enjoy the marriage bed at every opportunity—regardless of that damned stupid agreement.

He had never been stingy in the bedroom. He would see to it that she found a measure of enjoyment in his arms. Unless he was gravely mistaken, that should not prove too great a hardship for either one of them. She was a deeply passionate woman who would bloom nicely under his most excellent tutelage.

A slow smile of satisfaction spread across his lips. If their previous encounters were any indication, he would suffer through this deuced arrangement quite nicely. He had no reason to be nervous. None whatsoever. He felt the tension ease from his taut muscles. Yes, marriage would have definite advantages. His bride's lessons would commence this very night. He could scarcely wait to be done with the deuced formalities.

He scowled at his eagerness. His impatience to introduce his bride to the sensual world surpassed all comprehension. It was not as though he had never made love to a woman before. But this was different. Tonight, it would be his wife he worshiped with his body. They might even make a baby together.

He loved dear little Annabelle with all his heart. But fatherhood was not a condition he had ever fancied before in his life. He could not imagine the depth of feeling for a child of his own loins. Certainly, the love one felt must be even more intense. He never realized how much he wanted a child. He sniggered softly. It was ironic, given that he had spent most of his life trying to avoid that particular dilemma.

At long last, the soft strains of music drifted through the church. Hunter's heart thudded against his ribs. The time had arrived. Tradition dictated that he face the altar while his bride walked up the aisle, but the insane desire to turn around and watch her walk toward him threatened to overpower him.

He quelled the urge. This whole thing was affecting him far too seriously. He needed to get a hold of himself. It wasn't as though theirs was a love match. He was marrying her because he had disgraced her and, more to the point, because Ian had threatened to call him out. Definitely not the stuff of which romantic dreams were made.

Feeling her presence at his side, he glanced down at the

woman who would shortly grace his household and, more importantly, his bed. His heart gave a slight squeeze at the sight of her. She looked like an angel. He assumed the gown belonged to her sister, for no London dressmaker could have worked such a miracle in the allotted time. His gaze drifted over her bent head, bowed in uncharacteristic submission. He clasped her small, delicate hand in his. It felt like ice.

His brows sloped downward. His angel was pale and frightened. The discovery disturbed him.

Why, he wondered, as he recited the words the rector had spoken, did she look so utterly depressed? He was in the midst of swearing to worship her with his body and to endow her with all his worldly goods. And she looked ready to be ill. It did not sit at all well.

She was supposed to be glad. Happy. Grateful that he had whisked her from the jaws of her vicious guardian. Pleased that he had agreed to her outrageous premarital stipulations.

Instead, she looked like a scared little rabbit. It was bad enough that her left hand had been stiff and reluctant as he had slid the shining gold symbol of ownership on her third finger. But the fact that he was forced to lean down to hear her promise to cherish, honor and obey him nettled him to the core.

He reminded himself that she was young and undoubtedly nervous. Lord knew what she had heard about marriage. He gave her a small smile of encouragement, which was met with a cold, somber expression.

His mouth thinned. So much for sympathy, he thought with a derisive scowl. This was not the sort of day he had envisioned for his wedding day. Not that he had ever dreamt of living through such a day. But he did expect his bride to be happy. Weren't all brides joyful?

"You may kiss the bride," the rector said with a beaming smile. He closed his leather-bound Bible and crossed his hands reverently over his chest.

Hunter turned to face the woman who was his wife before God. He clasped her by her shoulders and turned her to face him. Hell's teeth! She seemed to be fashioned out of wood. He drew her statue-still figure against him. Gazing down at her, he was intent on deciphering her unfathomable mood. But she kept her gaze averted from his assessing gray eyes. Worse yet, she made no move to accept his kiss. Lifting her bowed head, he angled her face to receive his kiss. And then his arm slid around her waist, and he caught her hard against him. She grimaced and closed her eyes in revulsion.

Anger ignited deep within him. Repulsed, was she? Well, too bad. She was his wife now, his to do with as he pleased. She would endure a kiss from her husband at the altar whether she welcomed it or not.

His head swooped down. His lips crushed hers in a bruising, punishing, angry kiss. Her hands curled into fists against his chest. She pushed against him. But his iron grip tightened around her, imprisoning her against his hard, cruel, unyielding body. He heard her groan in protest and the passion drained out of him. He had never forced himself on a woman, and he would be damned if he would start with his wife.

Lifting his head, he loosed the blaze of his furious gaze on her. Her breathing was ragged, he noticed with a surge of male satisfaction. A look of staggering dismay was etched on her ghostly stricken face. But she uttered not a word.

So be it, he thought with cold fury, as he took her by the hand and roughly marched her down the aisle toward the back of the church.

He strode past the small gathering of tearful well-wishers. She had made her feelings patently clear. No wonder she had demanded he agree to those ludicrous conditions prior to their wedding. What a fool he was to imagine she was a blushing bride. Her insistence was born of contempt, not maidenly fear.

She truly did not wish to be his wife. His lips twisted into

an angry snarl. The whole notion of marriage no doubt offended
her delicate sensibilities. What had she said to him? *Even if I
were foolish enough to marry a notorious rake—which I am
not—I would scarcely choose you.*

Fine. He comprehended the circumstance all too well. Once
he had gotten her with child, he would leave her in the country.
Good riddance. He only hoped she would bear him a son. He
did not wish to have to be involved with the little witch any
more than courtesy demanded.

He would find his comfort in the arms of a mature widow.
Lady Astor struck his fancy. It would not take long to come
to a mutually beneficial arrangement with her. His little wife
need not worry. She would have her quiet country life. He fully
intended to leave her there for the next twenty years. She could
write her fill.

Hunter managed to stand stoically at the back of the church
and endure the saccharine well-wishers with cold indifference.
He wanted to be done with the pomp and circumstance. His
bride, he noticed with irritation, showed more warmth to virtual
strangers than to her lawfully wedded husband. It was only
when Ian suggested they should depart for the wedding breakfast that she darted a glance in her husband's direction. Her
gaze collided with his haughty, frigid expression and quickly
skittered away. In far too bright a voice, she suggested to her
sister, "Why do you and Ian not travel to the wedding breakfast
in our carriage?"

Ian gave her a look of surprise. "You should be alone with
your husband," he reminded her gently.

Hunter did not miss the look of horror that crossed his wife's
face.

"That is not strictly necessary, Ian," Amanda remarked,
quickly warming to the idea. She, at least, had the good grace

to consult the groom. "Have you any objections to our accompanying the bride and groom, my lord? Perhaps you would like time alone with your beautiful bride?"

Hunter's icy gaze never left Sabrina's ghostly face as he said, "No, not at all. My bride and I owe you a debt of gratitude. Who else, under the circumstances, would have offered to host our wedding breakfast?"

Sabrina bowed her head. Her nervous hands fidgeted with her small white bouquet of roses.

"The streets are crowded at this hour of day. It could take quite some time to arrive at Berkeley Square. I welcome Ian's company," he said unkindly.

"Then, it is settled," Amanda exclaimed with nauseating cheer.

The two girls hooked arms and descended the stone steps to the street. Their two heads were pressed together—chattering, no doubt, about some meaningless feminine trifle, Hunter thought with annoyance.

Ian turned toward his friend and smiled broadly. "I can scarcely believe it!"

"Believe what?" Hunter asked, his gaze riveted to his reluctant bride.

"I never thought I'd see the day when you got caught in the parson's trap." His hand came down on Hunter's back in a hard slap. "Congratulations, you are now a respectable married man. How does it feel?"

Hunter snickered and looked away. It felt dreadful. He would give anything to undo the last week of his life. What the devil had he been thinking? They would never suit, much less find happiness. He must have been mad to offer for the chit.

Ian laughed. "Matrimony has a way of insinuating itself into your life whether you like it or not." His warm gaze drifted over his beloved wife chatting with her sister at the base of the church steps. "They are quite a pair."

"Indeed, they are," Hunter replied, his voice cool and reserved.

"Mind you, I doubt you stood a ghost of a chance once they'd set their sights on you."

Hunter's head turned sharply. "What do you mean, set their sights?" he asked, his gray eyes narrowing into silver slits.

"Come along, old man," Ian teased with a wry sideways glance at his friend. "You know as well as I do, no man ever gets married because he wants to. We are all cajoled, pushed and finally seduced into it. Not that we regret it, mind you."

Hunter's face hardened to stone. "No. I did not know. How *precisely* was I cajoled into this marriage?" he ground out.

Ian chuckled. "I, myself, was surprised at the level of deceit involved in your particular case."

"Were you?" Hunter mused, his irate gaze fixed on his bride. "Why is that?"

"You should be flattered, old boy. You were hand selected from a long list of eligible bachelors."

"Is that a fact?" Hunter bit out.

"Amanda is convinced reformed rakes make the best husbands," Ian explained. "I am afraid I'm to blame for that misconception. You'll never believe it when I tell you," he said, unable to conceal his jocularity. "But she actually felt sorry for you. Bachelors are never happy, don't you know?"

Hunter's jaw clenched. "Am I to understand," he ground out, "that your hopelessly romantic wife took it upon herself to pawn her wayward sister off on me?"

A look of astonishment crossed Ian's face. "Never say, you actually believed that Banbury tale about being ruined? If I know those two," he remarked as he descended the church steps with Hunter beside him, "it was all a carefully orchestrated plan to snare the notorious Hunter."

Hunter's handsome face contorted with resentment. Oh, yes, it was all patently obvious to him now. The mercenary little chit had manipulated the situation with amazing finesse: The carefully orchestrated escapades that drew him in to repeated scandalous circumstances. The teary-eyed, stoic performance in front of the harsh grandfather. The coy refusal to Hunter's insistence they marry. It was all very well done, indeed.

"I cannot tell you how ecstatic Amanda was when you stumbled into that ridiculous, compromising situation all on your own. How *did* you two end up in Lady Declaire's bedroom?" Ian asked, his shoulders shaking with mirth.

Hunter went rigid, contempt evident in his every feature. "Why, your scheming sister-in-law contrived to meet me there, how else?" he replied, his temper near the boiling point.

Ian laughed. "I would not put anything past her." He caught sight of his friend's lethal countenance and frowned. "I say, you aren't by any chance vexed, are you? Amanda was concerned that you might not find their machinations as diverting as I. She swore me to secrecy. But I assured her you had an excellent sense of humor."

Hunter watched the coconspirators climb into his carriage. "Did you?" he murmured, contemplating murder.

"You don't really take exception to being led astray by feminine wiles?"

Turning toward his friend, Hunter flashed a frigid smile. "Of course not. As you say, all women are guilty of cunning and deceit."

"I must say, it was deuced clever of our little Sabrina to refuse you so adamantly at first. Nothing like a challenge to spur a man on, would you not agree? When poor Amanda heard the news, she nearly swooned for fear that you might have retracted your offer."

One end of Hunter's mouth lifted in a sneer. "Her little sister is a sound judge of character. She knew that once issued, it was unlikely I would withdraw my offer."

Oh, yes, the wily little charlatan had made an excellent match for herself. He had twenty thousand a year and Lindhurst Manor. What a fool he was to have believed in her. She had played him like a fiddle. He couldn't credit his stupidity. At the ripe old age of two and thirty, had he actually gotten tangled in such an obvious web of deceit? The mere idea infuriated him. No one forced his hand, least of all a hapless child. When he reflected on the guilt he had suffered, believing himself responsible for her, he could explode.

As the conveyance wound its way through the bustling city streets, Amanda and Ian engaged in forced idle chatter. Sabrina managed to issue the occasional complaisant rejoinder. Hunter, however, sat in brooding silence and wrestled with the unbecoming urge to throttle his bride. He could not credit the guileless woman he had come to know as being capable of such heinous deceit. Ian had as much as admitted her female treachery without an ounce of shame. She was a practiced little actress, just like every other woman he had ever known. The only thing fresh and new about her was the packaging.

The wedding breakfast proceeded without incident. The grueling three-hour affair consisted mostly of mindless chatter and romantic toasts. Teeth clenched, Hunter sat at the head of the table, not once deigning to address his bride.

The insipid guests grated on his nerves. They all seemed too animated. Their laughter sounded coarse to his ears. He could not abide another person wishing him happy.

"When do you leave for the country?" Hunter's good friend, Freddy Thompson, asked, munching on a slice of wedding cake. A piece of the very same confection lay conspicuously untouched on Hunter's plate.

"I am in no hurry," came Hunter's terse reply.

Sabrina's worried gaze flew to her husband's rigid face. She looked unnerved by his remark. "I thought ... we were to leave this very day?"

He fixed her with a hard look. "No," he uttered with decisive coolness. "I have business to attend to in London."

Given the state of his unholy marriage, he intended to continue his pursuit of the villain who impregnated Julia and abandoned her, prior to traveling to Kent for the dreaded interment. The sooner he suffered through the necessary period of time as man and wife and deposited the urchin at Lindhurst, the better.

"You should be pleased, my dear," Freddy told Sabrina.

Dragging her gaze from her scowling husband, she essayed a bright smile. "Why is that?"

"Your devoted husband must desire a long honeymoon if he chooses to finish his pressing business in London before undertaking the journey," Freddy teased with a wink.

Hunter offered no comment. He sat mutely at the head of the table, his countenance stark and forbidding.

Freddy's quip fell on an awkward silence. He cleared his throat and mumbled something about the delightful wedding cake.

A mantle of red spread over Sabrina's cheeks. She ran a nervous finger over the gilded edge of her cake plate.

Hunter's gaze weighed heavily on his bride. If the cunning little virago thought her feminine wiles would soften him, she was gravely mistaken. He was not a man who suffered deceit easily. If she was miserable, she had no one to blame but herself. He threw his napkin down on his uneaten piece of wedding cake and got to his feet.

"Come, let us away."

Sabrina was glad of the timely reprieve, however ill meant. Her husband's harsh demeanor throughout their interminable wedding breakfast had her nerves in shreds. She could scarcely recall a more grueling episode.

She felt perilously close to weeping, a self-indulgent pastime she had given up years ago. And yet it took a supreme effort not to burst into copious tears. She couldn't credit her pathetic weakness. She dearly hoped she was not turning into a watering pot.

The only thing that saved her from sobbing was the sure and certain knowledge that her brutish husband would be pleased to see her break down under the strain. And she refused to give him the satisfaction. Besides, she knew from experience, self-pity was a useless waste of her time and energy.

The customary pleasantries finally endured, the wedding day celebration drew to a close. The four family members gathered by Hunter's carriage in a solitary circle.

"Sabrina, you were the most lovely bride I have ever seen," Ian remarked with a sunny smile.

"Indeed, you are," Amanda cried, and pressed a kiss to her sister's pale cheek. "What a wonderful mistress of Lindhurst you will make, dearest."

Sickened by the sight, Hunter stated with abrupt rudeness, "It is time we left."

Heedless of the gawking onlookers, he caught his bride by the arm and gruffly steered her toward the open door of his carriage. Sabrina glanced over her shoulder at her concerned sister and brother-in-law and tried to smile. They waved goodbye. Amanda blew her several kisses and wished her happy.

"Get in," Hunter said curtly. At seeing his dark, forbidding expression, her lashes fluttered downward, and she climbed inside his private carriage.

The carriage lurched forward, carrying her from the people she loved most into a new and uncharted existence as the notorious Hunter's wife. Try as she might, she was unable to loosen the painful knot in which her stomach was twisted. She shivered with trepidation. What had she gotten herself into with her foolish, headstrong ways? Total ruin was eminently superior to marriage.

Sabrina could feel her husband's dark, penetrating stare, but she remained glued to the conveyance wall. Keeping her gaze fixed on the mundane events transpiring beyond the window saved her from a confrontation with the ominous stranger she had just sworn to honor and obey till death do they part.

She sensed, at long last, when his burning gaze drifted from her. Her breathing came a little easier. Stealing a covert glance at his chiseled profile, a dead weight settled on her chest. His jaw looked to be fashioned from granite.

The furious expression he wore was horribly familiar to her now that they were man and wife. Gone were his roguish eyes and teasing manner. Reluctantly, she admitted she preferred the playful rake to the ogre he had transformed into seemingly overnight. What had she done to deserve his censure? As if sensing her scrutiny, he turned his cold, gray eyes to hers.

"Happy, dearest?" His smile was a travesty.

She dropped her gaze. Her tongue darted nervously between her parched lips. "My lord, I fear I have displeased you in some way," she said, making a stab at cordial conversation. "Pray, tell me what is troubling you so that I may remedy your displeasure."

Your deceitful nature. "Nothing is troubling me," he replied, his tone like ice. "Certainly nothing that my *devoted* wife could remedy."

She stiffened at his sarcastic barb. "I could hardly lay claim to devotion, my lord," she replied in a voice that held a note of challenge. "Any more than you could swear your undying fidelity and expect me to believe it."

He flashed a humorless smile. "Ah, yes, our mutually beneficial agreement. How clever of you to insist upon it before the ceremony.''

Nonplussed, she stared at him and tried to fathom his strange mood. ''Neither one of us wished to marry,'' she reminded him pointedly.

''Even so,'' he said, his gray, stormy eyes gleaming with raw acrimony, ''you must be quite pleased with yourself.''

''What cause do I have to be joyous?'' she asked with a hint of bitterness.

''Why, you've married a man with twenty thousand a year and three enviable estates. I'd say you've done very well. Very well, indeed.''

She disliked his insinuation heartily. ''I care little for such luxuries, I assure you, my lord,'' she countered, her mien cool. ''It is evident, however, you are of a different mind altogether. Nothing I may say will invoke your good opinion.''

He uttered a derisive snort. ''A novel experience for you, to be sure.''

If he intended to continue in this implacable mood, their union promised to be intolerable. She drew a weary sigh and turned her attention once more to the bustling world out the window.

Sabrina barely had time to admire the elegant, dark green marbled foyer of Hunter's fashionable town house. The moment they arrived, he barked instructions at his stodgy butler to have his bride's possessions installed above stairs. A light supper was to be prepared for Lady Lancaster and served in her boudoir. Hunter would be going out directly.

''If you will follow me, Lady Lancaster,'' he said in a brusque tone that brooked no disobedience.

Without so much as a backward glance in her direction, he

strode down the narrow hallway toward a small sitting room. She had no choice but to trail submissively behind him.

When they were alone, he addressed her, the strain of maintaining civility evident in his terse manner. "The servants will be only too happy to accommodate you; you need only ask."

"What of you, my lord?" she dared to inquire, curiosity making her bold.

He hesitated for a moment before he told her in no uncertain terms, "I have some personal matters to attend to and shall dine at my club this evening. For the present, it would be best if you tried to rest. We've a long night ahead of us," he told her with a meaningful glint in his eye.

The color drained from her face. "A long night?" Her voice sounded high-pitched even to her own ears.

He leaned his elbow against the mantel and stared at her for a long, charged moment. His steely gray eyes glittered with inexplicable anger and something else she could not quite discern. "The arduous task of greeting all your servants awaits you, my dear. I know you wish to make an excellent impression as the new Lady Lancaster," he remarked with thinly veiled sarcasm.

"Yes, of course. How foolish of me. I quite forgot about my household duties. Rest assured, I shall not disappoint you, my lord."

He fixed her with a sardonic look. "A word to the wise, my dear," he averred sharply. "It is ill advised to make promises you cannot keep."

"Is that the voice of experience?" she flung back at him before she could halt her tongue.

His withering and cold gaze stabbed at her. "I am sure your eagerness to revel in the spoils of your excellent marriage will help you endure the strain of being married to me," he said bitterly.

He strode across the room to gaze out the window as if he could not bear to gaze upon her.

What had she done to incur his wrath? Sabrina could do little more than stare at the ominous man with his proud, angry back to her.

Spoils of marriage? What that cryptic remark was meant to convey she could not imagine. ''I am sure I shall weather the storm quite well,'' she murmured on a miserable sigh and quietly left the room.

Chapter 10

It lacked the hour of ten that evening when Sabrina's bedroom door swung open. She looked up. Her startled gaze collided with her husband's piercing gray orbs. He had shed his wedding clothes and wore superfines that fit like a second skin, she observed with a hard swallow, and a linen shirt that bared a healthy portion of inviting bronze skin.

"I'll see to her ladyship's needs for the rest of the evening," he told her maid, his eyes dancing with devilment as he stared at Sabrina.

Sabrina flushed crimson at his blatantly sexual insinuation. "That will be all, Fanny," she said softly.

"Yes, milady," the skittish maid replied with a quick curtsey. Darting a nervous glance at his lordship, Fanny scurried from the room like a frightened mouse.

Sabrina willed the rampant butterflies in her stomach to settle down. No cause for concern; after all, they had an agreement.

One thing nagged at her, however: what was he doing in her bedroom?

His slow, seductive gaze roamed over her. Unnerved, she felt herself grow warm and quickly looked away. She shook off her trepidation. Even if her husband was behaving strangely, he would never go back on his word. A sinking feeling invaded her stomach. Or . . . would he?

"Would you care for something to drink?" he asked, sauntering toward her, crystal decanter in one hand and balloon glass in the other.

Sabrina's head snapped up. A drink? Did women of his acquaintance drink?

He chuckled softly at her look of surprise. "A glass of brandy, perhaps?" he offered amicably, and took a swallow of the amber liquid. "I am afraid I am all out of lemonade and ratafia at the moment."

He was mocking her, of course. "No, thank you," she replied with prim curtness and resumed the braiding of her hair. She tried to project an outward calm. In reality, however, her heart galloped almost painfully in her chest. She couldn't quite believe she was married. And to the notorious Hunter.

She was his. To do with as he pleased . . . whenever he pleased. A dizzying current of excitement ran through her. What would she say if he pressed her to perform her marriage duty this evening? She caught her lower lip between her teeth. Egad, what then?

The stack of novels she had cast haphazardly on the end of the bed caught Hunter's eye. He cocked his dark head to read the binding. *Ivanhoe.* He gave her a blank look of surprise.

"You've read *Ivanhoe?*" he asked, amazed by the discovery, for he had scarcely managed to find time to crack the binder.

"Naturally, I've read it. I *can* read, my lord," she muttered tersely. "I've been given to understand my penmanship is more than merely passable. And I still have all my teeth."

"I've noticed," he remarked, riffling through the pile of novels: *Coelebs in Search of a Wife*, *Evelina* and *Glenarvon*. "They are almost as sharp as your barbed tongue."

He snatched Lady Caroline Lamb's *Glenarvon* from the pile. "Where the deuce did you get this?"

Sabrina frowned at his reflection in the mirror. "I suppose," she muttered on a bored sigh, "you are shocked that I have read it."

Shaking his head, he tossed the scandalous book on the bed. "On the contrary, you never cease to amaze me. Tell me," he drawled as he dropped into the chair beside the crackling fireplace, "is there no end to your eccentricities?"

Her chin came up. Hateful man! Ooh, wouldn't she love to wipe that arrogant smirk off his far too handsome face.

"Indeed not. I've read all of Byron. And most of Shelley, too," she told him with an imperious air.

One ebony brow elevated slightly. "Have you, indeed? *Prometheus Unbound*?" he queried with maddening condescension.

She scowled at him. That book had only recently been published. He knew full well she could not possibly have read it. "No. *Frankenstein*," she replied pointedly.

He flashed an indulgent smile. "How'd you like it?"

"Not at all." She wrinkled up her nose in disdain. "What utter rubbish. Reanimating a dead person, it is preposterous to imagine a current running through each one of us."

A satyr smile spread across his face. "Oh, I don't know." His hooded, deeply sensual gaze raked over her gossamer-thin nightgown. "Looking at you right now, I don't have too much trouble believing that."

My! He *was* wicked! The way he was looking at her would put a harlot to the blush. Never before had she been on the receiving end of a purely lustful gaze. Her cheeks flooded with color. She lowered her gaze. She felt like an inexperienced lamb in a hungry lion's den. And yet, she found herself strangely excited by the dark, imposing man who was her husband. Mercifully, he changed the subject.

"I don't suppose your grandfather had any inkling of this unusual pastime of yours?"

She pulled a face. "Heavens no. Ian gets the books for me."

"Ah." Hunter took another sip of brandy. "Dear old, helpful Ian. What would we do without him?" he mocked.

She set her brush down and turned to face her taunting spouse. "I happen to be very fond of Ian."

He gave her a frigid smile. "Nice, cozy little family circle," he opined with scorn.

Her eyes flashed with temper. "*Nice* is not a word that leaps to mind where you are concerned."

The firelight glow cast his face in a saturnine light. "Marriage not all you hoped it would be, *dearest?*"

"How could marriage to you be something any girl hoped for?"

His impressive male figure unfolded from the chair. In a heartbeat, he crossed the room to where she sat. Craning her neck back, she stared up at him. Dark and forbidding, he was a man who could easily bend a frail female to his will. But she was not frail, she reminded herself with a hard gulp.

Acutely conscious of his raw masculinity towering over her, she got to her feet. It was a futile attempt to diffuse his intimidating power and size. And it failed. What had she gotten herself into? she wondered with a spine-tingling shiver. How on earth would she survive the kind of intimacy Amanda had described, with an implacable, angry man like him?

"It doesn't hurt that your husband has twenty thousand a year," he ground out with icy contempt.

"I daresay, it does little to make you more agreeable to my way of thinking," she replied, despising the breathless quality of her voice.

His angry gaze threatened to devour her whole. "No?" he snarled. His hands closed over her arms, dragging her against his rock-hard chest. "My zest for life poses a problem for your mercenary little heart?"

Anger flared in her breast, loosening her tongue. "My heart is not in the least mercenary, my lord," she told him brusquely. "But even if it were, what possible difference could it make to you?"

His piercing silver gaze flickered across her face. "I assure you," he told her bitterly, "it makes no difference to me, one way or the other, provided that when I choose to bed you, you are warm and willing in my arms. And you please me to my satisfaction."

She drew in a shocked breath. "We had an agreement," she insisted, her voice laced with trepidation. "You said—"

He fixed her with a level stare. "Your naivete astounds me."

"But you gave me your word," she insisted, her voice nearly shrill with panic.

As if dealing with a temperamental child, he offered her a benign smile. His tone, however, was curt and steel-edged. "I am your husband. I'll decide what should be done with you. And when."

The color drained from her face. "You cannot mean to—"

"I intend to secure my heir by the new year. Your beautiful, ripe body is the only advantage I am likely to enjoy from this blasted arrangement. I've no doubt I'll find some measure of comfort in your arms."

His crudity heightened her trepidation no small degree. She swallowed. Her throat felt as hard as flint. But her indomitable spirit would not allow her to back away from a confrontation.

Casting a defiant glare at him, she spat, "You comport yourself like an offensive boor. I have no intention of submitting to you. It would be best were you to leave before you make

an even bigger fool out of yourself.'' Having thrown down her
gauntlet, she held her breath and braced herself for his response.

For a scant moment, she thought he might heed her advice,
but then he uttered a low growl of desire and crushed her to
him.

Before she could protest, his open mouth came down on
hers, hot, wet and demanding. His arms tightened around her,
imprisoning her intimately against his strong, solid, masterful
body. He smothered her lips in a bruising, passionate kiss.
Impatient hands tore at her nightgown, eager to feel her soft,
silky skin beneath his palms. His hand slid down her back,
branding her with his searing touch, and smoothed over her
hips, caressing her soft curves, grinding her hips against his,
making her all too aware of the effect she was having on him.

At first, he thought her moans were from pleasure. It did not
take him long to realize he repulsed her.

He pushed her away. ''What the devil is the matter with
you?'' he panted, his face flush with desire. ''Why do you
recoil in disgust every time I touch you?''

She turned her back. ''Please . . . leave me,'' she choked
out, clutching the bedpost for much needed support.

''Devil take it, madam, I am your husband,'' he told her
roughly.

Hurt and angered by her rejection, he reached for her. She
shied away from him. ''By God, I've the right to touch you,''
he growled, and caught her nightgown in his fist, partially
baring her back. What he saw gave him pause. ''Good Lord,''
he breathed. Her back was covered with black-and-blue marks.
''What happened?''

She tugged her nightgown over her shoulder. ''It is nothing,''
she said with a sniffle that told him she was crying. ''Pray, my
lord, do not concern yourself.''

At seeing the cruel evidence of abuse, his resentment dissolved instantly. Whatever else she might be, she certainly did not deserve to be beaten like an animal.

He told himself he was not softening toward her. He was still livid with her deception. But that did not prevent him from feeling compassion.

He took her by the shoulders and turned her to face him. "I do concern myself." Cradling her tear-stained face between his hands, he lifted her gaze to his. "Who did this to you?" he asked softly, the pads of his thumbs brushing the tears from her cheeks.

Her lashes drifted downward. "Can you not guess?"

He frowned with cold fury. "That heartless brute," he ground out. "He did this to you?"

She nodded and hugged her waist. "I believe the expression is caning, my lord. Ordinarily, I am put on bread and water and locked in my room. The very worst he'd ever done was cut my hair. Apparently," she said, mopping the tears with her sleeve, "bringing disgrace on his good name was the final straw. Total ruin warranted something a trifle more drastic."

"When?" he demanded, his anger waxing by the minute. "When did he do this to you?"

"Directly after your interview. I am afraid he took a rather strong dislike to you, my lord. He does not enjoy having his nose tweaked. And I am afraid, you tweaked it rather hard."

Hunter swore under his breath.

"My wicked indiscretion deserved severe punishment. Goodness knows he has a formidable temper." She winced at the memory. "I wonder if it might not have been better for us both had you not come," she said, gingerly inspecting the condition of her back. "It would seem to be excessively poor form for a Bennett to be compromised by a rake, but stooping to marriage is beyond the pale."

His brows snapped together. "Precisely, how often has this sort of thing happened?" he asked, his tone grim.

"This is the first. And I hope the last time." She tried to smile but sniffled instead. "Unless, of course, you own a cane?"

He did not look amused. "You must see a doctor."

She shook her head and tried to put a bright face on an utterly mortifying circumstance. "I'll feel right as rain in a few days. It is just a bit tender at the moment," she remarked, wincing.

He thrust his fingers through his thick black hair. Bloody hell. No wonder she had been stiff and reserved in the church. The condition of her back certainly went a long way toward explaining her lackluster attitude at the altar. The embrace he'd given her must have hurt.

"Why the devil did you not tell me?" he snapped, his anger directed at himself rather than at her.

She shrugged and grimaced for her effort. "I was . . . humiliated." Her eyes welled with tears. "I—I did not want you to know."

He caressed her red, blotchy cheek with his palm. "Did you think that likely, given that we are man and wife?" he asked, his tone softening.

She blinked away her tears. "I don't see why not."

He dismissed her naive assumption with a deep frown. "No," he said, dropping his hand, "you wouldn't."

"The embarrassing truth would have remained a secret had you honored our agreement," she grumbled, dragging her sleeve along her running nose.

He fixed her with a sardonic stare. She looked like a child. Corrupt blood must run in his veins. He was sorely tempted to pull her into his arms and smother her swollen, rosebud lips with his own.

"Our so-called agreement allowed for a change of heart, if you will recall."

"You never intended to honor our agreement, did you?" she asked, her voice nearly cracking with emotion.

He frowned slightly. "Enough about that damned foolish agreement," he replied irritably.

"You lied to me."

"Not . . . exactly," he said with a good deal of discomfort. What the devil was the matter with him? Tonight was his wedding night. By all rights, *she* should be apologizing to *him*.

She fixed him with a frosty glare. "I think you are despicable."

His gray eyes turned cold and distant. "Regardless of your fine opinion of me," he told her brusquely, "you will see a doctor first thing tomorrow morning."

She nodded, and issued a dutiful, "If you insist, my lord."

His jaw clenched. What he would not give to get his hands on her hateful grandfather. "You will never see that vicious old man again. Do you understand me?"

She smirked at him. "You've no need to worry, my lord. He has disowned me."

"Good riddance. Nothing like this will ever happen to you while you are under my protection. I am not given to uncontrollable fits of rage."

"That is immensely reassuring, my lord. What, pray, am I to do when you decide to break your word and pounce on me?" she asked flippantly.

"I did not pounce," he bit out. "And if memory serves," he said, letting his sultry gaze drift over her, "you did not seem to mind overmuch. Until I touched your back, you seemed to enjoy being pounced on."

"I did nothing of the sort," she countered sharply. But the hot color suffusing her cheeks told him differently.

He massaged the back of his neck. "It is getting late," he said on a weary sigh. "You need some rest. I'll send for the doctor first thing tomorrow."

"Does this mean you intend to honor our agreement after all?"

He gave her a hard look. "You have precious little to fear from me this night."

"Fiddle-faddle!" she cried. "You are evading the issue, my lord."

He refused to dignify her childish reaction with a response. His feet carried him across the threshold of his bedroom. He slammed the connecting door shut with a resounding thud. He shook his head and wondered what the devil *fiddle-faddle* was meant to convey.

Having spent the better part of a sleepless night digesting the ramifications of her predicament, Sabrina decided it was totally unpalatable. Just because she *was* married to Hunter did not mean she had to *stay* married to him. She could easily get an annulment, or even a divorce.

She did not have a moment to lose, for she intended to announce her intentions to him this very morning. Honor had been served. He had done the noble thing. He had married her and saved her good name. What difference would it make to him if they annulled their farcical marriage?

Very soon now, she would have her quiet country life, and he could return to his rakish ways. Both of them would be blissfully happy. Or, at least, as happy as they had ever been prior to meeting.

She heard footsteps shuffling across Hunter's room. She stiffened. After last night's exchange, she dreaded their next encounter. Taking a deep, fortifying breath, she decided it was now or never. A quick, nervous examination of her reflection in the mirror made her frown.

She bit her lip. Oh, dear. Her pale yellow muslin morning gown and white lace cherusse made her look like a spinster.

Oh, bother! What did she care? It wasn't as if Hunter found her attractive in the least. On the contrary, Grandfather was entirely correct: no man would ever admire her looks. She was too unconventional to be considered even remotely attractive. She tore her gaze away from the reflecting glass, for it never contained a satisfactory image.

Mustering her courage, she assured herself that this was for the best and dove headlong into the fray.

Nevertheless, her hand shook as she clasped the doorknob to the connecting door and tapped lightly. There was a momentary hesitation before she heard him utter a gruff, "Come."

She opened the door and froze. To her amazement, he was standing before her shirtless. Obviously fresh from a bath, his wet hair was slicked back from his handsome face.

Her heart galloped in her chest. Heavens. If possible, he looked twice as handsome as usual. Her fascinated gaze pored over his hard, lean body. She gulped. She had never seen a man half-naked, or otherwise. The effect was rather . . . unsettling.

She knew his body was formidable. She had felt his hard, sinewy muscles beneath his shirt. But his bare chest was broader than she had imagined. And his shoulders were much wider than her mind could ever have conceived. He was quite magnificent, she thought on a dreamy sigh.

Her greedy eyes pored over his taut, firm stomach that rippled down to his nicely tapered waist. It looked not unlike the washboard the servants used for scrubbing. Thick black hair covered his well-defined chest. She had to quell the urge to touch him, to weave her fingers through his coarse hair and savor the solid muscles hidden beneath. Heat crept into her face.

Flustered, she tore her fascinated gaze away and forced herself to look anywhere but at her splendidly made husband in all his seminaked glory.

"I'm sorry . . . I—I didn't realize you were . . . were indisposed," she stammered nervously. In an effort to shield her acute discomfort, she turned around aimlessly in search of her own room.

"I am not indisposed," he replied with curt indifference and dismissed his valet, who was lurking obediently in the background. When they were alone, he fixed her with a chilling glare. "What is it you wanted?" he asked, his voice stiff with civility.

She could not bring herself to look at him. He was far too tempting. She would further embarass herself by ogling the man. Lowering her lashes, she said in a voice that did not sound at all like her own, "I have been thinking—"

He cocked a dubious brow. "Have you, indeed? This is becoming a rather unfortunate habit."

Pricked by his insult, she lifted her defiant gaze to his.

Regarding her with a cynical smirk, he put his hand on his narrow waist emphasizing his powerful thighs and his tapered hips. "What is it this time, my sweet?" he asked in a voice that dripped condescension.

"I want a divorce," she told him bluntly.

"You *what?*" he thundered, truly amazed by her audacity. After twenty-four hours of the marriage she had manipulated him into, she had the impudence to demand release.

In two angry strides, he closed the distance between them. His powerful, hard, lean body moved with lithe grace. She took a step back from his encroaching wrath. Her back collided with the door.

"I—I want a divorce, or an annulment, if you prefer," she repeated, trying to remain calm. "It matters not to me."

"There has never been a divorce in my family," he ground out, pinning her against the door. "I do not intend to break with tradition. In other words, madam," he said icily, "the answer is unequivocally no. No divorce. Ever."

Incensed, she slapped her hands on her hips and glared up at him. "Why not? After all, my lord, we are hardly in each other's pockets."

His savage expression loomed perilously close to her face as he leaned down, trapping her between two powerful, well-toned arms.

"I have no intention of disgracing my family with the scandal of divorce," he said, fighting for control over his temper. "Our marriage is steeped in sufficient controversy as it is, do you not agree?"

She flushed in unspoken accord. "Fine." She cleared her throat. "If not a divorce, then an annulment."

His gleaming eyes narrowed into dangerous silver pinpoints. "Under the law, you are my chattel, my property, to do with as I please. And I say there will be no divorce. The only thing that is going to separate us, dear heart," he said brutally, "is death. I suggest you get used to being Lady Lancaster."

"Ooh!" she railed, stamping her foot. "You are impossible! You did the noble task of marrying me. Your family will not suffer if we get an annulment."

"There will be no annulment!" he roared.

"We clearly do not suit," she protested with energy. "There is no reason to remain in this mockery of a marriage—"

"My dear girl," he said harshly, "it is of little consequence to me whether we suit or not. If necessary, I will eliminate any possibility of an annulment, bruises or not."

She recoiled in dismay. "Pray, my lord, do not be vulgar. You make your point with brutal clarity."

"Good," he said in a lethal tone, and turned away from her to prowl the room like a caged panther. "I cannot credit your insolence. You got what you wanted," he lashed out cruelly. "You thought to escape the consequences of your scheming *and* to garner a yearly income from your gullible husband, is that it? Well, unpalatable or not, you asked to be Lady Lancaster. And I come with the title, madam.''

Outraged, she cried, ''How, precisely, did I ask for this? I had no wish to marry you.'' Tossing her curly mane over her shoulder, she crossed her arms over her heaving chest. ''I dislike you heartily. You have nothing to recommend you. Your character is churlish and argumentative. Furthermore, my lord husband,'' she panted with fury, ''your main inclination is to be unkind and selfish.''

The pulse in his cheek throbbed with a vengeance. ''Are you quite finished assassinating my character?'' he asked through clenched teeth.

She arched her chin defiantly. ''For the moment,'' she replied tersely, ''yes.''

His chiseled features set in a furious scowl. ''Since you are such an excellent judge of character, pray tell me your opinion of a young woman who, in collusion with her dear sister, contrives to entrap a man, a very affluent man, mind you, by spinning tall tales and waxing deceit. Have I etched an accurate portrait of your character, do you think?''

Her eyes widened owlishly. ''I never did any such thing,'' she gasped. ''You conceited, arrogant man! How dare you flatter yourself into thinking I set my cap for you. I would have to be stark raving mad to desire you for a husband.''

His disdainful gaze swept the length of her. ''Perhaps you are stark raving mad,'' he taunted, for he obviously discredited her heated rebuttal. ''It would be consistent with my lack of fortune.''

She fixed him with a frosty gaze. ''My lord,'' she blustered with contempt, ''understand me when I say *you* are hardly the quintessential husband and the very last man I should ever wish to marry.''

His silver gaze sharpened. "Is that a fact? Why, then, did your beloved brother-in-law confess your wretched scheme to me not five minutes after you'd secured your position as my wife?"

Her brow furrowed in confusion. "*Ian* told you this fantasy?" She was all astonishment.

"Fantasy?" he muttered with scorn. "I wish it were. Your jubilant sister confessed your contrivance with relish."

Sabrina looked more confused than ever. "Amanda?" she echoed, dumbfounded. "What does she have to do with this?"

Slowly, the truth dawned. A sense of dread enveloped her. She slumped down on the edge of the bed. No wonder Amanda had plied her with enticing details of the infamous Hunter.

"I'll strangle her," she hissed under her breath. "The meddling, foolish, hen-witted romantic. How could she do this to me?" she groaned, her head in her hands.

He uttered a derisive grunt. "You don't figure largely as the victim."

"My lord," she moaned, as her fingers washed over her miserable face, "I fear we have both been the pawns of a most heinous cupid."

He gave her a dark, skeptical look. "If you expect me to believe you are innocent—"

"Oh, do come along. If I had wanted to trap you, I could have easily done so at Holmes's garden party."

"If memory serves, you did try," he countered coolly.

"To achieve ruin, *not* marriage. A simple confession from me relating the salient points of your scandalous kiss in the library would have elicited a harsh demand for a marriage proposal from dear old Grandpapa. Of that, you must have no doubt."

He did not look convinced.

"How can you be so dimwitted as to believe I play a part

in securing for myself a fate that promises to be worse than death?"

He fixed her with a crushing gaze. "It is you who are dimwitted if you think for one moment this performance will sway my opinion."

She was utterly nonplussed. "I scarcely would demand release if I'd invested time and energy to lure you to the altar. Even your colossal ego will allow that much."

He shrugged. "Marriage to me is not all you had hoped."

"I commend you, my lord," she snipped with sarcasm, "you have, at last, arrived upon the truth."

"Indeed, I have. You, my dear, are a grasping, cunning young woman who'll go to any lengths to get what she wants."

Her dander rose. "Oh! You are beyond the pale," she cried, her frustration growing by leaps and bounds. "Would I have insisted on our nuptial agreement if I were eager to wed you? I care not one farthing for your money, your title or your splendid home," she told him bitterly. "It is my heart's desire to be free, to pursue my intellectual interests. Not marry an egotistical, puffed-up lord who is conceited enough to believe I trapped him into an unwanted marriage."

Hunter gave her a dark look.

"If you do not believe I have provided a faithful description," she imparted on a huff, "you may ask Amanda for the true narrative of events."

"Your sister will produce a similar fabrication, of that I've little doubt."

Flabbergasted, she stared at him. "You think I intended to be caught in Lady Declaire's bedroom?"

His mouth was a grim line of reproach. "I doubt the circumstances were of great import."

Her mouth fell open. "Is your conceit boundless? In your infinite arrogance, you actually imagine I purposefully trapped you?"

"I do not imagine it," he told her, his expression as cold as ice. "I know it."

She was at her wit's end with the maddening man. "In that case, pray, why did I refuse you? If I were eager to snare a wealthy mate, I scarcely would have dared spurn your offer for fear that you would have retracted it." She threw the words at him.

He offered her a twisted smile. "Ah, but you are a clever little minx, are you not? As an avid student of human nature, you knew all too well that what seems unattainable to a man becomes a burning necessity."

She blinked at him in complete astonishment. "You think . . . you truly believe, I purposefully refused your offer in order to arouse your interest?"

A wicked gleam lit his gaze as it drifted, with excruciating thoroughness, over her flushed face and heaving bosom. One end of his enticing mouth lifted slightly. "Among other things," he imparted with hateful mockery, "yes. Now, if this charming little interview is at an end, you may do me the honor of getting out of my sight."

She gaped at him, incredulous. The arrogance of the man was untenable. How dare he insinuate she was a liar? She, set a trap to snare him? It was unconscionable. The very last thing she wanted was to be the wife of a boorish, conceited buffoon like him. Her blood boiled.

"Nothing," she flung back at him, "would give me greater pleasure. Your insufferable attitude is too much to be borne." Turning on her heel, she fled the room in a whoosh of yellow muslin.

A scant hour later, the elderly Dr. Ennis was summoned. Hunter chose, to Sabrina's acute dismay, to remain present during the humiliating examination. Silent and brooding, he stood, arms clasped behind his back, watching her with those piercing gray eyes.

It was mortifying. The single pleasurable moment was derived when the doctor made the assumption that Hunter was responsible for his wife's condition. Affronted, Hunter swiftly assured him to the contrary.

Dr. Ennis pronounced Sabrina's back "bruised" and offered some salts for daily use in a warm bath.

It was unsettling the way Hunter watched her fumble with her nightgown. In a vain effort, she tried to shield her nudity from his dark, penetrating eyes. She could not fathom why her husband stood mutely at the side of the bed. The doctor had taken his leave.

She chafed beneath his smoldering gaze and asked him pointedly, "Was there something you wished, my lord?"

Slowly, he tore his scorching gaze from her round, firm breasts shielded only slightly by her thin cotton nightgown and raised his eyes to hers. "As soon as you are able to travel," he told her curtly, "we shall leave for Lindhurst."

One eyebrow arched slightly. "We?" she queried brazenly. "I thought we meant to lead separate lives."

The muscle leapt in his cheek. "I intend to accompany you only for the sake of appearances," he said tightly.

"Yes, of course. Appearances. Pray remember, my lord," she said coolly, toying with the lace cuff of her nightgown, "I have no illusions of a romantic honeymoon. You are free to return to London with all possible haste."

He placed his hand on the headboard and leaned down. His dark, finely carved features sharpened with animosity. Her instinct was to lean away from him, to slink back into the pillows. She quelled it.

His eyes flickered with pure rage. "Never fear. You will realize your ambition, my sweet," he told her in a deadly voice.

Her heart lodged in her throat. "What ambition is that?" she dared to ask, despising her quivering voice.

"I fully intend to leave you in the country, pursuing your intellectual interests, till you are old and gray."

Chapter 11

Several days later, as Hunter descended the steps of his town house, his mood was not further improved by the torrential downpour that pounded without mercy upon his back. The thunderous crack that traversed the darkened sky came as little surprise to his jaded ears. Foul weather suited his disposition and his fortune of late, he thought as he climbed into his waiting carriage.

As the conveyance lurched forward, he scowled at his own lack of foresight. Had he actually been foolish enough to envision a romantic honeymoon in the country with his child bride? The little chit's duplicity nettled him even now. How dare she act the wronged innocent when all along she had connived and weaseled her way into his home and his deep pockets? After more than a decade of blissful freedom and sexual foraging, he had done the one thing he had sworn never to do. He let a coquette dupe him.

Gad, he thought, throwing his endless legs onto the opposite seat, the past few days had been a living hell. He was eager to quit the lavish town house that had once been his bachelor refuge. Every room seemed to smell like his wife. He could practically *feel* her presence permeating the entire household. Only this afternoon, he had come across a lacy, scented handkerchief, with the initials S. B. crookedly embroidered across the top, lying on his favorite reading chair. How dare she invade his private sanctuary with her soft, enticing femininity?

The woman was obviously useless with the needle. In fact, he could not think of any ordinary female pastime at which she excelled. Still, he never noticed before how luxurious and shiny her coppery hair was. He longed to reach out and touch it. It would feel so damned good to run his fingers through her soft tresses and inhale the sweet scent.

He had never taken notice of the endearing habit she had of running her tongue over her lips when she was nervous or deeply engrossed in thought. He had been tempted on those occasions to cover her delectable mouth with his own.

The chit was deucedly inviting. Not at all what he wished to be confronted with at the breakfast table each morning. She was far too desirable for his liking. He could not believe how incredibly appealing she looked garbed in the modest, schoolgirl gowns that fit all too snugly over her soft, round bosom. They were not meant to be the least bit provocative. But the deuced gowns were driving him wild. He was becoming aroused just thinking about her!

It simply would not do. He must keep his mind on more grievous matters, like finding the scoundrel who had impregnated Julia and abandoned her in her hour of need. He despised having Sabrina under the same roof. Her very existence grated on him as a constant reminder of his gullibility. His fingers massaged his temples. He concentrated on banishing the silly wench from his mind, and met with his customary lack of success.

The carriage turned down Mount Street and ground to a halt outside Paine's modest town house, the contents of which, Hunter had on good authority, were being auctioned to settle his mounting debts.

The sky had graciously ceased its wet deluge, allowing Hunter to mount the stone steps in relative comfort. Interrogating a man of dubious character was not how Hunter had envisioned spending his honeymoon. Perhaps it was fitting. He should have kept his mind fixed on his goal, to discover the man responsible for Julia's downfall, and not been led astray by a redheaded, wild urchin.

After what seemed an eternity, a butler of advanced years opened the door. Reluctantly, he led Hunter through the conspicuously unfurnished foyer, down the bare-walled hallway, and into a drab-looking drawing room which appeared, for the time being, to have retained its original furnishings, however modest.

Hunter glanced around the dimly lit room. It smelled musty from stale tobacco and cheap liquor. Dust clung to the drooping curtains, diminishing their original brilliance.

A presumably inebriated Paine reclined, his clothes and hair in complete disarray, across a once stylish striped chaise that presently showed signs of excessive wear. At recognizing an intruder in his private hell, Paine struggled to pull himself up and focus his bloodshot eyes.

Hunter frowned at the image before him. Tales of Paine's demise were greatly underestimated. His pockets had obviously been to let for quite some time. Hunter's disgusted gaze crept over the dingy cravat that looked as though it had not been pressed in days. The soiled, once green velvet cutaway was frayed around the edges.

He would not allow himself to pity the desperate fool who had destroyed himself over the turn of a card. He was involved in something nefarious. Hunter was bound to determine what.

Paine's hooded eyes narrowed on Hunter's face. "Who the devil are you?"

"Hunter Lancaster, Earl of Greystone. *Julia Lancaster,*" he said pointedly, "was my stepsister."

Paine sat bolt upright. "You! You're the one who got that deuced runner on my tail. What the hell do you want?"

"Some information. I should very much like to know why a group of men would choose to wear a certain gold emblem."

Paine snickered and reached one arm down to grope the floor. "None of your damned business," he retorted viciously, and lunged suddenly toward Hunter. A flash of metal glinted before Hunter's eyes. Instinctively, he kicked the dagger from Paine's hand. Paine lunged toward him with murder in his eyes. Hunter sidestepped the punch and countered with a hard right to the whelp's jaw, which sent him stumbling backward.

Shaking his head to clear it, Paine growled with rage and leapt forward, taking a swing at Hunter's jaw. Hunter ducked and landed a hard fist in the cad's stomach, followed by a powerful blow to his opponent's chin, which sent the man to the floor in a disheveled heap.

Hunter stooped down and picked up the knife off the floor. Examining the object with a critical eye, he asked gruffly, "Who are you protecting?"

"Go to the devil," Paine snarled.

Hunter tapped the jeweled dagger against his palm. "I need a name," he said with brisk impatience. "I suggest you tell me what it is I wish to know before I lose my temper and put this dagger of yours to good use."

Paine wiped the blood dripping from his mouth with the back of his hand. Staggering to his feet, he tested the condition of his split lip. "What have I got that you'd want to know about?" he asked, taking a swig from a half-empty bottle of cheap brandy.

"I want to know the significance of the snake and the maiden."

He shrugged. "I don't know."

Hunter smirked. "I think you do. And if your information is worth my while, I'll compensate you. Handsomely. Judging from the current state of your affairs," Hunter drawled, casting a critical glance around the room, "you can scarcely afford to be difficult. Now, why would a group of men all wish to don identical rings?"

Paine raked his hands through his greasy brown hair. "If you want to know about the club, you've come to the wrong man. I've been excommunicated."

"How sad for you," Hunter muttered with scorn. "Who founded the disgusting club?"

Paine shook his head. "I've already told you, I'm out."

"Mmm. But you know about the others." Hunter yanked Paine forward by his shirt collar. "I want to know which one of you destroyed Julia," he said in a low, ominous voice.

Paine wrenched himself free. "It wasn't me," he said, slumping down on the chaise. "I don't go for respectable types," he sneered.

"No?" Hunter bit out, his savage expression perilously close to his adversary. "Then, which one of your charming cohorts does?"

Paine nervously ran his shaky fingers over his chin. "He'd kill me if I told."

"I might just kill you myself if you don't," Hunter snarled. "I know about your charming pastime. You, Hobson, and Everly."

"So what?" Paine laughed. "It is no crime to seduce a woman, even if she is untried." He grinned at Hunter with salacious pleasure. "It is just more of a challenge, especially when she puts up a fight."

Hunter took Paine by the shoulders and shook him hard

enough to rattle his teeth. "Give me the other two names," he ordered in a ferocious growl, "or you won't get a farthing from me."

"Shelton. James Shelton," Paine burst out. "He was one of us."

Hunter's eyes narrowed. "He knew Julia?" he asked roughly. "Is he the one? Who put her name in that revolting book?"

Paine shook his head. "I won't give you *his* name. Not for a thousand guineas."

Sickened by the seedy scenario, Hunter shoved Paine from him.

"I suggest you contact your friends at the club. I am sure you could blackmail the man I am looking for quite effectively now that you've proven yourself such a loyal follower. Oh, and when you see him," he advised in a tight, rigid tone, "tell him I intend to kill him. Has that permeated into your liquor-soaked brain?"

Paine swallowed audibly and nodded his head.

Hunter threw the dagger at the dust-covered mahogany table at Paine's side. The blade sliced into the top and gyrated for a few seconds from the force of the throw.

Utterly repulsed by the scene he had just witnessed, Hunter made his way from the dingy town house. God, he thought. Lord God. Had Julia been raped by one of those men? The mere thought made his stomach churn.

Distracted by the disturbing revelation, he hurried down the stone steps. Not taking notice of the other occupant on the sidewalk, he careened into a rather tall, slender gentleman.

"I say, I am sorry, old man," Hunter heard a male voice cry out.

Not focused on the present, Hunter managed to issue a curt apology and continued on his way.

"Hunter Lancaster, is it not?"

Hunter stopped and turned around to confront the faceless
body he had bumped into. "Yes?" he replied, his tone abrupt.

The tall, impeccably dressed blond man smiled amicably and
extended his hand. "George Wilkinson. We met some years
ago. My property in Kent borders on your family's estate."

"Oh, yes, of course," Hunter replied, shaking the man's
hand. The Wilkinsons were one of the most prestigious families
in England. Hunter had a vague recollection of meeting
George's father some years past. He was renowned as an honorable gentleman with a pristine reputation. Hunter knew very
little about the son. "Good to see you," he murmured politely.

Wilkinson smiled with warmth. "I do believe congratulations
are in order."

Hunter's brows snapped together. "Congratulations?" he
echoed testily.

"On your recent nuptials," Wilkinson supplied. "I hear tell,
your bride is as radiant as she is youthful," he said with a
feline smile. "You are, indeed, a fortunate man."

Hunter grimaced inwardly. Fortunate? He was anything but
fortunate. "We must all consider our obligations to the peer-
age," came his noncommittal retort.

Wilkinson emitted a sigh. "True, true," he muttered. "I can
scarcely conceive of a woman of my acquaintance capable of
diverting conversation, let alone worthy of my good name,"
he intoned airily.

Eager to disengage himself from the innocuous conversation,
Hunter imparted with curt civility, "Perhaps someday you will
share my good fortune."

"Perhaps," Wilkinson allowed. "It may be too much to
hope for. But you must also allow me to extend my most sincere
condolences on the loss of your stepsister. I met her only briefly
while on holiday in Bath some time ago. The waters can work
wonders."

Hunter offered a slight smile. "Yes, my father visits Bath religiously."

He released a sigh. "I cannot recall a more agreeable nature than your sweet stepsister possessed. I do believe I heard that she married an Italian count some time ago? There was a child, a little boy, was there not?"

"No." Hunter shook his head. "A girl."

A pause hung in the air. "Ah," was all the man said.

"She is my ward," Hunter explained.

"How delightful for you both. Still," Lord Wilkinson said with a doleful smile, "it must be devastating to lose someone so young and extraordinary as little Julia."

"Yes," Hunter replied sadly, "it was a tremendous loss for my father and myself."

"How tragic." Wilkinson glanced up at the town house from which Hunter had recently taken his leave. "I must be away before the next downpour."

Hunter's ebony brows knitted. "Never say *you* are associated with the likes of Paine?"

"Sad, but true," the tall man remarked, plucking a frilly handkerchief from his breast pocket. "The devil owes me an absolute fortune," he lamented with a sniffle.

Hunter snickered. "Don't expect him to make good on his losses."

"Alas, I fear," Wilkinson remarked, stuffing his hankie into his pocket, "he is perilously close to Fleet prison. I've learned my lesson. Never take pity on a friend in need."

Hunter smiled at the dandified man. "Generosity of heart is best reserved for charitable institutions."

Wilkinson bared his pearly white teeth in a smile. "Ain't it true? Good day to you, sir," he replied with an exaggerated low bow.

Hunter lifted his beaver hat. As he watched the willowy man trot up the stairs to Paine's town house, Hunter shook his head.

He had no clear recollection of ever meeting George Wilkinson. Or for that matter, Julia mentioning their acquaintance. It was of little importance. Hunter had a multitude of concerns at the moment, not the least of which was what the devil to with his wayward wife? One thing was for certain; he could not trust himself to pass another night with that temptress near at hand. He was eager to dump her in the country and rid himself of that enticement for good.

Rays of bright yellow sunlight streamed through the casement windows of the Upper Brook Street town house dining room. Garbed in a pale blue cutaway, navy brocade vest and gray pantaloons, Hunter sat at the head of the enormous table awaiting the arrival of his breakfast. He hoped, by rising early, to avoid any contact with his bride.

It was bad enough that he was married to the little hellion. The constant temptation of a young, wildly attractive female at his fingertips made him cantankerous to say the least. He should, by all rights, give in to his base instincts and bed the chit. At least then he would get her out of his system. One thought prevented him from pleasuring himself in her beautiful, vibrant, highly responsive body—she had tricked him. He refused, regardless of how great the enticement, to act the part of a prize bull.

He heard the door open and swiveled around in his chair. He swore under his breath. The devil worked overtime of late. No sooner had he sworn to himself that he would not be lured by his bride than she appeared.

She took her seat at his side. Despite his stony expression, she offered him a bright smile. "Good morning, my lord. Mmm," she said, running her tongue over her lips in an enticing fashion that drove him wild. "I am starving this morning. What is for breakfast?'' she asked, wiggling her bottom on the seat of the chair.

Bloody hell. Hunter dragged his gaze from her cheerful expression. He would like nothing better than to run his hands over her round, soft bottom. He watched her shake out her linen napkin and drape the enviable item across her silken thighs hidden beneath her soft, white muslin dress. He found the tiny pink roses that dotted the fabric oddly alluring.

Forcing his gaze away, he took a gulp of coffee. Mercifully, Evans arrived, providing a diversion for Hunter's lustful thoughts. The butler presented her ladyship with a crisp copy of The *London Chronicle*. Unfortunately, a second later, he disappeared, leaving the newlyweds alone once more.

''I hope you do not mind, my lord,'' she said as she scanned the paper in search of a particular page, ''but I simply could not wait to see my article on Thomas Brown.''

Placing the article before him, she got to her feet. She draped her arm around his shoulder and leaned over to point out salient features of interest.

He could feel her breath soft and warm against his cheek. A smidgen more, and their faces would be touching. Feeling suddenly overly warm, he tugged at his collar and felt the uncontrollable urge to clear his throat.

The heat from her delicate body gently pressed against him threatened to send him over the edge. It took all his self-control to resist the urge to drag her across his lap and kiss her sensuous, rosebud mouth till she was breathless and weak and begging for more.

Hunter was vaguely aware she was gabbing about something, but did not hear a word she was saying. His gaze was riveted to her lovely profile. Her peaches-and-cream complexion begged for his touch. He had to ball his hand into a fist so as not to touch her.

He drew a deep breath. Her heavenly scent invaded his nostrils. Lord, she smelled good, just like fresh lavender.

"I am forever in your debt, my lord, for suggesting the topic. Mr. Hammersmith was quite impressed by my conclusions. What do you think?" she asked, turning her eager expression toward him.

"What?" he repeated stupidly, utterly lost in her incredibly deep blue eyes.

"About my article? Do you think I gave the topic a fair assessment?" she asked with barely concealed eagerness.

He swallowed audibly. He felt like a schoolboy with his first crush. This would never do! By God, the chit got under his skin. He did not like the effect she was having on him. Not one bit.

"I don't give a damn about the deuced article," he barked at her.

She inhaled sharply at his mordant tone. Stunned and visibly shaken by his surge of temper, she recoiled from him. Her startled blue gaze searched his stark, forbidding features.

By Jove, she had a nerve to stand there looking hurt and confused while he was waging a war with rampant desire and losing the battle! Those damn juvenile schoolgirl dresses were provocative as hell. She was driving him insane. Throwing his napkin down on the table, he got to his feet.

"Why the deuce don't you buy some decent dresses instead of wearing those old rags?" he asked her sharply.

She blinked at him in dismay. "I—"

"I expect my wife to dress better than a pauper's child."

Embarrassed heat flooded her cheeks; her lashes fluttered downward. "Yes, of course," she said quietly.

"I suggest you pay a call to Bond Street this morning." His gaze swept over her. "And for God's sake," he growled, his voice harsh with censure, "get rid of those skimpy, childish dresses. Burn them if you have to, but don't let me ever see you in them again. Is that perfectly clear?"

"But—"

"But what?" he snapped at her.

"I . . . have no money, my lord," she replied with a good deal of discomfort.

"Put it on account. I should think Madame Desjardin knows my tastes well enough by now to outfit *you* appropriately," he muttered with curt irritation.

She glanced at him in surprise. "Are you not coming?" she asked him, her voice anxious.

"I've more important matters that require my attention. We will shortly leave for Lindhurst. Prepare yourself for a solitary life in the country, madam."

She looked crestfallen. "But what—what about my work?" she sputtered, extending the paper to him. "Will you not give me your impressions?"

His derisive gaze swept over her paltry offering. "Why don't you pen an article on animal husbandry?" he asked with biting sarcasm. "You might learn something useful."

With that he stormed from the room, leaving his breakfast untouched and his dumbfounded bride deeply hurt.

Biting her lip, Sabrina expelled a doleful sigh. The workings of her husband's mind were beyond her. His mood swings were, indeed, baffling. From time to time since their marriage, she had caught him staring at her, a burning, hungry look in his eye. Usually, a gruff remark summarily ensued, and he would take himself off.

But what had she done to warrant his censure this morning? The man certainly had a formidable temper. She could not understand his violent reaction. And she was not at all sure an article on animal husbandry would be of interest to Mr. Hammersmith.

* * *

The first leg of the arduous journey to Lindhurst commenced in taciturn silence. Sabrina pretended to be interested in the countryside. It was not particularly appealing. Green fields punctuated by scattered cows chewing their cuds and heavy thickets here and there made for a dull ride.

When at last she could no longer endure the tense silence, she closed her eyes to rest. It was one thing to be stuck traveling with her recalcitrant husband, but quite another to endure his insufferable glowering.

She must have drifted off, for she awakened to a gruff voice in her ear. "Wake up." Her eyelashes fluttered open only to find her husband leaning over her. "We've arrived, Lady Lancaster."

"What time is it?" she asked, still groggy from her nap.

"Time to see your new home. This is your first glimpse at Lindhurst. I hope you find it worth your trouble."

Turning away from the hateful man, she came face-to-face with Lindhurst from the carriage window. Her breath caught in her throat. It was magnificent. An enormous, square stone facade on one side faced what appeared to be a lake and, on the other, sprawling woods. The famous Lindhurst gardens were, doubtless, at the back, for the front was adorned with a curved drive and a solitary fountain in the middle of the plush green lawn.

"It quite takes my breath away," she remarked in soft, admiring tones. "I have never seen such grandeur."

"Then, you must regard your circumstance as happy, indeed," came his cool reply.

She glanced over her shoulder at him; a hint of anger flared in her tempestuous blue gaze. "I cannot comment on my circumstances, only the majesty of your home, my lord."

"I am glad you like it," he muttered cruelly as the carriage rounded the drive. "You will be spending a great deal of time here."

The carriage came to a stop, and the footman lowered the steps for Hunter to disembark from the carriage. Sabrina placed her foot on the top step and lost her balance. She fell against her husband's chest. For a tense moment, she worried he might let her topple to the muddy ground. Then, all at once, she heard a derisive grunt and felt strong, capable arms encircle her waist to stop her fall.

She clutched his broad shoulders for support. His dark, penetrating gaze roamed her hectic face, his mouth close enough to press a kiss to her softly parted lips. She flushed warm at the prospect.

She reminded herself that he believed her capable of treachery and was scarcely likely to show her any measure of affection. Regardless of the longing she thought she saw lurking in his silvery depths, he detested her.

Flustered at being pressed intimately against her husband, who harbored a disgust of her, she averted her gaze. "Thank you, my lord."

Frowning, he set her down as if she were a tainted thing he could not stand to be near. Without further ado, he turned on his heel and marched into the house, leaving his wife to trail behind, flanked by two skinny footmen and hordes of baggage.

Sabrina was overawed by the regal household. The mahogany furnishings and plush carpets were, indeed, superb. Several large gold-framed portraits, boasting past generations of Lancasters, gazed down at her with stern disapproval. The expansive stairway cloaked in dark green velvet wound its way up to the first landing. It split in two different directions and vanished into the dark shadows that lead to the east and west wings of the house.

Sabrina sighed with appreciation. Every inch of Lindhurst was elegant, but not in the least overstated.

As she glanced around her at the magnificent home, she had to admit that the notorious Hunter lair was quite exceptional. Masculine in every detail, but that went without saying. She could scarcely imagine pastels in such a place.

An enormous portrait flanked by two crossed shiny sabers mounted on the opposite wall caught her eye. She approached the portrait to better admire it. It was obviously commissioned during the war. The handsome young man depicted in the life-size painting was garbed in a crisp red uniform.

She cast a speculative glance in her husband's direction. He cut a handsome figure then and now, she mused with a fanciful grin. He was conversing with a slim woman of advanced years who possessed a friendly face. This Sabrina took to be the housekeeper. Their exchange appeared to be complaisant.

He turned to his wife and issued a curt introduction. "Mrs. Putnam, I present my wife, Lady Lancaster."

The elderly woman smiled kindly at Sabrina. "We are, indeed, pleased to welcome her ladyship." She turned to address Hunter. "We were expecting you to arrive quite some time ago, my lord."

"My bride was not well enough to travel. But upon her recovery, she was eager to commence her honeymoon in the country. I was only too happy to concede to her wishes."

Sabrina shot Hunter a startled look which he ignored.

"All is in readiness," Mrs. Putnam boasted. "I aired the master bedroom as you instructed, my lord."

Hunter stiffened. "Have Lady Lancaster's things placed in the adjoining room."

A look of confusion touched Mrs. Putnam's round face. "But, my lord, your instructions were very specific—"

"The adjoining room will suffice," Hunter told her curtly.

"Very well, my lord. I shall have a fire lit immediately to take the chill off. I hope you will be comfortable, my lady."

Sabrina smiled at the conscientious woman. "You needn't

worry on my account. I am weary from the journey and wish nothing more than to recline with a warm pot of tea.''

Hunter's mouth pinched. How well she played the demure, unassuming bride in front of Mrs. Putnam.

"I am sure everything will suit your humble needs, my dear," he assured her coolly.

"I am sure it shall, my lord," she replied with equally forced civility.

Having recovered from her arduous journey, Sabrina decided to take an afternoon stroll rather than to face her scowling husband. As she headed toward the stairs, she heard a strange sound and hesitated. Either her ears were deceiving her or someone was crying. She strained to ascertain from where the sound was coming. It was definitely the west wing. As she moved down the long corridor toward the ecru marble steps, the sobs grew louder. It was a child crying. Hastening her gait, she thought she heard the soothing sounds of a woman's voice. It was coming from the room on her right. Curiosity got the better of her.

Without thinking to knock, she threw open the door and crossed the threshold. A few yards away an elderly woman, who could only be the child's nanny, shushed a blond-haired baby in a large rocking chair.

Sabrina opened her mouth to speak, but the gray-haired woman pressed her finger to her lips. The chubby little baby uttered a mewing sound. Slowly, the child's eyelashes drifted shut. Its mouth slightly ajar, the small bundle fell fast asleep. Little hands clung to the nanny's shoulders. Gently, the old woman placed the blond-haired cherub in the crib and lovingly tucked the soft blanket around the sleeping child.

"I—I'm sorry," Sabrina whispered to the kindly faced

nanny. "I heard a child crying. I was curious," she admitted with some embarrassment.

The woman's face wrinkled into a smile. "Little Annabelle is teething," she said, and led Sabrina into the next room.

Sabrina's brow furrowed in confusion. "*Who* is little Annabelle?" she blurted out before she had time to stop herself.

"*She* is my niece," a deep, caustic male voice remarked from behind her.

Sabrina whirled about and came face-to-face with a wall of pure masculine flesh and bone that could only belong to her husband. He looked exceedingly displeased.

"Good afternoon, my lord," the nanny said dutifully.

Hunter inclined his dark head in taciturn greeting. "Mrs. Edwards. I see you have met my bride," he intoned with a glare in Sabrina's direction. "How is your charge this afternoon?"

"Teething makes her a little cranky. She's cutting another tooth. Poor little girl. It won't be long before she has a mouthful. She'll be right happy to see you, my lord."

He smiled amicably. "I shall see her before dinner in the play room." Without further ado, his fingers closed over Sabrina's arm. Bidding Mrs. Edwards good day, he propelled his bride from the room.

"In future, madam," he growled against her ear, "if you wish to know if I have any byblows, I suggest you ask me, not the servants."

She opened her mouth to refute his vile accusations, but could not. Truth be told, she had been wondering whether Annabelle was his daughter. It was dreadfully improper to ask who the child was, but he should have told her.

"Had you bothered to inform your bride of the child's existence, I would not have been reduced to asking the servants," she countered sharply.

He came to a standstill in the hallway and gruffly released her. "Very well, if you must know, she is my stepsister's child.

She is my ward. *Not* my daughter. Which, I suppose," he intoned with contempt, "makes you her aunt."

Sabrina slapped her hands on her hips and glared up at him. "Precisely when did you intend to inform me of her existence?"

He shrugged. "I saw no reason to involve you in a private family affair."

Dumbfounded, she gaped at him. "Private family affair!" she sputtered at last. "I am your wife. I have the right to know."

"Perhaps," he allowed at his most arrogant, "though I do not ask that you spend time with the child. But I do insist that you be kind to her. I will not have her origins bandied about by you or the servants."

Sabrina struggled to control her temper. Between his infuriating conviction that she had lured him into marriage and his heartless belief that she would ever hurt an innocent child with a blunder of the tongue, she was perilously close to her breaking point.

"Do not concern yourself, my lord." Her voice was rigid with control. "I do not bandy gossip."

She turned on her heel and disappeared down the steps to seek refuge in the privacy of her bedroom. Why did he not return to London and leave her in peace?

Another week of connubial coexistence passed, surprisingly, without further incident. In fact, it proceeded with grueling, uneventful civility. Aside from the hours she spent playing with little Annabelle, Sabrina was decidedly bored. She had completed her interviews with the land steward and forwarded her article on animal husbandry to *The Chronicle*, although she had serious doubts whether it would be accepted. At present, she found that she had more time on her hands than she knew what to do with. This would never do!

She saw very little of her husband; save for meal time, they were constantly apart. When they were forced by convention to be in the same room, he uttered little more than a begrudging yes or no to the questions she thought to ask him. He was, it seemed, ignoring his wayward wife, a condition that grated on her, that was until the day she dared to enter his private sanctuary, the library.

She tapped lightly at the mahogany door and waited for his deep voice to resonate from within. "Come in."

He glanced up from his paperwork and did a double take. Evidently, her spontaneous interruption was not welcomed. Tossing his quill pen down, he sat back and regarded her in stony silence.

"I thought we might picnic," she said brightly.

"Picnic?" he echoed with blatant contempt for the pastime most people considered enjoyable.

"Yes. Come along, my lord, you must be vaguely familiar with the notion. Wicker basket. Wine. Delicious food. Soft, warm, inviting blankets. Glorious sunshine. Rest and relaxation. You have been on a picnic before, have you not?"

"Not since I was in short pants," he snorted, and resumed his examination of what appeared to be the estate books.

She rested her slender hip on the edge of his desk. "Well, then," she said, smiling down at his cross expression, "it should be a delightful pleasure for you to indulge in a childhood fancy."

His eyes met hers. "I do not wish to picnic," he muttered with thinly veiled hostility.

She drew a deep breath and held her ground. Lord knew, he was not making this any easier. But she was determined to establish some level of cordiality between husband and wife.

"You have to eat some time," she offered cheerfully.

He sat back and crossed his arms over his chest. "Now, why would my wife wish to picnic with the likes of me?" he asked nastily.

She ignored his jibe. She wanted peace not war, she reminded herself. "I thought that since we are going to be irrevocably stuck together for possibly the next ten to fifteen years, depending on how long you live, we might decide to get better acquainted."

His dark gray eyes sharpened. "Are you suggesting I'm old?" he asked through his teeth.

"Well," she said on a blithe sigh, "you are hardly sprightly, my lord."

"The devil I am not!" he growled, and slapped the leather-bound book shut.

She leaned forward, draping her body across his desk top. "Care to see if you can best me on horseback?" she asked, a mischievous glint in her eye.

He chuckled with derision. "You could never best me, madam."

A scampish grin spread across her lips. "We shall see, my lord, we shall see."

Chapter 12

The pounding of the hoofs beneath her mingled with the sound of her mount straining for breath. As the wind whipped at her face, tangling her hair beyond recognition, a thrill of exhilaration ran through her. She looked down at the green meadow whisking by beneath the horse's long strides. Glancing over her shoulder at her husband edging closer, she shrieked with delight and urged her mount forward with a tap of her crop on the dapple gray's rump. If she landed on her backside because she had foolishly urged her mount too fast, she would be mortified.

It was not, of course, a fair race. She was riding sidesaddle and lacked the advantage of clinging to the powerful beast with her thighs, which would have enabled her to fly like the wind as she had done countless times before, when her grandfather was not looking.

She doubted the ferocious Hunter would take kindly to being bested by his wife. Unwilling to give free rein to the great speed the animal was capable of, she eased back on the bit and let her husband take the lead.

She reached the designated elm in time to find Hunter waiting for her, his hands slung on his narrow hips. She jumped down from the saddle and twisted the reins around the tree branch. She turned to face her husband. Her heart tripped over itself.

His breathing was ragged from the strenuous ride. A fine sheen of perspiration covered his bronzed skin. He was staring at her. A blind woman could read the passion in his silver gaze. She was not green enough to misconstrue his thoughts.

"You have won, my lord," she said with a nervous smile. "I shall have to demand a rematch." Her eyes darted away from the fetching sight of her husband flushed with heat and sweat.

"We did not discuss my prize," he murmured, his voice like velvet.

"Prize?" She fidgeted beneath his smoldering stare. "I do not recollect mentioning any prize, my lord," she replied, and brushed past him.

"I doubt it will be worth much, given that my opponent let me win," he said, catching her by the arm.

She looked up at him in surprise. "I did no such thing. You bested me fairly."

He eased her closer to him. "Why did you pull back?" he taunted. His dark, sultry gaze ran over her face. "Afraid of what might happen if you give the beast free rein?"

She colored fiercely. "On the contrary," she tossed back tartly, "I know what will happen."

Wrenching her arm free, she walked a safe distance away. She heard his low, husky chuckle and despised him for it. Gazing idly about the plush green landscape, she pretended to be unaffected. In reality, however, the heady, overwhelmingly masculine scent of leather, sweat and horse invaded her senses and threatened to turn her knees to jelly. Her fingers fiddled with her hair, trying to repair the wind-blown mess, but achieved little success.

Hunter watched her struggle with her unruly hair and smiled. His wild, carefree wife was in constant disarray, he mused, surprised by how appealing he found her. "Allow me," he said from behind.

Reluctantly, she accepted his assistance. His fingers removed the last remaining precariously scattered hairpins and let her hair fall down her back. It was just as thick and soft and luxurious as he had imagined. Wrapping his hand in her hair, he grasped the back of her head and turned her to face him.

Her heart slammed against her ribs. Swallowing hard, she tried not to think how very much she liked his touch. Just having her near him, feeling his magnetism, was pure torture. She stared into his stormy gray eyes overflowing with his desire, and she knew he wanted to kiss her. Her breath quickened with yearning. Try as she might, she could not look away. Of its own volition, her body seemed to close the distance between them.

And then his arms enveloped her small frame, cradling her in the warmth of his strong embrace. His warm lips captured hers. His kiss was tentative and surprisingly gentle.

Despite her insistence on a prenuptial agreement, she knew she could not stop this from happening. She yearned for him to touch her, to kiss, to hold her. Yes. Oh, yes, she thought, swept away by the moment. She wanted him. And everything that went with him.

Instinctively, she parted her lips and clung to his sinewy arms. His kiss became demanding. His mouth moved passionately over hers, bruising her soft, pliant lips with burning desire. His fingers locked in her hair, holding her captive. Sliding her arms around his back, she leaned into him and returned his kiss with equal craving.

He scooped her up, cradling her in his arms, and walked

toward the lake. Laying her down on the carpet of soft grass beneath the enormous shady elm, he held her close, his mouth clinging to hers, devouring her sweet taste. He kissed her passionately, violently, as if he could not get enough of her. His tongue intimately entwined with hers. With a soft moan of pleasure, she joined the love play.

They lay together in the plush green grass, his body partially on top of hers. Helplessly adrift on a sea of desire, Sabrina lost all sense of reality. She did not want the exhilarating sensations to stop. His palm slid over her breast and boldly caressed her. The pad of his thumb rubbed against her sensitive nipple. It peaked beneath his touch. He deepened the kiss. His hands moved lower to caress her hips, her waist and beyond.

Alarmed at where this might lead, she realized their passionate interlude had gone far enough. She tried to pull away. But he moved on top of her, pinning her body beneath him. When she felt him tug at the buttons of her velvet riding habit, she reached up to stop his hand. He placed the offending member around her neck. She felt him reach inside her chemise. His large, warm hand covered her bare, aching breast. Rubbing his thumb against her already taut nipple, he squeezed it gently between his fingers.

Arching upward, she moaned against his mouth. She knew she was incapable of making him stop. Her body betrayed her. She craved the feel of his rough, calloused hands against her sensitive breasts. Then his mouth was at her breasts, showering them with kisses. Hot, wet and demanding, his mouth closed around each nipple and sucked hard. She gasped with pleasure. Threading her fingers through his thick raven hair, she clutched at him, never wanting the spiraling pleasure to stop. He trailed kisses along her shoulder and her neck. His teeth nibbled at her earlobe.

"*Sabrina,*" he breathed. "I've waited longer for you than

any other woman. I thought I might go mad. I had to touch you,'' he told her huskily.

She was too dazed to comprehend his meaning. Delirious from the newfound tempest of emotions raging inside her, she took his face in her hands and kissed his mouth. Grunting with pleasure, he kissed her back with fierce hunger.

"It will not do," he grated hoarsely against her lips. "I must have you." Fumbling for her skirt hem, his hand slipped beneath her skirt and slid up her leg to caress the inside of her thighs and in between.

She panicked. Passion dissolved into fear. Instantly, her mind began to function properly.

Did he mean here? Right now? In the middle of the day? On the grass?

Oh, no. She was not ready for this. She had barely survived marriage to the cantankerous man; she would never survive an afternoon of passionate lovemaking.

"Hunter," she gasped, pushing against him.

He did not budge. Not one inch. Instead, he kissed her while his fingers stroked her soft apex, creating the most exciting, mindless response deep inside her. She felt hot and breathless and weak.

"*Hunter,*" she whimpered, uncertainty mingling with fear. "What . . . are you . . . doing?" She panted with excitement caused by the tormenting pulse of his fingers. "You cannot think to . . . oh." She bit her lip against the aching pleasure.

He smiled down at her with a wicked glint in his eye. All the while, he teased her soft, feminine core with his probing fingers. "You'll see," he promised thickly, and kissed the sensitive spot behind her ear. The situation was getting out of control. She moved her head away, but to no avail. He kissed her neck.

"I—I don't want to see," she panted. "I've a very good idea what you are about. I am not . . . not ready for this."

Lifting his head, he stared down at her, his breathing labored, his face flushed with unrequited passion.

She was about to explain that someone might come along and that they should wait for privacy and a more appropriate time and surroundings. She did not want to be initiated into lovemaking with her skirt hiked up like some cheap tart taking a tumble in the grass. The hard expression on his face gave her pause.

He stared down at the beguiling woman lying beneath him. She was driving him insane. Those blue eyes of hers bewitched him.

If their previous encounter was any barometer, he knew she wanted him as badly as he desired her. Most women found him utterly charming. Why, then, were his actions boorish when it came to his own wife? Many marriages were forced and still did not end up like this.

It injured his pride that his wife shrank from his advances. It further bedeviled him that she was able to hold herself from him when he coveted her with mindless desperation. If possible, Madame Desjardin's creations were even more alluring than the childish, skimpy muslin frocks she used to wear.

He prided himself on his self-discipline. He was, after all, no young buck ruled by his emotions. He was in complete control at all times, except, it would appear, when it came to his young, extremely desirable bride.

His face was rigid with anger as he snapped, "It seems I've married a coquette. I should have known," he sneered cruelly. "You tempt a man beyond reason and then cry off. I know your sort."

"I suppose you are well acquainted with every sort of woman," she spat out, her chest heaving with rancor and hurt.

"Oh, I don't know," he murmured, letting his gaze slide over her face and partially revealed bosom with insulting thoroughness, "I've never tried your sort before."

"You bastard!" she hissed, and tried to slap his face. He caught her arm and held it firmly to the ground.

"Don't," he snapped, pinning her with his weight. "That is a nasty habit. One of which you'll find I am not very fond."

Her anger was only marginally outdone by her shame. Her wild, enthusiastic response to him disturbed her. She had to develop some restraint where her husband was concerned. She could ill afford such foolish sexual abandon.

"Let me go," she cried, squirming beneath him, "you . . . you . . . misbegotten pig!"

"It seems I am to suffer every kind of insult in this dreadful arrangement," he drawled with icy mockery, and abruptly released her.

"If you find yourself trapped in a miserable marriage, you've no one to blame but your jealous paramour," she flung at him bitterly.

His eyes narrowed on her flushed face. "Jealous paramour?" he bit out. "What the devil is that supposed to mean?"

"Your most excellent Lady Declaire."

"She was never my lover," he barked with irritation.

Sabrina gave him a crushing look. "Is that a fact? Pray, why then did she waste no time in spreading details of our scandalous encounter? Is that not the action of a scorned lover?"

His brow darkened. "Harriet Declaire?" he echoed on a furious growl. "I don't believe it," he derided. "What could she possibly hope to gain by doing such a thing?"

"I am at a complete loss, my lord. I thought *you,* could tell *me,*" she muttered with heavy sarcasm. "Whatever the reason, that horrid woman saw fit to divulge a rather sensitive scenario which reached the ears of a certain elderly gentleman who did not take kindly to learning his granddaughter was caught in Hobson's guest bedchamber with a notorious rake."

His skeptical gaze searched her face. "Do you expect me to credit this ludicrous story?"

"Quite frankly, I do not care what you believe, my lord."

He caught her chin and turned her face to his. "Are you claiming you never confessed to your grandfather?"

"Of course not." She jerked her head back. "Have you taken complete leave of your senses? Why would I confess? The very last thing I ever wanted was to marry you. It was only after the scandalous report was swarming all over London that Amanda insisted I confess all to Ian. I cannot believe he failed to mention the instrument of my downfall, given how generously he imparted Amanda's treachery," she muttered crossly. "Surely, he must have told you all that passed before?"

"I naturally assumed it was you who'd divulged the unhappy truth."

She gave him a rueful look. "My lord, I scarcely would have told that disagreeable old man anything as shocking as what took place in your carriage."

He stretched out beside her, resting his weight on one elbow. A slow smile spread across his face. "Shocking, eh?"

She was in no mood for jocularity. "If you think I delight in our current predicament, you have lost your wits altogether. We are stuck in a most disagreeable arrangement with little hope for relief. I swear to you, I played no part in procuring our dreadful union. Indeed, my lord, it is my fervent desire that you return to London and never come back. Is that the portrait of a clinging, smitten woman?"

His jaw tensed angrily. "I understand your feelings toward me perfectly," he averred curtly.

"I am vastly relieved to hear it." Her voice was laced with asperity. "At long last, the truth has finally penetrated your thick skull. We obviously do not suit."

He winced. By Jove, he had muddled it rather badly. He would like to murder Harriet Declaire, ring Ian's neck and paddle her meddling sister's backside. All three of them had had a hand in manipulating him into marriage.

He caressed the taut line of her jaw with his finger. "Oh, I don't know," he murmured, his tone warm and seductive. "We might suit."

"Don't," she snapped, and swatted his hand away. "I am not some plaything you may seduce on a whim."

He expelled a deep sigh and got to his feet. Booted feet slightly apart, he stood with his back to her.

She glanced down at her once neat, elegant riding habit now thoroughly disheveled and halfway unbuttoned. "Brute," she grumbled at his back, and hurried to set herself to rights.

He glanced at her over his shoulder, his greedy eyes raking over her. "Vixen," he replied, a hint of a smile hovering around his lips. He reached out a hand to help her up. She eyed the appendage with trepidation.

"I don't bite, Sabrina," he muttered, and snatched her hand, pulling her to her feet.

She smoothed the mass of wrinkles and brushed the bits of grass from her blue velvet riding habit. "I would not be surprised if you did."

He threw back his head and laughed. "No. I don't expect you would be."

She fixed him with a crushing glare. "This was a poor suggestion," she lamented. "I am sure you'd rather pass the afternoon in your library. I've plenty of reading to do."

He shook his head. "No," he countered fiercely. "I've spent more time looking over those damned ledgers than I ever intended. It was the best place to avoid having to deal with you."

She glanced up at him in surprise.

He offered her a crooked grin that had her heart beating double time. "Childish, I know," he laughed, "but nonetheless true."

Smiling tentatively, she asked him, "Shall we eat, then, my lord?"

"Mmm," he said, his scorching gaze threatening to devour her whole, "I am ravenous."

Rosy color crept over her cheeks. She turned away and walked toward the lake.

Hunter fell into step at her side. They walked in awkward silence toward the willow tree by the side of the lake where the delectable feast awaited them.

Amazed, Hunter surveyed the soft, inviting plaid blanket adorned with every sort of food imaginable. "You arranged all this?"

Shyly, she nodded, and fell to her knees to prepare a plate of cold meats and chutney for him.

He dropped down beside her. "Why?" he asked, his penetrating gaze fixed on her bent head.

She lowered her lashes, shielding her eyes from his searching gaze. Wordlessly, she shrugged her shoulders. She was not inclined to offer an explanation for fear that he would mock her. She was definitely not prepared to bare her soul to this taciturn stranger.

He lifted her chin with his index finger. His slumberous gray gaze held her captive. "Thank you," he murmured against her mouth, and pressed a tender kiss to her lips.

"You are entirely welcome, my lord."

"My name is *Hunter*," he averred with meaning.

"Hunter," she corrected, and busied herself with serving.

He grinned at her. "As I recall, you were a decidedly bolder lass before we were married. Where is the girl who demanded I ruin her reputation before dawn?" he asked teasingly.

She laughed and cocked her curly head to one side. "I was rather, was I not?" She gave him a small smile and met his gaze with an impish glint in her eye. "That girl is still here, I'm afraid," she said unhappily.

He raised a questioning brow.

"She is the respectable Lady Lancaster now with an image to uphold and proprieties to observe."

His hand slid around her neck; his thumb caressed her cheek. "Not with me, surely?" he insisted, a roguish smile tugging at his lips.

"Open the wine," she told him, pushing him away with a playful shove.

"I am glad you made me come. It has, indeed, been too long since I was on a picnic," he remarked as he filled their glasses. He took a sip and lay down on his back with a heavy sigh, one arm folded under his head. "It was never like this when I was a boy."

"No?" she asked, and placed a plate of food beside him. "What was it like?"

He set his gaze on the tree branches above his head. "Not like this," he replied, a sardonic lilt to his voice.

She wrinkled up her nose. "Is that good or bad?"

He turned to look at her. "This day," he said in an achingly soft voice, "is far superior to anything in my childhood."

Her face fell. "You cannot be serious? Was it really such a trial for you then?"

He drew a deep breath and turned on his side to face her. "My childhood," he told her dryly, "consisted mainly of solitude and tutors."

She looked confused. "But what about your stepsister?" she asked, biting into a slice of cold roast pheasant. "Amanda told me you were devoted to one another."

"We were. I was sixteen when my father remarried. My stepmother, Katherine, brought little Julia to live with us. Julia was barely two at the time. Not that Katherine cared a wit for me," he said bitterly. "She was only slightly preferable to my maternal mother."

Sabrina swallowed her food audibly. "Have you no fond memories at all?" she asked, appalled.

"I suppose I must. When I was very young, my parents were, well . . ." He flashed a rueful smile. "Let's just say, they were never devoted to one another. My mother was like me. Father did not approve."

Sabrina's eyebrows knitted. "Like you?" she echoed, taking a sip of wine.

He turned the full force of his roguish gaze on her. "Wild. Immoral. Wickedly sinful. It is in my blood, don't you know? Father detested us both."

"How awful that must have been for you."

He shrugged and downed the remainder of his wine in one gulp. "I survived," he muttered, and sat up to eat.

"Tell me what happened to Julia," Sabrina asked quietly.

He looked her in the eye. "I thought you knew," he said tersely.

Color flooded her face. Apparently, he had not forgotten her grand faux pas the night they had met.

She shook her head. "Amanda filled my head with wicked stories. Her intention is now patently obvious," she grumbled with irritation.

"I cannot credit her foolishness," came his sharp reply. "Surely, she must have realized that her scheming would wreak nothing but havoc?"

"I sincerely doubt she ever envisioned that debacle at Hobson's party. But, I daresay, she was not beyond using it to her advantage. If I know Amanda, she probably imagined you'd be overcome by love for me, and thought you'd give up your roguish ways," she intoned melodramatically, "in favor of my hand in marriage."

"Is that what she hoped?" His voice was like a satin caress. And his gaze, heaven help her, was hot enough to melt even the coldest heart. She cleared her throat and bowed her head. "Silly, is it not?" she mumbled softly.

He offered no reply. But she could feel the weight of his stare. It made her uncomfortable.

"What was she like?" she asked in an effort to shift the topic of conversation to safer ground.

"Who?" he asked, his sensual gaze drifting over her with unnerving slowness.

She took another sip of her wine. "Julia."

"Julia was . . ." He drew a deep sigh. "She was wonderful. Sweet. Trusting. Kind. Very beautiful. Everyone loved her."

"What happened?" Sabrina asked, offering him a slice of pear. "How did she . . ."

"Die?" he asked bluntly.

Sabrina nodded.

"She died in childbirth."

"Was she . . . I mean"—she dipped her head—"who was she—"

"She was never married," he interjected curtly.

"I see," Sabrina said quietly. She raised her eyes to his. "Then, who is Annabelle's father?"

He shrugged. "I've not the slightest idea."

She blinked at him. "But Amanda told me Julia died a contessa."

He gave her a sardonic look. "Your devoted Amanda is a wellspring of knowledge."

"It was not viciously meant. To be fair, she never thought ill of you. I expect you were not unlike forbidden fruit. It was her intention to make you seem dark and dangerous and wildly exciting."

He chuckled a little ruefully. "I am scarcely that."

Oh, yes you are, Sabrina thought, but held her tongue.

"Little Annabelle is, indeed, a contessa. It is not very difficult to acquire titles or feign marriages in Italy. I arranged it."

"Oh," she said after an awkward silence. "That was good of you."

He looked away. "It was nothing. It was a hell of a lot less than Julia deserved."

"What could you have done?"

"More. I managed it badly." He got to his feet and drove his fingers through his hair. "Do you know what they said after I buried Julia and news of Annabelle's birth reached the *tonnish* elite?" he asked her roughly.

Pain etched on Sabrina's features. "I'd rather not hear," she murmured quietly.

"It doesn't matter to them that a blackguard took her under his spell and got her with child and then deserted her," he said bitterly. "All they care about is whether the child is mine."

"Don't, Hunter," Sabrina implored him, "don't do this to yourself. Annabelle is yours now. She is an innocent child. What can it matter who her father is? She knows how much you love her. I hope, in time, she will come to have regard for me as well."

He gazed at her, admiration shining in his slate gray eyes. "What a rarity you are, my dear," he said softly, and dropped to his knees before her.

She glanced at him askance. "I suppose I must plead guilty to that trait," she allowed ruefully.

He reached out and brushed a stray curl from her cheek. "I know about your daily visits to the nursery." He smiled at her startled expression. "Mrs. Edwards tells me everything about little Annabelle. You are fast becoming her favorite playmate. I am more appreciative than I can say." He sighed wearily and dropped his hand. "Heaven knows, she needs more than I can ever give her."

"That is not true," Sabrina countered. "She needs you. Mrs. Edwards cannot stop talking of the child's devotion to you."

"Still, I am grateful for your kindness."

Self-conscious, she scoffed at his remark. "It is little enough for me to try to bring her some measure of happiness," she said with modesty.

"What of your husband's happiness?" He gave her a sensual smile that was designed to make her grow weak with longing. And did. "Have you no pledges for him?"

She lowered her gaze to her lap. "What would you have me say?"

He tilted her chin up. His eyes held her gaze with a burning intensity that fairly singed her. "Tell me you want me as much as I want you," he said, his voice hoarse with desire.

Her eyes widened. "My, you are quite direct, my lord. I scarcely know how to take you."

He chuckled softly. "Do not worry overmuch, my sweet." He caressed her cheek with his palm. "I'll be only too happy to show you how I like to be taken."

She flushed to her roots. "I shall bear that in mind, my lord," she murmured dryly.

He threw back his head and laughed. "You do that, my sweet." A quizzical expression crossed his face. "I own, you are not at all what I expected my wife to be."

Sabrina's heart turned to lead in her chest. She quickly averted her gaze. Of course she wasn't. She was scarcely what anyone would expect a lady of consequence to be.

"It's getting late," she said, a bit too quickly. "We'd best be getting back."

His eyes narrowed slightly. "All right," he replied with a shrug, "if you like."

He got to his feet and extended a helping hand to her.

Sated and replete, husband and wife rode across the plush green meadow toward the house in silence. Sabrina tried to shake off her feelings of inadequacy. Why should she care what the churlish man thought of her?

Oh, but she did care. Terribly. She realized with a jolt that she wanted to please him. Her forehead wrinkled in confusion, for she couldn't imagine why. After all, aside from a few wonderfully exciting sensual encounters, she barely knew him.

This afternoon was the first enjoyable occasion they had actually spent together since their marriage. But it was a pleasant day. More than pleasant. She had been sorely tempted to let him have his way with her in the grass.

Chapter 13

That night, after sharing the first companionable dinner with Hunter since their wedding, Sabrina found herself unable to sleep. After what seemed like hours of tossing and turning, she abandoned all hopes of peaceful slumber.

She sat up in the enormous canopied feather bed that threatened to dwarf her small figure and lit the taper on the bedside table. Several of her most coveted novels lay haphazardly piled on the table. Tempted to lift the cover and lose herself in the enviable prose, she reached out her hand for Jane Austin's *Emma*. Her hand fell shy of its mark. If only it were possible to find solace in a book.

She sighed and leaned back against the mountain of snowy white pillows behind her head. The events of this afternoon whirled about in her brain, tormenting her with possibilities.

What if she had let nature take its course? What if she had made love to Hunter? What then? How would she have felt afterward? She wrapped her arms around her knees and sighed.

She wasn't sure she was capable of giving her body to him without her heart. He had proved he could be cruel and rather difficult when the mood hit him. Why should she make herself more defenseless than she already felt?

Two arguments waged war in her brain, the first being that it was her wifely duty. Her nose crinkled. Duty never ranked very highly on her list of concerns. On the contrary, she thrived on nonconformity. The second argument was far more compelling and rather disturbing. She wanted him.

She wanted to feel his body pressed against hers, run her fingers over his taut, hard muscles, feel the warmth of his skin, bask in his heavenly, manly scent, and taste his hard, passionate mouth.

Heaven help her, she wanted to enjoy every measure of what a man had to offer a woman. She felt herself grow warm at the thought. What would it be like to touch his glorious naked body, welcome him into her bed, and her body, in the manner Amanda had described with such vivid and tantalizing detail?

Her lips ruffled slightly. No wonder he had been mildly amused by her prenuptial agreement. Given his wealth of experience with the fairer sex, he must have known sooner or later one, if not both of them, would give in to temptation. She just had not considered it would be sooner. At least, not quite this soon. And she never dreamed it would be her!

She glanced longingly at the connecting door that led to her husband's bedroom. She bit her lip. She could never bring herself to fling open that door, beg him to take her to bed and make passionate love to her. A frown marred her forehead. A yellow hue shone beneath the door. Every once in a while, it was eclipsed by a dark form that was undoubtedly her husband. He was pacing the floor. Why?

Perhaps this afternoon's outing had shaken him as well. Was he, too, searching for a way to persuade her into his bed? She scoffed at her ridiculous conclusion. The man was a renowned rake. He needed no assistance when it came to bedding women. She flung herself onto her side and hugged the blankets to her chest and prayed for sleep.

Sleep refused to come.

This was utterly stupid. She wriggled onto her back. She would never get to sleep at this rate. She sat up in the bed and cast a furtive glance in the direction of her husband's bedroom. Visions of the virile, handsome man clad in a dark brocade robe filled her mind. Did he have a satin robe? she wondered. If he did, she was certain it clung to his broad shoulders and sinewy chest with enviable closeness.

What on earth was he doing tramping to and fro in the middle of the night? Curiosity got the better of her. She wracked her brain for a reason to intrude on his insomnia.

He had brandy. She had seen the crystal decanter and glasses on the small mahogany table the day she had asked him to release her from their vows. Brandy. What an excellent notion. If nothing else, it might help her sleep. She threw back the covers and hopped from bed.

But then, of course, there was always conversation, she told herself as she scurried across the chilly room in bare feet and a modest white cotton nightgown. They could converse about. . . . She hesitated for a moment. Her forehead creased. What would they find to talk about? Whatever topic they chose would occupy their minds until they were ready to go to bed.

Separately. Of course.

A rush of tingling heat poured over her. She shook her head. No. She was not prepared to share his bed. She caught her lower lip with her teeth. At least, she didn't think she was. In fact, she was almost positive it would be disastrous, no matter how exciting his passion promised to be. She held her breath and turned the doorknob.

At seeing her head peer around the door, Hunter's pacing came to an abrupt halt.

"Sabrina," he breathed, his face a portrait of complete surprise. "What are you doing awake?" he asked, as if she were a disobedient child who should have been to bed hours ago.

Her heart flopped around in her chest. He did have a satin brocade robe. And it was clinging to his bare chest just as she knew it would. She gulped. He was naked beneath the heavy plush robe, she realized with a flush of delicious warmth. She forced her hungry gaze to his face.

"I ... um ... could not sleep." Her cheeks burned apple red. "I saw your light ... I am sorry," she murmured, and turned to take her leave. "I should not have intruded ..."

In a blink of an eye, he closed the distance between them. "No." His hand closed gently over her arm. "It is all right. I could not sleep either." He smiled slightly. "I am glad you are here."

Her startled gaze flew to his. "You are?"

"Mmm, hmm," he murmured, drawing her close. "I could not sleep either."

She wet her lips. "Why not?" she asked. Her voice sounded breathless and weak even to her own ears.

His gaze flickered over her face. "I fear my thoughts are preoccupied tonight."

"Mine, too," she admitted with a yearning smile.

He cocked an ebony brow. "I thought you were too young to suffer from such ailments?" he teased lightly. His breath was warm and soft and tickled her cheek.

"I am not so very young," she countered, mildly affronted. He was supposed to be swept away by passion at the sight of her, not remarking on her age.

"Yes," he said, pressing a kiss to her forehead, "you are." He drew a pensive sigh and dug his hands into the pockets of his plush robe. "Very young, indeed. Completely innocent of the ways of the world." He crossed the room and leaned a weary elbow on the fireplace mantel. "You've no idea what evil lurks in men's hearts."

She frowned in frustration. Splendid. He was in his patronizing mood again. She despised being treated like a child. The very last thing she wanted at the moment was a benevolent brotherly chat.

She slammed her hands on her hips. "I am all astonishment, my lord," she muttered with heavy sarcasm. "I had thought you were merely heartless. Alas," she said on an exaggerated sigh, "evil lurks mordantly where your heart should beat."

He looked up at her sharply. "Pray," he mocked coolly, "don't sound overly disappointed on my behalf."

"How could a mere child like myself hope to do otherwise?" She imbued her voice with an acerbic edge. "I warrant it is all part of the trial you face with a child bride."

He chuckled softly. His smoldering gaze poured over her like a sensual caress. "Is that what you are?" His voice sounded oddly husky. "My child bride?" he asked, closing in on her like a stealthy, dark predator.

Her stomach somersaulted. She backed away from his encroaching masculinity. Her legs bumped into the enormous canopied bed that loomed behind her like a blatant sexual reminder. She pressed her palms on the soft downy coverlet for support and forced herself to look anywhere but at the alluring wedge of bronzed skin. It was rather difficult, for his well-defined chest was directly at eye level.

"When you patronize me, how else should I feel?" she asked in a horribly small voice.

"If I condescend to you," he countered, leaning down, his handsome face perilously close to hers, "it is because I have the benefit of fourteen years more of life's experience."

She swallowed. "Yes, well," she rushed out breathlessly, "I daresay you have made several more blunders than I." Her fingers nervously toyed with the satin ribbon at the neck of her ruffled nightgown. His dark, sensual gaze followed the direction of her fingers. She dropped her hand and cleared her throat. "As for the remainder of your case, I see no evidence to support it."

He grunted and gave her a hard, withering look. "It's late, Sabrina." His breath was warm against her face. She shivered. "I am in no mood to argue with you."

Truth be told, in her current situation, her desire ran in a much more amicable direction as well. The conversation had taken a decidedly sensual turn. She found to her dismay that her brain ceased to function properly at approximately the same time her pulse started to soar, which, as a matter of course, was always when her husband was near.

"W-why could you not sleep?" she asked in an effort to change the direction of their disturbing, cozy little chat and quell her raging pulse.

He drew away from her. "I've been thinking about the instrument of Julia's disgrace," he said with a heavy sigh, and massaged the back of his neck.

Sabrina's brow snapped together. "I was given to understand you did not know his name?"

Hunter's jaw tightened. "I don't." He retrieved a large gold ring from his pocket and examined it with a dark brow. "But I will. In time."

"How?"

"I've hired a Runner to do some poking about."

Her eyes sparkled with intrigue. "Have you, indeed?" She plunked down on the end of his bed. Leaning back on her palms, she dangled her bare ankles like the child she swore she was not. "What savory clues has he unearthed?" she asked, barely able to contain her excitement.

He etched a crooked smile. "Not nearly what I had hoped," he remarked, gazing down at the gold object in his hand as though it held the key to the questions burning in his mind.

"That ring is like the one we found at Hobson's."

He glanced up at her. "What makes you think so?"

"I am not a fool, my lord. I knew the moment you saw it at Hobson's it had significance. Where did you get it?"

"Amongst Julia's belongings. It was tucked away in a locked drawer along with a love letter." He looked pained by the memory.

"Love letter?"

He crossed the room to the bedside table, retrieved a folded piece of paper from a wooden box and handed it to Sabrina.

She glanced quizzically at her husband and unfolded the worn parchment paper. It was heavy stock, obviously good quality, she observed, as her eyes scanned the flowery black writing strewn across the white page in startling black.

My own true love, how I miss you! It will not be long before we are together again, reunited in our love. I have missed you, my pet. What a treasure you are to me. So young and vibrant and innocent. I have never experienced such mindless devotion as what you give unselfishly to me. Do you truly love me, little one? Dare I hope to hear your soft profession whispered in my ear soon? You are never from my thoughts and always near my heart. Come back to me soon, my beloved, for I cannot exist without your love to guide me. I long to take you in my arms and make you mine for all eternity.

I am as ever, your most gallant knight.

Sabrina frowned slightly. She folded the worn parchment and handed it back to her husband. "Gallant knight is not a terribly helpful clue to his true identity. It was a man with whom she was obviously very well acquainted." She bit her thumbnail. "How many could there be?"

"Evidently quite a number," Hunter snorted with derision, "but none of wicked persuasion."

"Save for one," she said on a sigh.

"Yes, save for one," Hunter muttered pensively as he shoved the note in his pocket. "But I'll be damned if I can find him."

"Have you considered the possibility that the knight reference is genuine."

He cast a dubious look over his shoulder.

"Perhaps they met in a chivalrous context, or often rode together. Is that not possible?"

His tormented strides commenced once more before the burning embers in the fireplace. "How could I hope to ascertain such details of a relationship? To the best of my knowledge, she kept him a secret from the world."

"Not the world, surely?"

"She never made mention of any knight, gallant or otherwise, to me. We shared everything, she and I."

Sabrina planted her chin on her palm. "Obviously, he swore her to secrecy. Either that, or she was ashamed of her own conduct. Still," she thought out loud, furrowing her brow, "someone must know of this gallant knight."

"No one knows," Hunter fired back. "I've left no stone unturned. I've considered every possible avenue. I can find nothing."

Sabrina hesitated for a moment. "A girl usually confides in her mother. If she has no mother, a sister. Has she a close friend? A confidante?"

He stopped short. "To the best of my knowledge, *I* was her confidant," he intoned sharply, drumming his index finger against his very nicely made chest.

Sabrina frowned at him. "Oh, do come along, my lord. Don't be so sensitive. If she were involved with a man without the benefit of wedlock, she would, doubtless, *not* share the burden

with her overprotective stepbrother. It would have to be someone less—"

"Punitive?" he suggested with a hard glint in his eye.

She shifted uncomfortably on the gold satin coverlet. "That
was not the word I was searching for, but yes, someone she
felt would not deter her from what proved to be a disastrous
relationship. Can you think of no one she might have felt
safe to bare her soul? Under the circumstances, it would most
definitely have to be a woman. It is decidedly awkward to share
matters of the heart with a man."

One eyebrow elevated slightly. "You, I take it, are an authority on the subject?" he asked, his voice dripping mockery.

She gave him a frosty glare. Was it strictly necessary that
he behave like a pigheaded idiot all of the time? she wondered
with mounting ire.

"Certainly not," she snapped at him. "But I do know she'd
have to be stark raving mad to risk being caught." She folded
her arms over her chest. "I should think the disastrous consequences would be ever fresh in your mind, my lord," she added
with a meaningful glint in her fiery blue orbs.

His dark, crushing look told her precisely how much he
enjoyed her terse reminder of their forced nuptials. "You may
be right." He rubbed his chin thoughtfully. "I had thought not
to involve anyone else for fear of the gossip mongers getting
wind of it."

"Oh, but, my lord, the person of whom I speak would be a
trusted confidante. If Julia felt safe to bare her soul, we need
not fear indiscretion."

"It is possible . . . ," he allowed, "you may have a point."

"Why, thank you, my lord," she intoned with biting sarcasm.

He dismissed her remark by ignoring it. "But I can think of
no one in particular to whom she would entrust such a secret.
What is more, I cannot very well broach such a scandalous

topic in the hopes of finding her supposed confessor. I must think of Annabelle.''

"Of course you must. Whoever Julia's soul mate was, she would most definitely have kept in touch while you were abroad. Have you any recollection of a particular person Julia wrote to whilst in Italy?''

He shot her a dubious frown. "Our excursion was rather hasty. I assure you, I did not publicize the fact that my stepsister was increasing. I cannot think of anyone who knew our whereabouts. These things are best handled with the utmost discretion.''

"Even so," Sabrina replied, "I cannot believe she contacted no one during her confinement.''

"I recall receiving only one missive that seemed to upset her. I never understood why.''

Sabrina's ears pricked. "Do you recollect any of the pertinent details?''

He shrugged. "A few. It was about Lady Caroline Martin. Julia and she had been friends since childhood." He gave her a small smile that made her heart thump wildly in her chest. "I remember that much. It seemed to upset Julia when Caroline married. I've not the slightest idea why.''

"First thing tomorrow morning, we will pay Lady Caroline a call.''

A skeptical brow drifted upward. *"We?"*

"These things often require a woman's touch, my lord. You cannot expect Lady Caroline to divulge all to you.''

A dark frown marred his otherwise perfect features. "You are not to get involved in this. This is my affair; I will handle it in the manner I see fit. I've known Caroline most of her life. She has no reason to be uncomfortable in my presence.''

"If she knows our gallant knight, she will have every reason," Sabrina countered evenly.

One eyebrow elevated slightly. *"Our* gallant knight?" he echoed.

"I am your wife, my lord."

His gaze flickered over her like a satin caress. "Mmm," he said huskily, a slow smile creeping across his face, "I had noticed. I should recognize that gleam in your mischievous eyes by now. You are bent on interrogating poor Caroline, regardless of what I say."

Sabrina wrinkled her nose. "Interrogate is such an unpleasant word. I had something more civilized in mind, say an afternoon visit from Lord and Lady Lancaster. She does, I assume, reside somewhere nearby."

He gave her a sideways glance. "She married the old and very well respected Lord Geoffrey Eastmore, who has a formidable estate in Surrey."

She looked up at him in surprise. "Eastmore? I thought certain he was too old to be interested in marriage."

Hunter snickered at her choice of words. "On the contrary, I believe he is very interested in the marriage bed. That is the prerequisite for producing the Eastmore heir."

The heat of embarrassment scorched her cheeks. She quickly darted her gaze away from Hunter's amused silver orbs.

"Eastmore was looking for a young, healthy bride from a respected family. Evidently, Caroline was it. She must have come with an enormous dowry."

"I see. Very well then, my lord." Sabrina released a determined sigh. "We shall have to travel to Surrey."

He shook his head at her. "Without the benefit of an invitation? Permit me to remind you, your last impetuous jaunt resulted in our hasty marriage."

"In that case, you have little to fear from scandal. More important, my lord, have you the time, or the inclination, to await an invitation?"

His lips curled into a wicked grin. "I've known midshipmen during the war with better manners than you."

"Have you, indeed? I thought I recognized you in the portrait downstairs. I must say, you cut a rather dashing figure, my lord."

"You put me to the blush, madam. But you are quite correct; I am impatient to learn all that I can. I don't suppose it would do me any good to forbid you to come to Surrey?" he inquired silkily.

She smiled up at him sweetly. "I am afraid not. I am bound and determined to find out who is perpetrating these vicious crimes."

He knitted his brow in poorly feigned ignorance. "Vicious crimes? Whatever can you mean?"

"You think Julia's misfortune is related to Jane Greenly's death as well as I do. That hideous ring is too much of a coincidence not to be a valuable link. No use pretending, I am onto you."

His smile turned roguish. "You are, are you? Well, in that case," he murmured in what could only be described as a bedroom voice, "I'd best cooperate. Fully."

Sabrina's pulse skittered unbearably. "I think that would be best," she replied in a soft, throaty voice that sounded nothing like her own.

"I am fairly certain there is a group of men who belong to some secret society; at least, nobody seems inclined to discuss it. The snake and maiden insignia is the only link between them, thus far. It is possible Jane Greenly was their unwilling victim." He fell silent. A brooding expression overtook his face.

Sabrina slid her small hand over the top of his much larger one. "I know what you are thinking."

He stared down at her, his silver eyes serene and darkly compelling. "Do you?" he asked thickly.

She framed his face between her hands. "You must not think of poor Julia as a victim. It cannot be. The letter from her malefactor is, I believe, genuine. He must have loved her."

For a long moment, he stared deeply into her guileless blue eyes. Then he pulled her hands from his face and withdrew. He stood before the fireplace with his back to her. He put his hand on the mantel and stared down at the dying flames.

"You are supposed to believe in him," he said after a while. "That is why men like him are successful at destroying unsuspecting innocents. You all believe his honeyed lies."

"How could someone purposefully lie like that?"

"It happens all the time." His tone was cold and distant. "Men manipulate women with false declarations of their feelings every day."

"But why? What would be the object of such a heinous deed?"

He turned to face her. "Can you not guess?"

Yes, she thought with an unhappy sigh, she could. "Even so, such an arrangement could, at best, be short-lived."

He uttered a growl of frustration. "Is it possible that you are that naive? It suits the man's purposes. He wants nothing more than a romp between the sheets. He cares not how he connives, or whom he hurts."

"I see," she said quietly, and occupied herself with the examination of the floor.

Hunter was instantly contrite. He glanced over at her head bent in what he guessed was embarrassed discomfort. He closed the space between them. Cupping her chin, he lifted her face to his. "Forgive me, it was not my intention to speak harshly to you," he said in an achingly soft voice that made her weak with longing. "It is just that you are so like Julia at times. Young and inexperienced. You know nothing of the world."

She bristled. "I am not Julia. I am Lady Lancaster, your

wife. I know more of the world than you think," she flung at him.

He scoffed at her. "You know precious little, my sweet. Of that, I am glad," he said, gently caressing her cheek with his thumb. "It is not a particularly nice place to be. Don't be in too much of a hurry to grow up."

She jerked her head back. "Stop treating me like a child of twelve! I am a full-grown woman, a fact you seem to remember quite clearly when it suits your purposes."

His gaze turned sinfully seductive. Her stomach quivered. Before she could stop him, his hands slid around her waist. He dragged her to the end of the bed and pulled her close.

"You are quite right," he murmured as he let his eyes drink their fill of her gauzy white nightgown that thinly veiled her naked body. "You are a woman." His voice was smoother than black velvet. His softly seductive tone seemed to underscore the provocative, slow strokes of his thumbs against her abdomen. Her stomach muscles contracted. She drew in a sharp, startled breath. "Or had *you* forgotten?"

"No," she managed to reply, captivated by his smoldering silver gaze. "I . . . have not forgotten."

He smiled like a wolf about to devour a helpless lamb. "Good," he murmured against her mouth, "neither have I."

Warmest blue gazed into smoldering gray. Slowly, he pressed her down on the bed, blanketing her body intimately with his. His mouth moved against hers in a gentle kiss. Her silky arms wrapped tightly around his back. With a tortured groan, he kissed her, crushing her mouth beneath his.

Her eager body responded, burning with excitement from head to toe. She felt warm all over, and her heart was pounding wildly in her chest. It was as if she had run a very long distance. All these riotous reactions, and he had only kissed her. How would she survive the night? She had to gain some ground here or she would be lost.

"Hunter . . . I need—"

"I know what you need," he mumbled breathlessly as his hot, wet lips caressed the ivory column of her neck.

His hands were all over her, caressing her breasts, her waist and her hips, creating a powerful, burgeoning desire deep within her. He slipped her nightgown from her shoulder and trailed tiny kisses along her collarbone. His hand settled on her breast while the other was buried in her soft red curls, cupping her head in a light caress as his mouth tasted her intoxicating sweetness. He gently squeezed the round mound in his palm, and his thumb grazed the hardened nipple. Tension coiled deep inside her. Her breast ached. She leaned into his caress, desperate for more of what, she knew not, only that her beautiful husband held the key. His kisses ignited a fire within her.

His mouth found hers once more, and he whispered against her lips, "I never wanted a woman as much as I want you." He covered her mouth with his in a deeply erotic, passionate kiss. His hand slid down her back, pressing her slender form intimately against his. She felt the heat of his desire and, with a tiny moan, moved against him, devouring his lips with an ardor equal to his own. His hands tugged at her disheveled nightgown until her soft, luscious breasts were bared to perfection.

"You are beautiful," he breathed as his mouth closed over her taut peaks and gently sucked. "Perfectly beautiful."

She arched her back, and her hands delved into his raven hair as his tongue worked its magic. He lifted his head. His passion-filled orbs burned into hers. Gently, she cupped his face in her hands. Her thumb lightly traced his moist lips. He uttered a groan of desire and kissed her. Impatient hands rid her of her nightgown and tossed it on the floor. His eyes greedily traveled the length of her, scorching her creamy flesh.

Sabrina tried to shield herself, but he would have none of it. She felt a rush of heat surge through her body, excited by his frank, sensual perusal. She longed to boldly caress his rippled muscles that she knew lurked beneath his satin robe. Hunter's eyes smiled into hers in appreciation of her wanton admiration. He shrugged off his robe with haste born from his intense burning need. As he leaned down to kiss the valley between her breasts, the softness of her belly, the roundness of her hip and the inner flesh of her thigh, she realized she was breathless with longing. She could stand it no more. His intimate kisses fueled the fire of her already intense longing. Cupping his handsome, passion-flushed face between her hands, she pulled him to her and took his mouth in a torrid kiss that reflected the passion growing inside her. He spread himself over her. She felt the heat of his skin against her own, the tickle of his coarse chest hair against her aching breasts.

"*Sabrina,*" he breathed with aching softness as he kissed her neck and nibbled at her ear. He rained kisses all over her face and mouth. "I am not sure I can wait much longer. I've got to be inside you." He groaned, leaving her swollen, wet, ruby lips to cover her naked body in kisses.

He savored every inch of her with his hands, his mouth and his tongue. His touch excited her beyond all imagining. She was awed by the reaction he created deep within her.

She quivered and ached simultaneously. His name escaped from her lips on a tide of longing. She could endure such sweet torture no longer.

He pressed hot, searing kisses along her stomach. His hands caressed her narrow hips, the flat of her abdomen, and slowly moved to cup her breasts. She thought she would die if he continued this a moment longer. His lips captured hers. Her hands rippled over his hard-muscled shoulders, basking in the wonderful feel of him. He was magnificent. She caressed his neck, threading her fingers through his ebony mane. She uttered his name with a ragged breath. His lips moved to take her mouth in a savage kiss. As their tongues began their love play, each was hungry for a deeper sampling of the other. He nudged her legs open with his muscular thigh and settled against her. She could feel the heat and breadth of him against her warm, moist womanly flesh. Slowly, ever so gently, he eased into her. She felt her body open to him. Another wave of delicious warmth cascaded through her. She felt the fullness of him invade her completely and gasped in surprise at the raw burst of sharp pain. He cradled her head between his hands and kissed her face. She could feel the warmth of his breath on her face and hear the urgency in his voice as he whispered,

"Sabrina . . . Sabrina. My beautiful, wonderful wife."

She caressed his cheek and traced his lips tentatively with her fingertips. "Show me . . . I want to please you, but I don't know what you want."

He stared down at her, his face flushed with passion, his breathing ragged and his eyes brimming with emotion. His lips lingered above her mouth. He released a half groan, half laugh. "I have what I want." His mouth claimed hers in a torrid kiss.

Her arms went around him. Her mouth slanted hungrily over his. The initial ache of his intrusion faded as he moved inside her, withdrawing almost completely and then driving into her soft, wet sheath once more. His rhythmic movement rekindled her intense pleasure. Each quickened thrust created new waves of ecstasy deep within her. She could hear his hoarse, ragged breathing and feel the pounding of his heart against hers as he drove onward to new heights of pleasure. She had never known such bliss, such complete fulfillment, and all-consuming joy. Two hearts, minds and bodies had come together. Driven by their passion for one another, they soared to untold heights of pleasure. Their souls united forever in this one moment as man and wife.

"Sabrina . . . oh, God, Sabrina," he murmured breathlessly against her neck, his thrust hard and deep.

So filled with emotion was she, that she could utter no reply.

She did not need to; she knew what he was feeling, for she was feeling it, too. She turned her head in search of his mouth.

"Hunter . . . I—" she was about to say she loved him, but his movements increased to such a frenzied pitch that the words were lost on the tide of her fulfillment. Completely swept away by the moment, she uttered a moan of exquisite pleasure and clutched him to her. Glorious sensation of pure ecstasy blossomed deep inside her. The feeling was so potent and so overwhelming, she wondered if she could endure another moment without going mad with pleasure. It did not seem possible to reach an even higher plateau of delicious ecstasy. But he took her there.

"Don't . . . fight it," he breathed, loving her with hard, deep, fast strokes. "Let . . . it happen."

Waves of sublime culmination washed over her. She cried out his name. With a groan of supreme pleasure, he drove deep and climaxed inside her.

Chapter 14

Their passion finally spent, Hunter collapsed onto his back beside Sabrina. His breathing was coming hard and fast, and his body was covered in a fine dew of perspiration. He looked over at her. She gazed back at him with an expression akin to wonderment. Then, all at once, he smiled slightly and gently brushed her flushed cheek with the back of his hand. He pulled her into his arms. She felt him press a kiss to the top of her head and brush her damp hair away from her face. Snuggling against his chest, she listened to the comforting sound of his heart pounding beneath her ear and luxuriated in the feel of his strong, loving arms around her.

The sounds of the crackling fire combined with the gentle stroke of his hand along her spine lulled her toward sleep. His hand slowed and finally went limp against her. His breathing was slow and deep. She knew he slept. Thinking she ought to return to her own bed, she tried to move away from him, but his arms tightened around her.

"No. Don't go," he mumbled, stirring partially from his much needed slumber. "Stay with me." His arms pulled her closer. "I want you near."

She relaxed against his hard, muscular chest and smiled a secret little smile. Closing her eyes, she hugged the special moment to her heart and drifted off to sleep, content with the knowledge that her rakehell husband needed her.

Sabrina slowly emerged from her deep slumber and felt Hunter's hands on her body, caressing her, awakening her desire once more.

"*Sabrina,*" he breathed, kissing her cheek, her nose and her eyelids. His mouth moved to kiss her temple. "I've got to be inside you, my precious little one," he whispered into her mouth before he kissed her, smothering her lips with his own.

As his mouth slanted voraciously over hers, her arms slipped around his broad back, drawing him against her aroused body.

His lips moved along her soft skin. He nibbled at her shoulder and kissed her collarbone, her throat, her neck and then finally the back of her ear. Desperate to be kissed, to feel his lips upon hers, to taste him fully, she whimpered and turned her face toward his. His lips captured hers once more. Their tongues danced erotically together. His hands roamed over her body. She could barely contain herself; she wanted him with aching desperation.

His palm slid over her abdomen and pulsed against the apex of her thighs. "Are you ready for me, little one?" he murmured huskily against her cheek. His finger slid inside her snug channel. He smiled at her. She was dripping with sweet honeyed wetness and was more than ready for him.

She gasped with pleasure as his fingers stroked her. "*Yes, Hunter, yes.*" Her blood pulsated like a tempest through her body. She rocked her hips against him. "*Please, God, yes.*"

His arms around her, his body blanketed her with his warmth. She opened for him, her body craving an end to this sweet torment in their blissful fulfillment. He entered her, filling her completely with one powerful thrust. She cried out, catapulted to a world of complete rapture. A host of wonderful, spiraling sensations assailed her. His every movement heightened her senses. She never wanted the feeling to end. Their passion was all-encompassing. Nothing else mattered. They gave freely of themselves in this exquisite cleaving of man and woman.

In the afterglow of their lovemaking, she lay against him softly tracing the hard contours of his muscular chest.

"Hunter?" she whispered.

"Mmm," Hunter mumbled, his voice heavy with sleep.

"The night before our wedding, Amanda told me what to expect from the marriage bed. She mentioned there were ways to, ah, prevent . . . well, to avoid making, um, a baby."

That woke him! Good Lord. "What?" he burst out, shaking the cobwebs of slumber from his brain. His wife had a penchant for talking at all the wrong times. This was by far the most bizarre conversation he had ever had—especially in bed. He did not wish to discuss the prevention of babies with his wife. It made him deuced uncomfortable.

"I was wondering . . . did you—"

He stiffened. "No," he told her curtly. "You must know I did not."

"Oh. I did not think you had."

Devil take it! She sounded disappointed. He tilted her chin upward. "Sabrina," he imparted in a tone that brooked no disagreement, "I don't intend to either."

She looked dumbstruck. "Why ever not?"

His jaw clenched. "You are my wife, that's why not," he practically snapped at her.

She blinked at him. "What difference should that make?"

Draped across his chest, a lovely, naked invitation to pleasure, she was suggesting they abstain.

He sat up and dragged his hand through his tussled midnight hair. "All the difference in the world."

She sat up beside him. Tugging the sheets over her bare breasts, she gazed at him. Her wild red locks, damp from their lovemaking, cascaded down her back and shoulders like a siren temptress's. "I do not see why," she said, looking more desirable by the minute.

Hunter grimaced. "The natural result from our union is children," he muttered uncomfortably. "Surely you must be aware of that."

"That may be the natural course," she tossed right back at him, "but I am too young to become a mother."

He burst out laughing. "Is that what is worrying you?" he asked, caressing her soft, rosy cheek with his knuckles. "Your age?"

"I think it's a valid concern," she countered, her mien cool.

"You will be a wonderful mother," he assured her, kissing her softly on the mouth.

"Stuff and nonsense," she replied, shoving her palms against his chest.

He blinked down at her in surprise. Well, at least she had not shouted *poppycock* at him. Things were looking up. Now she sounded like a stodgy old man. But she did not look like one, he noted with a surge of white-hot desire.

"You mistake my meaning. I do not want a baby," she told him, enunciating each word quite clearly. "I've no desire to be endlessly breeding whilst you enjoy yourself in London."

"Fine," he agreed, and busied himself with kissing her delectable neck. "I promise to remain with you during your confinement, and afterward, if you like," he breathed against her skin.

She gawked at him. Incredulity mingled with anger. "You

are kindness itself, my lord. I should consider myself fortunate, indeed, to have such a generous husband.''

He did not miss the acid tone. ''A child would be good for you, Sabrina,'' he told her huskily as his forefingers caressed the valley between her breasts.

She swatted his hand away. ''No, my lord, a child would be good for you.''

He framed her face between his hands. ''Think of how devoted you are to little Annabelle. Do you not wish for a child of your own body? A child of our making, yours and mine?'' he asked her softly. She seemed to waver slightly. Good, he thought, her maternal instincts were his ally. ''We would make a beautiful babe together, you and I,'' he coaxed, kissing her on the mouth.

''Hunter,'' she murmured, sliding her hands over his, ''pray, listen to me. We must discuss the matter fully.''

He chuckled deep in his throat. ''I agree wholeheartedly,'' he whispered and trailed hot, wet kisses along her shoulder. ''Fully.''

She drew in a sharp breath. ''Unless you agree to—to use the um, proper, er, method,'' she declared boldly, ''I—I refuse to share your bed.''

He shook his head as if to clear it. ''What?'' he asked, looking dazed and confused by her declaration. ''What are you saying?''

She lowered her lashes from the hurt look on his face and toyed with the bed linen. ''Well, you would keep touching me.''

He tipped her chin upward with his forefinger. ''Are you refusing me your bed?'' he asked, his piercing gray gaze locked with hers.

She swallowed. Her gaze darted away from his penetrating stare. ''Not exactly . . .''

He flashed a smile of pure male satisfaction. "I thought not. Let us not have any more talk of it."

"Very well, my lord," she mumbled, and pulled back the bed linen.

He scowled at her. "Where the devil do you think you are going?"

"To my bed."

He uttered a growl of frustration and hauled her down on the bed. "The devil you are!" he grumbled, kissing her hard on the mouth.

Wrapping his arms around her, he cradled the soft, voluptuous woman against his hard, lean body. He told her gruffly, "I am in no mood for your childish games, Sabrina. Go to sleep."

"Yes, Hunter," she said on a lusty yawn, and settled comfortably in the succor of his embrace.

Almost before Sabrina's eyes flickered open she reached for her husband. The bed was empty. She moved her legs beneath the blankets and felt the soreness from their strenuous love-making. She pushed up on her elbow to survey the room. Judging from the bright sunshine peeking around the heavy brocade drapes, it was a glorious day outside. She lay back on the pillow with a delicious sigh. It was a glorious day inside, too. She lay quietly reliving the wonder of last night.

She wished Hunter had not abandoned her this morning. It made her feel slightly despondent. Almost as if last night's passion had been an aberration or a wonderful fantasy she alone had experienced. She hugged the blankets to her and let out a doleful sigh. Given his checkered character, it might have been little more to him than a moment's pleasure. What could she ever mean to a man like him?

"Thinking of me?" drawled a voice from the doorway.

Startled, Sabrina looked up. One look at his coal black hair, piercing gray eyes and perfectly chiseled features—she melted. Her heart thudded at the sight of him handsomely clad in tight fawn-colored breeches and a navy velvet coat. His lips curved into a slow, sensual smile. She felt the color rise in her cheeks as she recalled his hot, wet mouth all over her.

"Yes," she said with a swallow, "as a matter of fact, I was."

"Capital notion, my sweet," he murmured, his smoldering gaze drinking her in as he crossed the room to the side of the bed. "My thoughts are always of you. Only you." He pressed a kiss to her cheek. "Did you sleep well?" he queried, his tone sinfully suggestive.

"Yes, thank you." She gave him a small smile. "I . . . missed you this morning," she admitted shyly.

"Did you?" His lips curled into a wolfish grin, and he sat down on the bed beside her. "I am glad," he whispered, kissing her on the mouth. "I missed you, too."

She was immediately uneasy with his tender mood and the gentle caress of his thumb along her jaw. She knew where this situation could lead and she was ill prepared to deal with it. If last night was any indication, she was helpless to resist him. At this rate, she would be increasing by the end of the month!

The passion lurking in his smoldering gaze fairly singed her. A rush of heat swept over her. Good gracious, he was wicked. It was broad daylight.

His lips captured hers in a searing, persuasive kiss that banished all rational thought from her mind with amazing finesse. His arms tightened around her, pressing her snugly against the hard length of him.

"*Hunter,* it is light out."

He lifted his head and glanced over his shoulder. "So it is," he replied, and began to kiss her delectable rosy mouth once more. She moved her head, and his hot, searing lips found the quickening pulse at her throat. "Hunter . . . you are dressed."

Her complaint was acknowledged with a deep, throaty chuckle and several more heated kisses which threatened to drive her to the brink of control. "You're not," he murmured huskily.

"Should we not at least have breakfast?" she ventured, feeling awkward and unsure how to extricate herself from her current position.

His lazy, sultry regard made her pulse skitter unbearably. He frowned at her with playful admonishment. "It is nearly noon." His deep drawl swirled around her in a sensual caress. "You slept most of the day away," he murmured, watching as his hand cupped her breast and grazed her nipple. He smiled as her nipple turned rock hard beneath his touch.

She pushed his hand away. "Why did you not wake me?" she asked, embarrassed by the news.

He shrugged an indolent shoulder. She could not help but notice how well the velvet fabric clung to his broad shoulders, any more than she could squelch the memory of how she had clutched at those same shoulders while he drove into her with deep, long strokes that took her to unimaginable peaks of ecstasy.

He flashed a crooked grin. "I assumed you needed your rest," he said in a husky voice and pressed a kiss to the soft, enticing valley between her bare breasts. "It is customary for the bride to sleep in on her honeymoon."

Her cheeks pinkened. "Oh, is that all." She lowered her gaze to the coverlet. "I thought perhaps you might be . . . angry."

"Angry?" He chuckled softly and, lifting her face to his, kissed her on the mouth. "Now, what would I have to be angry about?" he drawled out, tucking a stray curl behind her ear.

She reached out and caressed his handsome cheek with her

fingertips. "Then, you are not upset about what we discussed last night?" she asked, her voice wavering with uncertainty.

"We discussed a great many things last night. To what, precisely, do you refer?" he asked, trailing kisses along her neck and bare shoulder.

She lowered her lashes to shield her discomfort. "You know what," she said softly.

"Ah." He sat back. "You mean your ridiculous refusal to bear me a son?"

Her eyes flashed wide. "Is that how you see it?" she gasped in dismay.

His hand gently brushed her tussled hair back from her face. "How else should I?" he asked with maddening nonchalance.

Astonished, she stared at him. "You might consider my feelings," she said tartly.

"As you might," he replied with a cool smile.

"Please, Hunter," she entreated him. "We are not enemies. Why must we remain on opposite sides of the issue? Can you not understand my feelings on the matter in the slightest?"

A look of utter incredulity touched his handsome face. Gawking at her, he uttered a short laughing sound. "You are not serious about this?"

He hadn't taken her objections last night to heart. All women wanted children. She was merely frightened. And justifiably overwhelmed. After all, her body had recently been introduced to the sensual world. Lovemaking was naturally alarming for an inexperienced girl of eighteen.

"I am in earnest, my lord," she said, her soft blue gaze locked on his staggered expression.

He lifted his gaze heavenward. "Lord, save me from feckless females," he muttered with a sardonic edge to his voice.

"I am not feckless," she flung back at him. "You said yourself I am young. I have so much of life to live, so many things yet to experience. We have time to make a baby. All the time in the world."

"No," he snapped in a curt tone, "I do not see. You are my wife. I expect an heir, Sabrina."

Taking his hand in hers, she pressed a kiss to his palm and rubbed her cheek against it. "I know you do. And in time, I will give you as many children as I can. But for now," she pleaded, "can we not get better acquainted with one another?"

He pulled away from her and stalked across the room to gaze stoically out the window. "We are well enough acquainted," he muttered with ill concealed irritation.

She drew a deep sigh. "Hunter, please, do not be cross with me."

He turned on her, his silver gaze glittering with resentment. "How do you expect me to feel?" he burst out, furious. "You are my wife. I desire your body. You have forbidden me to touch you," he gritted. "Is that not a faithful depiction of our future life together?"

"Please try to understand. I simply do not wish to—to—"

"Bear my children." He supplied in a tone that was decidedly cold and abrupt given his recent warmth.

She paled slightly. "Please ... Hunter ... don't," she begged, and wished the animosity between them would vanish. This was not at all what she wanted. Why could he not show her some small measure of kindness and understanding?

"What else am I *not* supposed to do?" he lashed out angrily.

She released a weary sigh. "You are being impossible."

He sent her a hard look. "I fully comprehend your feelings, madam," he told her, his slate gray eyes gleaming dangerously. "We shall see who is the intractable one."

She turned her face away. "You cannot make me bear you children," she averred with that characteristic defiance he found deuced annoying.

He snickered unkindly. "I could. If I so chose."

Her head turned sharply. She stared at him, a mixture of indignation and fear on her face.

He shook his head at her stricken expression. "I won't," he muttered with barely concealed contempt.

"Then . . . ," she asked tentatively, "you will respect my wishes?"

He hesitated before he spoke. "I give you my word. I will never force you. More than that, I cannot give."

Distress filled her gaze. "Then, we are at cross purposes, my lord."

A wicked smile softened his otherwise harsh features. "Not necessarily," he said, his tone treacherously soft. "You may change your mind and find you want what pleasure I can afford you. I believe I am not wrong, nor am I egotistical to claim you welcomed me inside you as much as I enjoyed being there."

Hot color burned her cheeks. She lowered her lashes and concentrated on her fingers toying with the satin coverlet. Wordlessly, she nodded her curly head.

A satisfied smile edged his mouth. "I thought as much." He knew it was true. Oddly, he wanted to hear her say it. His little vixen wife had come alive in his arms in a way no other woman had ever done. He was mildly disappointed that she had not verbalized her feelings, for he had little doubt as to his own. Hell, he wanted her right now. But he would wait.

"I don't think we need concern ourselves on this minor point. As an avid student of life, I am certain you will soon be eager to further your"—his lips twitched—"experimentation, shall we say."

Her face brightened. "Then, you will—"

His gaze frosted over. "No," he told her sharply. "I will not."

She folded her arms beneath her bosom. "In that case, my

lord,'' she imparted crisply, ''there will be no experimentation, sensual or otherwise.''

A sharp intensity blazed in his silvery depths. His mouth slashed in a grim, tight line of fury. By God, she had gall. No one dared dictate to him. How dare she draw up such a ridiculous marital accord and expect him to agree to it? It was too much to be borne. He clenched his jaw, grinding his teeth. She was a hellion, come from the netherworld to wreak havoc on his well-ordered life.

Planting his hands on either side of her hips, he leaned perilously close to her. His savage expression battled with her stubborn upturned face.

''You have thrown down the gauntlet, madam. I shall prove your worthy adversary, depend upon it.'' His voice was rough and deeply masculine.

He stood straight and gazed down at her with bleak, cold gray eyes.

''Get dressed,'' he commanded, his manner brisk. ''We must away. We've a social call to pay in Surrey. In this matter, at least,'' he said unkindly as he let his chilling gaze drift over her, ''you may prove useful to me.''

The color drained from her face. His tone was hateful. She could not believe after the intimacies they had shared he had transformed into a cold stranger once more. Disbelieving blue eyes searched his dark features for signs of emotion and came away wanting. Where was the man she had made love to last night? No one would guess he had spent the night locked in the throes of passion, worshiping her body.

''Very well, my lord,'' she mumbled, and pulled back the bed linen to get out of bed. She glanced down and saw the telltale signs of her lost innocence.

Her gaze flickered over the splattering of blood. Her face burned with humiliation. How proud he must feel. His lordship had bedded his wife at long last. His only regret was that she refused to act the prized cow and bear him a son. What a fool she was to believe in his honeyed words and searing kisses. She was a convenient vessel for his heir. Nothing more. Swallowing the painful lump in her throat, she draped the sheet over her body and tramped across the room in desperate need of a bath, though no amount of soap and water would wash the burning memory of their passionate union, or cleanse the deep ache from her breast.

Garbed in her prettiest lavender morning gown and deep purple velvet spencer, Sabrina gazed out the window at the geese preening themselves by the side of the pond in back of Lord Eastmore's estate. Neither she nor Hunter had exchanged a single word the entire way from Kent. He was cool, reserved and darkly handsome in his black great coat and beaver hat. Even in the face of total acrimony, her heart raced in his presence. One look into his stern, forbidding face and she sincerely wished she had not. His mood had not improved any. If possible, the detestable wall of polite coolness that separated them was fortified by smoldering anger.

He stood a tall, towering, dark figure beside the fireplace waiting for Lady Caroline to appear. A look of fierce determination was etched on his handsome face. Sabrina could well imagine the depth of his feelings at this moment. She longed to go to him and ease his worry, but she stifled the urge. No matter how much she wanted to throw her arms around his neck and beg for his forgiveness, she would not. He was behaving like a domineering, uncompromising boor.

Still, she could not endure this wretched coldness between them. Thankfully, Lady Caroline appeared, dispelling the chill in the room.

To Sabrina's dismay, the bedraggled woman blended into

the stark sitting room decorated predominantly in olive tones and puce remarkably well.

For his part, Hunter could scarcely credit how the young carefree girl he had once known could have aged seemingly overnight. Her brown hair lacked luster or shine. Her once bright brown eyes looked flat and devoid of all emotion. Perhaps that was what came of marrying a man old enough to be one's father.

What Caroline said took Hunter completely unawares.

"I knew you would come," she said quietly, folding her hands at her waist. "I knew. I dreaded this moment, but I knew."

Sabrina glanced covertly at her husband as if to say, *I told you so.*

He slanted her a dark look of irritation. "I must speak to you—" he rushed out.

Lady Caroline kept her voice low as she said, "You will want to know about Julia, I expect."

"You must tell me everything you can recall about the man who wronged her brutally," Hunter imparted in a blunt tone that won him an admonishing sideways glance from his bride.

The drawing room door creaked open. Out of the corner of her eye, Sabrina caught sight of the aged, white-haired, bushy-browed Eastmore making his way across the room. She clutched Hunter's navy velvet sleeve and shook her head at him.

Good heavens, she thought. Eastmore was ancient. He looked like a shriveled skeleton. He watched his wife with pale blue, watery eyes. Pinning a smile on her face, Lady Caroline nodded in his direction.

"We have visitors, my lord."

"So, I see," he grunted.

"Perhaps, you would care to offer Lord Lancaster a glass of port in the library?"

The old man snorted. Leaning heavily on his cane, he muttered a beleaguered invitation to Hunter to follow him. Hunter gave a silent nod to Sabrina, granting her license to interrogate Lady Caroline, and took his leave.

Chapter 15

"I had no idea Lord Eastmore was so—so—" Sabrina hesitated, grappling with the appropriate polite phrase to describe such a mismatch.

"Old?" Caroline queried with a slight smile.

Abashed, Sabrina nodded.

"Indeed. We rarely, if ever, make social appearances," Lady Caroline remarked. "Which pleases me as well. I have little desire to visit London."

Sabrina's brows drew together in consternation. Lady Caroline's admission seemed more than melancholy. She was depressed.

Lady Caroline forced a wan smile. "You mustn't feel sorry for me. My future is not that dreary," she explained, making a stab at optimism. "We lead a quiet, undisturbed life in the country which suits my needs perfectly."

Sabrina thought of her own bizarre circumstance and smiled. Apparently, not all marriages were made in heaven.

"Then, I am happy for you. It is seldom possible to find the suitable companion." Something she knew all too well. Was she not the woman who swore, at long last, she would be able to pursue her intellectual inquiries in peace and solitude? Was that not what she wanted? Of course it was, at the time. But now, after spending last night in her husband's arms, her conviction waned.

Lady Caroline lowered her gaze to the floor. "Only consider poor Julia."

Sabrina reached out and squeezed Lady Caroline's hand. "You know the identity of the gallant knight." Her assertion was not a question.

Lady Caroline nodded.

"I suspected as much. Can we not sit and talk awhile?" Sabrina offered, at seeing Lady Caroline's shoulders slump.

When they were seated on the dark brown velvet settee, Lady Caroline clutched her hands tight enough to cut off circulation. "She met him at the beginning of the Season, at Almack's. I became . . . acquainted, through a serious misfortune with a friend of his." She glanced at Sabrina and smiled sadly. "When I have offered an account of what tragedy I experienced, you will have little doubt why I am, today, Lady Eastmore. You must never think of dear Julia in the same light as myself," she hastened to add nervously, wetting her parched lips. "I will always believe, regardless of how it ended, hers was a love match. That he lead her astray, I can easily attest to, but I know he did not misuse her."

Lady Caroline gripped her knees with her hands. "I have never spoken of what happened, to anyone, out of fear that they would betray me to my family or to my husband. Only Julia knew the truth. It was not until after she had been so horribly wronged that I confided the vicious account to her."

Sabrina leaned closer and covered Lady Caroline's white-knuckled hand with her own. "You must not tax yourself. If it is too painful to relate all to me, then I beg you, reconsider. Lord Lancaster need only hear of Julia's circumstance, not yours."

Lady Caroline dabbed the tears that welled at the corners of her sad brown eyes. "I should like to impart the abominable act to . . . someone. It has been difficult for me to keep it locked away."

"In that case," Sabrina said with a sympathetic smile, "I am honored that you have paid me the great compliment of your confidence."

"Julia was seduced by a handsome, suave villain who swept her off her feet with honeyed words and romantic ideals. I was . . . not. He came upon me in the darkened bushes at Vauxhall Park. I could do nothing."

Lady Caroline was too engrossed in her own grief to notice Sabrina's sharp intake of breath.

"I was stunned. Shocked. He overpowered me with little difficulty. I was utterly helpless. The fireworks, you see, the cheers from the crowd, eclipsed my cries for help."

Sabrina cringed in horror. The thought of such a violent, forceful experience made her shudder with revulsion. She could not envision the beautiful expression of love that she had shared with Hunter turned into something heinous and cruel. Unsure of what to say, or how to lend comfort, she waited in silence for Lady Caroline to recover.

Her shoulders shook from the force of her tears. Sabrina hugged Lady Caroline, unable to think of any other way to soothe the poor woman who had suffered brutally at the hands of a man. Pulling away at last, Lady Caroline wiped the tears from her cheeks with the back of her hand.

Drawing a deep breath, she forged ahead. "A-after that, I knew I must marry. Immediately. I was terrified that my family, my father, would discover my hideous secret. So, I married. I married someone who would not know . . . would never learn of what happened to me.'' She lifted her red-rimmed, teary eyes to Sabrina's concerned face. ''You see, Geoffrey and I live separate lives. We scarcely see each other. He has never touched me, or even tried to kiss me, for which I am eternally grateful.'' She squeezed her eyes shut against the devastating memory. ''I could not . . . bear to . . . to be touched by a man ever again.''

''Were you well acquainted with this sinister man who attacked you?''

''Oh, yes,'' she said with staggering venom, ''I knew him. James Shelton. He was handsome, debonair, the picture of charm itself. He pretended to love me. And then . . .'' She bowed her head and emitted a tortured sob.

Sabrina rubbed her back while she wept. ''And his friend? Julia's lover, were you acquainted with him?'' she urged gently.

She shook her head and pulled away. ''She met him at Almack's a few years ago. He quite swept her off her feet.'' She sniffled. ''Of course, they were together in Kent. His estate borders on the Lancaster estate. It was there that he seduced her into his bed,'' she hissed with disgust.

Sabrina hesitated before she spoke. ''This man who attacked you, did he wear a ring that you can recall or perhaps a medallion?''

Lady Caroline blinked. ''A ring?''

''Yes, a gold signet ring.'' Sabrina drew a revolted sigh. ''I fear you would not forget such a piece. It is singularly hideous.''

Lady Caroline hesitated for a moment, struggling to remember. ''I recollect when I first knew him that he had a ring. Yes, I am sure he did. I remember, I inquired about it. He said it was a sign of prowess and laughed it off. He must have removed it. I don't recall seeing it ever again.''

Sabrina hugged Lady Caroline tightly. ''Thank you. I can imagine how difficult that confession must have been for you. I am sure my husband will be eternally grateful for your candor.''

Sabrina desperately needed to speak to Hunter. He must know the identity of poor Julia's seducer and not realize it. Whoever the blackguard was, he was obviously a master at pretense. She was, at least, glad to learn that Julia had not endured a similar hardship.

Anxious to hear what Lady Caroline had confided in his wife, Hunter hurried through their goodbyes and hastily handed her into their carriage.

Throwing herself against his chest, Sabrina clung to him for dear life. "Oh, Hunter, it is the most despicable thing I've ever heard," she cried in disgust.

Gently, he stroked her back, soothing her. "Tell me. What happened?"

"You cannot imagine how that poor woman has suffered at the hands of Lord Shelton," she choked out.

He stiffened. Shelton? Of course, he was the last one. "Yes, my love, I am very much afraid I can."

"He deserves to be locked up in Newgate to rot for what he's done to Lady Caroline and who knows how many others," she said with venom.

His arms tightened around her. "Not . . . Lady Caroline, too?"

Sabrina nodded. "Oh, Hunter, it was horrible."

"And what of Julia?" he asked in a taut, cold undertone that masked his deeper emotions.

She pulled away from him and managed to compose herself, but not without the help of his well-placed handkerchief on her cheeks. "You must understand, she believed herself in love." She sniffled. "Hunter, if it is any consolation, I do believe he must have loved her."

"Huh," he grunted in disgust. "Whatever that means."

Sabrina ignored his disparaging attitude toward love. He was merely upset. He was capable of love, and he did believe in it. He must.

He looked positively grim, however, as he demanded in a harsh tone, "What, precisely, happened to Julia?"

Sabrina swallowed audibly. "She was . . . seduced, but not . . . defiled."

His steel gray eyes ignited with a fiery intensity. "I suspected as much. Who?" he bit out.

"Lady Caroline knew only where they met and when he . . ." She lowered her gaze to her lap.

"Go on."

"They were together in Kent."

"Kent?" he blazed with raw hostility.

Sabrina nodded. "His estate is nearby where your family spent the summer. Evidently, they met a few years back in Bath," she said on a sniffle. "At least, that is where he took her under his spell according to Lady Caroline."

Alarm darkened Hunter's eyes. "Bath, did you say? They met in Bath?" He slammed his fisted hand into the velvet squabs. "By God, what a fool I've been."

"Do you know the identity of the gallant knight?"

He uttered a low growl of rage. "How could I have been such a dense fool?" He thrust his hand through his raven hair. "Of course, Annabelle is blond and she has brown eyes."

Sabrina's brows drew together. "What has that to do with Bath?" she demanded to know, her tone curt with impatience.

"Evidently," he said bitterly, "a great deal more than I realized."

"I am at a complete loss, my lord." Confusion meddled with her mounting impatience to learn the blackguard's true identity. "Dare I hope you have fallen upon a useful clue?" she asked in frustration.

Hunter's jaw set. "Indeed, I have. Wilkinson. George Wilkinson. He destroyed Julia. I am sure of it."

"Are you certain?"

"Oh, yes. I am absolutely certain. I paid a visit to the ignoble

Lord Paine, who is tittering on the brink of Fleet Prison. Whom did I run into outside Paine's town house, but George Wilkinson. I thought it odd at the time that he should inquire after Julia." He sniggered derisively. "I had no idea they were *intimately* acquainted. He was interested in the child as well. He seemed to think it was a boy. That must have appealed to his vanity." Elbows on his knees, Hunter clutched his skull between his hands. "How could I have been so deucedly blind?"

"Hunter," Sabrina said, touching his arm, "do not blame yourself. This recent turn of events is too horrific to imagine."

"He told me they'd met at Bath some time ago. He admitted he was always fond of little Julia. He even had the audacity to mention his estate bordered on the Lancaster grounds. I cannot conceive of such a man."

She shivered. "Nor can I," she said softly.

"There is more. I have hesitated to disclose the sordid details for fear of offending your delicate sensibilities."

She offered him a lopsided smile. "You need have no fear of that, my lord. I've survived the worst, I suspect. Nothing you tell me at this junction would come as a surprise to me."

"This group of nefarious men cavorts around London, preying on innocent young women. I am presently convinced that Wilkinson founded the disgusting male society. I am very much afraid the secret society's charter is to prey on virgins for sport. These men enter various names of debutantes into a book and place wagers. Winner takes all, so to speak."

The color drained from Sabrina's face. "I suspected something untoward, but I never imagined this. What will you do?" Her gaze was heavy with anxiety.

Hunter's hands fisted. "Bring the bastard to justice. We head for London with all possible haste."

Sabrina drew in a shocked breath. "London?"

"I've not a moment to lose."

She blinked at him, a look of complete surprise etched on her face. "B-but what of Annabelle?" she stammered, dismayed. "I never said goodbye."

He smiled slightly at her forlorn expression. This, from the woman who swore she would not bear him a child. He reached out his hand and rubbed his knuckles along her cheek. "I am sorry, my dear," he said, his voice thick with emotion. "I know this must be hard for you to understand. I've waited too long and wasted too much time already. I must confront the blackguard with the truth."

A compassionate smile touched her lips. "I understand how you must feel. To think," she murmured, feeling utterly desolate. "Julia loved him. Or thought she did. She gave herself to him. Willingly."

A resentful iciness cloaked his dark features. "He played on her emotions, you can be sure," he imparted coldly.

"Seduction is not a crime, Hunter," Sabrina reminded him softly, her thoughts suddenly turning to her own marriage. Had Hunter played on her emotions? Without a doubt, her husband was an expert at seduction. Her brow creased with pain. When he learned of her need to kindle a relationship rather than give in to his demands to bear him a son, he had been ruthlessly unkind. Did he harbor no affections for her, then? Was she merely a means to an end?

He turned the full force of his ominous gaze upon her. "Rape is," he countered fiercely.

Confronted with the reality of Lady Caroline's predicament, Sabrina mentally chastised herself for wallowing in self-pity.

"Yes," she said, fighting the revulsion that welled up inside. "It is. But, it will be terribly difficult to prove. How will you manage it?"

"Leave it to me. I will see that they pay. Every last one of them. Particularly, Wilkinson. Julia could not have been his only victim, of that I've little doubt. She fared only slightly better than the rest.''

''Oh, Hunter,'' Sabrina cried, distressed, ''it makes me shudder to think of Jane Greenly viciously murdered by one of these horrid men, Julia seduced by a conniving scoundrel, and now, Lady Caroline brutally—''

He crushed her to him. Covering her mouth with his own, he kissed her deeply, his passion banishing all worry from her mind.

Expelling a huge yawn, Sabrina pulled the soft cotton night-gown over her head and tied the pink satin bow at the neck. She was glad, she admitted as she wrestled with her unruly head of hair hoping to gain some semblance of order, to be back in London. After the arduous journey from Surrey and Lady Caroline's disturbing news, Sabrina was eager to lose herself in some much needed peaceful slumber. Satisfied that nothing short of a pair of scissors could bring her mane to heel, she gave up the fight and set the brush down on the dressing table.

''You look ready for bed,'' a deep, husky voice remarked from behind.

Sabrina looked up from where she sat to find her husband lounging in the doorway, his muscular shoulder propped against the doorjamb. Her stomach flip-flopped. His dark, smoldering gaze held a sensual gleam. She quivered.

He shoved away from the doorjamb and strolled toward her. ''Aren't you going to invite me in?'' he drawled in a silky tone.

Her back straightened. ''I was about to go to bed.''

His palm cupped her cheek in a soft caress. He leaned down and kissed her lips. ''Don't let me stop you,'' he murmured against her mouth. Hot color scalded her cheeks. He smiled.

"You are more beautiful every time I look at you," he whispered in a velvet caress.

Riveted to her seat, she stared into his mesmerizing silvery gaze of passion. Slowly he leaned down. His fingers caught the ribbon of her gown.

"I want to commit every inch of your soft, beautiful body to memory," he mumbled against her mouth as he tugged at the bow. "So I will never forget this moment." He covered her lips in a lingering, gentle kiss.

Her hand stilled his movements. "Hunter," she managed to say breathlessly, "it is late." Quickly getting to her feet, she slipped past him. "I am frightfully tired. You—you must be exhausted."

A low chuckle rumbled in his bare chest. He walked toward her, a faint look of amusement on is handsome face. She backed away from the encroaching male heat.

He paused and leaned one arm against the bedpost. His hooded gaze watched her as she ran her fingers through her hair nervously.

"Come here," he urged with a smile that fairly singed her.

She shook her head. Chuckling softly, he closed the distance between them. Her pulse did not fail to observe his brocade robe was parted, revealing a tantalizing portion of his broad chest and thick black hair. Her heart skipped a beat. She cursed herself for trembling. She quickly dropped her gaze. "You're breaking your word."

"No," he said, his voice achingly soft, and pulled her into his arms. "I am not." His mouth covered hers in a ravishing kiss. She felt his intense hunger, the desire to possess her completely, and she braced her arms against his chest. He tightened his hold on her, pressing her even closer against the hard length of him. His mouth moved to kiss her cheek, her face and throat.

"*Sabrina,*" he whispered against her skin, "you taste so

damned good, like honeyed nectar. And you smell delicious. I could devour you whole.''

She closed her eyes. A thousand delicious sensations rushed through her. She was weakening by the moment. She tried to lean away from him, but he crushed her small frame against him. "You are trying to seduce me," she moaned against his lips.

Smiling down at her, he arched a sooty brow. "Is that what I am doing?" he murmured softly as his mouth descended to kiss hers again.

She turned her face. His burning lips kissed her neck. This was not going according to plan. She was perilously close to giving in to him. His teeth nibbled at her earlobe, sending delicious shivers down her back.

She gulped. "Hunter . . . you promised."

He lifted his head. The firelight flickered on the ceiling, casting shadows across the room, making it difficult for her to see the expression in his eyes. His mouth lingered over hers. "So I did," he concurred thickly and pressed a kiss to the side of her mouth.

"A man's honor is his word," she croaked.

He chuckled softly. "I never said anything about kissing you." His breath was warm against her neck. He trailed his tongue along her collarbone and behind her ear. "Or touching you," he murmured, cupping her full breast in his palm. He teased the rosy tip into a hard pebble of desire.

His hands seemed to have a mind of their own. Touching her, teasing her, urging her body to respond. She felt the warmth of his breath on her neck and tingled down to her toes.

She turned her head to find his lips. "No . . . you . . . did . . . not," she managed between searing kisses. "But I know," she panted against his mouth, "where this will lead—"

He covered her moist, softly parted mouth with his own. "It

will lead where you want it to lead," he said, his voice ragged with desire.

He kissed her temple. His breath tickled her cheek. Gulping, she whimpered, "I don't think this is such a good idea."

"No? I think it is," he growled, his mouth capturing hers once more.

She could feel her treacherous body slipping. Another searing kiss and she knew she would be unable to resist his ardent passion. She suppressed the urge to wrap her arms around him and pull his hard, sinewy body closer.

Gracious, she was tingling all over. Oh, dear, she admitted with a soft moan, she was helpless to resist him.

"You are wonderfully soft and yet hard," he murmured, burying his face against her breasts. He kissed her bare skin above the dangling satin ribbon and slowly slid her nightgown off her shoulders. It dropped to the floor, foaming like a billowing cloud at her feet. His scorching gaze raked over her naked body. He cupped her soft mounds of creamy flesh in his hands and traced the rosy peaks with his thumbs. Leaning down, he took one pink jewel into his mouth.

Succumbing to the fire of his touch, she arched her back, filling his mouth with her full ripe breast.

"Oh, Hunter," she whispered on a cry of pleasure burgeoning deep inside her.

As his hand caressed the flat of her stomach, sending tiny little shivers all through her, she writhed against him. When his hand moved lower, she opened her eyes to look at him.

"I've a feeling we are . . . *ooh,*" she breathed as his finger found her sensitive core. "Playing with . . . fire. We—" She bit her lip to fight against the tumult of pleasure his rhythmic strokes evoked. "Should . . . not," she uttered breathlessly. His finger had eased deeper into her slick wet passage. His treacherous thumb teased the soft, sensitive nub of flesh.

"Ah, but we should, my beauty . . . and we shall," he vowed

with fierce determination as his mouth covered hers. Moaning into his mouth, she gave herself up to his savage kiss.

He fell to his knees before her.

"What are you doing?" she whimpered, feeling hot, breathless and weak.

He kissed her stomach, her abdomen, her hips. "Kissing you," he told her huskily.

"Yes . . . well . . ."

He kissed her searing flesh and ran his tongue over her sensitive skin, causing her stomach muscles to contract.

"I don't think . . . that is to say . . . I should very much like it if you . . ." Her lashes fluttered shut. As he parted her dewy petals with his fingers and his tongue sampled her sweet nectar, a moan of pleasure emanated from her throat. "Oh, . . . Hunter," she cried, clutching at his shoulders. She rocked her hips, desperate to reach the peak of ecstasy she knew lay just beyond this sweet heaven.

Swept away by burning desire, she was vaguely aware when two strong arms went around her and dragged her beneath him on the floor. She opened her mouth to speak, but he deprived her of the power of speech. His mouth came down on hers in a hard, passionate kiss that stole her breath and her reason.

She put her hands against his chest. "Hunter . . . ," she panted.

He leaned over and took her hand in his. He kissed her palm and then her wrist. He smiled down at her and slid her reluctant hands around his neck. His gray eyes shone with unquenchable desire. "Kiss me, Sabrina. I need to feel your body close to mine."

She ached for his possession. At his passionate declaration her body shivered. He leaned forward to sample her enticing mouth.

"*Hunter oh Hunter,*" she moaned softly against his kiss.

"I know, little one," he murmured thickly, burying his face

in her neck. "I am on fire as well. Do you want me to stop touching you?" he asked, kissing her temple, her cheek, the side of her mouth.

Uttering a moan of bittersweet surrender, she felt desire swell within her at the touch of his lips. She melted in his arms like quicksilver, kissing him until she felt dizzy and breathless with anticipation.

When she made no intelligible reply, Hunter rolled onto his side and drew her against him.

"I want you. I need you," he admitted on a groan. "Tonight, I need to know you need me."

Her eyes fluttered open, and she gazed into his steel, languid orbs.

"Make love to me, *please.*"

"Oh, Hunter," she whispered, her eyes glistening with unshed tears of joy.

He lifted her thigh over his hip, angling her body to receive him. "You have only to say the word and I'll stop," he told her huskily, his hips moving against hers. "But *please* . . . God," he gasped, straining against the tumultuous storm of passion raging inside him, "don't say no."

She caressed his passion-flushed cheek with her palm. "How could I? Please don't stop . . . don't ever stop loving me. Not ever." As the two became one, her lips parted in a soft cry of pure exultation.

He cast a tumultuous smile down at her. "No regrets?" he asked softly, his voice ragged with passion. "Please, Sabrina, say you want me as much as I need you," he muttered thickly.

She placed her hand on his cheek. "I could never regret anything we do together. I want to be with you, Hunter. I need you. Desperately. More than you know." She pulled his head down to hers. *"Love me,"* she whispered against his mouth. "Oh, *please, please* love me." She covered his mouth with hers, kissing him with all the emotion she had pent up inside.

Strong and sure, his arms tightened around her. He drove into her, loving her with deep, hard strokes that took them both to nirvana.

His lovemaking was passionate beyond all her expectations. She cried out his name on a blissful sigh of completion. As he strained against her, a heart-wrenching groan of surrender was torn from his throat, and his seed poured into her. Then, slowly, ever so slowly, the world came back into focus.

Throwing himself onto his back, he tried to catch his breath. He was oddly shaken by the experience of making love to his wife. He told himself it was the idea of his seed taking root in her womb that pleased him excessively. Despite her childish protestations, he hoped they had made a baby together. He wanted that bond. He longed to see her body swell with the fruit of his loins. She need not fear, he would see to it that she received the finest care. No harm would come to her.

So engrossed in his own thoughts was he that he failed to notice he had made love to his wife on the cold, hard floor.

"Good Lord, how did we end up here?" he mumbled, and pressed a kiss to her temple before scooping her up into his arms and carrying her to the soft, inviting featherbed. Laying her down, he pulled the covers around her. He smiled a bit sheepishly. He cupped her cheek with his palm.

"I am sorry," he said, his dark gray orbs brimming with tenderness, "that must have been uncomfortable for you."

A mantle of red spread over her cheeks. "I didn't notice," came her shy admission.

He got into bed beside her and leaned over her to kiss her tenderly on the mouth, slowly savoring her sweetness. "Are you tired?" he asked, brushing her tangled hair back from her face.

She nodded and turned her face away. "Yes," she said on a hard swallow. Wiggling away from him, she curled into a ball on the far side of the bed. "Good night, Hunter."

His brow furrowed. "Sabrina?" He placed his hand on her slender bare shoulder. "What is it? What is wrong?"

She shook her head, but he guessed from the tremor of her slight body she was crying.

He leaned over her. "Never say I hurt you?"

A cry of abject misery escaped her throat. She bawled in earnest. He pulled her onto her back. Gazing down at her, he looked darkly handsome and deeply worried. "Did I?" he insisted, his brow creased with worry.

"It is not that," she snapped, avoiding his penetrating stare.

"Then, what?" he coaxed, brushing the tears from her cheeks. "Tell me," he urged thickly. "Why are you crying?"

"I think . . . I'm falling in love with you," she replied on a heart-wrenching sob, turning away once again.

He went dead still. In love? With him? He almost said, "Don't," but bit back the words. This he had not anticipated. He raked his hand through his hair. No one had ever loved him. Ever. Struck dumb, he rubbed her back while she wept.

"This startling revelation makes you cry?" he asked with levity he did not feel.

She nodded and gushed fresh tears.

"Why?" he asked, his own voice on the verge of cracking.

"B-because," she sobbed. "You're a heartless rake who will never harbor real emotions for any one person, least of all me."

Choosing to ignore her assassination of his character, he cupped her cheek with his hand and lifted her tear-stained face to his. "Why least of all you?" he asked in a gentle, soothing tone.

She blinked up at him and sniffled. "Well . . . I am me. And you are—you are . . . *you.*"

He bit back the urge to laugh. "Yes. We are. But what does that have to do with anything?"

"You could never come to love me."

"And why is that?" he asked, gently brushing her hair back from her blotchy face.

"I am so horribly uncouth, awkward and ugly," she spat with disgust.

His brow darkened. "You are not ugly, awkward or uncouth," he countered sharply. He framed her face between his hands. "My God," he breathed, his gaze searching her unhappy face, "you are the most precious, rare creature I have ever beheld. Beauty like yours is not merely superficial; it is inside you, in your heart" he told her, his voice softer now, compelling, "And your beautiful, wonderful soul. That is what I cherish about you the most. Your uniqueness." Tears cascaded down her cheeks. He kissed them away. "I've never met a woman like you," he murmured gently. "And I've never felt more fortunate in my life to claim you as my own."

"Oh, Hunter," she cried, throwing herself against his chest, "I do love you. More than I ever wanted to. I cannot help myself."

He chuckled softy and hugged her. "Go to sleep, Sabrina," he commanded, his voice oddly low and uneven. He found himself stifling the peculiar urge to clear his throat.

She pressed a small kiss to his chest and laid her cheek against his beating heart. "Thank you."

"What for?" he asked, rubbing the small of her back with his palm.

"For saying all those wonderful things. I know you do not love me, but I am thankful for your kindness toward me." Feeling warm and cozy inside, she slept.

Hunter remained awake, contemplating the soft bundle lying in his arms. He had never even come close to being snared by cupid's arrow. Oh, he had admired their beauty and applauded their talents between the sheets, but fall in love with a woman? Never. His emotions had never been roused. Until. . . .

He glanced down at the naked woman asleep in his arms.

He smiled at the top of her untamed, curly head burrowed against his chest. She looked like a little elf. This small slip of a girl was *his* wife. She was the most precious thing in his life, too, he reluctantly admitted. No one had ever issued him a pledge of love and meant it. He was not inclined to believe this one either. It was simply the way she responded to passion. She mistakenly connoted mindless, overwhelming desire with love. He knew better.

Yet, he acknowledged as she stirred, shifting her small weight onto a more comfortable spot on his chest, her artless declaration made his heart swell with emotion he thought long dead. He drew a deep breath.

Lord, he wasn't actually falling for the oldest ploy known to man, or it seemed woman, was he? No. Of course not. Let her think she was in love with him if it made her happy. The concept was not entirely unappealing to him either, he realized with a jolt. In fact, he liked the idea very well, indeed.

Chapter 16

The following morning Sabrina descended the stairs to find her husband speaking to a rather dingy-looking man in the marbled foyer. Hunter glanced up and caught sight of her. His lazy, hooded gaze moved over her pink silk gown with blatant sexual appraisal that told her he found her appearance more than merely pleasing. A surge of happiness rushed over her.

His sultry gray gaze locked with hers. Her heart fluttered. His lips curled into a slow, sensual smile. And she knew he was recalling their passionate night of lovemaking. Color washed over her cheeks. She gave him a small, shy smile. His grin broadened.

"Ah, my dear, you are awake. Come," he said, extending his hand to her. "I want you to meet our Runner, Mr. Crawford. He's been helping us in our search for the villainous group. I sent him word last night that we had returned. He has some developments to relate."

Our Runner? Sabrina's heart soared. Her husband accepted

her as his equal. She was deeply touched that he was willing to share his most private concerns with her. He must have some feelings for her. At the very least, he felt gratitude. Wasn't gratitude as good a place to start as any?

The Runner looked slightly taken aback.

Smiling at the scruffy man's reaction, Hunter drew his wife to his side. Gazing down at her, warm admiration shining in his eyes, he told Mr. Crawford, "My wife has been an immeasurable help to me. It was she who discovered Hobson's involvement. I would never have considered questioning Lady Caroline were it not for my clever resourceful bride." He raised her hand to his lips for a kiss. Sabrina beamed up at him, her heart in her eyes.

Expelling an impatient breath, Mr. Crawford cleared his throat. "Milord, should we not get down to business?"

"Hmm?" Hunter murmured, lost in his wife's eyes. "Yes, by all means." His arm went around Sabrina's waist. Drawing her against his side, he clasped her hand in his own and escorted her to the library.

The Runner rolled his eyes heavenward and trailed behind the two lovebirds with their heads bent together.

"I done some pokin' 'bout," Mr. Crawford remarked when all three were comfortably seated in the library. "The Greenly chit was raped 'fore she died. What a mess he made o' her," he muttered in disgust. "She must 'ave fought 'im pretty 'ard. Caw, what a sight, poor lass. The way we figure it, he must 'ave strangled her while he was"—he darted a glance at Lady Lancaster and cleared his throat—"durin' the attack. He tossed her body in the river when he was through usin' her."

Hunter's glance slid across the room to his wife. Sitting by the sun-streaked window, she looked several shades paler than usual, but she offered him a wan smile. He dragged his gaze from her ghostly complexion and addressed the Runner, "Who did it?"

" 'Tweren't Hobson, he's got an alibi. Far as I can tell, Hobson ain't that deeply involved anyway. Must 'ave been Everly who done it."

"He, I take it, is nowhere to be found?"

Crawford flashed a toothless grin. "Right y'are, milord. Last we 'eard, he'd left for India."

Hunter uttered a disgusted snicker. "How convenient. What else have you to report?"

"Paine is dead."

Hunter sat forward. "What?" His face darkened. "When?"

Mr. Crawford scratched his balding head. "Near as we can tell, 'twas roughly a fortnight ago. You must 'ave been the last one to see 'im alive."

"Not quite the last. George Wilkinson arrived as I was leaving."

The Runner cocked a bushy brow. "Aye, is that a fact? Well then, I guess little Georgie is guilty o' murder."

"How did Paine die?"

" 'Anged 'imself."

Hunter shook his head. "I doubt Paine's death was a suicide. He was terrified to name the blackguard who founded the club. If my suspicions are correct, Wilkinson's behind Paine's death and the nefarious club."

"I agree." The Runner twisted his lips. " 'Tis 'ard to prove, milord."

"Mmm, quite," Hunter muttered pensively. "I assume all this came to light whilst I was in the country?"

"Aye, that it did. One o' them nobs came by t' see what Paine had t' sell. Found 'im swingin' from a rope. Been dead for days. Right stiff 'e was. He didna smell too pretty, I can tell you," the Runner said with a laugh. "He was a right lovely shade o'—"

"E-excuse me," Sabrina interjected, and fled the room, her hand clenched to her mouth.

Hunter got to his feet. Issuing a gruff apology, he fled the room in search of his pallid wife.

A few minutes later, Hunter found her. She was in the kitchen leaning over the scullery bucket. Mary, the cook, was pressing a cool cloth to his wife's neck.

He gave Mary a silent nod to leave them. "I'll look after her now."

He crouched down on his haunches beside his wife. Turning her pale face to his, he asked, "Not feeling quite the thing, are you?"

She nodded and wiped her dewy brow with the back of her hand. "I'm fine. It's just ... I—I knew Jane." Her lashes fluttered shut. "The way she died ... it is too gruesome." She emitted an abhorrent groan. "And to hear about that dead man—"

"Forgive me, I should not have allowed you to be present for the discussion." His voice was laden with self-recrimination. Helping her to stand, he drew her against him and held her close. "I'm sorry," he murmured, kissing the top of her curly head. "Crawford has been in the business for years. He's not accustomed to frail females," he teased her.

"I am not frail," she countered, slamming a playful fist against his chest. "Really, I am not. At least, not ordinarily."

"I think it is safe to say that descriptions of dead bodies and rape victims is something entirely new to you and not at all pleasant."

She leaned her head back to look at him. "But I want to be a part of it, Hunter. I want to help you find these vile men."

He smiled and framed her ashen face with his hands. "In future, madam, you may serve me best by not swooning."

She pulled a frown. "I was sick, my lord. I do not faint."

He grinned. "I am relieved beyond measure to hear it," he said lightly. "I despise woman who are prone to vapors and apoplexy." His smile faded. "Perhaps it would be best," he said, smoothing her hair back from her forehead, "if you retired above stairs until the interview is over. I am afraid these recent events are a bit grizzly."

"No." She shook her head. "I am all right now. I promise not to turn missish again."

He gazed at her with a skeptical eye. "You are sure you want to continue?"

"I must," she said with grave sincerity, "if I am to be of any help to you."

He shook his head at her. "You are a wonder." His mouth covered hers, pressing a quick, hard, covetous kiss to her lips. Taking her hand in his, he lead her back to the library.

Mr. Crawford shifted from foot to foot. "Beggin' yer pardon, milady," he said sheepishly, "I ain't used t' women about the place."

Sabrina offered him a kind smile. "Think nothing of it. I assure you, I am not by nature squeamish. Pray, continue," she advised, resuming her perch on the chair by the window.

He turned his attention to Hunter. "Like I were sayin', 'ard to prove Wilkinson's involvement in all o' this."

"I don't need any more proof," Hunter muttered with contempt. "I am satisfied the blackguard fathered Annabelle and is guilty of destroying the lives of God only knows how many other innocent young women."

"Aye. But what are ye plannin' to do 'bout it?"

"Catch the bastard and make him pay."

"But how?"

To Hunter's complete amazement, his diminutive wife sat forward and cleared her throat.

"As to that, I have given the situation a considerable amount of thought. I have a suggestion to make," she announced boldly. "I wonder, Mr. Crawford, if you would be good enough to give your honest appraisal of my scheme?"

The Runner looked slightly less stunned than his lordship. "I'll do me best, milady."

"I recommend we set a trap for this horrid man Wilkinson."

Hunter's eyes narrowed suspiciously. "What kind of trap?"

"An amorous engagement, similar to the previous circumstances where he lured his victims. Only on this occasion, Mr. Crawford, with your aid, of course, my lord, will catch the villainous cad."

"In the act, so to speak," Hunter supplied, his face set in stone.

"Precisely," she said, smiling with pride.

Hunter crossed his arms over his chest. "And who, pray, will play the part of his willing victim?" he asked, his tone brusque.

She blinked at him. "Why, me, of course. After all, we are fairly certain he founded the vile club that preys on defenseless, young innocents. Poor Jane Greenly attended Almack's every Wednesday. Given that Lady Caroline met Shelton at Almack's and she is certain that is where Julia passed time with her very ungallant knight, we know, or can safely assume, Almack's is where these dastardly men approach their victims. Who better to play the part of a young, defenseless innocent than myself?"

Uttering a half-bitten oath, Hunter vaulted to his feet. "The devil you will!" he growled. "Have you taken complete leave of your senses?"

"Have you a better idea?" she challenged.

His dark, stormy gaze pinioned her to her seat. "These men are killers," he said, his tone grave. "I don't intend to risk losing you luring that bastard into a trap, madam," he ground out.

"She may 'ave somethin' there, milord," Crawford remarked. "It's an idea."

"My wife," Hunter gritted fiercely, "will not, I repeat not, be bait for a man who seduces, rapes and ruins women on a whim. For God's sake, he founded the damned club where murderers and rapists figure largely as ranking members."

The Runner rubbed his razor-stubbled chin. "Y' right o'course. Still, in all, I must admit, 'tis one way to catch 'im."

"Fine," he fired back, wearing a path in the plush Aubusson carpet. "We'll use somebody else."

Mr. Crawford etched a pensive frown. "I doubt you'll find another woman brave enough—"

Hunter gave the Runner a quelling glance. "Or foolish enough," he intoned with meaning. "You, madam," he growled at Sabrina, "will do as you are told, or be brought to heel."

Sabrina pulled a face.

He glared at her with angry eyes.

Folding her arms over her chest, she looked away from him and arched her chin like a petulant child.

Swallowing audibly, Mr. Crawford tugged at his collar and mumbled, "I 'spect y'right, milord. 'Tis too dangerous."

"No," Sabrina countered with energy, "it is not. Hunter," she pleaded, getting to her feet, "please try to be reasonable."

Savage fury lit his silvery gaze. He was closer than he ever dreamt he would be to paddling his wife on her backside. He could not believe she had proposed such a perilous scheme. It was preposterous.

"You know it is the only way to lure him. He's onto you. For heaven's sake," she cried, throwing her arms in the air, "you sent a Runner to investigate his private club. He doesn't know me, or what I look like. You'll be a mere stone's throw away the entire time. What can he possibly do?"

"No," he snapped at her. "It is out of the question. It is too dangerous."

She uttered a derisive grunt of dissent. "It is not."

Stormy, slate gray eyes threatened to impale her. "I forbid you to do this."

She gawked at him. "Forbid me?" she echoed with a look of incredulity on her face.

"Yes," he snarled. "Forbid you."

She expelled an annoyed sigh. "You are just being stubborn. You know it is the only way to garner a confession from him."

"I don't need a confession," he spat venomously.

"What is it you are after? If not the truth, then what?"

Wordlessly, he stared down at her, tall, darkly handsome and very angry.

"Do you not want justice? After all this time, why are you refusing to do the one thing that will result in his capture?"

His hand slid around her neck. He pulled her roughly to him. Dark eyes glittering with raw emotion searched her face. "I cannot bear the thought of losing you," he admitted, his voice gruff with emotion.

Her heart swelled in her chest. Smiling up at him, she caressed his cheek with her palm. "In that case, you never will."

"Then, you agree to abandon this foolhardy plan?" he asked, relief evident on his features.

"If you truly believe it is too dangerous," she said on a sigh, "I've little choice in the matter."

His eyes narrowed on her face. "Why are you willing to admit defeat so quickly?"

She traced the hard line of his jaw with her forefinger. "I know when I am bested, my lord," she said softly.

"Just like that?" he asked, eyeing her skeptically. "You are relinquishing the argument? No attempts at persuasion? No wheedling for ground?"

She shook her head and locked her arms around his neck.

"When faced with an insurmountable foe, the only solution is to bow out gracefully, do you not agree?"

He arched a sooty brow. "An insurmountable foe?" A sensual gleam lit his silvery eyes. His hands slipped around her waist, drawing her snugly against him. "Is that what I am?" he asked her huskily.

Her heart tripped over itself. "I don't want you to be," she said softly. "Please, Hunter, let's not argue."

His mouth twitched. "I must confess," he said with a roguish grin, "there are other things I would much rather do with you."

Two blotches of red stained her cheeks. "I've the perfect solution to the problem," she said, smoothing her palms over his well-made chest. "If you are all that concerned for my welfare, I'll stay with Amanda until this horrible mess is cleared up and Wilkinson is made to pay for his heinous crimes."

Hunter heaved an enormous sigh. "If, as you say, he knows I am onto him, it might take some time to track him down. I would feel better knowing you were in safe keeping until I find the villain. Besides," he said with a crooked grin, "if I know the two of you, you'll need time to catch up on the latest *on-dits.*"

She blinked up at him. "I do not know about that, my lord. You were the person we liked to speak of the most."

He threw back his raven head and laughed. "You flatter me, madam." Kissing his adorable wife on the nose, he remarked in a dry tone, "Pray, do not plan any more weddings behind my back."

She scowled up at him. "*I* never did."

He leaned back and regarded her with a critical eye. "I am still not sure you are being entirely honest. But we've a criminal to apprehend, have we not, Mr. Crawford?" he asked, glancing over his shoulder at the red-faced man lurking in the corner.

The Runner cleared his throat. "Aye, milord," he replied

with a lopsided grin. "I was wonderin' when y' might get down t' business."

"Immediately. I intend to pay George Wilkinson a visit he'll not soon forget. Will you accompany me?"

"Aye, that I will. 'Twill be a pleasure to make that bas— er''—abashed, he glanced at Sabrina—"bloke's acquaintance."

Sabrina slipped away from her husband's grasp. "I'll leave you two men to your planning."

The following morning Sabrina disembarked from the Lancaster carriage to find her sister waiting for her at the door to Morely House with open arms.

"It is good to see you," she said, giving Sabrina a tight squeeze. "I was dreadfully worried when I did not hear from you. You cannot imagine the horrors I have suffered, not knowing how you have fared this last month. You must tell me how you are finding marriage," she said, linking her arm through her sister's. "He has not mistreated you, has he?"

Sabrina opened her mouth to reply, but her sister blustered excitedly, "No. Of course he has not. You look ravishing, dearest. Marriage clearly agrees with you. I must confess," she intoned gravely as the two walked toward the blue salon, "Hunter looked positively vexed on his wedding day, poor man. I could have strangled Ian for divulging my little secret. Oh, but tell me, dearest," she said, taking her sister's hands in her own, "you are not terribly upset with me for playing cupid, are you?"

Sabrina expelled a long breath. Retrieving her hands from her sister's grasp, she removed her blue beret with plumes. That discovery seemed like a lifetime ago. So much had transpired since then. She had been ready to commit murder when she had realized what havoc her foolish, romantically inclined sister had wreaked. Since then, her mood had mellowed. She was not sorry she had been forced to marry Hunter. Her only wish was that he cared for her, if only just a little.

Smiling slightly at her sister's hopeful expression, she shook her head. "No," she said as her fingers undid the tassels and cords of her pale blue redingote.

"I am in love with him. Though I doubt he shares my feelings," she said a little wistfully.

Amanda sank down on the settee and drew her sister down beside her. "You must give him time. Men need to adjust to married life. I daresay Ian was not in love with me at first. It took a full six months before he expressed any emotion at all. And then, he gushed like a schoolboy."

Sabrina gave Amanda a rueful look. "Amanda, he asked for your hand the morning after you met."

"That does not signify," she said with a dismissive wave of her hand. "He only did so because he thought I came from good stock and would bear him sons. He used those exact words the day he offered for me."

Sabrina looked slightly taken aback. "You cannot be serious? Why did you never tell me?"

Amanda shrugged. "He was by far the most eligible bachelor of the Season. I was madly in love with him. And I knew, with time, I could bring him around to my way of thinking."

"Well," Sabrina replied sarcastically, "he was right on that score. You have given him two healthy sons in as many years. He can find no reason to be unhappy with you." *Unlike Hunter,* she added silently.

"Mmm. But more importantly," Amanda said, a dreamy smile gracing her features, "he has given me his heart and a promise of eternal devotion."

Getting to her feet, Sabrina wandered over to the window. "I sincerely doubt I shall ever hear those words from Hunter."

She gazed out the window at the stylish barouches rolling down the cobblestone street.

"You will," came Amanda's assurance from behind. "I am certain of it. Else," she teased, "I should never have flung my arrow."

Sabrina cast a doleful smile over her shoulder. "How can you be so sure?"

Amanda blinked in surprise. "How can you doubt it?"

Sabrina turned away. *Easily,* she thought, *very easily, indeed.* Only last night, after he had made passionate love to her for the second time, she had lain in his arms and told him how deep her devotion went. He had remained silent. She was deeply hurt.

Her heart felt like lead in her chest. She was a lovesick fool. Obviously, his feelings were not involved. Nor would they ever be. She had long since given up on any possibility of refusing him her bed. For all she knew, she was already with child.

Like a fool, she had fallen prey to his expert charm and roving hands. She was, it seemed, helplessly in love with her husband—while he found nothing to recommend his wife aside from a fleeting moment's pleasure between the sheets. As far as he was concerned, she was simply a body in which to pleasure himself, an easily replaced vehicle for an heir.

But there was a way to win her husband's favor. She need only give him what he wanted most. She bit her lower lip. How difficult could it be? After all, it wasn't as if she would be doing something that was never done before; countless women did it every day. Why should she be afraid? She would be alone. She would make certain of that, in case anything untoward should occur.

She etched a bright smile and turned to face her sister. "Let's go to Almack's tonight."

Amanda looked dazed and confused. "But you detest Almack's," she burst out.

"Detest is far too strong a word," Sabrina countered. "Now that I am married, my attitude toward such banal outings has changed."

"Quite frankly, I do not know if I could convince Ian to escort us. He complained bitterly the last time I dragged him."

Sabrina flashed a conspiratorial smirk. "Come now, Amanda, I am certain there is precious little you could not persuade dear Ian to do."

Amanda gave her sister a sly grin. "I collect you are right. I shall wear my lavender silk," she said, springing to her feet. "Now, where did I put that voucher?" she asked, flying from the room in search of the coveted social prize.

Chapter 17

"I still think you should have worn a more suitable gown, Sabrina," Amanda remarked, eyeing her sister's drab white dress with disapproval. "You are Lady Lancaster now. Although, I daresay," she lamented with sarcasm, "anyone looking at you would think it. Why did you not give those plain, old dresses to Fanny?"

"I hadn't thought of it," came Sabrina's noncommittal reply. A slow smile crept across her face. Everything was working out splendidly. If Amanda thought Sabrina looked like a novice, then Wilkinson was bound to agree. With a little luck, *he* would approach *her,* saving her a great deal of angst, for she had never actually seen him. All she knew was that he was blond and brown-eyed. She could not very well approach every tall, fair-haired gentleman on the premises in the hope of stumbling onto the culprit.

The carriage wheels ground to a halt before the large Assembly Hall on King Street. Ian shifted on the leather seat. "I do hope Countess Lieven refrains from monopolizing all of our time this evening,'' he grumbled to his wife. ''I was bored stiff the last time you forced me to suffer through one of these blasted evenings. Hunter Lancaster would not be caught dead at Almack's. I'm relegated to escorting the two of you.''

''Yes, dear,'' Amanda replied, every inch the dutiful wife.

He glanced out the carriage window and groaned. ''Good Lord! What an abominable crush.''

Half an hour later, Sabrina entered the huge spare room that passed for a ballroom. A surge of excitement rushed over her. The thrill of the unknown never failed to entice her. Tonight was no exception. How pleased Hunter was going to be when she presented him with the villain.

Craning her neck, she let her gaze survey the sea of pastel dresses and swarming bachelors. She tried to no avail to spy any and all tall, slender, blond men with an evil look in their eye. Mr. Crawford surely must have received her note by now. She chewed nervously on her lower lip. The difficulty was going to be how to find Wilkinson. The rest of the details Bow Street could take care of.

She stood on her tiptoes and peered over the tops of the ladies' heads. To say the room was crowded would be an understatement. Ian was correct. It was a mob scene. This would never do.

''What *are* you looking for?'' Amanda demanded, her voice curt with reprimand.

Sinking down on her heels, Sabrina replied lamely, ''I—I thought I saw someone I knew.''

''It is generally best to wait to acknowledge their address,'' Amanda muttered in a fierce under breath.

''You are quite right,'' Sabrina mumbled. She caught her lower lip between her teeth. Oh, dear. This was more difficult than she originally envisioned. She could ill afford to appear obvious. Time, however, was of the essence. If tonight's scheme was going to be a success, she had to garner an introduction to Wilkinson and hope he found her worthy of his particular brand of charm.

It was not strictly necessary to dance the quadrille, or even elicit a waltz from the miscreant. She could just as easily win an introduction standing on the sidelines once she caught sight of him—if she ever caught sight of him. Oh, crumbs! It could take all night, provided he was actually in attendance *and* he found her worthy of his time.

On the other hand, she thought as she observed poor Ian cannoning his way through the throng of bodies with two cups of tepid tea in each hand, it might serve just as well to be formally introduced.

"I wonder," she ventured to ask, after sampling the lukewarm libation Ian offered her, "if you might do me the favor of pointing out a certain gentleman of whom Hunter has spoken?"

"If I am able," Ian allowed.

"Who is it you wish to meet?" Amanda asked, cringing at the tasteless contents of her cup.

"George Wilkinson," Sabrina remarked beneath lowered lashes. "I do believe his property borders my husband's estate in Kent."

Amanda's ears perked up. "Is Hunter planning a visit to Kent?" she asked, nearly bursting with excitement. "A trip to the seaside would be divine this time of year." Her voice dripped with envy.

Ignoring her sister's comment, Sabrina asked Ian pointedly, "Are you perchance familiar with that most excellent family?"

"Yes. I am. I doubt there is anyone who is not familiar with the Earl of Saunderson. It is probable that he is in attendance tonight. He is one of the regulars, I do believe."

Sabrina could barely contain herself. He was here. In a few

hours, she would have his confession, and Hunter would be proud and pleased with her cunning intervention.

"I am sure that if Ian sees him he'll be more than happy to point him out," Amanda interjected, patting her sister's hand. "At present, however, I collect my husband promised the first waltz to me," she remarked, sliding her arm through Ian's and nudging him toward the uneven dance floor.

Sabrina's face fell. If she knew Amanda, it would be some time before the happy couple rejoined the sidelines. Sabrina tried to cheer herself. Sulking against the wall might work in her favor.

Twenty minutes later, not a solitary soul had given her a second look. She was obviously not the proper lure for such a man as Wilkinson, or any man for that matter. Her heart sank. If only she were more attractive. Wilkinson would surely pick her out among the crowd. From all reports, Julia had been a beauty beyond compare.

Sabrina's mood soured. Hunter would be livid when he discovered she had involved Bow Street for naught. She would have sent poor Mr. Crawford on a merry goose chase.

"Good evening, my lady," a melodious voice murmured at her side.

Her head whipped around. Mutely, she stared in disbelief at the impeccably dressed, tall blond man gazing at her with slumberous brown eyes.

She gulped. It was him. Gracious, what a stroke of genius!

"G-good evening," she stammered.

He chuckled softly, apparently amused by her case of nerves. "I do believe I have had the pleasure of making your acquaintance, have I not?"

She shook her head. "No. We've never met."

"Really?" he asked, cocking a dubious brow. "I was certain, as I stood watching you, that you were by far the most beautiful creature on earth. I could not help feeling I knew you. But perhaps, it is because we were destined to meet.''

Gawking at him, she swallowed audibly. ''Destined to meet?'' she echoed stupidly.

An unfathomable emotion registered on his face. ''Mmm,'' he said, his lips twitching. ''Fate has brought us together, would you not agree?''

She blinked up at him. ''Fate?'' Good Lord, what a performance!

''You appear to be waiting for someone,'' he remarked, studying her intently beneath hooded eyelids.

She shrugged. ''No one in particular. This is my first time at Almack's. I must confess, I am a little nervous,'' she prevaricated, dropping her gaze to the floor. ''I really should not speak to a gentleman without the benefit of a formal introduction.''

He gazed at her quizzically for a moment before he etched a bow and said, ''George Wilkinson, Earl of Saunderson.'' His practiced charm grated on Sabrina like chalk on a chalk board. She found herself wondering if under different circumstances, she might have been his naive victim. The thought chilled her blood.

She drew in her breath and pressed her gloved fingers to her lips. ''Oh, my,'' she crooned with admiration, ''not *the* Earl of Saunderson?''

He smiled broadly. ''Pray, do not keep me in suspense. I am persuaded I have never gazed on such perfection. Whom do I have the pleasuring of addressing?''

Sabrina fought the urge to be ill on the spot. The man fairly dripped honey. She forced herself to giggle like a nervous schoolgirl. At least, she hoped she sounded like a schoolgirl and not a complete imbecile. ''Well, perhaps . . . just this once, given your fine upstanding reputation, I don't suppose it would be wrong. My name is Camilla. My grandfather is—''

''Very charming, I am sure. But it is *you* who interest me

at the moment," he countered smoothly. He bowed and kissed her hand. "May I say what a very great pleasure it is for me to make your acquaintance, Camilla?"

This was really too much! Sabrina quelled the desire to roll her eyes. No wonder he was successful at seducing unsuspecting young women. Even knowing what a monster he was, she could not deny his warmth and charm were disarming.

"I do?" she queried, essaying a wide-eyed, innocent look.

"I am anxious to learn everything I can about you. You," he said, his gaze drifting over her face in reverent appreciation, "intrigue me."

Sabrina had to quell the urge to laugh. This was really too much to be borne. "You flatter me, my lord," she said demurely, and batted her eyelashes.

"You must call me George, and I shall call you," he said, taking her hand in his and gazing deeply into her eyes, "precious."

The miscreant had a penchant for absurd nicknames.

"You flatter me . . . George," she murmured, slipping her hand from his clutches, but not before he pressed a kiss to the back of it. It would be easier than she thought to arrive at an unpalatable end with this malevolent fellow.

"You look overwarm, precious," he observed. "A breath of fresh air will make you feel more the thing."

Better and better, thought Sabrina with a coy smile. "It is a lovely evening. I am sure I would be only too glad to take a turn with you."

"Capital idea," he replied, and secured her right arm firmly through his.

As they traversed the hot, stuffy room which was filled to capacity, Sabrina cooed like a lovesick dolt at the man beside her. Out of the corner of her eye, she caught sight of Amanda tramping through the crush of guests in hot pursuit. Fixing her sister with a dark, menacing look, Sabrina gave a stern shake of her head that effectively halted Amanda in her tracks. Utterly perplexed, Amanda stared blankly at Sabrina and mouthed the words, "What are you doing?"

Scowling, Sabrina shooed her sister away.

"Is that woman an acquaintance of yours?" George's dulcet tones wafted through the air.

Sabrina cursed her meddling sister. She would ruin everything if she did not leave off. "Er, yes, but I would much rather spend time with you," she managed to say dreamily.

He glanced across the room. "She looks rather intent on stopping you," he observed.

"That is because she is jealous."

He arched a golden brow. "Is she, indeed?"

Sabrina darted a glance at the doorway lurking a few yards away. "Can you doubt it?" she asked, desperate to reach the exit before her sister ploughed her way through the crowd and demanded an explanation that might prove a trifle embarrassing.

He looked vaguely amused. "I should think droves of young bucks would line up for your hand, precious."

"Oh, no," she hastened to assure him, "you are the first."

"I am so glad," he murmured.

Taking her by the arm, he steered her outside, into the dark cover of night. *"Lady Lancaster."*

Iridescent moonlight cast the rows of black carriages in an ominous light. A small shiver crept up her spine. "Why do you call me that?" she asked, not daring to glimpse at the encroaching figure at her side. A sense of dread enveloped her. The street was virtually abandoned save for a few carriage drivers who were still awake. But they would not dare gainsay a gentleman. She was horribly alone.

"It is your name, is it not?" he replied quite calmly as he propelled her toward the curb. Only the bite of his fingers on her bare flesh belied his anger. "I was sure I recognized you.

I watched you on the sidelines and waited for your husband to appear."

Wincing, she tried to loosen her arm, but it was no use. "How did you know what I looked like?" she asked, darting a frantic glance around her.

He snickered at her naivete. "Come, come, my dear, I make it my business to know everything about your husband since he saw fit to make it his life's ambition to ruin my life. It is only right that I should return the favor. Besides, there is not a person among the *ton* who does not know Lancaster took a bride to avoid a scandal. Did you actually think if you played the part of the untried novice anyone would be fooled?"

Unaccustomed to being anyone anybody would take a second glance at, she had not considered her true identity would be well known. Talons of fear clutched at her. Hunter was entirely correct. Her plan was anything but foolproof. The problem was that she had realized her folly too late.

Wilkinson's carriage was scarcely two feet away. Panic rippled through her. If she got into that carriage with him she was as good as dead. Letting her legs go limp, she nearly collapsed on the ground. But he held her fast. His iron grip threatened to crush her bones.

"I suggest you put your legs to good use," he remarked on a bored sigh, "or I shall be forced to hurt you rather badly."

Grimacing, she stood up. "If you knew," she asked, barely able to draw a steady breath, "why did you go along with me?"

"Your husband is a rather tiresome fellow. He's cost me my club, caused me no end of difficulties with Bow Street, sticking his nose where it ain't wanted. I wonder how he'll feel now that the shoe is on the other foot, so to speak."

Swallowing audibly, she cast a last furtive glance over her shoulder at the deserted dark street. Where was Amanda when she needed her most? "If you let me go," she said, quaking with fear, "I promise—"

"You'll forget all about this little incident?" He chuckled nastily. "I wonder when you chits will come up with a more compelling incentive."

Her tongue darted nervously across her lips. "You must know my husband is a wealthy man. He'll pay you handsomely."

"Ah, yes, Hunter Lancaster would pay a pretty penny for such a rare gem as yourself. Not that I'd ever ask for anything as vulgar as money. What a curious, difficult man he is, too. I wonder how he will feel when he discovers his wife's been used by another man. I must confess, I rather preferred his stepsister. But you'll do nicely for the present."

His dark carriage loomed before her like the grim reaper of death.

"You won't get away with this. M-my sister saw you with me. It is only a matter of time before Hunter discovers what you've done. You cannot possibly think to get away with kidnaping me."

"Once I am through with you, you'll wish I had decided to kidnap you and asked for a king's ransom."

The color drained from her face. "I—I am not worth your time, really I am not."

"Nonsense, precious, it will be my pleasure. I do think it was extremely careless of your devoted spouse to use you to lure me in." He tapped his chin with his long white finger. "And, I daresay, out of character."

"He does not know anything about this," she blurted out, straining against his vice grip around her waist. "It was all my idea. Please," she cried, desperation making her voice shrill, "let me go. I swear I won't say a word. Why would I?" she asked, unable to stem the wave of tears. "You have done nothing untoward. You can let me go. I'd have nothing to report, nothing at all. I-it will be just a simple misunderstanding. No one need hear of it.''

He cocked a brow and threw open the carriage door. "He doesn't know, eh?'' he remarked, dismissing her pleadings by ignoring them. "How interesting.'' He grabbed her chin and turned her face into the silvery moonlight. "Then, we have time to get better acquainted before he realizes what's become of you.''

Repulsed, she squeezed her eyes shut. "Please,'' she sobbed, tears rolling unchecked down her face, "you don't have to do this.'' She darted a terrified glance into the black abyss awaiting her. "You are a respected peer of the realm, not some lowly criminal off the streets.''

He cocked his head to one side. "I reckon you are right. Of course, Paine was a rather vexing problem. Thanks to your meddlesome husband, I had to dispose of the pesky man. The devil talked too much. But I never actually tightened the noose. I mean to say, if kicking a chair out from under somebody is a crime, then we are all guilty of murder at some point, do you not think?''

Bile rose in her throat. Horrified, she stared at him. "Y-yes, y-you are right. Paine hung himself. You've nothing to-to worry about. Don't waste your time on someone like me. I am nothing. Nobody. I could never harm you.''

"On the contrary, my dear,'' he said with a chilling smile, "you are married to the thorn in my side.''

Sabrina never knew what hit her. The moment his fist collided with her face, the world went black.

"What the hell do you mean, she's not here?'' Hunter thundered at a tearful Amanda closeted in the small boudoir of Morely House the following dawn. "I left her with you for safe keeping!''

Seated on the pink velvet settee in her dressing gown, Amanda blanched at his mordant tone. "I saw her leave Almack's with George Wilkinson late last night," she said, issuing a tearful sob. "When I reached King Street . . . they'd gone."

"Why the devil didn't you stay with her?" he exploded with blistering fury.

"Be fair, Hunter, you know how headstrong Sabrina is," Ian said, rubbing his distraught wife's arms. "How could we possibly have known what she was scheming? It wasn't until Bow Street arrived with the startling revelation Sabrina had been plotting to catch the blackguard that we suspected something untoward. As soon as we realized what had happened, we sent word. What could we have done? I had no idea this Wilkinson was a villain. You might have, at least, told me. Had I known, I never would have let her out of this house."

Hunter dragged his hand through his hair. "Of course, you are right. Forgive me. The fault lies entirely with me. I might have known she'd try something like this." He slammed his fists against the mantel. "I was a blasted fool to trust her. Damned stupid chit will end up getting herself killed, or worse."

Amanda blinked up at him from beneath tear-dotted lashes. "What fate could possibly be worse than death?"

Ian patted her shoulders and said, "There, there now, don't fret. I am sure we shall find her. She'll be safe and sound in no time at all. You'll see."

"I should have realized she was conspiring the moment she asked to go to Almack's. To think," Amanda blubbered into her handkerchief, "I left her alone so that we might share a waltz, when all the time, that scoundrel was lurking on the sidelines waiting to pounce on my poor, unsuspecting sister."

Hunter cast a disgruntled look over his shoulder. Her insipid caterwauling grated on his nerves. He was all too aware of the gravity of his current predicament. He could do quite nicely without her tearful reminders.

"Hunter?" Amanda asked with a sniffle.

"Yes," he growled impatiently.

"You don't hate me for tricking you, do you?"

"Tricking me?" he barked, his thoughts preoccupied with more grievous matters. "What the devil are you talking about?"

"I tricked you. If not for my intervention, you might not have married my poor sister," she supplied with a gush of tears. "I know it was terribly underhanded of me, but I felt certain you'd suit."

He rolled his eyes heavenward. "Good God, woman," he spat at her. "How can you ask me such a question? Can you not see she is my life? I love her."

She offered him a miserable, small smile. "Well, even if she's . . . she's"—she could not bring herself to say the word—"at least . . . you loved one another for a . . . short . . . space . . . of time," she wailed, burying her face in her hands.

Hunter grimaced. He refused to consider that grim possibility. She was alive. She had to be. How could he still draw a breath if she were lying dead somewhere?

Pacing to the window, he planted his palms on the sill. "Where the devil is Crawford? He should be here by now. We are losing valuable time," he hissed vehemently.

"I am sure he is making a thorough investigation prior to presenting his report. Bow Street assured me, Runners are crawling the streets looking for her."

"Mmm. I am sure. With the same competence as they responded to her note," he muttered with a sardonic sneer.

"For all they knew, the note was a prank. After all, Crawford was on assignment with you. Issuing a plea for men to come to Almack's is a bit odd, you must admit."

Hunter fixed Ian with a chilling glare. "If this is your idea of helping matters, don't."

Ian looked instantly contrite.

Amanda sobbed even louder.

Rolling his eyes, Hunter expelled a frustrated growl. Unable to endure another moment of her blubbering, he muttered, "I need a drink," and stormed from the room to await news downstairs.

"I'll join you momentarily," Ian advised Hunter with a curt nod and tried to calm his hysterical wife.

Shortly after Ian joined Hunter's silent vigil, Crawford finally made his appearance. He looked grim, indeed, as he informed Hunter of his wife's whereabouts.

He shook his head. " 'Tain't good, milord."

Hunter's grip tightened around the glass, turning his fingers white. "Well?" he demanded, every cell of his body dreading the news that was to come, hoping against all hope that she was not dead, and knowing if she were he would wish to die as well.

" 'E's taken her," he told Hunter.

Hunter slammed his glass down on the table. "Where?"

"To 'is 'ome in Kent, most like."

Hunter swore under his breath.

"Are you quite sure?" Ian asked.

"Aye. Took a bit o' time, but we're fairly certain 'tis where 'e's headin' "

"Then, we've not a moment to lose," Hunter averred with icy precision, and headed for the door.

"Now 'old on a minute," the Runner cautioned. " 'E'll be ready and waitin', milord."

"Good," came Hunter's clipped reply. "I am more than ready to meet him," he said with burning contempt.

" 'E's got a good start. 'Twill be difficult to catch 'im."

"I'll have the advantage on horseback. The carriage will

slow him. You and your men follow, but Wilkinson is mine.''
With that, Hunter strode to the street door and wrenched it
open. Calling to the groom, he issued orders to saddle his horse
and was about to descend the stone steps when Ian grabbed
him by his jacket sleeve.

''Hold on, what are you planning to do?'' he asked, eyeing
Hunter warily.

Hunter yanked his arm free. ''Kill the bastard,'' he said
through his teeth.

''That is a matter for Bow Street,'' Ian insisted.

Hunter shook his head, his dark eyes glinting with hatred.
''I am not about to stand by and let those bumblers handle it
while he rapes and murders my wife.''

Ian weighed the circumstances in his mind. ''Very well,''
he said with a smile. ''If you are determined to kill him, at
least let me lend a hand. You never were a decent shot,'' he
said with welcomed levity and shouted to his butler to bring
his pistols.

Hunter clapped his hand on his friend's back. ''We must
away for Kent. Every second counts,'' he shouted, and flew
down the stone steps.

Chapter 18

Sabrina felt the swaying of the speeding carriage, heard the creaking of the wheels and opened her eyes. Slowly, she regained consciousness. Gazing up, she tried to focus through haphazard strands of hair, at the upside down portrait of a man sitting diagonally across from her. Momentarily confused, she frowned and pushed the hair out of her face.

As the man's face became clear to her, the events of the last evening surged to the forefront of her mind with a vengeance. She sat bolt upright. Her head careened. The horrifying realization was visible on her face, eliciting a derisive chuckle from her male counterpart in this travesty of horrors.

A dull throb originated where her jaw previously dwelt. Gingerly, she touched her fingertips to the side of her face, felt the swollen, bruised protrusion and winced.

"Tender, is it?" he asked in that hatefully dulcet voice of his.

She refused to honor that vicious remark with a reply.

"Where are you taking me?" she asked, pulling back the drape to peer out at the pitch-black landscape. "What is it you are after? If not ransom money, then what?"

His hooded gaze drifted over her disheveled appearance, lingering with insulting thoroughness over her snug bodice. He flashed a licentious smile. "You are a single-minded wench, I'll give you that."

"Aren't all your victims?" she asked, tossing him a hateful look over her shoulder. "Or do you frighten them into submission first?"

"Victims? Tut, tut. Victim is such an unattractive word. I prefer to think of them as playmates. After all, we are going to have such fun together, you and I. Who knows?" he said with a leer. "You might even find you enjoy it, if you let yourself."

"You're mad," she hissed at him.

He pulled a face. "You disappoint me, my dear. Surely, you can do better than that? Insanity would suggest that I was not in complete control of my faculties. And we both know that is not true."

Her eyes glowed with burning enmity. "You are a monster."

He uttered a nasty chuckle. "Don't delude yourself; I am no more a monster than your beloved Hunter. How many beds do you think he's graced over his lifetime, hmm? Too many to recall, I am sure." He shrugged his shoulders. "I merely have an unusual hobby. I like to deflower virgins," he imparted with a lascivious smirk. "And I am very good at it, too."

She glared at him, a spiteful glint in her eye. "Precisely how often did the gallant knight punch his favorite virginal playmate, Julia Lancaster, in the face?"

The smile slid from his face. "I would never hurt little Jules," he imparted roughly. "She was the most precious creature, the dearest thing in the world to me."

"I suppose that is why you got her with child and left her

to face the ignominies of scandal all alone?" Sabrina spat with venom.

"Shut up," he growled at her. His hands balled into fists. "So he read my letter. I suspected as much. Damn him to hell! He had no right to delve into my private affairs," he exploded, pounding his fist on the seat.

"My heart bleeds for you," she mocked him.

Lunging forward, he grabbed a fistful of curly hair and gave a hard yank. "I wouldn't be flippant, were I you," he snarled, smoothing his hand over the ivory column of her neck.

Squeezing her eyes shut, she fought against the urge to scream from the pain, for he was nearly tearing her hair from its roots.

"Should be quite a diverting exercise to bring you to heel. Of course, I don't normally sample used goods, but I'd be willing to make an exception in your case."

"I'll kill myself first," she vowed fiercely.

He threw back his head and roared with laughter. "We shall see, precious. We shall see."

As the carriage tore through the dark of night, Sabrina sat curled in a miserable ball and prayed Hunter would come to her rescue. Desperate to find an escape route, she glanced longingly at the door and debated flinging it open and leaping to her probable death. Anything would be preferable to enduring what the man across from her had in store, she thought with a shiver. And she might survive the fall with only a few broken bones, if that. It was worth a try. She tried to inch her way across the seat. Her self-sacrifice was never realized, however, for her captor spoke up: "Not much farther now. You can smell the sea," he remarked, closing his eyes and inhaling deeply. "I am always happiest in Kent."

Her eyes flew wide. "Kent? Why have you brought me

here?'' Her voice was taut with panic, for she now knew no one would come to her rescue. It was too much to hope. She was going to die at the hands of George Wilkinson.

Frowning, he gave her a derisive look. ''You are not overly bright, are you?'' He sighed and flicked an imaginary piece of lint from his velvet clad chest. ''None of you women are, I expect.''

The carriage slowed. Sabrina darted a glance at the door. It was now or never. She threw herself across the seat. Jiggling the handle, she shoved her weight against the carriage door. The door swung open. She fell from the carriage and would have landed face first on the hard ground were it not for the fact that she grabbed hold of the swinging door and hung on for dear life. Dangling from the speeding carriage, she glanced down at the dark, hard ground narrowly whisking by her head. Her leg was caught. Wilkinson was holding her. She felt him trying to drag her back inside. Frantic, she kicked at his face with her free foot. She wished she had donned her leather vamp boots instead of her soft, kid-soled slippers. The result was the same. Uttering a string of furious oaths, he released her. She tumbled from the swaying carriage head first to the hard, rough ground.

It took several seconds before she realized she had somersaulted into a rocky ditch. The breath was knocked out of her. Dazed by the fall, she sat up and tried to draw breath into her lungs. She caught a glimpse of the carriage grinding to a halt a few yards away. Catapulted by fear, she managed to get to her feet. She had not the slightest idea where she was going, but she ran as fast as her legs could carry her through the dark night.

She darted a glance over her shoulder. She could hear Wilkinson's angry growl. He was giving chase. She bit back the urge to scream and kept running.

The sounds of waves crashing against the rocks echoed along

the craggy shore. In the distance, a yellow light glimmered through the darkness. Hiking her skirts above her knees, she ran toward the only possible safe haven. Heedless to the rough terrain and shrubbery that scraped at her legs, biting into her flesh, she ran. Her one thought was escape.

By the time she reached the enormous stone edifice, she felt as though she had been running for miles. Exhausted and out of breath, she fell against the heavy wooden door and banged her fists, sobbing for help.

The door creaked open. A kindly faced butler beckoned her enter. Distraught and relieved beyond measure to have found succor, she stumbled into the dark hall.

"Thank you, thank you," she cried, clutching the elderly man's arm for support. "Please, you must help me. A man is after me," she said, gulping for breath. "He—he tried to kill me."

"Is that a fact?" a horribly familiar voice drawled out from a dimly lit staircase a few yards away. "We cannot have the poor young woman fearing for her life now, can we, Stevens?" George Wilkinson asked, coming into the light.

"No, my lord, we can't," the butler replied with a malevolent smile.

Shaking her head, she backed away from him. "No. No!" she screamed. She covered her face with her hands. "It cannot be!"

"Oh, but it is, my dear." Regarding her with a cynical smirk, he cocked his head to one side. "I must say, you are rather eccentric. I, myself, prefer the comforts of the carriage. Far be it from me to disparage the merits of a good tramp through the woods in the middle of the night. Invigorating, was it?" he asked, cruelly mocking her.

"My lord," a manservant said, entering the great hall from the shadows, "I hate to interrupt you—"

Wilkinson's head turned. "What is it?" he snapped angrily.

"Begging your pardon, my lord, but two men on horseback have just entered the grounds."

He turned back to her. His jaw clenched with rage. "That would be your annoying husband, I should think."

"Hunter!" she cried out, straining toward the door. But the butler held her fast.

"Take her to the tower and await my instructions. I'll handle these two interlopers." He grabbed her by the chin. "It won't be long now, precious."

She spit in his face. Slowly, he raised his hand and wiped her saliva from his cheek.

He chuckled softly. "You're a fiery little thing, aren't you?" he said, and slapped her hard across the face.

With a hard shove from behind, Sabrina stumbled into the dank, cold room which she assumed was the tower. The creaking iron door swung shut behind her with a loud thud. As her eyes adjusted to the darkness, she saw quite plainly that the tower had large, rectangular openings through which shards of silvery moonlight streamed. Getting to her feet, she staggered over to look out. Far below, the ocean crashed against the craggy landscape with a thunderous rage.

No hope of escape unless she leapt to her death. Tears pricked her eyes. She hugged her arms around her waist.

Behind her, the door creaked open and then slammed shut. Someone else was in the room. But who? *Oh, God, please God, let it be Hunter.*

She heard the rusty bolt slide into place, locking them both in. A flint struck, and a tiny flame of a single taper flickered, casting Wilkinson's maniacal face in an eerie glow. Oh, where was Hunter? She could hear her captor's labored breathing in the darkness. Obviously, he had hurried up the stairs that led to the tower room. Was her husband giving chase? Lord, she hoped so.

"Your husband is very persistent, precious. Do you think he intends to fight for you?" he asked as he traversed the darkened room in search of his prey.

Pressing her back against the damp wall, she held her breath and prayed Hunter knew his way to the tower. She had no idea how many stone steps she had been hauled up. Nor which direction the tower room faced. It was no use to try to call to him; the stone walls must be several inches thick.

The flickering light headed toward where she hid with her back against the cold, damp wall. "I sincerely hope not. I, for one, find it highly implausible that any woman is worth a man's life."

She slid her feet along the edge of the wall. The floor beneath her heel gave way, and she gasped in surprise. She reached out, her hand grasping the crumbling wall. It gave way beneath her clawing fingers. One glance over her shoulder at the white caps below and she vaulted away from the ledge. In her haste, she careened headlong into the arms of her foe.

"Here now, I've got you," his booming, amused voice cried out as he caught her around the waist. "Where are you off to in such a hurry, precious?"

Desperate to be free, she kicked at his shins, shoving against his chest like a wild animal helplessly caught in a trap fighting for its life. "Let me go, you vile bastard."

"Cheeky hellion!" he burst out, amused by her pathetic attempts to wrench loose. "You'll do nicely," he told her with a salacious grin as he tightened his grip, nearly cracking her ribs.

"Sabrina!" Hunter's shout echoed inside the stone stairwell.

"Here—" she tried to cry out, but Wilkinson's hand clamped down over her mouth.

Dragging her away from the insistent fists pounding at the

door, Wilkinson whispered against her ear, "It will take him quite some time to break down that door. Shall we pass the time with a favorite little game of mine? I am sure you'd like it."

She could hear Hunter calling to her through the door. Grimacing, she moaned against Wilkinson's palm.

"I don't imagine it would take you long to learn the rules," he grated against her ear. "I've a feeling you are the sort who'd rather fancy the pleasure and pain."

Wriggling against him, she shook her head. It was no use. With little effort, he dragged her along the tower edge, farther into the damp, cold darkness and farther away from Hunter.

"I've particular tastes for your sort," he said, caressing her smooth skin with his hand. "How long do you suppose it'll take before you are begging for mercy?"

A small click sounded in the darkness, like a pistol being cocked. "Not long," Hunter's deep, menacing voice drawled from behind, "but it won't come to that. And we both know it."

Nothing had ever sounded as wonderful to Sabrina's frightened ears. Hunter had come to her rescue. Thank heaven. She wasn't quite sure how she was going to maneuver her way out of her current predicament without him. In fact, she was quite petrified.

Clutching her around the waist from behind, Wilkinson swung around to face Hunter, using Sabrina's body as a shield.

His pistol aimed at Wilkinson, Hunter took a menacing step forward. "Let her go."

"Come any closer, Lancaster," Wilkinson growled, "and your precious bride goes over the edge." He motioned with his head toward the disintegrating ledge to his left.

Hunter stopped short. "It comes as little surprise to learn you'd hide behind a woman's skirts. This is between you and me. Leave my wife out of it."

Wilkinson hauled Sabrina's body hard against him. "Look who's come to watch our performance," he taunted, pressing his cheek to hers from behind.

Hunter's eyes glinted silver fire. "It's over, Wilkinson. There isn't going to be any performance."

"You think not? You've pestered me long enough. If you still want her, when I'm finished with her, you can have her," he sneered mordantly. "You'll not deny me the pleasure of making you suffer, Lancaster."

Hunter's jaw tightened perceptibly. He shook his head and pointed the pistol at Wilkinson's head. "Afraid not." His tight, controlled voice held a note of lethal warning. "She's a jewel well beyond your reach."

"Damn you, Lancaster. I loved Jules, but you couldn't leave it alone. You had to dig it all up. Why the devil couldn't you keep your nose out of it? It was between Jules and me. It was none of your concern."

"You are wrong. It was very much my concern," Hunter countered, his tone hard and ruthless. "It was stupid of you to insist that club members wear that disgusting emblem. It was the one thing that linked the incidents together. I expected you to be more clever. You should have run away to India with Everly when you had the chance. You cannot escape now. The grounds are crawling with men."

Wilkinson darted a glance down below. Flickering yellow torches could be seen traversing the grounds amid the distant shouts of men.

"Give yourself up, Wilkinson."

"Never," he snarled, and threw Sabrina at Hunter.

Hunter caught her. His pistol fell to the floor.

Wilkinson snatched it from the ground. "Now who's got the upper hand?" he asked with a pompous snicker. "I'll kill you. And have my way with the girl."

"I wouldn't count on it," Hunter replied, pushing Sabrina

behind him. "You haven't got the guts to put down the pistol and face me like a man."

"Hunter, no!" Sabrina cried, clinging to his arm. Ignoring her protest, he pushed her away. "Don't, Hunter. He'll shoot you."

"That's right, my dear," Wilkinson drawled amusedly. "You think you are so superior," he spat with contempt at Hunter. "You're not. We are a lot alike, you and I. How many women have you seduced in your time? Too many to recall, I should think. Nothing wrong with celebrating our male prowess, now, is there?"

Hunter shook his head in disgust. "We are nothing alike."

Wilkinson snickered. "That's what you think. Shall I tell you about your adorable little stepsister? Dear, sweet Julia was a whore. I did not have to seduce her. Don't kid yourself into believing it was rape. She wanted it. She even begged me to—"

Snarling like a savage beast, Hunter pounced on Wilkinson. As the two men fell to the ground in a death struggle, the pistol was thrown free. Sabrina's frantic gaze searched the dark dirt floor for the weapon. In desperation, she fell to her knees and felt the ground with her fingers. Distraught with fear, she scrambled across the floor on her hands and knees. With frenzied movements, she searched the ground until she felt the cold hardness of it. Her fingers wrapped around the smooth wooden stock. She dragged it from the ground. As she got to her feet, she did not stop to think about whether or not she could actually kill a man. She knew what she had to do. She had to save the man she loved.

"S-stop!" she cried out shakily, trying to take aim on Wilkinson. But it was difficult to get a clear shot. As soon as Wilkinson came into range, Hunter's fist collided with his jaw. Wilkinson fell backward, only to have Hunter jump on top of him, pummeling his face with murderous fists.

"Stop, I say!" she cried in frustration, pointing the large black object at the two men.

Footfalls sounded on the stone steps, the door was thrown wide and Ian rushed in. He darted a quick glance in Sabrina's direction before trying to haul Hunter off his adversary.

"You're killing him, man," he shouted, dragging Hunter away from the vile culprit. "You cannot think to escape, Wilkinson. Give yourself up," he advised, holding Hunter back.

Shaking his head, Wilkinson managed to get to his feet. He dragged the back of his hand across his bloodied face. Weaving to and fro, he turned to look at Sabrina. His gaze traveled to the pistol in her hands. He threw back his head and uttered a hearty laugh. Before anyone could stop him, he threw himself over the tower ledge, tumbling to his death on the rocks below.

Ian ran to the edge, gazing down at his mangled body now claimed by the rushing waves. He shook his head. "He wreaked his own revenge in the end."

"What about his victims?" Hunter asked Ian roughly. "Where is their justice?"

Ian shrugged and stepped away from the crumbling ledge. "His death, I suppose," he replied, his tone somber.

Hunter's mouth set in a grim line. "His death won't bring back Jane Greenly, it won't erase Lady Caroline's pain, nor will it alter the fact that Julia died with a broken heart, believing herself in love with that villain."

Ian released a heavy sigh. "At least, you've put an end to their secret society. There is some solace in that."

"Not enough," Hunter said bitterly. "It could never be enough."

Sabrina dropped the pistol on the dirt floor and rushed to Hunter's side. Collapsing against him, she buried her face in his shoulder. "Oh, Hunter, Hunter."

His arms, strong and sure, closed around her. "It's all right," he assured her, the rich timbre of his voice calming her. "He's dead. You're perfectly safe now. I've got you.'' He turned his head and brushed his lips against her temple. He held her in his arms, running his hands over her. It was some time before he had convinced himself that she was all right.

Ian watched the happy couple. He smiled slightly. ''I hope this has been a lesson to you, young lady?'' he teased Sabrina, his tone sharp. ''You might have been killed were it not for your heroic husband.''

Tears trickled down her cheeks. ''I know. I've been such a fool.''

Hunter cupped her face lovingly with his palms, the pads of his thumbs catching the tears as they fell. ''We both have.''

So engrossed in one another were they that they did not take notice when Ian quietly slipped away.

Tenderly, Hunter kissed Sabrina's lips. ''I thought I'd go mad not knowing if you were dead or alive or what that bastard had done to you,'' he told her, his voice thick and unsteady. ''It made me realize what an idiot I've been.''

''You? An idiot? I don't believe it.'' She smiled dreamily up at him. ''It is beyond the realm of possibility.''

He smiled down at her, enjoying her teasing. ''I was damned selfish. When I thought I might lose you,'' he said, caressing her cheek gently with his palm, ''I deeply regretted the time we'd wasted. Oh, my darling,'' he murmured, pressing a gentle kiss to her lips, ''we can wait as long as you wish for a child. I had no right to press you.''

''Oh, Hunter ... Hunter, you are magnificent, my love,'' she gushed, showering kisses all over his face and clinging to her husband for dear life. ''Truly, a splendid husband. For all your selfishness, I love you dearly.''

His arms tightened around her. He expelled a deep, gruff laugh. ''You are quite an original, my dear. Thank heaven you are safe.'' He hugged her to him, squeezing her tight as if he had to prove to himself she was really alive.

When at last Hunter leaned back to look at her, he asked, "Are you certain you are all right?" Brushing her tangled hair back from her face, he scowled at the bruise marring her porcelain skin and ran his fingertip lightly over the discoloration.

She nodded. "I've never been better," she said, fighting back the rush of tearful relief that was eager to flow. Rather than gushing like a river, she busied herself with the absurd task of straightening her husband's disheveled coat and cravat. "Where did you ever learn to fight like that? I was amazed by your agility, my lord."

Hunter gave her a rueful look. "I'll give your regards to Gentleman Jackson when next I see him," he drawled, locking his arms around her waist.

"Thank heavens you came when you did," she said, adjusting his collar tabs with loving care. "Or I might have joined the ranks of his poor, unsuspecting victims," she said with a shiver.

"Mmm," he muttered curtly, and slapped her playfully on her bottom.

She gave him a startled look.

"I am still reeling from your deception." He fixed her with a stern look. "I suppose I should consider myself fortunate he did not stoop to killing my wayward wife prior to my arrival." His tone was extremely sarcastic.

She colored slightly. "As to that, I am ever so grateful you saw fit to follow. I do not know what I would have done had you not come to my rescue."

"I cannot credit your stupidity. For God's sake," he breathed, "you might have been killed. And, I might add, very nearly were."

"I know it was foolish. But I very much fear obedience has never been my forté, my lord."

A grim frown touched his lips. "Neither is sound judgment," he countered brusquely.

"You mustn't be cross with me, Hunter," she said gently, tracing the hard line of his jaw with her finger. "I did it for you."

His brow darkened. "For me?"

Lowering her gaze, she nodded. "I wanted to make you happy. I thought if I managed to catch the villain, you might . . ." Her voice trailed off.

"I might what?" he pressed, his manner softening.

"Love me," she replied in a voice so low he had to strain to hear her.

"You little fool," he said, his voice hoarse with emotion, "don't you know you are my life, my love, my all? I love you. Oh, my darling Sabrina, how could you doubt me?"

"Well," she said, blinking back tears of joy, "you never said."

"Was fighting to save your life not enough to impress upon you the depth of my feelings?" he asked, his gray eyes brimming with tenderness and love.

She smiled coyly. "I must confess," she remarked with a rush of relief, "I was never so happy to see any one person in all my life."

"Neither was I," he murmured huskily, pulling her close. And then, his arms went around her, and he crushed her to him, smothering her mouth with a deeply possessive, passionate kiss.

Epilogue

Two weeks later, a letter arrived for S. K. Hughes at the Lancaster Upper Brook Street town house address.

"Hunter, you will never believe it when I tell you," Sabrina cried, bursting into the library where her husband was occupied penning his correspondence. "I've received a letter from Mr. Hammersmith at *The Chronicle*. He enjoyed my last article so much, he's requested I write an article on Thomas Erskine, who has recently written, *Internal Evidence for the Truth of Revealed Religion*."

Seated behind his desk, Hunter raised his eyebrow. "Has he really?" came his disinterested reply as he continued with his business. "Jolly good for him."

Rushing toward the desk, she said with excitement, "And there is more." She hopped onto the desk, swinging her crossed ankles to and fro as she read aloud, "The proprietor would very much like to met S. K. Hughes in person Friday, eleven o'clock, at the Fleet Street office." Sabrina's face fell. Slowly, she folded the crisp ivory paper and slid it back inside the envelope.

Hunter glanced up at his wife, who had suddenly gone from jubilant to depressed. "Why so glum?" he asked, setting his quill pen aside and sitting back to examine his wife's unhappy expression. "I should think you'd be ecstatic."

"I cannot possibly go," she lamented, sliding off the desk to wander aimlessly around the room.

Leaning back in his chair, Hunter folded his hands behind his head. "And why not?" he asked, admiring the sway of her narrow hips.

She expelled an annoyed sigh and swiveled about to look at him. "Vexing man," she said, her tone cross, "you know perfectly well why not. I am a woman."

A wicked gleam shone in his eye as his dark, sultry gaze roamed seductively over her with slow precision. "Mmm," he drawled wickedly, "I've noticed."

She gave him a withering look. "Hunter, be serious," she imparted on a forlorn sigh. "It's important."

His expression sobered. "What has your being a woman to do with meeting the proprietor?"

"Once I meet him and he discovers my deception, I'll be through. No more S. K. Hughes," she muttered with a petulant frown, and folded her arms at her waist.

"Not necessarily," Hunter allowed, getting to his feet. He crossed the room to where his distraught wife stood. "The proprietor might have an open mind. After all, your stories have been well received in the past. S. K. Hughes is gaining a following among readers. The proprietor could be persuaded to overlook your gender."

"But consider the alternative. How will I ever be able to indulge my intellectual side without S. K. Hughes?"

Hunter bit back a smile and hugged her to him. "We'll think of something. In the meantime," he advised, tilting her down-turned face to kiss her lightly on the mouth, "you'd best send your reply."

She did not look hopeful.

Framing her face with his hands, he coaxed gently, "It will be all right. You'll see."

Sabrina's nerves were in tatters as she sat in the newspaper office outside the proprietor's door waiting to be admitted. She had no idea how he would view her scandalous deception. Even if, as Hunter suggested, her articles were well regarded, no proprietor in all of London would openly employ a female reporter. It simply was not done. Her only hope was that he agree to continue her subterfuge.

Mr. Hammersmith appeared in the doorway and motioned for Sabrina to enter. Gathering all her courage, she got to her feet and marched into the proprietor's office. Her feet carried her across the threshold, then stopped short. There, not five feet from her, sat her husband, happily installed behind a walnut desk. Bold as brass, he addressed her, a look of cocky amusement on his face, "Hello, my darling. Surprised to see me? I must say you look positively ravishing in that dress. Pink becomes you. Come over here and give us a kiss."

"Why, you," she fumed, slamming the door in her wake. "Deceitful, dishonest, low-down swine."

He held up his hands to ward off her verbal attack. "Now, hold on a minute, I am not the one who pretended to be someone I wasn't."

"No," she stormed, slamming her palms down on the desk, "you just neglected to tell me you knew the truth. You knew all the time I was S. K. Hughes."

Leaning forward, he shook his head. "I had no idea. Hammersmith oversees the day-to-day operations. I am not all that involved with the paper. I merely own it."

"Ooh," she cried, stamping her foot with temper. "The performance you gave, 'the proprietor might be open-minded.' When I think of how I suffered," she ranted, fists clenched at her side, "and worried and agonized over this meeting. Ooh! I could kill you." She slanted him a dark look. "And that ridiculous suggestion that I write about animal husbandry. I've never been so infuriated in all my days," she complained.

He threw back his head and roared with laughter. "Never said Hammersmith actually agreed to print it? Well?" he inquired, his shoulders shaking with mirth. "Did he?"

"I am not quite sure what he plans," she confessed with a good deal of reluctance. "I haven't actually received a reply from him as yet."

"I shouldn't wonder," Hunter muttered, brushing the tears from his eyes.

She crossed her arms over her chest and drummed her fingers against her arm. "Perhaps the proprietor would save S. K. Hughes the embarrassment and pull the article."

He inclined his head amicably. "Agreed."

"You are the lowest of lows. I shall never forgive you."

His hand snaked out and caught her by the wrist. "Darling," he said, dragging her down into his lap. "I wasn't serious when I suggested you compose an article on ewes and rams."

"Well," she grumbled, piqued by his amusement at her expense, "how was I to know? You can be rather moody and difficult from time to time. I never know what to think."

He brushed a lone curl back from her forehead. "Has life with me been a trial for you, then?" he asked in a husky undertone.

Scowling, she gave him a disgruntled look. "You are a beast."

His compelling gray eyes gleamed with concern. "Have I truly made you miserable?"

"Oh, no, Hunter," she cried, throwing her arms around his

neck and hugging him. "I do love you. And I am happier than I ever dreamed possible."

"Except for when I'm moody and difficult and keep things from you?" he teased, retrieving her arms from around his neck to look at her. "Like the future of your sacred S. K. Hughes? Which, by the way, promises to be long and fruitful. You may write for the paper as long as you are inclined."

"Thank you, Hunter. But I very much suspect my journalism days are numbered."

He gave her a quizzical look. "What do you mean?" he asked, his voice a velvet murmur. "I thought I married the girl who'd be happy to wile away the hours in the country, provided, of course, she had her intellectual pursuits to occupy her time?"

"Well . . . you did. I felt that way then."

He looked at her askance. "And now?"

She heaved a sigh. "Now . . . I am not so sure."

"Not so sure?" he echoed incredulously. "I don't believe it."

She laughed. "Strange but true. You see, I've found something more . . . interesting to occupy my time."

He cocked one ebony brow. "Such as?" he queried silkily.

"You. And . . ."

"And?" he prodded, a curious look on his face.

"Our baby."

He stared at her, a blank look on his handsome face. "Our baby?" he whispered softly. "What are you saying?"

Beaming from ear to ear, she said, her tone dry, "I should think it was rather obvious."

"So soon?" he asked stupidly.

"I am afraid so," she said with a deep sigh.

Gazing deeply into her eyes, he asked, "you don't . . . mind?"

She cupped his face with her palm. "How could I mind? The child is yours."

''Sabrina,'' he breathed. His hand slid over the top of hers, and he pressed a kiss to her palm. ''You are a treasure.'' He wrapped his arms around her and kissed her deeply. He pulled back suddenly. Frowning slightly, he lifted her chin to look at her. ''How long have you suspected?''

''A few weeks.''

A dark scowl clouded his features. ''You mean to say you risked your safety and that of our child,'' he intoned gravely, ''on a ridiculous folly with Wilkinson that might have meant your death?''

''Well, no, at the time, I wasn't positive I was actually carrying your child.''

His eyes narrowed on her face. ''When *precisely* did you know?''

''Last week.''

''And you waited until now to tell me?''

She gazed up at him with artless blue eyes that were always his undoing. ''When did you want me to tell you?''

''The moment you suspected,'' he snapped.

''Why?''

''*Why?*'' he asked, gawking at her. ''Well,'' he sputtered, ''so that I could take care of you. Good Lord,'' he burst out, ''I made love to you last night.''

''Yes,'' she said with a dreamy smile, and rested her cheek against his shoulder, ''I remember.''

He looked disconcerted. ''You should have told me you were with child,'' he said awkwardly.

''So that you could see to my every need?'' she queried, arching a dainty brow. ''Make certain I did nothing too strenuous?''

''Naturally.''

Heaving a sigh, she folded her arms at her waist. ''In that case, I wish I had waited to tell you.''

He looked slightly taken aback. ''You need me to look after

you," he said, his voice, like his expression, warm and deeply tender. "To see to your every need and prevent you from doing anything that might cause you discomfort."

"Making love to the man I adore does not cause me discomfort."

One end of his sensual mouth curved upward. "Well, then, my beautiful, wayward wife," he drawled out in soft, seductive tones, "I definitely think you need more bed rest."

His dark velvet promise made her grow warm. "Mmm," she purred, winding her arms around his neck. "I quite agree." Tugging his head close, she pressed a kiss to his lips. It was all-encompassing and full of love.